Western Writers of America Presents

Great Stories of the West from
Today's Leading Western Writers

Edited by
Paul Andrew Hutton

ᴸᶠᴾ

La Frontera Publishing

Cheyenne, Wyoming

ROUNDUP!
Western Writers of America Presents
Great Stories of the West from
Today's Leading Western Writers

An Anthology

Copyright © 2010 Western Writers of America, Inc.

Cover illustration from the original acrylic on canvas painting by Thom Ross "Moonlit Vendetta" © Thom Ross. All rights reserved, used with permission. Cover image photo by Patrick Bennett.

Cover design, book design and typesetting by
Yvonne Vermillion and Magic Graphix

Printed and bound in the United States of America
First Edition

First Printing June 2010

Library of Congress Cataloging-in-Publication Data

Roundup! : Western Writers of America presents great stories of the West from today's leading Western writers / edited by Paul Andrew Hutton. -- 1st ed.
    p. cm.
A collection of fiction, non-fiction and poetry.
ISBN 978-0-9785634-7-9 (pbk.)
1. American literature--West (U.S.) 2. American literature--20th century. 3. West (U.S.)--Literary collections. 4. Western stories. I. Hutton, Paul Andrew, 1949- II. Western Writers of America.
PS561.R68 2010
810.8'03278--dc22

                            2010014294

Published by La Frontera Publishing
Cheyenne, Wyoming
(307) 778-4752 • www.lafronterapublishing.com

In Memory of Elmer Kelton

PREFACE

The Western Writers of America originated in 1951 with an exchange of letters between noted genre writers Nelson Nye and Tommy Thompson. They recruited four other writers—Harry Sinclair Drago, Norman A. Fox, Wayne Overholser, and Dwight Newton—wrote a constitution, collected dues, established the celebrated Spur Awards, and elected officers to create the WWA in 1953. Nye also edited the *WWA Roundup*, which has since evolved from a mimeographed newsletter into a sophisticated and colorful journal published six times a year. The focus of early WWA publication efforts was on annual anthologies, beginning with *Bad Men and Good: A Roundup of Western Stories*, published by Dodd Mead in 1953. Since then over forty anthologies have been sponsored by the WWA. The present volume is a continuation of this proud tradition, but it is also quite different from previous WWA books.

At the suggestion of La Frontera Publishing's publisher, Mike Harris, this WWA anthology is envisioned as a sampler of the best of current western fiction and nonfiction by WWA members. The twenty-seven authors (among them Elmer Kelton, who died while this book was in press and to whom it is dedicated) have penned both fiction and nonfiction stories, as well as poetry and a novella. The authors include WWA Wister Award winners for lifetime achievement such as Kelton, Robert Utley, Matt Braun, Richard Wheeler, and Andrew J. Fenady, as well as many Spur Award winners and several fresh young writers.

The organization is thematic, with sections on the Native West, the early frontier, the traditional West, the Wild West, and the contemporary West. Within each section works of fiction, nonfiction, and poetry are featured. From 113 submissions a WWA board of editors—Johnny D. Boggs, Cotton Smith, Candy Moulton,

Melody Groves, Larry Sweazy, Rod Miller, Robert Conley, and the anthology editor Paul Hutton—selected the pieces featured here.

Special thanks are due to Mike Harris, who suggested this project and saw it through to fruition, Elaine Nelson, Meg Frisbee, James Ersfeld, Bobby Daniels, and the WWA editorial board.

Paul Andrew Hutton

TABLE OF CONTENTS

TRADITIONAL WEST

NATIVE WEST

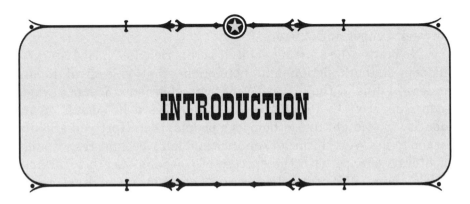

INTRODUCTION

By Paul Andrew Hutton

Many serious scholars, who spend a considerable portion of their lives debating such points, place the birth of the Western at 1823 with the publication of James Fenimore Cooper's *The Pioneers*. Some grumble that the more enduring and clearly superior *Last of the Mohicans* in 1826 deserves the honor of inventing this distinctly American art form. The point is well taken, but then others argue that the tales of Captain John Smith, colonial Indian captivity narratives, or John Filson's marvelous little chapter on the life of Daniel Boone in 1784 (so clearly influential on Cooper) are the true origin point for the Western.

Then there are those who give all credit to that talented Harvard dude, Owen Wister. He captured the imagination of the world with his 1902 novel *The Virginian*. It was Wister who turned the American cowboy into a national symbol—albeit with considerable help from William F. Cody, Frederic Remington, Charles Russell, and Theodore Roosevelt.

This debate has found expression among historians in the endless argument over Frederick Jackson Turner's 1893 "Frontier Thesis." Turner saw the American national character, and thus American exceptionalism, as an outgrowth of the frontier experience. His critics counter that the frontier was but one of many forces that shaped the new nation. The argument is one between "process" and "place," with the strongest modern interpreters

1

of "place" led by the engaging Patricia Nelson Limerick of the University of Colorado. It is exactly the same literary debate as between Cooper and Wister.

No matter the starting point, it is this rich and varied literary history—in both fiction and nonfiction—that is central to an understanding of the distinct American character. It has always been this way. In the 1820s Americans were in search of an identity that might unite them as a people. Both North and South looked to the West. Frontier America suddenly became respectable in literary circles with the success of Cooper's "Leatherstocking Tales." Samuel Woodworth's song "The Hunters of Kentucky," celebrating the prowess of Kentucky and Tennessee militiamen at the 1815 Battle of New Orleans (where every man was "half a horse and half an alligator") swept the nation in 1822 and became an informal campaign song for future President Andrew Jackson.

Border dramas, as they were called, such as "Nick of the Woods" and "The Lion of the West" (based on the life of Davy Crockett) became all the rage on eastern and European stages. The rise of Jackson and other Western political figures, including the frontiersman Crockett, symbolized a political and cultural shift from the East to the West. Timothy Flint's bestselling biography of Daniel Boone, the martyrdom of Crockett at the Alamo, the celebrated adventures of Kit Carson and John Fremont, the California Gold Rush, and the romance surrounding the great migration to Oregon (immortalized in Francis Parkman's *The Oregon Trail*), all served to change the frontiersman, once disdained by the guardians of American culture as a dangerous symbol of low breeding and anarchy, into the very idealization of an evolving national character.

A ghastly Civil War wrought this all asunder. A great Westerner, the grandson of one who had followed Boone through the Cumberland Gap into Kentucky, redeemed the dream and restored hope to the nation. Abraham Lincoln, through the Homestead Act and his sponsorship of a transcontinental railroad, also set in motion the forces that created a new trans-Mississippi West. Out of this a new epic arose. This story united a divided nation and forever cemented a unique national identity for a richly diverse people. A fresh generation of heroes emerged to be celebrated in the popular dime novels that horrified parents and literary critics alike—the gunfighter-lawman Wild Bill Hickok, the heroic soldier George Custer, the scout Buffalo Bill, the outlaw Jesse James, the Indian statesman Sitting Bull, the wild cowgirl Calamity Jane—and from them came a story rich in romance and boundless optimism yet also burdened with a sense of nostalgia for a dying past. Buffalo Bill Cody, who had lived the reality of the conquest of the West as a Civil War soldier, railroad buffalo hunter, and army scout, put it all into a grand extravaganza in 1883 and took it on the road. His "Wild West" enthralled two generations of Americans and Europeans, creating the clichés and conventions followed by innumerable writers, poets, and filmmakers yet unborn.

Owen Wister, who was no stranger to the conventions of Cody's show, enshrined the virtues of the stalwart Westerner in his 1902 classic novel. A year later Edwin S. Porter presented the world with the first film to tell a story, and also the first Western film, with his *Great Train Robbery*. Within a generation a mighty new industry emerged from Porter's primitive cinematic tale, with fully one-third of its production devoted to Westerns. Thomas Ince and John Ford, William S. Hart and Tom Mix, Charles Kenyon and Betty Burbridge, Gary Cooper and Joel McCrea, Nunnally Johnson and Alan LeMay, Gene Autry and Roy Rogers, Frank Nugent and James Warner Bellah, Budd Boetticher and Howard Hawks, John Wayne and Clint Eastwood, Walon Green and Michael Blake, John Sturges and Sam Peckinpah, John Fusco and Kirk Ellis and a host of other remarkable talents refined the Western tradition in motion pictures and television over the past century.

The stunning commercial success of Max Brand and Zane Grey inspired a host of lesser and better talents who flooded a booming short and long-form fiction marketplace hungry for Western stories. From Jack London and Emerson Hough to Ernest Haycox and Eugene Manlove Rhodes and from Walter Van Tilburg Clark and Dorothy Johnson to Luke Short and Jack Schaefer, they worked and refined their craft over half a century of startling change in literary tastes. For every Willa Cather, Mari Sandoz, John Neihardt, A. B. Guthrie, and Conrad Richter, who produced works celebrated by literary critics, there were a dozen prolific writers of popular fiction churning out romantic tales of frontier adventure for such national publications as *McClure's, Collier's,* the *Saturday Evening Post* or a host of garish Western pulps that entertained countless readers through years of economic boom, depression, and war. It was the grand age of the printed word, and talented Western writers found a ready market for their labors.

As a cadre of successful Western pulp writers (publishing regularly in *Argosy, Blue Book, Dime Western, Ranch Romances* or *Ace High*) moved into the short novels eagerly sought by the expanding postwar paperback book houses, they began to consider the need for a professional writers' organization for the Western genre. The success of Anthony Boucher and the Mystery Writers of America initially inspired them. Sensing that the days of the pulps were numbered, they sought to create an organization that might celebrate a rapidly changing genre and give it higher national visibility. Thus was born the Western Writers of America.

Founded in 1953 by six Western writers—Harry Sinclair Drago, Norman Fox, Dwight Newton, Nelson Nye, Wayne Overholser, and Thomas Thompson—the Western Writers of America rapidly expanded. The first issue of the organization's journal, *The Roundup,* appeared in April 1953. After heated debate—as common then as now in a contentious, egocentric, and passionate outfit—it was decided that selected writing awards would be called Spurs and the first were given at the 1954 Denver conference for books published in 1953.

The first WWA anthology, *Bad Men and Good*, with a foreword by Luke Short, was also published by Dodd, Mead and Company in 1953. Among its fourteen short stories was John Cunningham's "The Tin Star," soon to be turned into the classic Western film *High Noon*. This was followed by *Holsters and Heroes* in 1954, published by Macmillan, and the WWA anthology was on its way to a quarter century of annual publications. Over forty WWA publications, both fiction and nonfiction, were to follow presenting an incredible array of literary talent.

The organization was a huge success, its membership swelling and its anthologies selling briskly in both cloth and paper. In 1954, Westerns outsold mysteries as the most popular fiction genre. Within five years Westerns also dominated the new medium of television, with forty-eight Western programs airing by 1959. The incredible success of television, however, spelled doom to the glory days of printed genre fiction.

Western Writers of America responded to this changing marketplace, expanding its membership and the Spur Awards from book authors to include short story writers, script writers for both film and television in 1969 and 1971 (and eventually documentary script writers after the boom in that field in the 1990s), as well as non-fiction authors in both long and short-form categories, juvenile authors of both fiction and non-fiction, poetry, audio books, and song. The Spur Awards emerged as a prestigious brand name reflective of high quality writing in a wide variety of formats.

The shifting publishing marketplace with its new technologies has worried many in the field so that WWA conferences of recent times have been marked by much lamentation over the demise of the Western genre. Similar discussions went on during the 1950s and 1960s as well, even as the marketplace boomed. This sense of malaise comes despite the phenomenal success of Larry McMurtry's *Lonesome Dove* as both novel and television miniseries, the cable television success of *Into the West* on TNT, *Deadwood* on HBO, and *Broken Trail* on AMC as well as the long-running *Real West* documentary series on A&E and the History Channel, as well as recent Western nonfiction bestsellers such as *Undaunted Courage* by Stephen Ambrose, *Son of the Morning Star* by Evan Connell, *Blood and Thunder* by Hampton Sides, and *A Terrible Glory* by James Donovan. After a fifteen-year drought there has also been a remarkable revival of the big-screen Western with the two *Young Guns* films by screenwriter John Fusco, the Michael Blake-scripted *Dances With Wolves,* Clint Eastwood's *Unforgiven,* Kevin Costner's *Open Range*, the McMurtry-scripted *Brokeback Mountain*, and the Coen brothers' *No Country for Old Men.*

Despite these recent triumphs, genre Westerns are clearly in decline. Louis L'Amour almost single-handedly kept the traditional Western alive for a generation. Even after his death he still commands more rack space than many of his talented rivals. Several Western writers who once jockeyed with Louis L'Amour for shelf space have now been elevated into more lofty literary circles. Scholarly papers are presented, college courses offered, and thoughtful dissertations written, on the high literary works of Elmer Kelton, Max Evans, Richard Wheeler, Bill Gulick and others. Genre fiction just isn't what it used to be.

Many Western authors are now reclassified by publishers and book retailers as historical fiction while other writers have shifted to the more lucrative romance genre, although the novels still retain frontier or Western settings. Several noted writers, like Jim Harrison, Annie Proulx, Cormac McCarthy, and Jane Smiley, write novels that eastern critics do not recognize as Westerns. A new genre of Southwestern border stories in both fiction and nonfiction has recently emerged. Many of the best new Westerns are contemporary in setting and often they are mysteries. Tony Hillerman dominates in this field, with many following in his wake—all writing a new and different form of the Western.

The Western Writers of America, while weathering rapid changes in literary tastes and the entertainment marketplace, has sought over the last half-century to identify and reward the finest work in the field. The Spur Award has held its place as one of the most prestigious and recognizable literary awards in the world. WWA anthologies have set a standard of excellence in the field while providing entertainment to thousands of readers and keeping the Western short story alive.

Be it "place" or "process" the story has always been the same —the land, the people, the struggle for family, for wealth, for equality, for justice—the American dream. It is a story not just of the West, but recognizable by all mankind, a story that defines who we are as Americans. It is the image we most often project to the world. The dream of the frontier, of a new beginning, of the chance for redemption—the dream of Jefferson and of Hawkeye, of Nick of the Woods and of Davy Crockett, of Mr. Oakhurst and of Mr. Lincoln, of Andy Adams and of Teddy Roosevelt, of the Virginian, of the Ringo Kid, of Elinor Pruitt, of Will Kane, of Willie Boy, of Ranse Foster, of Ma Joad, of Shane, of Woodrow Call. It is the spirit of these characters—both real and imagined—and the spirit of countless others that animate the Western story and the Western Writers of America.

The Western story is America. That story defines who we are as a people—no matter where we or our ancestors come from. As we face the future we will adjust as we have in the past to new tastes, new technologies, new literary markets, fresh visions of the human condition. The Western Writers of America tell human stories—illuminating the past, redeeming the present, informing and entertaining, grieving and celebrating—we are writers and we take that responsibility seriously. The stories and poems in this anthology are reflective of that grand tradition.

TRADITIONAL WEST

LEFT BEHIND

By C.K. Crigger

We was lost. I knew it, Ma knew it, shoot, even my little sister Faith knew it. And Pa? Pa blustered.

"We'll make camp alongside this river." Pa pointed through the pouring rain at the swollen stream. Shoot. One of many tumbling through these towering North Idaho mountains, it ran fast and loud. One thing sure, the river'd get where it was going faster than we would, 'cause not only was we lost, we didn't know where we was headed.

"It's too high to ford anyways," Pa told Ma. "I'll park the wagon yonder under them trees and start a fire. You and the young'uns can get warm, Rosemarie, and everyone'll feel better."

Shoot, I knew who'd be starting the damn fire and it wasn't Pa.

Ma, too worn out to talk, nodded and bent over my little brother Andy, trying to keep him out of the wet. Pa reined our team of mixed-blood Percherons into a cluster of cedars.

See, Andy was sick. Had been for a couple days now, keeping us awake at night with his coughing, and worrying Ma with a fever she couldn't bring down. Ma was sick, too, but her problem was different than Andy's. Ma's belly was pooching out that way it did just before a new brother or sister arrived. Since Andy, who was six years old, none of them babies had lasted longer than a month or two. Ma cried something fierce when they passed, but Pa always said, "Don't you take on so, Rosemarie. We'll just start us another."

9

So then we'd have a burying and I'd put a little cross over the grave with a name and a date carved on it, which seemed to ease Ma. They always named the boys William, and the girls Mary.

One by one, we'd leave those little crosses and the graves they guarded behind when Pa took a notion to move on. Shoot, Pa always took a notion to move on. And Ma would look back with her face sad. I sure hoped this time would work out different.

"Grady Edenfield, I'm talkin' to you."

At the tone of Pa's voice I snapped out of my woolgathering and said, "Yessir," without the least idea of what he wanted. When he sounded like that, it meant he was nursing a big thirst, no surprise considering the weather and Andy's being poorly and Ma's condition. He always got itchy when Ma was about to pop or when his traveling plans got interrupted. Pa got itchy a lot.

I caught Ma mouthing, "Wood," proving me right about the fire. There was plenty of dead limbs laying on the ground under the cedars, kept dry by the drooping branches. I had a good fire going in no time, and Faith helped me throw a tarp over some bushes to make a shelter to keep the rain off. Ma settled Andy under it and got a pot of water boiling so's to brew him a potion.

Didn't work, though. He kept right on coughing, and I saw Ma wiping little sprickles of blood off his mouth. His skin had turned awful pale. Shoot. I knew what that meant. I turned away so Ma wouldn't see me scrubbing tears, and saw Pa saddling Fore, one of the Percherons.

Faith had seen him too. "Where you going, Pa?" she asked.

This dragged Ma's attention from Andy. "Mark? What...?"

Pa settled his floppy old hat tighter on his head. "I'm going back to that town we passed yesterday. I'm going to get a doc out here for Andy."

Ma's lips tightened. "That was a pretty small town, Mark. There may not be a doctor there."

"Then I'll go on until I find one." Pa snapped the reins, making Fore shake his big old head.

Ma snugged the blankets up around Andy's neck. "That could take days. I'm..." She made a funny gesture. "I don't have days. Send Grady. He can do it."

Shoot, yes, I could do it. I'd've liked something warm to eat first, but I saw how worried Ma was so I walked over and tried to take the reins.

He jerked them out of my reach and said, "He'd be too slow, or he'd get lost and never find the town."

"Shoot," I said, "we're lost already, but I can backtrack as good as anybody. I'll do it, Pa."

He cuffed me alongside the head. "Don't backtalk me, boy. Rosemarie, get me some of that leftover cornbread and bacon to eat while I ride. Hurry it up. The sooner I'm gone, the sooner I'll be back."

Ma stared at him. "You can't just leave us like this, Mark. You haven't even set up camp properly. I'm going to need your help."

"I'll go," I said again. "I'll hurry, Ma." This time I got hold of the reins and started clambering up on Fore—a mighty stretch of my foot to the stirrup, I can tell you—when Pa grabbed me by the belt and flung me off onto the ground.

"Oomph!" I was glad it was muddy or it'd've hurt worse.

"Mark!" Ma was crying a little now, not too loud because Pa didn't like it.

He pointed at Faith. "You, child. Bring me that cornbread."

Seeing me all full of mud and with my ear swelling, my sister, her eyes big, hastened to obey.

Ma stood up like she was lifting a house, her face white as paper. "The baby is coming."

"Women's business," he told her. "You don't need me. You've been through it plenty of times, and the girl is old enough to help."

Pa swung up on the horse and glowered down at us until Faith ran over and handed a packet of food to him.

"Expect me when you see me. I'll be back when I've found a doctor for the boy." With that, he kicked the horse into a ponderous gallop back the way we'd come. What had the name of that town been? St. Maries? Or had that been the one before?

Faith squished her toe around in the mud. "Is Pa going to buy whiskey, Ma?"

Ma sighed, sank down beside Andy as if her bones ached something fierce, and dabbed his forehead with the wet cloth. "I expect so." Her head drooped, hiding her face.

Shoot. There wasn't no "expect" to it.

Andy died in the night. We was all, Faith and Ma and me, awake to see him go. Faith thought she'd see the Lord our Savior come take Andy's soul up to heaven, but I told her it was too dark.

11

Ma, her head bowed, was folding Andy's hands over his chest when all the sudden she reared back with a shrill yell, dang near scaring Faith and me into falling into the fire. Faith screeched, too, their noise scaring poor old Aft, our other horse that I'd picketed just beyond the firelight's reach.

Ma stifled her cry and gasped, "I'm having the baby."

Now my sister, being only eight years old, didn't rightly know what that entailed. Ma had a habit of dropping her babies at night, so Faith always missed the big event. But I knew what was going on, having seen a few critters birthed in my time. Faith was gonna have to grow up quick, because it didn't look like Pa would be back. Her and I would have to see Ma through.

I remembered what the women had done last time. "Set some water to boiling, Faith," I said. "And look for those flour sacks Ma's been saving up. I reckon those are to wrap the baby in."

Ma, clamping her mouth on another pain, nodded approval.

That rainy night seemed like it was going to last forever, what with Andy passing and Ma hurting so she couldn't even talk. But dawn came at last, and with it a breeze that blew the clouds away. Blew away the new baby's life, too, without it ever having drawn a real breath. Faith, despite everything, managed at the last minute to sleep through the birthing. Wisht I could've.

"Boy or girl?" Ma eyes was closed, like maybe she'd have less to forget if she never looked at the body.

"Another William." I wrapped the poor little mite in one of the flour sacks and placed him beside Andy. Two brothers in one night. I figured that must be some kind of record.

We sat around most of the day waiting for Pa. When she wasn't sleeping, Ma had spells of crying, so Faith cried, too. I just did what had to be done, which was stake Aft in a nice patch of meadow grass I found, gather more firewood, and cook up some beans for supper. While I was doing those chores, I was thinking on where we could bury my brothers. Tomorrow they'd have to be planted whether Pa was back or not.

So that's why I ambled to the top of a little knoll overlooking the river. With the water going down, the river was as pretty a stream as you'd care to see. The knoll was a good place to put the boys, I thought, well beyond the high water line, and with a good view.

I'd drug a shovel along with me and started in digging the grave. When I figured it was big enough, and deep enough—shoot,

Andy and William together didn't amount to much—I stuck the shovel in the pile of dirt and looked around while the sweat dried on my face.

That's when I noticed a log cabin nestled on some rising ground a couple hundred yards east of the ford. We'd missed seeing it through the rain, but I sure was glad to spot it now. Whoever lived there was bound to help Ma.

When I ran over to the cabin, though, I found the place abandoned and no help to be had. The cabin was in good shape, or would be once somebody cut new leather hinges for the door. The two rooms was empty as a walnut shell except for a note stuck up on a bent nail.

Ain't no gold in this crick, it said. *You want this place, yer welcome to it. I'm moving on.* It was signed *Jackson Parth.* The note reminded me of Pa.

I told Ma about the cabin, but she said as how we'd better stay at the ford so's Pa could find us. Happened he didn't make it by nightfall, nor by noon the next day when it came on to rain again.

"We've got to bury the boys," Ma said.

Faith, her eyes big, looked over at the shelter where the boys was covered with a blanket. "What about Pa?"

"I don't think we better wait on Pa," I said. To tell the truth, my brothers was getting a little ripe.

Ma took a shaky breath. "You're right, Grady. We can't wait for Mark. Help me up."

She and Faith had been sleeping in the wagon while I slept under it, which ain't so bad in warm weather, but gets damn uncomfortable on wet ground.

Ma seemed light as thistledown as I pulled her up, and I wondered if she was strong enough to attend the burying. Howsomeever, she insisted on carrying little William while I toted Andy, and with Faith trailing along, we all got to the hole I'd dug. We lay the boys in and I covered them up. We didn't have much of a ceremony. Ma said a prayer, we all cried, and that was that. Me and Andy'd had some good times and I was sorry as I could be they was over.

Afterward, I pointed out the cabin and Ma insisted we go over for a look-see. Faith ran ahead, but I stuck with Ma who was still walking slow. She kept twisting her head this way 'n that.

Admiring the countryside, I reckoned, same as I had done. Just so happened the sun had come out, warming us up and making the river sparkle like jewels.

I could tell she liked the cabin. She read Parth's note three or four times before folding it and putting it in her pocket. A little smile crossed her face. "Mr. Parth may have come up empty, children, but it looks to me like *we've* struck gold."

"What do you mean, Ma?" Faith asked.

"I mean we've got a ready-made home here, Faith. Your brother is right. This *is* a fine, strong cabin. We can fix it up a little and be snug as bugs."

"Until Pa comes for us," Faith said.

"Hmm," said Ma.

I made Ma stay in the cabin seeing as she was too weak to be walking all over creation, and Faith and I went and loaded anything we'd unloaded back into the wagon. Then I hitched up Aft, which was kind of awkward with a harness meant for two, though we got to the cabin just fine. We spent the rest of the day moving stuff inside. Hoping we wasn't making a mistake and just making more work for ourselves, I fixed the door hinges, swept out the dirt and mouse droppings, and we was set. Shoot, it felt just like home.

In fact, that night as Ma rested in her rocking chair in front of the fire I'd built on the hearth, we decided we didn't want to leave. None of us did. It was like we made a pact.

Ma got strong again pretty quick when she wasn't worn out from being constantly on the move, caring for sick young'uns, or working on another baby. Faith pitched in and we managed the work. Shoot, I was twelve years old, a man, or would be once my voice changed, and I set out to do a man's work.

I repaired the pole corral behind the cabin so we didn't have to hobble Aft anymore. I chopped enough wood to last a month, stacking it under the house eaves where it'd keep dry. Shoot, I even built a sorry looking table and a bench for us to sit on. Faith brung in early blooming flowers she found, and Ma...well, Ma visited the boys' graves up on the knoll every day.

As for Pa, there was no sign he was ever coming back for us.

I'd been hunting the day our first visitor stopped by. We was glad to see him, too, since we'd been living here better'n a month all by our lonesome.

From halfway up the mountain, I'd seen the man crossing the river at the ford. About then a nice three-point buck hopped in front of me and I flung up my grandpa's old rifle and shot it. I was right gleeful, too, since this would be the first fresh meat we'd had in a while, except for prairie chickens and rabbits. Shoot, I'd druther have venison any old day.

Anyways, when I'd lugged a deer hindquarter down the mountain to the cabin—thinking I'd have Aft pack the rest of the carcass home before dark—I found a feller sitting in our kitchen drinking coffee out of Ma's best cup.

"This is Mr. Juris, Grady," Ma said. "He heard your gunshot and stopped to investigate. Then he saw our smoke and thought he'd better say howdy."

"Looks like you had good hunting, Grady," he said.

I nodded and shook the hand he offered. "Have you seen my Pa?" I asked.

"Sorry. Your mother asked that, too. Like I told her, I'm just passing through." His nose twitched as Faith pulled the Dutch oven from the fire and the scent of prairie chicken stew and dumplings wafted out.

"You'll eat with us, Mr. Juris?" Ma poured the man more coffee.

He glanced around, which made me examine our surroundings with new eyes. The contents of our wagon was set around, but it didn't do much to fill up the space. We weren't using the second room. Ma and Faith slept on a narrow bed in the corner, and I slept on a pallet in front of the fire. We felt more comfortable if we stayed together.

"Are you sure I wouldn't be putting your family out, Mrs. Edenfield?" he asked gently. Guess he could see we didn't have much in the way of supplies.

Ma's shoulders stiffened. "My son does well by us, with his hunting. Tomorrow we'll feast on venison."

Mr. Juris smiled. "Yes, ma'am, I can see that."

So Mr. Juris ate supper with us, put his horse in the corral, and helped me pack the rest of the deer out before dark. He camped in our dooryard, joining us for venison steak and flapjacks at breakfast, and when he left, we found a dollar on the table for our trouble.

Two days later another traveler stopped by. He, too, ate a meal with us, and when he traveled on, left a dollar on the table.

15

The next night there was another, and the day after that, a man and his wife. They took our spare room and paid *three* dollars.

We was getting rich, or so I figured until Ma, with a worried look on her face, drew me aside. "Grady, " she said, "do you think you could hitch Aft to the wagon?"

"What's wrong, Ma?" I had visions of her being sick again.

"We need to go into that town and buy supplies. We're almost out of flour and sugar, and the coffee is the same as gone. We've had too many visitors."

"Yeah, but those folks all paid. We got us some cash."

"Yes." She had a strange look on her face. "We would've been destitute without them since your father took all our money. We might've been starving by now."

"Not with me and my rifle," I said, standing proud.

She drew me to her in a hug. "Yes. At least he left that behind."

No need to remind her the rifle hadn't been Pa's anyways. It'd belonged to Ma's Pa, and he'd willed it to me. But then I figured she hadn't actually forgot. She was being *sarcastic*.

With the top off the empty wagon, after a little rerigging it wasn't too much for Aft on his own, so the next morning I took off alone. There'd been another feller arriving cold and hungry during the night, and now Ma didn't want to leave the place empty, or let Faith stay by herself.

That was fine with me, because I planned on asking a few questions around town. The first was at the store, 'cause buying supplies was the most important chore on my list. Shoot, sure didn't take long to spend six dollars, I can tell you, but I managed to wrangle a handful of lemon drops for Faith along with the staples.

Turned out the storekeeper hadn't seen Pa, but he told me there was a doctor in town, so that's where I went next.

"Sorry," the doc said. "Four weeks ago, you say?" He shrugged. "Your father didn't come here."

When I told him about Andy, and Ma losing the baby, he shook his head. "Sounds like your brother had pneumonia, and your Ma...well, son, sometimes babies just aren't meant to be."

Shoot, seemed like most all of Ma's weren't meant to be.

My next stop was the livery stable, figuring the hostler was the one to have seen Pa and Fore. "Sure I remember," he bellowed.

Guess he was deaf. "I got five dollars for helping sell that big old horse to one of the loggers hereabouts. One of his team got crippled by a runaway log and they had to shoot it."

Made me sick, Fore being in danger. Damn, Pa, anyhow.

"And my Pa?" I persisted. "Where did he go."

"Hell, I don't know. I sold him a saddle horse and away he went. Somebody'd told him there was a silver strike in the Coeur d'Alenes and he didn't want to miss out."

"Was he drunk?"

The feller got a crafty kind of look on his face. "Well, now, I sure couldn't say about that. I didn't ask, and he didn't tell."

Shoot!

"You want to sell that horse you got there?" he asked. "I could give you a good price."

I'll just bet he would. Skin me alive is what he'd try to do. "Nope," I said.

I made the rounds of the three drinking establishments, and learned Pa had been at all of them. Not that anybody knew his name. What they remembered was the fight he got in and that he'd broke a man's arm. Mining strike, my eye. Pa had run from an angry crowd, and nobody knew which way he'd gone.

Shoot, I guess I knew which way he hadn't. But here was a curious thing. When I got back home and told Ma, she shrugged like she didn't even care.

The garden was up and growing, my last trip into town I'd finagled some laying chickens, and by mid-summer, we was running a regular hotel. Ma had a few dollars set aside, and it seemed we was doing better than ever in my memory.

Every day Ma walked to the knoll and visited my brothers' graves, but she didn't seem near as sad as she used to. And then early one morning a feller by name of Kemper Bacon visited our cabin.

Turns out Kemper was the logger that bought Fore from Pa, and now he was looking to buy Aft.

"He ain't for sale." I glared at the man standing in front of Ma and me with his hat in his hand. He was a big feller with scarred arms, a couple of missing fingers, and a craggy face darkened by sun and wind. "I heard your other horse got killed. I ain't letting Aft go get hit by no runaway log."

17

"And I ain't planning on letting another good horse get killed," Kemper shot back. "Fired the sonsabitch—sorry, ma'am—that caused the accident."

That was something.

"Truly, Mr. Bacon," Ma said, "we can't let the horse go. We need him."

"You don't need a horse that heavy for a garden and some haying." Kemper cast a knowing eye over the meadow. "These big horses eat more'n an elephant. Are you folks prepared to see this one through the winter?"

Ma chewed on her lower lip. "We'll manage."

He left, but returned a week later. This time he had Fore hitched to a wagon alongside a bay mare two hands shorter than him. Kemper caught my disparaging stare.

"Kind of funny looking together, ain't they? Maddy is lazy, too. Lets poor old Fore do all the work."

Faith squinted up at Kemper. "That isn't fair."

"No, it isn't, but until I find another horse as big as Fore, I reckon he'll have to put up with it."

"Mr. Bacon," Ma said, wiping her hands on a towel she'd grabbed up when he interrupted her bread-making, "I know what you're trying to do. But really, we're fond of Aft. We were fond of Fore, too, and it breaks our hearts to part with either of them. My father trained them, you see, and he's gone now. It seems disloyal to him."

Kemper scowled. "Then why the hell—begging your pardon, ma'am, little missy—did your husband sell this one?"

Ma looked down at the ground and Kemper, sensing that was a road he didn't want to travel, tried another tack. "It's a shame to break up a good team."

"Yes," I said, "and they're full brothers. It ain't right to break up brothers, either."

Kemper kind of settled into the ground and when he spoke, his voice was gentle. "Guess that's the point I'm trying to make."

My face got hot as fire. Shoot, that Kemper Bacon was a twisty bugger. Ma held firm, though, and during the next week, I stepped up my efforts by scything more grass from the meadow and bringing it in to dry for winter hay.

Then it was a Sunday and as was becoming a habit, Kemper showed up driving a buckboard with the horse Maddy and her twin hitched to it. Shoot, did I ever envy him that buckboard. I was tired of using a peeled down prairie schooner every time I needed to go to town.

He'd hit at dinner time, so he sat down at our rickety table to eat with us and the guest staying in our spare room. Afterward, he had another proposition.

"What I'll do," he said, a hopeful look on his face as he swallowed the last of his coffee, "is trade the team I'm driving today, along with the buckboard, for Aft."

I could see Ma was thinking it over.

"And," Kemper added, "I'll bring in my crew and we'll log out that hill above the meadow. It'll give you a sunnier spot for the garden and hay field. I'll take expenses and you can have the profit. Logs are going high, right now. They need timbers in the mines."

Ma looked at me. I sure hated to let Aft go, but Kemper's deal was a good one. Before either Ma or I could say anything, he sweetened the pot.

"I'll add another room onto your hotel, and build a barn and woodshed."

Ma's eyes widened and she took a deep breath.

"I can't do more than that," Kemper said.

"No," Ma said. "I know you can't."

Kemper started getting that hang-dog expression, until she said, "And you won't have to. I'll take your deal, Mr. Bacon. I just ask that you treat both those animals right."

Which, naturally, he promised to do.

To tell the truth, the bay mares were easier for me to handle than the Percherons. Oh, not because Fore and Aft were ornery. They was just too big for a boy.

Like Kemper had promised, the barn got built, the room added on, and he came to stay in the extra room while they was logging the hillside. Paid his dollar a day, too, regular as could be. He was good to my sister. He was awful nice to my Ma, and shoot, he even tolerated me.

Then, on the very day I saw Kemper steal a little kiss from Ma, everything changed.

It was evening. Kemper and two of his crew, Mr. Juris, who'd spread the word about Ma's cooking, and a married couple passing through, was sitting at our supper table. Faith was serving pie made from huckleberries she and Ma had picked up on the mountain. We was all laughing when Pa strode in like he owned the place. He was duded up with high-heeled boots and a leather vest; a six-shooter hung at his hip. He looked like an outlaw and he stunk of whiskey.

Our laughter died. Ma stood up, her chair falling over behind her. "Mark!"

"Hello, Rosemarie," he said.

"Where have you been all these months, Mark?"

Pa's eyebrow arched up like it always did when he was looking to belittle her. "Away. I see you're entertaining. With all these men here, I hope you've been making money, because I need a stake."

I guess it was an insult, because Ma turned dead white. "Men? What are you insinuating?"

"Yeah," said Kemper. "What *are* you insinuating."

Pa set his hand on the pistol butt. "Mind your own business, mister. I'm talking to my wife."

I could see he disremembered Kemper, even though he'd sold him our horse. I could also see he didn't scare Kemper none.

In a voice soft as kitten fur, Kemper said, "My friends are my business, Mr. Edenfield, and *I* ain't in the habit of letting down the people I care about."

Sounded to me like Kemper could insinuate as good as anybody.

Ma broke in, her words tumbling over themselves. "After you abandoned us, Mark, Grady found this house. Mr. Juris has been kind enough to recommend my cooking, and Mr. Bacon, his men, and these people," she nodded at the married couple, "are paying for their supper."

Pa's hard gaze roamed the room. "How did you get money to start?"

"The cabin was here. Our friends helped make it better. I'm running a hotel, Mark. A small hotel."

She didn't say who'd helped, or that she'd filed homestead papers on the land yesterday, and that Pa's name was not on them.

Pa, he just acted like our hard work meant nothing. "Pack up, Rosemarie," he said. "We're moving on."

Everybody went still. Ma's hand went to cover her heart. "Aren't you even going to ask how Andy is, Mark? Or our new baby?"

20

He shrugged. "I suppose the new one died, as usual. And the other boy? Well, he always was puny." He turned to me, "Boy, get packed. And hurry it up. I ain't got time to waste."

Which meant he probably had somebody on his heels and they was mad.

Ma looked at me and Faith before letting her gaze drift to Kemp. "No," she said.

Pa got a bug-eyed look. "What did you say?"

"I said no. This family isn't moving again. I'm staying here, Mark, with my live children and my dead babies and I'm giving them a home. You can keep on traveling the rest of your life. I don't care anymore."

He slapped her so hard she fell, and he knocked me to my knees when I tackled him. Last, he tried to fight Kemper Bacon, a bad idea. When Pa woke up, at Kemp's suggestion he climbed atop his horse and rode off toward town.

"A man who'll abuse his wife and children don't deserve them," Kemper said.

That was the last time we seen Pa. About six months later we heard he'd been killed in a brawl somewhere in Colorado. It was a long way from home.

Shoot. I guess Pa was lost then, too.

THE RELUCTANT SHEPHERD

By Elmer Kelton

Hewey Calloway had not been to town in more than eight weeks. Now he had two months' cowboy wages in his pocket and was riding in for a well-earned celebration. Upton City might never be the same again.

Knowing how hung over he would feel by the time he emptied his pockets, he almost dreaded it.

Sister-in-law Eve would have a lot to say afterward, but she had a lot to say about almost everything. He respected her strong opinions about responsibility, sobriety, and thrift, but he did not share them. Now past thirty and proud of maintaining his bachelorhood against contrary advice from almost everybody around him, he felt it was his right to spend his money and his off time in any way he saw fit. Even tight-fisted old rancher C. C. Tarpley understood that his employees had to vent steam occasionally. Otherwise, their work suffered, and C. C. could not stand for that.

Hewey hoped he might be lucky enough to run into old drinking compadres such as Snort Yarnell or Grady Welch. But if they weren't there, he could holler loudly enough by himself.

He reached deep into memory, reliving rowdy adventures he had enjoyed in times past, recalling the many pleasures and glossing over the pain that inevitably followed. People like Eve kept telling him that at his age he ought to slow down and find a place to settle. But he felt not one bit older than when he had been twenty. He was going to have a good time whether anybody else liked it or not.

He was humming a shady little dancehall ditty when a distant sound first reached him. He listened intently, but for a moment or two could not make out what it was. Then it came clearer. He recognized the bleating of sheep.

"Sheep!" he exclaimed, though no one could hear him except his horse. "Biscuit, old C. C.'ll bust a blood vessel."

This was Tarpley land, and C. C. hated sheep like the devil hates holy water. Hewey did not exactly hate them; he just refused to acknowledge their existence.

He rode in the direction of the sound. Soon he saw a flock moving slowly westward, each sheep pausing to graze, then trotting to catch up. A black and white dog kept pace, its tongue lolling. When an animal paused too long, the dog ran up and nipped at it. The nearby sheep tumbled over each other in their haste to give the dog room.

A tarp-covered wagon, drawn by two mules, rolled along slowly on the upwind side, out of the dust stirred by the flock's tiny hooves. A horseman followed the sheep, not allowing the drags to linger long in one place. The man was hunched over as if half asleep.

I'm fixing to wake him up good, Hewey thought. As a Two Cs hand, it was his job to see after C. C. Tarpley's interests. C. C. was definitely not interested in having sheep cross his cattle range.

Hewey knew this was a tramp sheepman with no land of his own, moving across country and fattening his animals on other men's forage. It was a common enough practice, though it was increasingly frowned upon as more and more Texas state land fell into private ownership.

Hewey had a cowboy way of assessing a man's horse before he made any judgment about the rider. This horse was old, in bad need of being turned out to pasture. The saddle appeared to be just as old, somebody's castoff. The bridle was patched, the reins of cotton rope instead of leather. The only thing not old was the rider. Hewey guessed him to be in his mid to late twenties.

"Hey, you," Hewey said, "don't you know this is private land?"

The man raised his head. Hewey knew at first glance that he was sick. His face had a gray look. The eyes were dull. In a weak voice the man said, "Thank God you've come along. We need help."

"You'll sure need help if C. C. Tarpley finds you here."

The young sheepman pointed toward the wagon. "My little boy, he's awful sick. I'm afraid we'll lose him. My wife's not much better."

"What's the matter with them?"

"I think we got ahold of some bad water."

Hewey said, "I don't know as I can be any help. I ain't no doctor. You need to get your family to town."

"But I can't leave the sheep. They're all we've got. They'd scatter, and the coyotes would get a lot of them."

Hewey did some mental calculation. At the rate the sheep were traveling, it would probably take three, perhaps four days to reach Upton City. He wondered if these people had that much time.

He said, "I'll go take a look at your wife and boy. But like I said, I ain't no doctor." He pushed Biscuit into a lope and overtook the wagon. A young woman held the leather reins. Like her husband, she appeared to be asleep. When she turned her gaze to Hewey, her eyes were dull, her skin sallow.

Hewey said, "He tells me you got a sick boy in that wagon."

"Terrible sick," she said, her voice so quiet that Hewey barely heard it.

Riding alongside, he lifted a loose corner of the tarp. Inside, on blankets, lay a boy with eyes closed. He could have been asleep, or even unconscious.

The man had followed Hewey, but the old horse was slow in catching up. He asked, "What do you think?"

"I think you've got some mighty sick people. You need to leave the sheep and get these folks to Doc Hankins as quick as you can."

"I told you, the sheep are all we've got."

There was a saying in cow country that the only thing dumber than a sheep was the man who owned them. This man was proving the point, Hewey thought.

He said, "Well, then, you'd better speed them up."

"You can't hurry sheep."

Hewey shrugged, fresh out of arguments. "Well, when I get to town I'll tell Doc Hankins. Maybe he can ride out in his buggy and meet you."

He moved ahead, coughing from the dust raised by the sheep. It would take at least the first two drinks just to wash his throat clean.

25

Even after he had traveled half a mile, he could still hear the bleating. He could not understand the thinking of a man willing to gamble three lives on a flock of sheep. If they were his, he could easily ride off and leave them to take their chances with the coyotes. Cattle did not have to be pampered and protected like that. Too bad the family did not have a herd of cows instead of a flock of helpless sheep.

He tried to think ahead to the good time he would have in town, but his mind kept drifting back to the woman and to the boy lying in the bed of the wagon.

Dammit, Hewey Calloway, he thought, they're not your responsibility. What if you'd taken a different trail to town? You never would have seen them.

But he had seen them. Now he could not shake free from the images. Cursing his luck, he turned Biscuit around and put him into a trot, back toward the sheep. The woman hardly looked up as Hewey passed the wagon. The man on horseback had dropped behind the flock again. Hewey rode up to him. "Mr. Whatever-your-name-is, hurry yourself up to that wagon. You're goin' to town."

"But the sheep..."

"I'll see after the damned sheep. Just leave me that horse and a little grub to pack on him. And see that you make them mules trot."

"Do you know anything about handling sheep?"

"No, but I learn fast. Get goin' before I change my mind. It's half changed already."

In a short time the wagon was rumbling along the trail toward town, the mules stepping high. Confused, the dog followed it a little way, then turned back toward the flock. It looked at Hewey with evident mistrust.

Hewey said, "Dog, I hope you know what you're doin', because I sure don't." He watched the wagon a minute, then turned to stare at the slowly moving flock. He thought about Upton City waiting in vain to welcome him and his wages. But here he was, stuck with a bunch of snot-nosed woollies.

Some days, he thought, I've got no more sense than a one-eyed jackrabbit. He reserved some of his frustration for the sheepman, who ought not to be dragging a family across this dry desert in the first place.

26

Biscuit had been trained to be a cow horse. He seemed bewildered by the sheep, but no more so than his owner. Watching, Hewey gradually came to see that he did not need to do much except follow, and occasionally to help the dog push stragglers along. The sheep moved westward at their own pace, like molasses in January.

From the corner of his eye he caught a furtive movement off to the left of the flock. The dog suddenly snapped to attention, then barreled off in pursuit of a coyote. It came back after a time, panting heavily. Blood was drying around its mouth. Coyote blood, Hewey surmised.

In admiration he said, "I wonder what they're feedin' you. I'd like some of it myself."

Late in the afternoon the dog chased down a jackrabbit and ate it. Hewey realized the animal was not being fed at all. It was making its own living. He told the dog, "You ought to be workin' for C. C. Tarpley. At least he feeds good."

He worried about how he would get the sheep to bed down. To his surprise, they did it on their own at dusk, instinctively pulling into a fairly compact band. The dog circled them a couple of times, chastising a few independent-minded ewes that tried to find a sleeping place a little away from the others.

A while after dark, Hewey was reminded why sheep tend to bunch up at night. He heard a coyote howl, answered shortly by another. He had always enjoyed listening to coyotes. He regarded them as a natural element in the landscape, helping give this part of the country its unique character. They had never represented any kind of threat to him before. But tonight was different. These sheep were vulnerable, and like it or not, he was responsible for them. He saw the dog listen intently, then trot off to circle the flock. He had staked Biscuit on a long rope to graze. He saddled the horse and moved off after the dog.

He had no gun. If a coyote showed itself, he could do little except run at it with his rope and chase it away. The dog was a weapon in itself. Somewhere ahead, in the darkness, Hewey heard the yipping and snarling that indicated a fight. In a while the dog appeared, acting proud of itself.

Hewey grinned. "Dog, if I ever get in a fight, I want you on my side."

Next morning, while he fixed a meager breakfast of coffee, bacon, and baking powder biscuits, he wondered how he would go about getting the sheep up and off the bed ground. They took care of the problem themselves, rising to their feet and grazing in the dawn's warm light. They began to drift. The dog moved tirelessly, starting them in the right direction. Hewey had little to do but move a few of the lame and lazy, then follow.

Herding sheep ain't as tough as I thought, he told himself. The dog does most of the work.

The flock moved no faster than yesterday. At this rate he figured they might reach town by tomorrow evening, or more likely the day after. A cow herd would have made the distance in half the time, a steer herd even less. A determined turtle could leave these sheep behind.

Toward noon, he saw what he had feared most, three cowboys riding toward him from the east. He had not wanted anyone to see him here. He had swamped out a saloon a few times, but never had he sunk so low as to herd sheep. He could only hope these men were all strangers.

He was not that lucky. A tall, lanky rider grinned, a gold tooth shining as he approached. He exclaimed, "Hewey Calloway! When did old C. C. start runnin' sheep? And why ain't you already quit?"

Reluctantly Hewey reached out his hand and shook with Snort Yarnell. With Snort spreading the word, it would not take two days for everyone within seventy-five miles to know about Hewey's disgrace.

One of the cowboys guffawed. "This can't be the Hewey Calloway you've told us about, Snort. He was supposed to be eight feet tall and a ring-tailed tooter. My, how the mighty have fallen."

Resentfully Hewey said, "I'm tryin' to get these sheep off of C. C.'s range as quick as I can. I don't suppose you fellers would like to help me?"

Snort still grinned. "I don't suppose we would. We got our reputations to think of."

Snort had a reputation as a top hand when he was sober but a hell-for-leather carouser when he wasn't. He asked, "Where's the owner at? Did you shoot him?"

"I don't have a gun with me. Besides, you know I can't hit a barn from the inside. I got these sheep on my hands by tryin' to do some sick folks a favor."

He realized they did not believe him. They probably thought C. C. had fired him and he had to accept whatever job came along. It had happened before, but things never became so serious that he was forced to herd sheep.

The laughing cowboy looked to be about twenty, just old enough to think he knew it all and had nothing more to learn. If he didn't stop laughing, Hewey was of a mind to teach him something new.

Stiffly Hewey said, "I've told you how it is. If that's not good enough, you can go soak your head in a water bucket."

Snort shrugged. "No use gettin' on your high horse, Hewey. If that's the best story you've got, stick with it. Me and the boys are headed for town to do somethin' we'll worry about for a month."

Hewey had never seen Snort worry about much of anything. He said, a little enviously, "You-all have a good time."

Snort said, "We'll drink a toast to you, and to your woolly friends."

They rode away, leaving Hewey thinking about going to Canada or someplace where nobody knew him.

He had hoped no word of this would get back to C. C. That hope was dashed now, for Snort had never kept a secret in his life.

The dog seemed finally to accept Hewey. It trotted along at his side when it was not busy bringing errant sheep back into the flock.

At least not everybody will be lookin' down on me, Hewey thought.

The dog chased after a coyote late in the day and came back exhausted. It laid down in the scant shade of a greasewood bush and panted while the flock moved on. But its sense of duty soon brought it back to Hewey's side.

Hewey said, "If I could ever find a woman as dependable as you, I might get married."

Eve was dependable, but brother Walter was welcome to her. Along with her many good traits, including being a world-beating cook, she carried a few liabilities such as a tendency to burden him with criticism and unsolicited advice.

Hewey did not sleep much that night. He kept hearing coyotes. He imagined them skulking into camp and dragging off helpless lambs. He had heard that coyotes sometimes ate them alive. He kept Biscuit saddled and made several circles around the bedded flock. That seemed to please the dog.

If I ever get this bunch to town, he thought, I'll never wear wool underwear again.

He watered the sheep at a dirt tank which belonged to C. C. He knew the old man would consider the water hopelessly contaminated and unfit for cattle, but even sheep had to drink. The dog plunged in and swam across the tank. On the opposite bank it shook itself, then jumped back in. Hewey considered doing the same, but the sheep had muddied the water too much.

The sun was almost down on the third day when he caught first sight of the stone courthouse and the tallest windmill in Upton City. He realized he would not be able to get the sheep all the way to town before night. He would have to camp one more time. The realization of being so near, yet so far, chapped him like a wet saddle.

He thought about Snort and the fun he must be having. He wished he could run all these sheep over a cliff, but there was not a decent cliff anywhere this side of the Davis Mountains. Be damned if he would drive them that far.

Approaching town the next morning, Hewey loped ahead to the wagonyard to open the gate into a large corral. He saw the stableman walking toward him from the barn and shouted, "Sheep comin' in."

"Been expectin' you," the stableman answered back.

So much for secrecy. Damn Snort Yarnell, he thought.

He knew how to pen difficult cattle, but he had no idea how to go about penning sheep. They approached the open gate with suspicion, a few ewes almost starting in, then running back into the flock. The stableman grabbed a ewe and dragged her through the gate despite her stiff-legged resistance. Several ewes made a tentative move to follow, and then the flock surged through like water from a broken dam. Some in their haste bumped heavily against the gateposts. The dog finished the job by pushing a last few reluctant sheep through the opening.

Hewey tied Biscuit to the fence while the stableman closed the gate. He said, "You were lookin' for me?"

The stableman replied, "When those sick folks hit town, they said some cowboy was bringin' in their sheep. They didn't know your name. Then Snort came in, and we all knew Hewey Calloway had turned sheepherder."

"I owe Snort a good cussin' out."

"You won't have any trouble findin' him. He's over yonder under the shed with the two punchers he brought along."

When cowboys came to town they usually slept on cots or on the ground at the wagonyard rather than pay for a room at the boarding house. No one as yet had built a hotel in Upton City.

Hewey asked, "What about the sick folks?"

"Doc Hankins fixed them up pretty good. Says they ought to be able to travel in three or four days."

Hewey walked with the stableman to the open shed where the cots were. The smart-talking young cowboy was leaning against a post, bent over and holding his stomach. The other squatted on the ground, moaning, his eyes glazed. Snort Yarnell sat on the edge of a steel cot, holding his head in both hands. His face was pale as milk.

The stableman said, "They haven't drawn a sober breath since they hit town. Now they're payin' the fiddler."

Hewey found it in himself to feel sorry for Snort, a little.

The stableman said, "If you hadn't got yourself saddled with those sheep, you'd be in the same shape now that Snort is. You're lucky."

"Awful lucky," Hewey said sarcastically, thinking of the good time Snort must have had.

A wizened little man in slouchy clothes and a battered felt hat came walking down from the boarding house. Hewey groaned as he recognized C. C. Tarpley.

Hewey said, "I was hopin' he wouldn't hear about these sheep. I reckon I'm fixin' to get fired."

A scowl twisted C. C.'s wrinkled face. He declared, "I thought you were workin' for *me*. What's this I hear about you bringin' those sheep to town?"

Hewey had been trying to decide how best to tell him. He said, "Wasn't nothin' else I could do, C. C. Sick as them folks was, and as slow as they were movin', there's no tellin' how long they might've had their sheep on your land. I was tryin' to get them off of it as fast as I could."

This implied that Hewey was just trying to do the boss a favor. C. C. would appreciate that more than the thought of doing a favor for a sick family. The old man was not often given to doing favors for anybody.

31

C. C.'s scowl slowly faded as he thought it over. "I never looked at it that way. You done right, Hewey."

Relieved, Hewey said, "All in the line of duty, C. C."

The old rancher started to turn away but paused. "By the way, how long have you been gone from the ranch?"

Hewey counted on his fingers. "This is the fourth day."

"Looks to me like you've had enough holiday for now. You'd better be gettin' back to work."

Hewey's disappointment went all the way down to his toes. "Yep, reckon I had."

He stood with hands shoved deeply into his pockets as C. C. walked away. The stableman said sympathetically, "There'll be a next time."

Hewey felt the roll of bills he had intended to spend on celebration. He drew them from his pocket and extended them to the stableman, holding back one to buy his dinner. He said, "Those sheep are goin' to need some hay, and that dog deserves a good chunk of beef to chew on. With what's left of this, I wish you'd make sure those folks' wagon has plenty of groceries in it when they leave."

Smiling, the stableman placed a hand on Hewey's shoulder. He said, "You're a better man than you know, Hewey Calloway. Even for a sheepherder."

Hewey grunted. "Don't blab it around. I've got my reputation to think of."

He untied Biscuit and swung into the saddle. "See you in a couple of months. I'll throw a real party next time."

He was already dreading it.

GRANDMA'S HOPE CHEST

By Dusty Richards

In early summer there were long columns of cattle headed for Abilene that went by for days on both the west and east side of Jenny Lynn's soddy. Their polished long horns shone in the bright sun when the twelve-year-old stood on the rise and squinted through the dust and glare at their snake-like procession.

One day in late afternoon a cowboy rode by as she watched the parade. A tall, lean young man who wore bull hide chaps, snub-nosed boots, and spurs that jingled like silver bells. He removed his hat and wiped his un-tanned forehead on his sleeve. Then he asked her name.

"Jenny Lynn Prior." She bowed her head politely to the man on horseback.

"You must live on that homestead?" He motioned his big brimmed hat toward their low-walled soddy.

"I do with my maw and paw."

"Guess you've got a milk cow?"

"We sure do. Sarie, but we've got her tied up so's she don't runoff with them Texas cows of yours."

He looked back at the passing line and laughed. "I guess that would be a problem."

She wrinkled her nose. "She thinks she belongs to buffalos too."

He nodded. "You figure she'd raise another calf?"

Jenny Lynn smiled and agreed.

"I get one tonight, I'll bring him to you in the morning."

She looked at him troubled. "I ain't got a dime to pay yeah, mister."

"Ain't no matter. He'll be free."

"Why would you do that?" The Kansas wind swept her dress against her legs and she was forced to press her skirt down.

"Cause he'd never make it to Abilene." He started to rein his horse around to leave.

"Wait, wait, what is your name?"

"Bonner, Clint Bonner." He tipped his hat and was gone.

Sunrise was only a purple slit on the horizon when she led Sarie in to be milked outside the front door. Her mother took up the three-legged stool, set the pail down and seated she began forcing streams of snowy milk in the bucket while Jenny Lynn held the lead rope.

At the sound of silver bells, she whispered to her mother. "He's coming maw. I hear him. He's coming."

"Who's coming?"

"Mister Bonner and he has a calf for me. I can hear him bawling."

Bonner reined up, nodded at them, and stepped down with the newborn in his arms. Set on the ground, the little critter could hardly stand on his buckling legs. Sarie licked him, and he moved beside her, managing to get a little milk from her udder.

"He looks happy enough," Bonner said, then he swung up in the saddle, tipped his hat. "Good day ma'am and good luck. You sure have a fine daughter."

The calf was christened Billy Bonner and in the fall her father led the fat calf off to town and returned with a small cedar chest for Jenny Lynn. That box became a hope chest for my great grandmother. She stowed the things she felt necessary in preparation for that "someday" event.

Today that old chest still smells rich of the cedar wood. In it are the short letters bound by a pink ribbon that he wrote to her every two or three months. And from when she turned sixteen there is a wedding license for Jenny Lynn Prior and Clint Bonner. He was twice her age, but to a girl who lived in a soddy, he was her prince charming. And the folded Lone Star Quilt she made for their bed is beneath those items.

Traditional West / Fiction

RETURN OF SMOLAN GRANT

By Cotton Smith

Jubal Butler stood in the doorway of the Gypsum, Texas, saloon. Home after four years as a Ranger. He knew most of the men inside, but it still felt strange.

A circle of dust flittered from his shotgun chaps as he stepped inside. Long dark hair waved along his shoulders. Wearing no hat, he looked more Apache than white man. Trail dust mingled with beard stubble. His left arm was carried oddly at his side.

"My Lord, is that you, Jubal? Thought you were dead!" The bald-headed saloonkeeper yelled.

Jubal smiled. "Close, Will, but I'm breathing."

Everyone turned and immediately noticed the double-action Colt Thunderer carried in a cross-draw holster on his bullet belt. A second matching revolver rested in his belt. Each gun had ivory grips inlaid with a small circle of turquoise. Several whispered concerns; several smiled.

The saloon patrons remembered him as a young man with a fierceness matched only by his best friend, Smolan Grant. Bold and reckless. Absolutely fearless. And dangerous. Both becoming Rangers surprised most.

"Heard you—an' Smolan—were killed," a townsman with long sideburns shouted from his table, "Some God-awful gun fight between you—an' rustlers. On the border it was. Are you all right? Are you still a Ranger?"

35

"I am now. I am not." He smiled again at the double answer.

"Well, Smolan sure ain't dead. Been robbin' banks. Has a gang," a gangly cowboy declared, waving a beer.

Jubal nodded. "Heard that. Last time I saw Smolan was a year ago. We left the Rangers then." He didn't say why or where he had been since then.

Other men hurried to Jubal Butler, eager to shake his hand. He grimaced when one grabbed his left arm. The stiffened arm was slow in movement, soft in strength; even making a fist was difficult.

"Sorry, Jubal. Didn't realize. You're hurt." The store clerk with graying hair frowned.

"That's all right. Takes time to heal."

A chiseled face carried a horizontal scar along Jubal's right cheek. Another result of that border war. He listened quietly as the crowd around him spoke of drifters telling of a gunfight two years ago, a vicious battle between rustlers, Jubal Butler and Smolan Grant, and an Apache scout. The tales always ended with the death of all the participants.

He indicated the fight was true, but the only dead were the rustlers. He grimaced and said, "And a good friend...Kuruk."

"What kinda name is that?" a wide-faced cowboy asked.

"Kuruk was a Mimbreno Apache. A shaman. A healer. He scouted for us. Gave me this."

From around his neck, he held up a long, leather thong holding a small, uneven piece of clear quartz. To Kuruk, it represented life-giving water and one of their gods. Jubal's eyes said he didn't expect to be questioned about it anymore.

As he walked farther into the saloon, someone mentioned his older brother, Milo, now owned the family ranch, the largest in the region. Their father had died after a fall from a horse three years ago. Jubal's face didn't react; he said nothing. He already knew, having stopped at the Lazy B before coming to town. It was awkward; the brothers had never been close.

Seeing Tilly at the ranch, and learning of her marriage to Milo, had been a shock. Seeing their one-year-old son, James, was another surprise.

A raw-faced townsman in a dark, three-piece suit said, "Hey, do you remember Tilly Teagle? Real good-lookin' gal? She married Milo. Can you believe it?"

Jubal's eyes widened. It was still hard to believe. The letters she had sent to Smolan Grant and his constant talk about her had convinced him they would be married. Of course, that was before Smolan turned outlaw—and the town thought both were killed. Tilly had asked about him, but Jubal knew nothing she didn't. Milo called Smolan a name and Tilly got upset. What really bothered Jubal, though, were her eyes. An invitation to him was definitely there.

Smolan had loved her since the first day she attended their one-room county school. Every boy had been in love with her at one time or another. She had a teasing smile that made a boy weak and tongue-tied. Later on, she had a body that was a tease in itself.

At the bar, Jubal accepted a glass of Irish whiskey, poured from a bottle kept hidden. "On the house, Jubal. Glad you're back," the bartender said. "What're your plans?"

The young gunfighter sucked down the whiskey. It was hard to think. He wasn't sure why he had come back. He heard himself say he would be moving on soon.

"Wish you would stay, Jubal. Gypsum needs a marshal," the bartender wiped the bar surface. "Marshal Huggins...you remember him. Died a week ago. Pneumonia."

"I'm sorry to hear that. He was a good man."

Two weeks later, three riders ambled down Gypsum's main street. Well-armed strangers with horses better than most ranch mounts. No one noticed them or their horses, except Marshal Jubal Butler, drinking coffee and watching from his office window. A morning ritual, since becoming the town's peace officer. He wasn't sure why he had made the decision. Maybe he owed Gypsum something. Kuruk told him the spirits guided a warrior to the right path.

Unaware of the developing danger, townspeople went about their daily tasks. Freighters and wagons rumbled along the street. In the background, the steady ping of the blacksmith's hammer provided the illusion of a normal day.

"Well, and a good morning to you, Marshal Butler." He muttered to himself, knowing the strangers meant bank trouble.

Earlier he had sent his two part-time deputies to check the saloons on the far end of town. He wished they were with him. Now there wasn't time to get them.

37

He slammed his cup down on the desk and yanked on his dark, pinstriped coat with the badge pinned to the lapel. It took time to get his stiffened left arm into the sleeve. Jubal checked his Colt and returned the gun to its holster. The second revolver was taken from his desk, checked and shoved into his belt.

As the strangers pulled up at the hitching rack in front of the bank, Jubal eased from his door, keeping to the shadows. Any attempt to warn the town of the coming holdup would only get somebody hurt or worse. This was what he was hired for. Gypsum would know soon enough. One way or the other. He touched the piece of quartz hanging from his neck and muttered a warrior's prayer Kuruk had taught him.

Outside the bank, one horseman stayed mounted, holding all the reins, while the other two outlaws went inside. A freight wagon rolled past and the marshal walked along its far side until he got closer. As he reached the bank, Jubal drew his Colt and stepped away from the wagon.

"Mornin', stranger. Wrong town to try making a withdrawal."

The man jumped in his saddle and reached for his pistol.

"Wrong choice, too. Pull that gun real slow. With your fingers. Let it drop," Jubal declared. "Now, out of the saddle and let go of all those reins."

"What is this, lawman? Me an' my friends jes' came to town."

"I know. I'm the welcoming committee."

As the man dismounted, Jubal clubbed him on the head with his gun barrel. The outlaw crumpled into an odd-shaped coil at the marshal's feet.

Holstering his gun, Jubal slapped the horses hard. All three snorted and ran toward the far end of the street. A water trough enticed them to stop. He drew his pistol again, stepped onto the planked sidewalk and took a position against the building to the right of the bank door.

Several townspeople stopped on both sides of the bank, uncertain of what was happening. One woman asked her husband why the new marshal had knocked out that man; her husband shushed her.

Jubal motioned for them to leave.

"My wife's in there, Marshal," a tall man said, fiddling nervously with the gold chain on his vest.

"She'll be all right—unless you keep talking," Jubal said softly.

"You'd better be right. My money's in there, too," the businessman bristled, turned on his heels and walked away with the others.

Minutes later, the two bank robbers burst through the bank door. Both carried filled saddlebags. It took an eye blink to realize something was wrong. No horses. Their comrade lying in the dirt.

"Drop your guns," Jubal said. "You're under arrest."

The closest man in a battered derby spun toward him with his cocked revolver. A stocky outlaw hesitated, then turned in Jubal's direction as well.

The young marshal fired five times. Fast. In one long bellow. Three bullets hit the derby-wearing outlaw as he fired wildly. The other two hit the stocky man in the right shoulder and arm and his revolver crashed on the sidewalk. Twisting backwards, the closest bank robber slammed into the other and collapsed in front of him. The outlaw's derby flew away and his gun thudded uncontrolled onto the sidewalk. His saddlebags plopped next to him.

Jubal holstered his Colt and drew the second.

Holding his hand to his right shoulder, the stocky man stared down at his dead companion and dropped his saddlebags to the sidewalk.

"Smart choice," Jubal said.

"You'll be sorry, lawman. When Smolan Grant hears about this, he'll kill you an' destroy this piss-ant town," the outlaw blurted.

Smolan Grant? Was this his gang? Of course, he couldn't come into Gypsum without being recognized. Was this revenge for chasing him out of town years ago?

"Hey, Aaron, come out and get your money. It's safe," Jubal yelled at the bank president. He touched the quartz around his neck and whispered thanks.

From the far end of town, his two deputies came running. Soon Gypsum was abuzz with the daring of their new marshal, and Jubal's deputies returned to their tasks.

An hour away, Milo Butler's roan heard the growing sound behind them before he did. Jubal's older brother was thinking about Tilly.

After thinking about her during a few hours of branding and calf cutting, he had decided to go into town and invite his younger brother to Sunday dinner. He liked having Jubal back, but hadn't said so. It would please Tilly; she was always complaining about not having any company, being alone. Having Jubal there would make her happy.

Milo's horse stutter-stepped. Thundering past horse and rider came a brand-new carriage pulled by two matching bays. Tassels lining the short roof snapped in the breeze. Sunlight sparkled from the silver spokes of the wheels.

"Easy. Damn you, easy."

Milo yanked the reins hard as the surprised roan shied away. He shoved his legs forward to stay in the saddle, angry to be caught off-guard.

The driver's blonde head turned toward Milo; long hair swung with the movement. A toothy grin of recognition followed. Light blue eyes sought the rancher's mind as the driver waved.

Smolan Grant!

Milo hadn't seen Smolan Grant since that son of a town whore had been run out of Gypsum. But everybody had heard about Smolan's recent bank robbing spree. Holding the reins tight, the rancher watched the carriage disappear down the road and turn west, toward the abandoned county schoolhouse.

"Should'a killed the sonvabitch. Probably came to rob our bank. Damn." He licked his parched lips and spurred the horse into a lope. Like his late father, he was a hard man with hard ways. Usually finding something to grumble about every day.

Locked-away heat passed through Milo's body as his mind released the shadows of catching Smolan with Tilly in her father's barn when they were teenagers. Milo had nearly killed him with his fists. Jubal showed up unexpectedly and stopped him. Jubal whipped him that day—the first time Milo had been beaten. By anyone.

It was also the day their father heard the news and disowned his younger son. Shortly after that, Smolan and Jubal left Gypsum. Smolan was forced to leave; Jubal wanted to be with his friend.

Milo gritted his teeth at the painful recollection. Today, Smolan looked just as confident as he always did, yet different. He was dressed in a gray, three-piece suit and a matching curl-brimmed hat with a wide silk band. From under his coat, two pearl-handled revolvers were carried in twin shoulder holsters.

Tilly reentered Milo's mind. She was usually there. Like some eternal rose. His greatest prize. But she had been angry with him this morning, more than usual. She had started off telling him of an article she had read about a train ride to San Antonio and how much fun it would be. He said it was impossible at this time of the year. She said that's what he always said, regardless of when it was. That was true; he liked being on the ranch. Saw no need to leave. He wished she would understand.

Her last words as he left were, "Tell James goodbye before you leave."

They had been married for two years. Milo had asked her at least a dozen times to marry him before she finally agreed, after the stories of the reported deaths of Smolan and Jubal. In the last few days, though, she had been particularly irritated. Almost as bad as when she heard Smolan Grant was alive and robbing banks.

Lately, letters from some eccentric aunt had set her off again. One had come just last week. He'd never heard of the woman; Tilly offered to read it to him since he couldn't read well. He wasn't interested in hearing from a crazy old woman and said so.

He had another reason to see Jubal now: Smolan Grant.

Entering town, Milo Butler yanked the roan to a hard stop in front of the marshal's office and swung down. He wiped his mouth with his shirt sleeve. He was wondering why his brother came to that barn on that particular day. He hadn't thought about it before.

From behind him came a familiar voice. "Hey, Milo, you missed all the excitement."

The rancher spun toward bank president, Aaron Kinson. "Been workin'. You wouldn't know about work. Wha'd I miss?"

"Three strangers tried to rob the bank," Kinson said, waving his arms for emphasis. "Your brother stopped 'em. All by himself."

"What were you doin', Kinson? Wavin' loan papers at 'em?"

Milo chuckled at the man's quick departure and headed inside the marshal's office.

Turning in his chair, the lawman said, "Mornin', Milo. Got that young'un riding yet?"

Milo grunted.

Like their father, Milo wasn't an easy man to like, but he was his brother. Jubal changed the subject, leaning back in his chair.

"How's spring round-up going?"

The raw-boned rancher was two inches taller and twenty pounds heavier than the marshal, but their younger-day fisticuff outcomes were actually about even, in spite of what Milo liked to say.

41

Milo waved his hands to stop the conversation. "Guess who I just saw in a real fancy carriage?"

"The governor."

"Hell no. Smolan Grant."

"Smolan Grant? You're joshing," Jubal said.

"Why would I ride all the way to do that?"

"Anybody with him?"

"Just him an' two fancy pistols."

"Good. Three of his friends are in here." Jubal motioned toward the cells.

"Heard that. They don't look so tough to me," Milo snorted. "He was headin' for the old schoolhouse."

"What's he going there for? How long ago?"

Milo cocked his head to the side. "Now see here, I ain't one o' your deputies. Hour, maybe. Go see for yourself."

"I aim to do just that."

Milo glanced at the weapon rack against the far wall. "Maybe, I'll just go along with you."

"No. I don't herd cattle; you don't go after outlaws."

"Think I'm afraid of Smolan Grant?"

"Well, you're the only Butler who isn't."

From the jail cell, the bowlegged outlaw yelled, "You'd better be scared, lawman. Once he hears we're in here, he'll come an' kill all you bastards."

Jubal's eyes told him to be quiet and he did.

Milo started for the cell and Jubal told him to stay where he was. The hot-headed rancher didn't like being told what to do, but he didn't move. Something in his brother's manner was unsettling.

The other outlaw asked quietly, "Say, aren't you Jubal Butler? Smolan said you were Rangers together. Saved your life."

Jubal glanced at the cell without speaking.

"Said you were good with a gun. Almost as good as him," the outlaw continued.

"Thought you'd gone to live with Apaches. Didn't know you was the law here."

Jubal's glare indicated he was through listening.

Milo looked at the cells. "Bet you heard o' me, too. Milo Butler. Own most of the range 'round here. Helped run Smolan outta town."

"Never heard of you."

42

"Damn. You boys don't know nothin'. No wonder you're in there." Milo spat.

Jubal pulled the Colt from his holster, checked the loads and reholstered it. "Milo, I don't think you've ever forgotten Smolan took a shine to Tilly."

"Don't be stupid."

The rancher walked to the desk and leaned toward Jubal. "Recall another skinny kid who liked her once, too." He twisted his face. "Say, I was wonderin'...how come you showed up that day, you know, the time I caught Smolan messin' with my girl. In Teagle's barn."

A strange look passed across Jubal's face. "Why in the world were you thinking about that?"

"Came to me when I saw that bastard."

Jubal nodded. "Guess I was looking for Smolan. Who can remember that far back?"

"You should'a let me kill him." Milo paused. "I didn't see you comin', you know. That's how you beat me." He grinned.

Without responding, the lawman stood, shoved the second gun into his back waistband and covered the weapon with his coat. "Smolan saved my life. He'll be asked to leave. I won't arrest him."

Milo turned to leave and stopped. "Hey, near forgot what I came for. Want you to come for Sunday dinner." He waved his arms. "Tilly don't know about it yet. Figured she'd like the company. Maybe you two could sing. Afterward. You two always did like singin'. Around that old piano of ma's." His face twisted for an instant. "Hard to believe both are gone. Ma for over ten years, I reckon."

"Appreciate the invite, Milo. Be fun to spend some time with your son."

"You know I'd like you with me at the ranch. Let you buy in. Real cheap."

"Not a cattleman, but thanks."

Frowning, the rancher looked down at his boots. "Say, go with me to that ladies' store across the street, will ya? Need to get Tilly somethin' pretty. You're better at that stuff than I am."

"Don't need to go. There's a red hat in the window. New. Saw it yesterday," Jubal said. "Thought of Tilly right away."

"Why'd ya think o' her?"

Jubal smiled. "She's my brother's wife, remember?"

Milo grinned for him a wide grin and pulled on his weathered hat brim. "Maybe I'll go take her that hat right now. See you on Sunday."

"Look forward to it."

Standing in the doorway, Jubal watched his brother disappear into the shop and reappear moments later. Milo spurred his horse into a run as soon as he hit the saddle. In his left hand was the red hat, held like it was a dead chicken.

Jubal's mind went to Smolan. Why had he returned? Revenge?

Leaving his deputies in charge, he got his horse from the livery and headed toward the abandoned schoolhouse. As he pulled up in front of the aging structure, sounds of scuffling could be heard inside. The fancy carriage sat nearby.

A voice called out, "Heard you were livin' with the Apaches. Didn't know you were the law here. What happened to ol' Marshal Huggins?"

"Came back here, instead. Didn't know you were going to take up robbing banks," Jubal responded. "Marshal Huggins died. Pneumonia. Nobody wanted the job." His mind warned that Smolan might start shooting. They hadn't parted well.

Smolan stepped through the doorway and onto the worn steps. His opened coat flaunted the holstered twin revolvers.

"So how's your big brother anyway? Saw him coming here."

"Doin' real fine, I'd say. Got the ranch. Married Tilly. They have a boy."

Smolan looked down at his well-shined boots as he cleared the steps. Jubal was surprised at his lack of reaction. Obviously, Smolan already knew of Tilly's marriage. How?

"So what brings you out here, lawman? Got a feeling it wasn't to chat."

"Wish it were," Jubal leaned forward in his saddle, deciding not to dismount. "I want you to leave."

"Didn't plan on staying. Just waiting on some friends."

"They're not coming," Jubal cocked his head to the side. "One's dead. The other two are in my jail. Nothing keeping you."

"Now, hold on, Jubal. Don't push me."

"I should be arresting you." Jubal straightened in the saddle. "Your friends tried to rob the bank."

"Why'd you come back to Gypsum, anyway?" Smolan asked, took a deep breath and stared off into the distance. Without waiting for an answer, he turned toward Jubal again. "Think you can take me?"

Jubal's shoulders rose and fell. "Didn't come out here for trouble. Came as an old friend."

"How's the arm?" Smolan moved easily away from the schoolhouse toward the carriage; his thumbs curling around his belt. The movement pushed the handles of his revolvers forward.

"Getting better." Jubal lifted his left arm two feet from his side, then patted his horse's neck.

"Think it'll ever be right?"

"Doc says no."

"Too bad." Smolan took two more steps to his right. "I saved your life, you know. Kuruk was already dead."

"Yes, I'll always be thankful for that—and always sorry he died trying to save me."

Smolan looked away again. "Still can't believe you took on that bunch all by yourself. Well, you and Kuruk. Killed eight. I got the last two. After you went down."

"Didn't have much choice. They came at us."

Smolan pointed at Jubal's necklace. "Apaches say that thing saved your life. After Kuruk gave it to you, he died. You believe that stuff?"

"Lots of things I don't understand, Smolan." Jubal brushed his hand over the necklace. "He told me to listen to the spirits. Said they would tell me what my path should be." He shook his head and changed the subject. "So, why are you here, Smolan?"

Inhaling deeply, the cocky outlaw rocked on his heels. "The boys were supposed to meet me here. Guess they won't now. Lot of memories here, though. Wanted to see it again." He chuckled. "Remember when we put a frog down Tilly's back?" A frown introduced the change in his voice and subject. "Tilly should've married me, Jubal. She thought I was dead. We loved each other. That bunch of assholes ran me out of town—or we'd gotten married then."

Jubal pulled on his hat brim to keep the sun from his eyes. "Well, you did rob Johnson's store even if it was just for fun. As for Tilly loving you, doesn't matter now, does it? She married Milo. Let's get back to your leaving."

45

The remark silenced both men. Jubal sensed Smolan considered shooting, just for an instant. A flicker in his eyes. Jubal had seen that look before. When they were on the same side.

"What about my men? The old marshal wouldn't have been able to stop them." Smolan broke the uneasy calm. "They'll expect me."

"You can't save them."

"Looks like I'll need some new friends." Smolan reached the carriage, glanced at the schoolhouse, then back at Jubal. "You didn't answer me. Why did you come back?"

"Wasn't sure until now. Guess the spirits brought me here. To stop you."

"You afraid of me, Jubal?"

Jubal took a deep breath and said, "Don't think either of us would like the outcome."

"Oh, so you think you're pretty good."

"Like I said, I came...for old times."

To emphasize his friendly intentions, Jubal slowly pulled the revolver from his holster, leaned over in the saddle and dropped it on the ground in front of his horse.

Smolan reciprocated by laying both of his guns on the carriage floor, then asked, "Not carrying the other? Always liked those guns."

"Will I need it?"

Smolan chuckled and shook his head. "Why do you think I came back?"

Jubal took another deep breath. "Tilly."

From the schoolhouse came a shriek and the door flew open. Red-faced and frantic, Tilly Butler ran at him. Her soft face was streaked with the tears of being discovered. Her crimson dress struggled to cover her ample bosom, where one button had been forgotten in her hurried redressing.

Halfway to Jubal, she stopped. "Oh, Jubal, I...didn't want you to..."

In an even voice, Jubal explained Milo had come to town to buy a special red hat for her. He left out Sunday dinner.

"It'll go well with that dress." He motioned toward her.

"Ohmygod!" Tilly blurted, stopping halfway to him, her face pale. "Oh, Jubal, please understand. I'm not a bad woman. I thought you both were dead." She lowered her eyes and stood, shaking.

46

Jubal shifted his shoulders. He wanted to be anywhere but here. He slapped the reins against his leg. "Milo is your husband. It was your choice."

Tilly lifted her head. "Your brother is a pig. He beat me. Beat me hard. Hit our son, too."

Shaking his head, Jubal shifted in the saddle and said, "Tilly, I'll believe a lot of things about Milo. But not that. He loves you—and James."

"I left Milo a letter. At the ranch." She tried to smile. "I can't stay with him. I just can't. I want to be with Smolan." Her eyes pleaded.

"Where's James?" Jubal asked.

"He's inside. He's coming, too," Smolan Grant declared.

"Please understand, Jubal," Tilly said and ran inside.

Smolan shook his head. "Made me mad as hell when I heard she was married. To your stupid brother, no less. Sent her a letter signed 'Aunt Bess.' Found out she thought we were both dead. Sent her another to meet me here. Today." His shoulders rose and fell as he continued, "Real sorry you found out, Jubal. I really am. Didn't figure on seeing you again. When I left, you were taking Kuruk's body to bury him in the mountains. Mumbling something about the Apache way."

With that, he left and returned alone with a suitcase in his left hand and a sack of supplies in the other.

"Think we'll go to San Antonio first. Got some fine dress shops there." He laughed. "A nice bank, too."

In spite of himself, Jubal chuckled, then leaned forward again in the saddle. "You're on the run. What kind of life is that for Tilly—and James?"

"Is that what this is really all about? Are you going to try to stop me—for your big brother?"

Twenty feet from the carriage, Smolan saw movement on the horizon. A rider appeared, racing toward them. In one motion, the outlaw dropped the baggage and grabbed both pistols from the carriage floor as he recognized it was Milo Butler.

"I was right," Smolan snarled.

"No, Smolan. Leave now. I'll go talk to Milo."

Smolan spun toward Jubal with both guns.

Leaning against the right side of his horse, Jubal yanked free his backup gun in the same motion. His coat flapped behind him. Smolan's first bullets cut the air where he had been. Jubal emptied his gun into Smolan as the outlaw fired again. Jubal's horse staggered with the impact of the bullets and began to fall. Jubal kicked free as the animal collapsed.

Smolan lurched against his carriage and slid to the ground, ending in a grotesque sitting position with his head resting on his bloody chest. Both of his guns exploded into the dirt and fell from his hands.

Jubal lay on the ground, trying to catch his breath. His left leg was bleeding. Finally, he struggled to his feet and picked up his first gun. Limping over to Smolan, he kicked his pistols away.

From the building, Tilly came, screaming, "You couldn't let me be happy, could you? You bastard! You wanted me for yourself."

"No, you're my brother's wife." Ignoring her continued ranting, Jubal laid his hand on Smolan's shoulder. "You didn't...give me...a choice, old friend. Ride on. Kuruk is waiting."

Milo's roan reined up. In his right fist was a Winchester. He studied the dead Smolan, then Jubal's dead horse, then glanced at his brother.

Tilly avoided his stare as she knelt beside Smolan's lifeless body, stroking his unseeing face.

"Hope this was worth it to get away from me." Milo shoved the Winchester into its saddle sheath and dismounted. "I'll take my son. That carriage'll take you anywhere you want to go."

He stepped toward Jubal, yanking free his neckerchief. "Lemme tie this around your leg. Then I'll give you a ride to town, little brother. You can hold my son. I'll ride behind. We've got some catchin' up to do."

48

CHIRICAHUA APACHE LEADERS: A COMPARISON

By Robert M. Utley

"Geronimo!" So shouted World War II paratroopers as they jumped, thus allowing time to clear the airplane before pulling the rip chord. If the Apache leader's name did not resonate around the world before the war, almost everyone now recognizes the name.

Although never a chief, Geronimo is almost universally credited as the greatest of Apache war leaders. His handful of followers, including families, challenged two of the best of the U. S. Army's Indian-fighting generals, led their soldiers in fruitless pursuits through the most rugged mountains on the continent, and until the last constantly eluded even the warriors of his own people who had enlisted as army scouts to help run down their kinsman. Geronimo's surrender to Brig. Gen. Nelson A. Miles at Skeleton Canyon, Arizona, on September 4, 1886, brought to an end four centuries of Indian warfare on the North American continent.

Students of the Chiricahuas, but one of the Apache tribes, recognize others who proved to be outstanding political, social, and cultural leaders as well as highly successful war chiefs. How does Geronimo compare with such luminaries as Mangas Coloradas, Cochise, Victorio, and even the aged Nana? Their names, if known at all, do not excite the public imagination like Geronimo's. Yet all boasted war records that invite comparison with Geronimo.

Mangas Coloradas dominates the early decades of the nineteenth century and even the divisions of the Chiricahua tribe.

49

He eventually succeeded in blending elements of three bands into a personal following, but came to exert strong influence over all and the fourth as well. Organization and terminology are confused both in the sources and in scholarship, but here the four are identified as Chihenne, Bedonkohe, Chokonen, and Nednhi. The Chihenne (Warm Springs) ranged the mountains along the western side of the Rio Grande in New Mexico, the Bedonkohe to their northwest in the Black Range and the Mogollon Mountains, the Chokohens (or Chiricahua proper) in southeastern Arizona, and the Nednhi in northern Mexico. The three that came to take on a separate identity under Mangas's immediate leadership were Chihenne, Bedonkohe, and Chokohens.

Mangas Coloradas dominated not only by influence, but also by physical stature. His height of six feet seven towered over all gatherings of Indians. He was not essentially a man of war but of peace, a skilled diplomat, generous, wise, a gifted orator, and a visionary. Until the 1860s, he generally got along well with Americans. But his hatred for Mexicans knew no bounds. Occasionally he camped near Janos, Chihuahua, and traded while negotiating with Mexican authorities. But Sonora, its eastern boundary shared with Chihuahua at the crest of the Sierra Madre, remained a lifelong obsession that cost many lives. He led repeated raids into Sonora, often accompanied by his protégé Geronimo. Courage, bravery, and fighting excellence stamped him as unrivaled both in war and raid.

Mangas Coloradas's greatest triumph occurred in January 1851. Early in the month two formidable raiding parties, each numbering about two hundred warriors, swept south into Sonora. Mangas led Chihennes, Bedonkohes, and Chokonens. The last included Geronimo and Mangas's son-in-law, Cochise, destined to reach top rank among the Chokonens and become Mangas's closest ally in future warfare. These plundered their way south as far as Hermosillo. The other party raided along the western foothills of the Sierra Madre. Both turned toward home at the very time the federal forces were changing commanders.

Hoping to head off the two groups of Apaches, the Sonoran governor ordered Capt. Ignacio Pesqueira and Capt. Manuel Martinez each to enlist a force of fifty national guardsmen and unite to fight the returning raiders. On January 20, they spotted a dust cloud heading north toward them, and they set up an ambush in a beautiful valley bordered by low hills called Pozo Hediondo. As the vanguard of the Apaches approached, the guardsmen attacked and easily drove them back into the hills, forcing them to abandon three hundred head of stolen stock. But behind these warriors rode the rest of the raiders, with Mangas and his band herding about a thousand horses. The pursuing Mexicans, now greatly outnumbered, collided with Mangas. For three hours they fought, sometimes hand to hand. Every Mexican officer went down, dead or wounded, and only fifteen men still stood to fight.

When all the Apaches joined the battle, they outnumbered the hundred Mexicans. But rarely did Apaches fight so fiercely and in such united fashion. Mangas Coloradas deserved full credit for keeping the Chiricahuas so well in hand, setting a personal example of courage, and leading his men to such a stunning victory. In this battle alone, Mangas Coloradas established his claim to be the greatest of Apache war chiefs.

Mangas continued through the 1850s to raid into Sonora while maintaining periodic relations with Janos, Chihuahua. As the decade drew to a close, however, his attitude toward Americans changed. His favorite abiding place was Santa Lucia Springs, just south of where the Gila River flows out of the Black Range before turning west toward Arizona. Lands surrounding the Chihenne country saw increasing numbers of Americans, many traveling west to the California gold fields. They were an unsettling intrusion, especially as the overland route to the Pacific ran not far south of Santa Lucia Springs. Moreover, the U. S. Army began to establish forts to guard the overland trail. The critical event, however, occurred in the spring of 1860, less than thirty miles east of Santa Lucia. Prospectors found gold in the Pinos Altos Mountains and set off a rush that led to the founding of the town of the same name. The miners were a rough set. They did not get along with any Indians, and they preferred to shoot rather than talk. Mangas and his warriors raided and skirmished with these miners and even fought a pitched battle on the outskirts on Pinos Altos itself.

Meantime, the Civil War had broken out in the East. The Regulars abandoned their forts and hastened to the war zone. Apache hostilities grew fiercer. Confederates seized Mesilla on the Rio Grande and Tucson, far to the west, and sought to invade New Mexico until routed by a hastily assembled Union army. Mangas played no part in these events, but continued to war with the miners who were tearing up his treasured mountains to get at gold.

Mangas hated these intruders, but never with the ferocity directed at Sonora. He would have much preferred peace. By 1862, however, he confronted a new presence in Apacheria—a brigade of California Volunteers incorporated into the Union Army and dispatched to the Rio Grande to help drive the Confederates back into Texas. Brig. Gen. James H. Carleton, a tough old veteran of the Regular Army, commanded. Cochise asked Mangas to bring his warriors to Apache Pass, where vital springs drew the overland trail through the Chiricahua Mountains, to head off the advancing bluecoats. The warriors of both chiefs set up an ambush on slopes overlooking Apache Springs. On July 15, 1862, Carleton's advance guard marched into a storm of bullets that prevented them from reaching the springs. The Apaches, however, had not reckoned on "wagon guns," and they were soundly whipped by bursting artillery rounds. In the aftermath, Mangas himself fell with severe wounds. As the Indians drew off, they carried Mangas south to Janos, Chihuahua, where he remained while a local doctor treated his wounds.

Back in his home country by autumn, Mangas now wanted to bring his fighting days to an end and settle at Santa Lucia. He had passed his seventieth birthday and was tired. But the miners still regarded him as the cause of all their Indian troubles, and they wanted his scalp. So did the Californians Carleton had left on the lower Rio Grande under Brig. Gen. Joseph R. West. When Mangas sent a peace-making proposal directly to Carleton in Santa Fe, the general advised his subordinate in the south, "Mangas Coloradas sends me word he wants peace, but I have no faith in him." Instead, West was to organize a formidable campaign to root out and exterminate all Apaches.

In January 1863, Mangas counseled widely on his effort to bring about an end to the fighting. He proposed to journey to Pinos Altos himself and talk about peace. Victorio, Geronimo, and Nana all advised against trusting the Americans. Mangas went anyway. A mixed force of soldiers and prospectors hid in Pinos Altos, having conveyed a willingness to talk peace. As Mangas and his bodyguards entered the town, the citizen leader, Jack Swilling, an old Indian fighter turned miner, walked out to confront the chief. After a few words, he signaled, and instantly a force of men with rifles emerged from the buildings to encircle the Indians. Swilling told Mangas he was now a prisoner and to dismiss his bodyguards, which included Victorio. Mangas complied.

Swilling, of course, lost no time turning Mangas over to General West. Thrilled to have the leading war chief in his custody, West had him closely guarded. During the night, as Mangas lay next to a campfire, soldiers applied heated bayonets to his feet. As the old man rose to remonstrate, they shot him dead.

Both Carleton and West gloated over their triumph—having seized the foremost Apache leader in the Southwest and killed him as he "tried to escape."

That the greatest of Chiricahuas, renowned as the foremost war chief, was at heart a man of peace is an irony. This giant of a man whose wisdom and character had welded all the Chiricahua bands into a unity rare among Indians wanted a quiet life of peace so badly that he ignored all his principal advisers, who urged him not to trust the Americans. He trusted them. They betrayed him and killed him.

The mantle passed easily to Cochise, hereditary chief of the Chokohens, a formidable war leader who had married Mangas's daughter, fought at his side, and, still in his fifties when Mangas died, retained the youthful vigor that slowed Mangas in his last years. Except for towering height, Cochise embodied most of the characteristics that marked Mangas—wisdom, dignity, generosity, fighting skills, and the capacity to influence and lead people. His homeland embraced the Chiricahua and Dragoon Mountains of southeastern Arizona, but, like Mangas, he came to enjoy stature among all the Chiricahua bands. He led many destructive raids into Mexico, and almost certainly he took part in the Battle of Pozo Hediondo in January 1851. But his distinction in recorded history is in war with Americans. By the time of Mangas's death, Cochise had already shifted his hostility from Mexicans to Americans.

Cochise's antagonism was grievously provoked by the so-called Bascom Affair early in 1861. Summoned by a rash young army officer devoid of judgment, Cochise met Lt. George N. Bascom in Apache Canyon, near the Butterfield stage station in Apache Pass. Falsely accused of stealing a white boy, Cochise learned he would be held as hostage for the boy's return. Suddenly he drew his knife, slashed the wall of the tent in which he confronted Bascom, and bolted up the side of the canyon amid a hail of rifle fire. Bascom seized Cochise's brother, wife, and several warriors who had accompanied him, and in turn Cochise seized a Butterfield employee. Taking position in the stage station, Bascom remained adamant against releasing his hostages until the boy was returned. Cochise gathered warriors to contest the blundering young officer. Even Mangas Coloradas showed up. After a week's standoff, in which several fights occurred, Cochise decided to withdraw. As Geronimo recalled, "we killed our prisoners, disbanded, and went into hiding in the mountains."

At the summit of Apache Pass, Bascom hanged his male prisoners to a stand of oak trees and rode away. The bodies dangled there for months.

Justly infuriated, Cochise launched a war against Americans that lasted a decade. Travelers on the overland trail, stagecoaches, way stations, occasional ranches—all fell under relentless attack as Cochise vented his rage. It intensified a year later, in July 1862, when he united with Mangas Coloradas to confront the California Column at Apache Pass. That he lost that battle did not affect his continuing war against Americans, and that American soldiers lured his father-in-law to his death in 1863 only intensified his hatred of Americans.

Carleton's soldiers made no headway in blocking Cochise's raids. They built a military post, Fort Bowie, in Apache Pass near the critical springs. Other posts were reoccupied. When the Civil War ended and the Volunteers departed, Regulars took their place. Constant campaigning and an occasional skirmish exerted little influence on the course of the war. Meantime, Arizona's population expanded, as the postwar years brought new immigrants from the East. Tucson boomed, largely on government contracts to feed and supply reservation Indians and the army in its campaigns against Cochise.

The government made repeated overtures to try to open talks with Cochise to bring the war to a close. No emissary could even get close to him, remote in the "Cochise Stronghold" deep in the rugged Dragoon Mountains. Finally, in 1872, a peacemaker succeeded. With the help of one of Cochise's few white friends, Tom Jeffords, the one-armed "praying general" of Civil War fame, Oliver O. Howard, accompanied only by his aide, went with Jeffords to the stronghold. After days of talk with the deeply suspicious chief, General Howard persuaded Cochise to call off the war. In return, Cochise demanded, and received, a reservation in his own homeland and Tom Jeffords as his agent.

Arizonans did not like the arrangement. They distrusted the management of Tom Jeffords. Cochise seems to have honored his pledge to stop raiding in Mexico, but he tolerated Indians from other reservations flocking to the Chiricahua reservation, which bordered on Mexico, and using it as a base for raids against Mexicans.

Cochise did not live to see the fate of his reservation. He died of disease in 1874. His son Taza, who had been groomed for the chieftainship, replaced him, but he died during a trip to Washington, D.C., to talk with government authorities. Taza's younger brother Naiche replaced him, but he lacked the strength either of his father or brother, a failing partly remedied by strong ties to Geronimo.

Jeffords and his reservation came to an inglorious end in 1876, when the government decided to concentrate all Apaches on parched, disease-ridden bottoms of the Gila River named San Carlos. Opposition to the move split the tribe and led to violent rifts. Some moved peacefully, but others, like Geronimo, took refuge in Mexico.

No other chief commanded the stature of Mangas Coloradas or Cochise to exert power and influence over all the Chiricahua bands. But the effort to gather all Apaches at San Carlos produced another great Chiricahua war leader—Victorio.

Although allied in raids and war with Mangas Coloradas and Cochise, Victorio preferred the haunts of his own homeland. A Chihenne, or Warm Springs, he and his people lived in the mountains surrounding the Warm Springs, or Ojo Caliente. These springs gave rise to Alamosa Creek—Cañada Alamosa— which drained from the Black Range to the Rio Grande. This land Victorio deeply believed had been awarded to his Chihenne people by Ussen, the life-giving creator of Apache cosmology. Ussen had commanded the people of the Warm Springs country to care for and live in it forever. It was sacred land.

Thus Victorio came to the chieftainship of his band as a man of peace who also practiced all the skills of Apache war and raid. Twenty years younger than Mangas Coloradas, he had nevertheless risen to the leadership of his people before the great chief was killed. Through the 1850s, sympathetic government agents sought to create a reservation at Warm Springs and in the Alamosa Valley. They failed because of a village of Mexicans in the valley where the Apaches traded plunder for arms, ammunition, and whiskey. In 1872 the government moved Victorio and his people from their sacred homes to a new reservation to the west. Only months after the move, General Howard, en route to make peace with Cochise, met with Victorio and agreed that the new Tularosa reservation was too high and cold. Victorio was finally allowed to go back to Ojo Caliente pending a decision by the government.

The government waffled until 1876. Then, applying the policy of consolidation, Victorio and his people were forced to go to San Carlos. The chief did not stay long, but led his warriors in a breakout. Cornered by military units, he was "temporarily" settled at Ojo Caliente while the government tried to decide what to do with him—give him a Warm Spring Reservation or move him back to San Carlos. For three years, rumors periodically swept through the people that the army was coming to take them back to San Carlos. Victorio vowed to die rather than return to that place. On September 4, 1879, he declared war, sweeping down on the herd guard of Troop E, Ninth Cavalry, killing all the herders, and driving forty-six horses into the mountains.

The Victorio War of 1879-80 pitted the canny chief and a force of warriors fluctuating between fifty and two hundred (Mescalero Apaches from east of the Rio Grande came and went) against the black soldiers of the Ninth U. S. Cavalry. Victorio knew every ridge, hill, mountain, canyon, and ravine in the mountains west of the Rio Grande. Constantly pursued and occasionally attacked by troopers under the dogged Maj. Alfred P. Morrow, he repeatedly eluded a decisive fight. When his stock broke down, he easily replenished them by raiding ranches and settlements. The cavalrymen had no such resupply and rode their horses almost to the death.

Morrow benefited from the occasional loan of units of Chiricahua Apache scouts from Arizona. Superb trackers, they never lost Victorio's trail. The war spilled over into Mexico, with Morrow losing a battle that might have been decisive but for the exhaustion of his horses and men. Victorio ranged through Chihuahua slaughtering Mexicans before re-crossing the border to continue to fight the Americans. In confessing his frustration to a fellow officer, Morrow paid high tribute not only to Victorio, but also to the Apache scouts:

> I am heartily sick of this business and am convinced that the most expeditious & least expensive way to settle the Indian troubles in this section is to employ about 150 Apache Indian scouts and turn them loose on Victorio without interference of troops except general instructions from the officer conducting the campaign. I have had eight engagements with the Victorio Indians in the mountains since their return from Mexico and in each have driven and beaten them but there is no appreciable advantage gained, they run but make a stand at another point where possibly ten men can stand off a hundred, kill a number and lose none...I leave here tomorrow and will stick to Victorio's trail so long as a serviceable animal or an able soldier is left but I still think that the pursuit is an unprofitable one and Indians should be employed on the principle of fighting fire with fire.

Morrow was right, but once again he pushed Victorio so hard that he crossed into Mexico to rest. Mexican troops and American units invited across the border gave him no rest. After twice trying to breach the cordon of Tenth Cavalrymen who blocked him from crossing Texas to the Mescalero reservation, he resolved to go west to the Sierra Madre of Mexico and join with Juh's Nednhi Chiricahuas. He never reached there.

On October 13, 1880, Col. Joaquin Terrazas and more than three hundred Mexican troops fell on Victorio and his people camped at a lake at the foot of three desert elevations called Tres Castillos. The Apaches scattered up the rocky hillside during the night, but the next day were systematically hunted down and slaughtered. Only a few men escaped, and Terrazas rounded up sixty-eight women and children and sold them into slavery.

Victorio had demonstrated his fighting skill in contending for more than a year with the black troopers of two regiments, the units of army scouts recruited from their own Chiricahua tribe, Mexican forces, and even a contingent of Texas Rangers. This was not the usual raid for plunder, but full-scale war, a rarity in relations between white and red. Victorio fully demonstrated himself the equal of Mangas Coloradas and Cochise.

Nana, a prominent chief in Victorio's band, escaped Tres Castillos. He had led a party in seeking more ammunition and returned just in time to see the fight from afar. Nana had married Victorio's sister (although some sources say Geronimo's sister) and, although a chief with his own following, sided with Victorio until Tres Castillos. An old man, in his seventies during the Victorio War, he was scarred and crippled, and he walked with a limp. Even so, in a fight he outshone many a younger warrior and proved an exemplary war leader. He went with Victorio to San Carlos, broke out with him, and fought by his side throughout the Victorio War. After Tres Castillos, he took the remnant of the Warm Springs people on west to the Sierra Madre.

Despite his long record of fighting with the other Chiricahua chiefs in raids against Mexicans, Nana's renown as a war chief is remembered mainly because of the exploits of one month in the summer of 1881—"Nana's Raid." Seeking revenge for the slaying of Victorio, he led a party of Warm Springs warriors out of the Sierra Madre and struck where Victorio had struck, in the rough mountains of western New Mexico. During one month, he repeated Victorio's deeds, killing between thirty and fifty white settlers, capturing herd after herd of horses, and eluding pursuing cavalrymen with the same zeal and success as Victorio.

Nana's Raid places him in the front ranks of Chiricahua chiefs. At his age and with his infirmities, he showed himself as skilled and successful as Victorio—in the same mountains, against the same white ranchers, and against the same black cavalrymen. Returning to the Sierra Madre, he allied himself with Geronimo, surrendered with him in 1886, and accompanied him into imprisonment in Florida and Alabama. He died in 1896 at Fort Sill, at least ninety years of age.

Clearly, these Chiricahua chiefs demonstrated exceptional leadership and personal bravery in plundering raids and in warfare itself. They commanded the admiration and loyalty of all the Chiricahua bands. Their names all resonated with the Americans and Mexicans who talked peace with them or fell victim to their aggressions.

Geronimo's name gained as much fame among his own people and among Americans and Mexicans. Over the years, however, the names of Mangas Coloradas, Cochise, Victorio, and Nana faded in public consciousness while Geronimo remained, for most people, the embodiment of Apache warfare.

Born a Bedonkohe about 1820, after gaining warrior status Geronimo fell under the influence of Mangas Coloradas. Most of the Bedonkohes did too and gradually merged into Mangas's following. The Bedonkohe range lay just north of Santa Lucia Springs, Mangas's favorite resort, and Geronimo had been born not far distant in the mountain valleys of the upper Gila River. He could not claim a chieftainship, but he emerged as one of the fiercest and most skilled of Chiricahua warriors. Together with Mangas, he both traded with and raided Mexicans, the former at Janos, Chihuahua, the latter in Sonora. He often rode with Cochise and with Juh's Nednhis in Mexico. He participated in the Bascom Affair of 1861 and the Battle of Apache Pass in 1862, although what role he played is unknown.

Thick, squat, perpetually scowling, of erratic behavior, a personality that offended and alienated many of his own people, Geronimo seemed the opposite of the statuesque Mangas Coloradas. By the 1880s, however, he emerged as a war leader because he was the very embodiment of Apache warfare. Aside from mastery of cunning, stealth, endurance, perseverance, ruthlessness, fortitude, and fighting skill, he mastered the essence of Apache fighting qualities, a consummate adaptation of man to environment.

The Apache country of New Mexico, Arizona, Chihuahua, and Sonora featured vast expanses of sand and stone, islands of rocky peaks webbed by treacherous canyons; widely scattered and uncertain water holes; cactus, mesquite, prickly pear, and a profusion of other flora armed with thorns; snakes, scorpions, centipedes, tarantulas, and Gila monsters. Temperatures soared to 120 degrees in summer and fell to chill depths at night in winter. Such country surrounded Mexico's soaring Sierra Madre, whose tortuous peaks, ridges, and canyons afforded refuge from any pursuer. Apache warriors had been reared to adapt to such conditions and use them to their advantage in war. Whites—Americans or Mexicans—found the landscape more daunting than the enemy. Like the Chiricahua chiefs, Geronimo knew exceptionally well how to exploit such conditions.

Nurtured well by Mangas, Cochise, Juh, and others great leaders, Geronimo excelled at raids in Mexico, often with Mangas, but frequently with a few or many recruited for such a foray. His hatred of Mexicans exceeded even that of Mangas, and for good reason.

After Pozo Hediondo in January 1851, Geronimo with Mangas and others crossed the Sierra to Janos to trade. Meantime, the change in Sonoran commanders had taken place. Col. José María Carrasco led a strong Sonoran force across the mountains into Chihuahua, and on March 5, he attacked several rancherías outside the town before entering the town itself. Geronimo returned to his camp to find it destroyed. "I found my aged mother, my young wife, and my three small children among the slain," he remembered many years later. "I was never again contented in our quiet home. I had vowed vengeance upon the Mexican troops...and whenever I saw anything to remind me of my former happy days my heart would ache for revenge upon Mexico." Whether he got the details right, he probably did get his emotions right, for he ravaged Mexico mercilessly for almost thirty years.

At this time he was still known by his true name, Goyahkla. When he emerged as Geronimo is unknown. A number of speculative theories have been advanced to explain the change. Most likely, since the Chiricahuas operated so much in Mexico, he simply adopted a common Mexican name, in English Jerome. Before the 1870s, he had taken this name, and it first began to appear in white sources.

Geronimo's hold on the American imagination, however, dated from the 1880s, by which time he had been located on the White Mountain Reservation north of San Carlos. Management and police of both reservations trace a complicated pattern during these years, keeping Geronimo constantly suspicious and ready to bolt at the slightest provocation. He and equally disgruntled Chiricahuas broke away three times in the early 1880s. Once an army officer coaxed him back. Next Brig. Gen. George Crook, with almost exclusive reliance on Apache scouts, tracked him through the Sierra Madre so relentlessly that he consented to come back to the reservation. The third occasion once again led Crook into the Sierra Madre and another agreement to surrender. Geronimo aborted this effort at the last minute, and Crook yielded his command to Brig. Gen. Nelson A. Miles, to whom Geronimo surrendered on September 4, 1886.

The prominence of Geronimo's name springs almost entirely from his course during the offensives of Crook and Miles. Although

Geronimo and others raided occasionally both in Arizona and New Mexico and in Sonora, the bloodshed served mainly to keep the public eye riveted on the attempt to run down the elusive Chiricahuas in the virtually impenetrable Sierra Madre. This was not war. It involved no fighting leadership, only the ability to elude the pursuers. Crook's Apache scouts proved so successful in keeping the quarry on the run that Geronimo finally agreed to talks and finally to surrender, twice to Crook. Miles, pressured to use regulars instead of scouts, had less success, although his probing columns endured the most severe hardship imaginable. It fell, however, to two Chiricahua scouts, directed by Lt. Charles B. Gatewood, to make the contact with Geronimo that led to the final surrender to Miles.

As Americans watched in suspense for five years that featured the name of Geronimo above all others, he so deeply embedded himself in the popular mind as the preeminent Indian war chief of all time that it remained securely there. Although the Sierra Madre campaigns were almost entirely about pursuit, not battle, the focus stayed on the name Geronimo. The Chiricahuas were sent East as prisoners of war. Geronimo largely disappeared from public view during the six years of imprisonment at Fort Pickens, Florida, and Mount Vernon Barracks, Alabama. But after the Indians, still prisoners of war, were moved to Fort Sill, Oklahoma, he attained some celebrity making crafts with his signature. Driving an auto and wearing a top hat in Theodore Roosevelt's inaugural parade in 1904 reinforced the public fascination. He died at Fort Sill in 1909, still a prisoner of war but still a fixture in people's imagination.

In comparing Geronimo with Mangas Coloradas, Cochise, Victorio, and Nana, a close student would be drawn to the conclusion that he compared favorably with all of them as a fighting warrior but did not rise to their stature as a fighting leader. Yet his name, lifted to fame by the Sierra Madre campaigns, will always overshadow theirs.

SOLEDAD CANYON

By John Duncklee

Past the jungle of rich men's castles
The canyon's mouth opens to the mountain's soul
Canyon walls covered with grasses
Some shrubs here and there
A place apart
A place to share
A place about which to wonder
The old windmill sucking air
Empty tank
Empty trough
Empty corral half torn away
Sad yet happy with the wind
Stoic in the sun
Strong against the snow
Receptive to the rain
The stream at times
The sound of its life
Sublime muted by the wind yet there
Once herds driven from the slopes
Cowboys, fat cattle, slick horses
Hungry buzzards without a meal
The scolds and hoofbeats
Riatas singing
Hats shading eyes

Chaparreras guarding legs
Steel shoes clinking on rocks
Sweat
Bawling calves and sorrowful mothers
Robbed each year
A tough way of life
Yet fulfilling for its toil
Beautiful for its place
Gone are the cowboys
Gone are the cattle
Gone are the yells
Gone is the singing rawhide
Rutted road to the other side
Still there
No more wagons drawn by teams
No more loads of groceries and salt
Soledad means loneliness or isolated place
But one cannot be lonely there
Unless one is lonely with oneself

Soledad is at peace.

NATIVE WEST

THE FAST DANCING PEOPLE

By D.L. Birchfield

Professor Tuskahoma told himself that an Indian was entitled to have a mid-life crisis just like everybody else.

If silly white professors could have one, so could he.

He was sure he had read that somewhere. Maybe it was in the Bill of Rights. *All Indians in this Republic shall be Entitled to a mid-life Crisis just like Anybody else.*

If another day went by without getting much done—so what? He was on sabbatical, a hard-earned, long-overdue sabbatical. What better time for a professor to have a mid-life crisis?

He poured another stiff glass of scotch and soda and popped an old tape of himself into the VCR. The tape—lightly edited scenes from a movie that had never been finished—might have launched a career for him in Hollywood.

If that film had been finished, he might have taken that critical step from Broadway child star to Hollywood actor, at about the same time his sister had done that. He might even have gotten to be as famous as she was now.

Everything had been right, except they ran out of money, the movie never got finished, and that was that.

Instead of becoming a Hollywood star, he'd bitten the dust but good in trying to be a stunt man, falling off, and getting shot off, so many horses, so many times, he had no idea how many bones he'd broken or how many horse wrecks he'd had.

He'd been left with nothing but the frustration of that half-finished movie, and his dream of being the action-adventure heart-throb of the nation. The vividness of that dream hadn't faded, thanks to that old tape he'd just popped into his VCR.

Watching that tape had always acted like a therapeutic elixir, taking his mind off any problem—a balm for his deeply wounded psyche. But, to his disgust, he'd discovered that he could no longer count on that tape having the power to do that.

For some reason, watching that tape now made him think about the one thing he was trying the hardest to forget—his most recent failed attempt to get married, the most spectacular failure in a long succession of failed attempts to get married.

He'd been watching that old tape anyway, while stubbornly *trying* not to think about how pathetically he'd bitten the dust in pursuing that high-spirited, high-maintenance brunette.

He'd also been trying not to think about other things lately, like how jealous he'd become of his sister's success.

That thought struck a nerve so raw that he'd only gotten halfway across the living room toward his big easy chair when he stopped, contemplating the tenderness of that sore spot. He stood in the middle of the room, sipping his scotch and soda, thinking about that, and thinking about some of the men he'd known who hadn't survived their mid-life crisis.

Mid-life was when a lot of good men bit the dust in a big way. He could see how he might be ripe for that.

Nobody had warned him that by becoming a professor he'd suffer the frustration of disappearing into the oblivion of a self-contained, self-important vacuum.

But how many more years could he endure, condemned to publishing deadly boring gobbledygook in peer-reviewed academic journals, which had a few thousand university libraries for subscribers, but no readers, no readers anywhere, not even on any campuses, except for a few silly graduate students who wanted to be professors, who read them to learn how to write gobbledygook, so they could begin thinking in gobbledygook. Then they would become irretrievably weird enough to be condemned to the oblivion of professors, by adhering to the credo of university faculty everywhere—that if the dean could understand their peer-reviewed journal article, it wasn't academic enough.

Meanwhile, America woke up every morning holding its breath until it found out who his darling ding-a-ling sister might be dating next. And to think they'd once been a team, the talk of the town on Broadway, the toughest town in the world to do that.

In that moment, he could see how deeply he was bogged down in those emotions. He could see himself going under in that quicksand—going down...down...gone.

He had an uneasy awareness that he'd better put this mid-life crisis behind him and get on with his life, while he still had one. Better men than him had gone under.

He stood there thinking about that until he'd drained his glass of scotch and soda.

He backtracked across the room and picked up the half-empty bottle of scotch, taking it with him to his big easy chair across from the TV. Once seated, he took a good, long swallow straight from the bottle, popping the cork back in with a little more force than he'd intended.

He let out a deep sigh. He wanted to watch that tape again. If he tried hard enough, maybe he could find emotionally neutral things in it to be thinking about. That might work.

Maybe he could try remembering things that had been going on around him during the filming, things the cameras hadn't shown, something like the last scene in *Postcards From The Edge*, when the movie audience got to see what the actors were seeing.

He was tired of feeling sorry for himself. Somehow, he had to get over that failed romance. Just move on. Get that woman out of his system. If she'd loved him, they'd be together, but they weren't together, and that was that.

He picked up the remote control and hit the PLAY button.

The tape began to roll, and, as always, he was soon mesmerized by it. This time, watching himself in that old, half-finished movie, he had quite a bit of success finding emotionally neutral things to think about.

He was almost able to filter out any thoughts about what had been going on in his own life lately, almost. This time, what he saw, filtered through the lens of his deepening mid-life crisis, was something like this:

Late in the day, as the sun was setting and a big full moon was rising, Ishtiliwata (the Braggart) waited, crouched high on a dusty hillside far from home, wearing nothing but a loincloth.

He was listening to them coming, listening to the yelping of the camp dogs. They were hot on his trail. Dead on.

In another moment or two they'd be right on top of him, the whole snarling pack. But he stood his ground, waiting for them.

In the foreground of the Technicolor panorama was a smattering of *Artemesia tridentata*, *Stipa comata*, and *Sporobolus cryptandrus*, immediately establishing the location.

As if to dispel any doubt about the setting, in the distance, for as far as the eye could see, was a great rolling expanse covered with C_4 warm-temperate, perennial grasses. Those grasslands appeared to consist primarily of *Bouteloua dactyloides*, known alternatively as *Buchloë dactyloides*.

Any number of other species of the *Bouteloua* genus were also readily apparent, including *Bouteloua gracilis* and *Bouteloua curtipendula*.

Hmmm. For some reason, that genus was named in honor of that famous Spanish botanist of the early 19th century, Don Claudio Boutelou. Did that make any sense? Name something that only occurred in North America after some Spaniard, no matter how famous he might have been?

Ishtiliwata was concealed in a dense thicket of *Prunus americana*, at the edge of a clearing.

Hmmm. That big, half-mown hayfield was off-camera right behind everybody, with that farmer impatiently waiting for them to finish, so he could get the rest of his hay cut for baling, with that half-cut hayfield having left the whole hillside heavily laden with the aroma of $C_9H_6O_2$—the distinctive sweet smell of fresh-cut hay.

A big yellow dog was the first one to come bursting into the clearing, leading the eager, headlong-plunging pack.

By the time that big yellow dog had gotten well launched into the clearing, Ishtiliwata had loosened the leather thong on his elkskin bag.

The whole howling pack was bounding into the clearing as he gave a mighty underhanded heave of the bag, gripping the bottom of it tightly at the critical moment, launching the *Mephitis mephitis* toward that big yellow dog with just the right amount of energy to make a nice demonstration of Heidelbacher's First Law of the Physics of Bodies in Motion—a body placed in motion

70

will remain in motion until the amount of energy that placed it in motion has been expended.

The tumbling skunk regained its balance quickly, well before all the energy that had placed it in motion had been expended.

As soon as it was on its feet, still being propelled toward the dog, and instantly alarmed at the jam Heidelbacher's First Law had put it in, the skunk began dancing around, turning its butt toward the dog, as it lifted its tail and lost no time in launching a glistening yellow stream of $CH_3CH_2CH_2CH_2SH$ straight for the dog's eyes, or, to be exact, at a target spot squarely between the dog's eyes.

By then, the big yellow dog had been expending so much energy himself that he was within four or five meters of the skunk, too close for any *Mephitis mephitis* to miss its target.

The dog had time to give one loud, startled, anticipatory yelp, while digging all four feet into the ground, straight-legged, pushing at the earth with all the energy it could muster, desperately trying to expend more energy now than it had been expending, while no doubt vehemently cursing all of Heidelbacher's Laws, particularly his second one—to stop a body in motion requires the same amount of energy as the energy remaining from the amount of energy that placed the body in motion.

In desperation, the skidding dog was ducking his head, hoping to dodge under that dancing skunk's liquid missile.

But the *Mephitis mephitis*, a rocket-science congenital whiz at applied physics, in launching its stinking stream of butyl mercaptan, had accurately calculated the extraordinarily complicated and ever-changing effects of all the energies that had been expended upon both of those collision-course bodies in motion, countered by all the energies that were being expended against that, made even more complex by the horizontal dancing-drift of the skunk, the vertical down-drifting of the dog's head, the wind direction and speed, relative humidity, barometric pressure, and quite a number of other factors, instantly working out all the formulas, which would require two and one-half blackboards to illustrate, mathematically, with a piece of chalk, for precisely when, and with what amount of energy, to execute the launch of his liquid missile, and where, precisely, the eyes of that desperately skidding and ducking dog would have skidded and ducked to at the moment of theoretical *Maximum Targeted Impact*.

71

It was at a spot almost exactly half-way between those two ever-more-widening eyes, a spot that was surely within .48 to .52 of being precisely half the distance between them, that the $CH_3CH_2CH_2CH_2SH$ liquid missile impacted its target, as the little rocket scientist who had launched it was well launched himself in a hurried exit into the thicket of *Prunus americana*, leaving a stinking, howling, blinding fog of chaos in the clearing.

A nearly naked young woman came bursting into the clearing just in time to see, and smell, the impact of that missile.

She threw her arms out wide, sideways, while desperately trying to throw herself backward, trying to form a break for the buck-naked, headlong-rushing brats behind her, attempting to give them some much-needed help with Heidelbacher's Second Law.

The dim light, and the mesmerizing motion of her mammary glands, alternately swirling, bouncing, and jiggling, caused Ishtiliwata the frustration of having to stare with great concentration in trying to see if the glands exhibited the distinctive markings of the people he sought—a modest dab of red paint at the very end of the gland. Finally, she stood still long enough for him to see that he had, indeed, found the *Fast Dancing People.*

But why should buffalo grass and grama grass be named for Claudio Boutelou? Why should it be called the Bouteloua *genus at all? And if it should be named for some foreigner, some Spaniard, why not his brother? Don Claudio had a slightly younger brother, Esteban, who had also been a part of the pathetically feeble birth of what the Europeans called botany. How did those siblings end up with only one of them being famous? Hadn't they been a team?*

It was getting dark when the hubbub in and around the clearing finally died down. Ishtiliwata crawled out of the plum thicket smelling like a *Mephitis mephitis*, like all the dogs.

He was one of them now.

Hadn't the Boutelou siblings done their best work together, when they were young, long before Esteban died? And didn't Don Claudio's collection, his famous herbarium, consist mostly of other collections, ones that had been put together by Clemente, Lagasca, and Cabanilles?

With little to worry about now from the dogs, Ishtiliwata slowly worked his way down to the village along the river, reconnoitering the horse pen, the object of his quest.

To try to make it back home with a prize breed mare from these people had accounted for many of his own Choctaw people who had gone missing, never to be heard from again.

He didn't intend to be among the missing, and he didn't intend to walk all the way back home. He had bragged that he would return mounted on the best breed mare in their entire *Fast Dancing* herd.

He would accomplish that great deed by doing exactly what the old ones back home had told him, that, whatever you do, don't touch any of their poles.

These people were not only, for as long as anyone could remember, the *Fast Dancing People*, but, more recently, as time goes, they had also become the *Sacred Pole People* as well, ever since they had acquired their greatly coveted horses.

They kept most of their sacred poles in the center of their dance grounds, in the center of their village, fashioned into an elaborate, impressive structure. Once any particular pole got to be sacred enough, it got to be a pole in their horse pen.

Somehow, he had to get the best breed mare out of their horse pen without touching any of their sacred poles, and without raising any alarms among those *Fast Dancing People*.

It was a game the *Sacred Pole People* were willing to play.

They did not lack confidence either in the power of their fast dancing or in the power of their sacred poles.

The old ones back home had warned him that the power of those poles was said to be very great. To touch one, or to cause one to touch the ground, well, you might just as well go drown yourself in the river.

All day long, the *Sacred Pole People* had been preparing for some wild, frenzied, night-long session of dancing. They valued those pole-sanctifying sessions so highly, at every full moon, that he had been assured, if he could strike at that time, there wouldn't be anybody but boys on guard.

And so he had formed his plans and had searched the buffalo plains accordingly. He'd passed up quite a few encampments, until he had seen, from a distance, the arrangement of this particular horse pen. This village seemed a bit short of ripe-enough sacred poles. Perhaps the mass of poles in that elaborate structure in the center of their dance grounds hadn't quite gotten sanctified enough yet.

73

Perhaps that was why a loop of the river formed three sides of their big horse pen. There, beneath the topsoil of that peninsula, what looked like probably an uplifted bedrock intrusion of horizontally folded igneous rock presented an impervious barrier to the river, forcing the river to find a way around it. The banks of the river all along that peninsula were so steep they didn't require any fencing. They were almost cliffs. Almost.

Some deep cuts in those riverbanks, along a few eroded fractures in that rock, provided access to the river at a few places where the water appeared shallow enough to be a good crossing.

All of those river access points were blocked by pole fences, with two or more boys standing guard at each one.

A lot of boys were guarding the horse pen along the long fence at the base of the peninsula, where the horse pen nearly abutted the tall teepees at that end of the village.

It was a big village, with a lot of horses, and the horse-pen peninsula was a big one, plenty big enough for Ishtiliwata to walk among the herd without being seen, far from the boys who were guarding the fences.

There were several unguarded, unfenced places along the riverbanks of that big peninsula where he thought he could probably get a horse down to the river. The trick would be to do that without being seen or heard by any of the boys.

He waited until the frenzy in the village had been going on long enough for the boys to have grown bored listening to it, and even more bored guarding the herd of sleeping horses.

He would have waited even longer, but he caught a lucky break when a big snarling dog fight broke out along the fence line at the base of the peninsula, where some hot-to-trot canine seductress had come trotting along, with every male dog in the village trotting along behind her.

He'd been thinking about slipping into the river and drifting down it until he came to some good place to get into the horse pen that way.

But it looked like all of the boys, from all around the herd, had gone at a dead run to watch the hubbub the dogs were making. They were paying no attention to anything else.

He saw his chance to crawl under the fence while their backs were turned.

And, just like that, he was among their horses.

74

But what if Esteban had been the driving force between those two siblings, and Don Claudio had merely been the one who lived long enough to get the fame? Don Claudio lived a lot longer than Esteban, until sometime in the 1840s. 1842? Had he still been alive when Willkomm visited Spain, the winter of 1844-45? No. Willkomm referred to him as the late Don Claudio Boutelou. Esteban had been dead for a long time by then, about a quarter of a century. It wouldn't be the first time something like that happened—-the driving force ends up not getting the credit. Would that be worth investigating? Probably not. No reason to think Esteban might have played a larger role, and it was Don Claudio who had been the student of Cabanilles.

Ishtiliwata walked through the whole herd, finding one mare after another that he thought might be the best one, until he had narrowed it down to two, a black one and a brown one.

He couldn't choose between them, so he let them choose.

He wanted the most spirited one.

That turned out to be the brown mare, who would hardly let him get near her.

She seemed to think he might be a skunk.

He wasn't quite sure how he would manage to get mounted on her, once he'd gotten her away from there, but, after a lot of soothing coaxing, she finally let him approach her.

After a lot more coaxing, she finally let him touch her, and then, after a lot of dogged persistence, she finally let him touch her all over, until he'd begun thinking that he could probably just mount her right there, when all hell broke loose.

The snarling, stinking-to-high-heaven pack of dogs, apparently not understanding that they weren't supposed to cross any sacred pole barriers, suddenly came boiling in among the horses.

Some of the dogs were fighting with each other, and some were chasing other dogs. The horses found none of that very comforting.

The herd began bolting, rushing away from the dogs.

Without thinking, and not sure if he had coaxed the brown mare quite as much as she might need coaxing, he ran beside her for a few steps, then, throwing caution to the wind, deciding it was now or never, he pounced, mounting her easily.

When the other horses stopped, the brown mare stopped too.

She didn't seem to mind at all that he was mounted on top of her, leaving him a bit chagrined at not having pounced sooner.

75

He was thus surveying the scene, pretty sure now that he could just ride her, very slowly, all the way to the riverbank, when two of the fighting dogs got a little too close to some contrary old nag.

The old nag kicked one of the dogs pinwheeling, kicked him directly under the brown mare.

The dog, disoriented no doubt, and determined to get in another lick of his own, jumped up and bit the brown mare squarely on the teats.

Heidelbacher himself, had he witnessed what happened next, might have been inspired, in describing it, to set aside his rather dry and unpoetic Laws in favor of an old Latin proverb: *Per aspera ad astra*—"through difficulties to the stars."

The brown mare was a bit deceptively deliberate in expressing the full range of her emotions.

She double-bucked him.

The second buck was one he would never forget.

First, she lifted him gently in the air, giving him nothing but air to hold on to, and then, as he was coming down, as he was thinking—if that's as rough as she gets, I can ride her anywhere—that high-spirited, high-maintenance brunette sent him sailing for the moon.

High in the sky, near the top of that trip to the stars, as he was starkly outlined against the backdrop of that big, full moon, he caught a quick glimpse of the boys, arms outstretched, pointing at him, yelling an alarm.

What happened immediately after that, he wasn't quite sure.

Sitting on the ground, disoriented worse than that pinwheeled dog, he was slow in realizing that the brown mare, teat-bitten mad, was wheeling and kicking everything in sight.

The whole herd began stampeding toward the village.

He regained his senses and got to his feet barely in time to keep from getting trampled, seeing the black mare, not far away, the one he regretted he hadn't chosen.

But, maybe, if he could still snag her, everything would work out *hoke*. With a desperate fling, he managed to get mounted on her.

The herd didn't stop. With no regard for anything sacred, the horses pushed down the pole fence and kept going.

Holding on for his life, frantically clinging to that long flowing mane of black hair, there was nothing he could do but try not to fall off, try not to get trampled by that unstoppable mass of pounding hooves.

But wasn't the Bouteloua *genus supposed to have been named in honor of* both *siblings? So why does everyone act as though it was mostly in honor of Don Claudio? Hadn't they published as co-authors? Maybe it* would *be worth looking into. Late-18th and early-19th century Europe might not be a bad place to wallow around for awhile, with the European contemporaries of Gideon Lincecum.*

Like a runaway freight train, the herd plowed into the village, wreaking havoc left and right, collapsing teepees, sending meat racks flying through the air, and sending *Fast Dancing People* scrambling madly to get out of the way.

Lincecum. Hmmm. Now that might be worth looking into, a comparative study, see if any of Lincecum's European contemporaries had what he had, that irrepressible curiosity, and discipline, to lay on his belly for days on end, staring at ant beds, and then get his study of Texas fire ants sponsored for publication with the Royal Society by none other than Charles Darwin, and, long before that, before moving to Texas, having the foresight to spend all those weeks with that Choctaw Alikchi, traveling the Mississippi countryside, carefully cataloguing the medicinal properties of plants for his medical practice, at a time when American medicine was still barbarically Medieval, still practicing blood letting, which was how George Washington's doctors killed him, and believing in the administration of allopathic poisons, like mercury, which killed god only knows how many Americans of that era. See if any of Lincecum's European contemporaries had his range, his capacity to make significant contributions in so many different areas—botany, medicine, zoology. What else? Linguistics. He wrote a grammar of the Choctaw language. What else? And Lincecum was entirely self-taught, in everything. He only had, what? A total of four months in a one-room, backwoods, Georgia schoolhouse, at the illiterate age of fourteen.

The horses gained even more speed as they neared the center of the village.

The black mare was flying when she suddenly found herself coming face to face with a *Fast Dancing* man who had backed up as far as he could go, with his back nearly against the towering mass of their sacred poles.

Ishtiliwata's wild ride on that black-haired beauty came to a stop with such sudden force that he was launched straight over the top of her head, smack into the chest of that *Fast Dancing* man, who was immediately inspired to demonstrate Heidelbacher's Eleventh Law of the Physics of Bodies in Motion—a body in motion colliding with a body at rest will place the body at rest in motion with the same amount of energy as the energy remaining from the amount of energy that placed the body-in-motion in motion.

That *Fast Dancer* was propelled backward with such great force into the base of those sacred poles that the sound of their cracking and splintering could be heard even above the noise of the stampeding horses.

Amid all the dust and chaos, Ishtiliwata staggered to his feet, finding himself surrounded on three sides by *Fast Dancing People*.

They were pointing at him, shouting things in such a way that he didn't feel any need to have any of it translated.

Some of them had knives in their hands, and some had tomahawks, and some were beginning to recover from their shock enough to start stepping toward him.

There was only one place to go, and that's where he went, scrambling madly up the side of their tottering and cracking, rapidly collapsing sacred pole contraption.

It clearly hadn't been designed to support anyone's weight. That possibility had apparently never occurred to anyone.

He got to the top of it just in time to get a good look at the entire village pointing at him and screaming their outrage, before the whole thing tipped a little too far forward and came toppling down to the ground with a great crashing sound.

He rode it all the way down, right into the heart of their sacred dance grounds, smack into the middle of dozens and dozens of suddenly transformed *Hopping Mad People*, hopping mad to get their hands on him.

He landed on his feet, thrown so violently into a headlong trajectory that he Heidelbachered with quite a few *Fast Dancers* before he had expended the energy of his headlong, splattering plunge into the mass of them.

Suddenly, an opening appeared, and he found himself reunited with that teat-bitten-mad brown mare.

She was wheeling and kicking nonstop in a rapidly rotating tight circle, making Heidelbacher proud, employing quite a parade of *Fast Dancing* volunteers to illustrate any number of Heidelbacher's Laws, putting on an impressive display of high-spiritedness, launching those volunteers out of sight toward every quadrant of the compass.

He jumped in beside her and grabbed a big handful of her long flowing hair. Clinging to it desperately, with a mighty leap he mounted her again, praying that she didn't want to put on another display of her bucking ability.

But she was ready to run.

She rocketed after the other *Fast Dancing* horses.

Every horse had passed through the village by then and was disappearing into the moonlit night, disappearing into a cloud of dust as thick and as eerie as any fog.

So there would be no doubt among the *Sacred Pole People* who had been among them, as Ishtiliwata went galloping away, he threw back his head and screamed the ancient Choctaw battle cry as loud as he could scream it.

The tape faded to black, as that triumphant braggart boasted and taunted his way into that dusty darkness, proudly mounted on the ride of his life, herding toward home every horse in that entire *Fast Dancing* herd.

Professor Tuskahoma sat staring at the darkened screen, a little drunk, a little sleepy.

He wondered, idly, if anyone had ever counted how many of those sacred poles he'd touched, how many he'd caused to touch the ground.

He yawned.

Maybe that was why the movie never got finished.

Why he'd been unlucky at love.

Why his sister got famous and he didn't.

But it was just a movie script. Written by one of those fool Western writers.

Probably not even an Indian fella.

And surely not one of the *Fast Dancing People*.

He yawned again, and he scratched his head, thinking about that.

Naw, surely not.

79

MURDER AT NAVAJO MOUNTAIN

By Kent Blansett

amuel Walcott was drawn to the West. Like many of his time, he sought adventure and wealth there. Walcott had married in 1854 and lived a reasonably prosperous life in the bustling east-coast city of Baltimore, Maryland. He and his wife Rachel were surrounded by Victorian routine, comfort, and custom. The Walcotts were not unlike most easterners who had fancied stories about fame and fortune in the West. Newspapers in the east typically printed fantastic stories of fortune seekers from Sutter's Mill to the Comstock Lode to the Black Hills. In 1880, Walcott teamed up with friend James McNally and headed west to seek his fortune in mining and homesteading. McNally, from Albany, New York, was much younger than Walcott and was also caught up in dreams of western fortune. Little did the two men understand what was in store for them when they partnered up to risk it all in the great American West.

Eventually, Walcott and McNally reached the thriving railroad community of Durango, Colorado. Located in southwestern Colorado, Durango had grown prosperous from the recent mining boom in the San Juan Mountain gold fields. Prospectors from across the country had flooded into the Four Corners. Durango grew fat off the thousands of miners intoxicated with gold fever.

Walcott and McNally divided their time between prospecting and homesteading. Both soon acquired several pieces of property around Durango and Ouray, Colorado. Walcott, when time afforded, wrote back to his Rachel in Baltimore. In one letter Samuel lamented that he was too busy to write, but had managed to dictate a letter with the help of Emily, a family friend. The letter dripped with themes of depression, melancholy, sickness, and death. Walcott confided to his wife that his health was poor. He was beside himself and grieved over the recent death of a neighbor. In one of his letters, he elaborated on the mounting tensions between Americans, Utes, and Navajos in and around Durango.

Rumors flourished among Durango settlers that all Navajo silver came from a mine, whose location remained sacred and protected by headman Hashkeneeni's people. The myth of the mine grew to such legendary status that many speculated it was the real reason behind the 1879 Meeker Massacre. Walcott and McNally, driven by the failure of their business in and around Durango, were no doubt inspired by this grand Four Corner's Eldorado. The two men sought out to find their fortune in this secret silver mine protected by the Navajo.

Uncertainty darkened Walcott's mood about his prospecting trip into Arizona Territory, as a letter to Rachel attested. After a long winter in Durango, he and McNally loaded up their wagon with provisions and headed for Utah Territory. Passing through Fort Lewis, Colorado, the two men soon reached Mitchell's Ranch, about seven miles from the Colorado border and within the southeastern part of Utah. The small ranch was located along the mouth of Montezuma Creek, and was a prime camping spot for the weary travelers.

Mitchell, the Mormon proprietor of the ranch, had a twisted and suspect reputation in the area. Most locals did not trust his dealings: his crooked business relations were suspect by everyone in the Four Corners area, including both Navajos and Americans. Mormons had also been suspected in supplying arms to Utes and Paiutes to war on nearby settlements and prospectors. In February of 1880, the killing of two American prospectors had fueled local suspicions of an alliance between Mormons, Utes, and Navajos. A later investigation determined that the prospectors had more than likely been killed by a band of Utes or Paiutes, but settlers around the Four Corners were set on suspicion of mischief by their Mormon neighbors.

During the month of March, old man Mitchell had had a "disagreement" with a Navajo customer, and without hesitation he had fired the first shot, instantly killing his client. Newspapers around the country covered the gunfight. A month later, news of the story was printed in *The Sun*, a Baltimore newspaper, arousing the fears of Walcott's wife. Arte Johnson, one of the survivors of the gunfight, had provided the details of that fateful day.

On the morning of the fifteenth of March a group of eleven Navajos entered Mitchell's store. Johnson, a stage driver and his crew were there, gathering provisions for their next stop in Durango. About fifteen soldiers and another twenty cowboys were around the store. It was a busy day at the ranch. Old man Mitchell got into an argument with one of the Navajo traders and when they both reached for their guns, Mitchell shot his assailant dead. A gunfight ensued between Mitchell, soldiers, ranch hands, and the twelve Navajos. The other Navajos pulled their dead friend from the store and fled from the scene. The ranch was quickly fortified for fear of a Navajo reprisal attack by a suspected 800 warriors. For the next few days the entire ranch was on alert, but no counter attack from Navajo forces ever came.

Despite the anti-Mormon rumors and recent gunfight, Walcott and McNally desperately needed Mitchell not only for provisions but also for advice. They were passing through unfamiliar territory and relied on Mitchell for his knowledge of the land. Mitchell, who had resided and traded in the area for four years, was familiar with the geography of the region, knowing the best sources of watering holes, trails, and places to acquire feed for their mounts. Acting upon Mitchell's advice, Walcott and McNally unhitched their wagon and left it at the ranch. The terrain was too rugged for their wagons, and ease of mobility was crucial for prospecting. By utilizing only pack horses they could cover more territory in less time. It was an efficient solution for prospectors tracking in a mountainous country.

After a few days, Walcott and McNally departed from Mitchell's ranch with a team of horses and their dog. They vanished into the vast and desolate Monument Valley, passing rock formations that jutted toward the heavens like enormous petrified redwoods. It was clearly a distant world far different from Baltimore and New York. The two prospectors pushed on through the sagebrush, juniper, and cactus, into a land and topography foreign and unfamiliar to both. Their horses, loaded down with provisions and supplies, sank into the red earth, making the journey slow and grueling. As they traversed more deeply into Arizona Territory and onto the Navajo Reservation, the terrain became even more treacherous. After a long and perilous ride the two men reached the domed-shaped Navajo Mountain, a sacred site for the Diné. In Blessing-way cosmology it represented the female head of a chain of mountains called Earth Woman. Covered in pines and surrounded by steep mesas and flats, the mountain was a day's work just to circumvent. Navajo Mountain was rumored to hold the secret Navajo silver mine, and its foothills made the perfect base camp for the weary and wind blown travelers.

Navajo Mountain had been a stronghold for the Diné in previous wars against both Spaniards and Americans. A few scattered Diné communities were in this region, managing their sheep herds on traditional lands passed down over the generations. The area also contained two traditional shrines on its crest, each maintained for centuries by clan leaders, societies, and the local communities. Walcott and McNally had not only entered a new territory, they were in a spiritual country. Neither of them could speak the Diné language, nor were they familiar with the customs or traditions of the people.

For many Navajo, the memory of the 1860s—the Long Walk and eventual internment at Bosque Redondo—were recent searing memories. It was an oppressive memory that forged not only a dislike, but also a deep sense of distrust for all Americans. For years the Four Corners was known for violent clashes, raiding, and political strife. The powers of the headmen and chiefs to maintain peace was in constant flux with the influence of the agents at Fort Defiance, Arizona. At times, young Diné warriors would often ally with Utes and Paiutes to raid settlements in and around the Four Corners. The unseen border that Walcott and McNally had so innocently crossed placed them at a dangerous crossroad.

Not long after the haggard explorers established their base camp, several miles south of Navajo Mountain, they were approached by their new neighbors. While herding, Hashkeneeni-begay—Son of Putting Out War—and his wife ran across the path of the two migrants. Hashkeneeni-begay figured that the two men might be in need of some provisions and motioned to one of his prized sheep. Walcott acknowledged the potential for trade, and properly offered tobacco to him and Bililakaih—His White Horse—a young man traveling with Hashkeneeni-begay. After smoking, the Americans followed the couple and the young man to their herd a short distance up the trail. Walcott and McNally were reluctant to choose a sheep and postponed their trade till the morning.

At sunrise, when Hashkeneeni-begay awoke, he rounded up some horses for his mother, who was in the process of moving. On his way back home he passed by Denetsosi—Slim Navajo—and Bililakaih slaughtering a sheep. He asked what they were doing field dressing a sheep so early. Denetsosi and Bililakaih told him that they were killing a sheep for the Americans camped up the road. Perplexed, Hashkeneeni-begay decided to ride ahead to the American camp and inquire why the Americans would be trading with Denetsosi instead of him. When he arrived at the camp, Walcott and McNally were sitting by the fire, stoking the hot coals to cook breakfast. Walcott was bundled up in a brown canvas coat, to take the bite off the cold mountain air. He gestured for Hashkeneeni-begay to join them. Hashkeneeni-begay nervously agreed to.

Not long thereafter, Denetsosi and Bililakaih arrived at the American camp with fresh mutton and corn. They laid out their provisions on a nearby bush and joined Hashkeneeni-begay by the warm crackle of the fire. Walcott and McNally scrambled to find a skillet and utensils to begin cooking their breakfast. The three Diné watched as the Americans ate and drank their coffee. Walcott and McNally never offered any food or coffee to their guests. Accustomed to different manners, the three men were astonished as the Americans gave their remaining leftovers to their dog, and pitched the rest of the coffee.

Walcott stalled his impatient guests even longer, sending McNally for the horses. As McNally disappeared into the junipers, Walcott reached into a saddlebag for his binoculars and began to survey the land. He motioned for Hashkeneeni-begay to join him and look through the spyglass to locate where their horses were grazing. While they busied themselves with the binoculars, Denetsosi took inventory of the camp for possible trades. He spotted a scabbard that contained a rifle, lying near the campsite, and his curiosity got the best of him. He asked Bililakaih, the young boy, to go check out the gun.

Walcott noticed the young man standing by the gun. Denetsosi asked Hashkeneeni-begay to inquire about the gun or a horse for trade. Walcott refused and became upset when he noticed Bililakaih untying the scabbard to examine the rifle. Walcott gestured for the young boy to leave his gun alone. While Walcott was distracted, Denetsosi and Hashkeneeni-begay held a secret conversation. Hashkeneeni-begay, the son of headman Hashkeneeni, told Denetsosi that they should kill the Americans for being so rude. Then he called for the young Bililakaih to come over. Hashkeneeni-begay told the lad that they were going to kill the Americans, and the young man agreed.

Despite the protest of Denetsosi, Bililakaih approached the rifle and began to take it out of the scabbard. Hashkeneeni-begay walked over and picked up an axe, catching Walcott off guard. Worried, he confronted Hashkeneeni-begay and grabbed the handle of the axe. Hashkeneeni-begay told the American he only wanted to see how sharp the blade was, and Walcott turned the handle loose. He then turned around to see the young boy about to pull out his cherished 1873 model Winchester rifle. As Walcott reached down to grab his prized gun, Hashkeneeni-begay planted the axe squarely into the back of his head, killing him instantly.

Excited, Denetsosi grabbed the rifle and a small pistol. Having heard the commotion, old man Dagaa-yazzie—Small Mustache— came into the camp. Surprised by the dead man, he asked the three what had happened. Denetsosi pointed to Hashkeneeni-begay and said that he had killed the American. Just then, they heard McNally approaching with the horses and panicked. Hashkeneeni-begay snatched the Winchester rifle from Denetsosi and fired off several shots at McNally. McNally fell off his horse and quickly tied the horses together to make a shield. Hashkeneeni-begay fired four more shots killing all three horses and began to unload the gun on the American.

McNally hid between the dead horses as bullets split and popped overhead. Dagaa-yazzie, the old man, told them to draw out the American's fire so he could sneak up close and shoot the American while he was reloading. He crawled within twenty-five feet of McNally and found cover behind some tall grass. The gunfight continued, as bullets splintered off juniper branches. Dagaa-yazzie slowly leaned beyond the grass to get a better view. McNally fired a shot which hit Dagaa-yazzie below his left eye and exited from his ear. The old man laid there for awhile in shock, and then he stood up, ran a short distance, and collapsed. Fearing that their companion was mortally wounded, the two Diné men and young boy raced him back to the headman, Hashkeneeni's hogan. They asked for Hashkeneeni's advice and counsel over this situation.

That night a large party of Diné returned to the camp to find that McNally had vanished. Not wasting any time, the elder Hashkeneeni led his son and the others to track down and kill McNally. The tracking was slow, and periodically they had to lite matches to stay close to McNally's trail. By morning the searchers had picked up his tracks, and a separate party found his foot trail. Hashkeneeni-begay suddenly heard shots fired. When he arrived, he saw the bloodstained body of McNally. Denetsosi returned to the prospector's camp and burned the blood stained blankets and saddles. He buried Walcott's body in a shallow grave some distance from the campsite.

By June 1884, interim Navajo Agent John Bowman was thrown into the middle of an investigation into the murders of Walcott and McNally. At first, rumor had pointed back to Mitchell's ranch and a Mormon connection to the murders. Documents found in the wagon left at Mitchell's ranch fueled speculation that Walcott was murdered for a large sum of money he had deposited in a Denver bank. By the end of June, with three months passed since the murders, testimony gathered by Navajo scout 'Pete' at the beginning of May 1884 was the only solid evidence on the case. The above account was given by Denetsosi to Navajo Scout 'Pete' who out of fear of retribution blamed Hashkeneeni-begay for both of the murders. Contradicting Denetsosi, Hashkeneeni-begay, Bililakaih, and his father Hashkeneeni rode into Fort Defiance and offered their own version of the story. Due to Denetsosi's testimony Hashkeneeni-begay was now the prime suspect. It was now vital to have Bililakaih, the only other eyewitness, to corroborate their stories and prove Hashkeneeni-begay's innocence.

According to Hashkeneeni-begay's account, the young Bililakaih went to look at the American's gun a second time. Walcott swore at the young boy, picked up an axe lying nearby, and chased him. He then turned the axe toward Denetsosi, and Hashkeneeni-begay grabbed the handle just before Walcott brought the blade down onto Denetsosi. Struggling, Walcott slowly reached for his pistol, but not as quickly as Hashkeneeni-begay freed the axe and knocked Walcott out cold. Denetsosi ran over and confiscated the pistol and the Winchester rifle. Bililakaih found another smaller pistol and handed it to Denetsosi, just then Walcott began slowly coming around. Denetsosi walked over, took hold of the axe, and hit Walcott three to four times in the head, killing him.

Also, according to Hashkeneeni-begay's testimony, Dagaa-yazzie came across the scene startled and confused, and the elder asked what had happened. Denetsosi explained how Hashkeneeni-begay saved his life, when McNally's return startled them. Dagaa-yazzie suggested that they kill the other American. Denetsosi reached for the Winchester, jumped into his saddle, and galloped at full stride towards the unsuspecting McNally. He fired three times but the gun only snapped; McNally reached for his pistol in self-defense, but Denetsosi had turned back towards the camp to retrieve a gun that worked. Bililakaih, the young boy, pleaded that they should call a truce and let the American go. Dagaa-yazzie disagreed and feared that the American might take vengeance on an innocent Navajo family if he was allowed to escape. Assuming the worst, the old veteran gave his horse a solid kick and charged at McNally, and the gunfight commenced. Dagaa-yazzie was wounded and they let McNally go until evening, when they tracked him down and killed him.

Bowman, the exasperated interim Navajo Agent, was faced with two conflicting testimonies, no bodies, and growing pressure from federal officials for an arrest. Back in Baltimore, Rachel Walcott, distraught over the news of her husband's death, had hired lawyer Fred Fickey, Jr. to pressure federal authorities for an answer. As though Bowman lacked enough challenges, now an eastern lawyer was on his case, demanding justice. Bowman sent word throughout the Navajo Nation that he wanted to arrest all those involved in the killing of Walcott and McNally. Bowman scheduled a council meeting with all the Diné Headmen and Chiefs. By the end of July 1884, Denetsosi and Dagaa-yazzie had turned themselves over to the authorities. Both were promptly taken to Fort Wingate, New Mexico, to await trial.

Bowman then contacted the War Department for military assistance in the capture of his prime suspect, Hashkeneeni-begay. By August, First Lieutenant H.P. Kingsbury of the Sixth Cavalry was dispatched out of Fort Lewis, Colorado, to rendezvous with Navajo Agent Bowman at Keam's Canyon by the eighteenth of August. Bowman arrived a few days early to counsel with 400–500 Diné Headmen and Chiefs. He demanded that Hashkeneeni-begay be turned over at once for trial. Agent Bowman threatened his audience, suggesting that congressional appropriations would be suspended if the "renegade" was not arrested. The delegates replied sharply to Bowman's demand and declared that the remaining fugitive was no longer a Navajo. Hashkeneeni-begay had relinquished his political ties to the Navajo, and had since been adopted by a band of Utes living in the northwestern part of the reservation. They explained that the Utes who had adopted him were well-armed and recently had joined with two other Ute bands rumored to have killed two Navajo scouts under Captain Perrine. The Diné Headmen and Chiefs cautioned Bowman that the Utes were preparing for war, and would not hesitate to defend and protect Hashkeneeni-begay as one of their own. Bowman cringed at the prospects of all out war with the Ute Nation. But there was more to the story than Bowman realized and there was no simple solution.

Bowman was soon joined by Lt. Kingsbury and his troop of the Sixth Cavalry. He updated Kingsbury on the situation. Bowman promptly sent a Navajo scout out to locate the Ute camp where Hashkeneeni-begay could likely be found. Several days later, the scout returned and reported that he had spoken with the fugitive Hashkeneeni-begay. He refused to surrender to Bowman.

On August 19, 1884, Bowman, with the Sixth Cavalry escort, marched out of Keam's Canyon to initiate a surprise attack against the Ute stronghold harboring the "fugitive." The march was long and arduous as they traveled some sixty-five miles through canyons and washes under a blistering sun. Tired and thirsty, after a two-day ride, they attacked the Ute camp, only to find it empty and abandoned. Everyone at the camp had scattered in different directions, making it impossible for the scouts to locate a main trail to pursue. Bowman, frustrated and incensed, abruptly called off the search, fearing that the Navajo scout had betrayed him by announcing their intentions to the Utes. He ordered the cavalry to rest and patrol the Ute camp for the next three days. Bowman then asked for a couple of Navajo scouts to join him in locating the murder scene and to aide in recovering the bodies of Walcott and McNally.

Agent Bowman had promised the widow, Rachel Walcott, that he would retrieve her husband's body and return it to Fort Lewis for a Christian burial. As the party made their way into the crime scene, they discovered the charred remains of Walcott's dog, as well as clothing, blankets, and a saddle. A few yards off were the skeletal remains of a horse, presumably killed in the gunfight with McNally. As Bowman surveyed the site, he tried to recreate the chaos of that fateful morning. One of the Diné scouts quickly returned with the news that he had located a shallow grave south of the campsite. Bowman nervously collected his thoughts and rode out to the shallow grave. Amidst the scorching August heat, Bowman watched as the scouts dug up the grave and exhumed Walcott's badly decomposed body. Upon close inspection, Walcott's remains provided Bowman with all the answers he needed. Tied to Walcott's left ankle was the rope Denetsosi had used to drag the body to its final resting place—the soft sandy foothills some distance away from Navajo Mountain. Bowman observed a critical detail: Walcott's skull had been bludgeoned several times, indicating the cause of death. Not once, as Denetsosi's testimony suggested, but repeatedly, as Hashkeneeni-begay had informed authorities at Fort Defiance.

It seemed to Bowman a case of self-defense. A relieved Bowman had before him the evidence he desired most. He called off the search for McNally's remains, for the only person who knew McNally's whereabouts was still at large. The steep walls of the mesa forced the scouts into an impenetrable thirty-miles of a complex system of interwoven ridgelines. The slope of the land made the task of locating McNally's remains impossible. Bowman returned to the campsite with Walcott's body. He was forced to make a choice; should they push on to Fort Lewis, Colorado as planned, or return to Fort Wingate? Lt. Kingsbury, still fuming over the Navajo scout's betrayal, agreed to escort Bowman to Fort Wingate, an easier route to traverse than Fort Lewis.

On August 31, 1884, Rachel Walcott said her final goodbyes to her husband as his body was laid to rest at Fort Wingate. The Christian service was brief, and by the next morning the Widow Walcott left for Colorado to take stock of her late husband's assets. No one had yet been tried for the murder. Walcott and her lawyer, Fred Fickey Jr., were furious. Someone had to be held accountable. Eventually Hashkeneeni-begay turned himself into authorities based on Bowman's new evidence. The trial took place in Apache County, Arizona Territory, ending in a verdict of not guilty by reason of self-defense.

Interestingly, the trial took place in an Arizona county heavily populated among other settlers with Mormons. This only exacerbated local suspicions that Mormons were somehow linked to the deaths of Walcott and McNally. More importantly, the not guilty verdict demonstrated that the Mormon community had to maintain justice out of necessity. Not only did they have strong economic and missionary ties with the Navajos, but they also lived in the shadow of previous conflict, as did their non-Mormon neighbors. The Apache County Court had to avoid any economic or military reprisals that a guilty or unjust verdict might elicit from the Navajo. From 1884-1885, Governors Lionel A. Sheldon of New Mexico and Fredrick A. Tritle of Arizona collectively warned their territories that any slight altercation might spark another war with the Navajo. Despite anti-Mormon sentiments, each Territory was concerned about the outcome of the trial.

By 1902, Rachel Walcott had sold all of her possessions in Baltimore, Maryland, and relocated to Ouray, Colorado, to manage her late husband's homestead. Six years earlier, her lawyer had pressured the widow to sue the Navajo Nation for compensation over her husband's death. Together they drafted a petition to the Commissioner of Indian Affairs for ten thousand dollars compensation for the murder of Samuel Walcott. It was a desperate attempt that failed to materialize any return for the widow. After a short stint as Navajo Agent, Bowman retired from the agency when D.M. Riordan returned to resume his post. Only one individual, Hashkeneeni, the Diné Headman who killed McNally, served a short sentence in St. Johns, Arizona. The body of James McNally was never recovered, and to this day remains lost in the Four Corners.

The story of the murders quickly grew into local folklore in the Four Corners region. Rumors spread that McNally killed Walcott in a rage of silver fever, and that he had disappeared into the backcountry forever. The Mormon connection continued, revealing the religious tensions harbored in the region. Violence was central to this story, because it reinforced and redefined the territorial borders of the American Southwest. Out of this violence emerged a dramatic legacy of expansion and colonialism.

There was true American justice for the Diné involved in the gunfight. As much as Agent Bowman was a player in the investigation, so too were the Navajo scouts, Diné, Ute, and

Paiutes who protected Hashkeneeni-begay. Navajo Tribal politics and intertribal connections with the Ute had spared Hashkeneeni-begay from a hangman's court. Between Federal and Tribal politics, east and west, this story highlights a climate of fear on all sides of the political, cultural, legal, economic, and military frontiers.

Caught amidst the changing tides of Federal Indian Law of *Ex parte Crow Dog* (1883) and the Major Crimes Act of 1885, the Diné plea of self-defense was recognized by the Arizona Territorial Courts. This legal case became the Scottsboro Trial of the American West. It signaled the end of a period of Navajo history and the start of a new beginning, as the Navajo Nation now reinvented their political dominance within the Four Corners region.

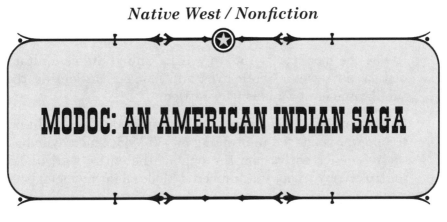

MODOC: AN AMERICAN INDIAN SAGA

By Cheewa James

The two men faced each other in the freezing November dawn.
Second Lt. Frazier Boutelle stood coatless in his blue U. S.
military uniform. He had taken off his coat an hour before, knowing
that he might need to have the free movement of his arms. He and
thirty-nine other U. S. Army military men, including a doctor and
four men handling the pack train, had ridden through the night
from Ft. Klamath, located in what today is the state of Oregon.
They'd come fifty-six miles in penetrating sleet and ice. The
numbed men found themselves frozen to their saddles at times.

The Modoc man standing in front of him had a jagged scar
running across one cheek. It had given him the name of Scarfaced
Charley. He and other Modocs had awakened to the amazing sight
of soldiers in the midst of their Lost River village, today part of
northern California.

Suddenly both men lifted their weapons and gunfire rang out
at exactly the same time. Neither man on that windy, snow-swept
ridge could have known the great significance of the first two shots
of the Modoc War, discharged simultaneously in the conflict that
became know as the Lost River Battle.

Those shots, fired November 29, 1872, did not kill a man, but
they would result in huge suffering and anguish to settlers, Modocs,
and U. S. Army soldiers throughout the first half of 1873. The shots
also signaled the beginning of a period that would profoundly and
irreparably affect the destiny of the Modoc people.

The Modoc War of 1872-83 stands as an amazing conflict in United States history:

- It was the most costly Indian war in United States military history, in terms of both lives and money, considering the small number of Indians who battled.

- By the end of the six-month war, over 1,000 U. S. military troops were engaged in bringing 50–60 Modoc men, who had their families with them throughout the entire war, under control. Army troops outnumbered Modoc fighting men about 20 to 1.

- The Modoc War is the only Indian war in American history in which a full-ranking general, General E. R. S. Canby, was killed.*

Were it not for the George Armstrong Custer fight at the Little Big Horn against the Lakota and Cheyenne only three years after the Modoc War, the Modoc conflict would probably be remembered as the most significant Indian confrontation in America's western history.

The Modoc War involved only one relatively small group of American Indian people. However, it is a riveting example of what happened across the United States as non-Indian settlers, landowners, and military persevered in efforts to continue western expansion. The Modoc saga is one that belongs equally to California and Oregon. But the end of the war would see Oklahoma become a part of this poignant story.

In war it is tempting, but simplistic, to label the warring factions as "right" or "wrong," "good" or "bad." War spawns cruel acts, but it also brings humane actions on both sides. The complexity of any war asks that naïve, one-dimensional conclusions not be drawn. War itself is the true evil.

Roots of War

For many millenniums the Modocs had inhabited 5,000 square miles in northern California and southern Oregon. Their population

---

* Custer was not a full-ranking general at the time of his death.

fluctuated between 400–800 at any given time. They were water people and made much use of waterfowl and fish. They used tule reeds to make baskets, canoes, sandals, and coverings for their homes and used seeds from the wocus, a water plant, to grind into food. Their semi-nomadic patterns took them to the right places at the right times for their hunting, fishing, and food-gathering activities. Then the last move of the year brought them back to the favored areas for building their winter homes, called *wickiups.*

Above all, the Modocs loved their land. It was, in every sense, their world. The environment sometimes could be adversarial, but Modocs knew ways to cope. They understood the land. It was that knowledge that made them powerful in combat.

The Modocs were never a united tribe, coming together only in emergencies like war. Rather, Modocs lived in bands surrounding Tule Lake and along Lost River and other tributaries near the lake. The bands were autonomous, with each band having its own leader and governmental base.

The first non-Indians came into Modoc territory somewhere in the middle of the 1800s. Small pox followed shortly after that. The Modocs, like most of the Indians in their area, suffered great casualties as they lacked immunity to the disease.

But Modocs were to remember an incident in late 1852 even more vividly. Ben Wright was the stuff from which legends are made. With his long, curly hair and swaggering style, he was a notorious Indian killer who often bragged of the number of noses, fingers, and scalps he had taken from fallen Indians. It was Ben Wright and his men who rode into a Modoc camp under a white flag of peace and killed over thirty men, women, and children. Wright's meaning of a white flag was to be engraved in the minds of Modocs.

The traditional life of the Modocs ended with the Treaty of 1864. Although the treaty was never officially ratified, in 1869 the Modocs were coerced onto Oregon's Klamath Reservation along with the Klamath and Yoohoskin band of Snake Indians. When the Klamaths, who greatly outnumbered the Modocs, began to harass the Modocs at fishing and attempts to cut timber, they sought help from Indian agent Capt. O. C. Knapp, a Union Army veteran who was not particularly happy with his role of Indian agent.

It was at this time that one Modoc emerged who was destined to stand out in Modoc history above all others. His name was

Keintpoos, translated as "Having-the-Waterbrash" (pyrosis or heartburn), probably referring to his stomach problems. But his Indian name was not the one people would remember. Keintpoos became known as Captain Jack.

Three times Captain Jack met with Knapp with no action resulting. Finally, on the last visit, Knapp swore at Captain Jack and accused him of being a chronic complainer. Jack spoke no English, but through his interpreter he replied, "If the agent does not protect my people, we shall not live here. If the government refuses to protect my people, who shall I look to for protection?"

With those words, Captain Jack and more than 300 Modocs left the Klamath Reservation in April of 1870 and returned to the ancestral Lost River land. Eventually some 130 Modocs drifted back to the reservation, under the leadership of Old Schonchin.

Some of the Modocs spoke English, although the tribe as a whole still used the native tongue. They adopted clothing similar to the settlers around them. Dungarees, shirts, and work shoes had long replaced the skins and tule sandals of their ancestors. Most had their hair cropped short and had muzzle-loading rifles with powder horns. Only the very old Modocs carried bows and arrows.

Yreka, California, had flamed to life at the western boundary of Modoc traditional land when gold was discovered in the vicinity in 1851. Modocs often looked for work there as house servants. Ranchers and farmers in the area would use Modocs as ranch hands.

The Modoc language was difficult on the tongues of the non-Indians, so Modocs were re-named. Shkeitko, meaning "left-handed man," was given the name Shacknasty Jim. Some say it is because of his mother's untidy housekeeping. Slat-us-locks became Steamboat Frank. He was named in recognition of the deep, resounding voice of his foster mother (who later became his wife). Boston Charley was very fair and Black Jim, very dark. History has recorded the colorful names of historically well-known Modocs like Curley Headed Doctor and Scarfaced Charley. But lesser known Modocs had names that make one wonder who dreamed them up: Greasy Boots, Big Duck, Old Longface, Skukum Horse, Humpy Joe, and Tee-hee Jack.

Modocs, except for those who followed Old Schonchin back to the Klamath Reservation, continued to live in their ancestral homelands for over two years after leaving the reservation, until that fateful November 29, 1872, morning when the first attempt was made to return the Modocs to the reservation by attacking Captain Jack's village on Lost River.

A bungling of military orders and a lack of clarity as to whether government officials or the military branch was really in charge brought too few men to the Lost River village. Some thirty-five fighting soldiers were not enough to bring the Modocs into submission, even with the element of surprise on the side of the military.

Captain Jack's village was burned to the ground. Modocs claimed an old woman was burned alive in her *wickiup*. The military claimed that did not happen. History has obliterated the truth, but there was no doubt that war had come. The Modocs fled into the surrounding sagebrush, headed for the nearby water of Tule Lake. There, with only the clothes they had escaped in, men, women, and children began the cold, miserable trip in canoes headed south across the lake. They were headed for the desolate lava beds on the other side of the lake, where they would take their stand against the military. In that land, known today as the Lava Beds National Monument, they knew they could use the land against their enemy.

During the chaos and fighting at Captain Jack's village, a group of civilian men, with no military orders and without the soldiers even knowing they were there, raided a Modoc village across the river from Captain Jack's people, killing women and children.

In revenge, a group of Modocs from that village rode out around the shores of Tule Lake and killed fourteen settler men— only men, an unusual act in the war tactics of 1873. Normally there was no distinction made between men and women. Henry Miller, long time friend of the Modocs, had been out riding the Thursday afternoon before the fateful Lost River Battle. He had assured Modocs he encountered that he knew of no plans for soldiers to be in the area. Because of the military's neglect to warn settlers of an impending attack, he had no idea there was a problem. Out riding on the day of the attack, he saw a band of Indians and raised his hand in greeting. He was shot from his horse and went to his grave never knowing what hit him—or why.

97

A Killing Time

Historical writings on the Modoc War have not made much note of the role of women, either Modoc or settler, in this war, but some of the bravest and most poignant stories are those associated with women. The settler women whose homes were raided and men in the family killed left a page in history that is not forgotten.

William Brotherton and two of his sons were shot and killed while cutting wood. Joseph, Brotherton's fifteen-year-old son, was with neighbor John Schroeder, who tried to escape the Modocs on his horse. Schroeder did not succeed, the Modocs shooting him from his horse.

In the confusion, Joseph ran for home. Sarah Brotherton, seeing her son fleeing the Modocs, rushed to meet him with a revolver in her hand. Her younger son called to her to come back, then opened the door and followed her. Turning to the boy, she ordered him back to the house, told him to grab his father's Henry rifle, elevate the sights to eight hundred yards, and blast away at the Modocs. This he did, with his younger sister wiping and handling the cartridges. Sarah grabbed her older son and raced back to the house. Barricading the door with freshly purchased sacks of flour, she pushed loopholes in the house walls, converting her home to a fortress. The family, with Sarah shouting orders, bombarded the Modocs with rifle fire, keeping them at bay. Finally the Modocs left, but it was not until the third day that help finally arrived at the Brotherton homestead, and the beleaguered family was rescued.

The reaction to the settler killings was one of shock and horror, and it reverberated across the nation. Modocs from other bands were also affected by the killings. The Hot Creek band, which lived on the western boundary of Modoc land under the leadership of Shacknasty Jim, had lives very separate from those in Captain Jack's village. Seeing that war was coming, they made the decision to turn themselves in to military officials at Ft. Klamath, where many of the soldiers were based. They wanted nothing to do with Captain Jack's war. Rancher John Fairchild, who hired many of the Hot Creek Modocs and even paid a small rent to them to live on his ranch, agreed to escort this band of Modocs to Ft. Klamath.

But the Hot Creek band, numbering approximately fourteen men and thirty women and children, was intercepted on the way north to the fort by a group of inebriated settlers who threatened to murder any Hot Creek that tried to cross the river. Even Fairchild could not contain the frightened Hot Creeks, and they bolted in fear. They rode to the south, eventually joining Captain Jack in the lava beds.

One can only wonder what would have happened if the Hot Creeks had not joined Captain Jack's fighting force, which only numbered thirty to forty men. Would there even have been a Modoc War? Fate intervened and sent Captain Jack fourteen more men, enough to make him feel he could wage a war rather than offer surrender.

Preparing the Stronghold

The Modocs realized that war had come.

Their battlefield was in a major lava flow in what is today the Lava Beds National Monument in northern California. The field of harsh, jagged rock results from volcanic activity over the last half-million years.

The Modocs' natural fortress was known as Captain Jack's Stronghold. To the south of the stronghold was no-man's land—torturous black lava as far as the eye could see. The terrain was so uneven and rough that no one ventured into it. The stronghold was bordered on the north by Tule Lake, which provided water to those inside the lava walls of the Modoc war camp. As the weather warmed, water was a major survival issue.

Captain Jack, with Schonchin John second in command, chose this rugged landscape because he knew that the land itself would be a wicked enemy of the army troops. The Modocs, in contrast, knew the lay of the land and how to use it. The lava flow was part of their forebears' tribal domain. They had used the ice caves for food storage and water. The warmer caves were temporary hunting lodges.

The addition of the Hot Creeks brought the number of fighting men with Captain Jack to between fifty and sixty. The Modoc army was a young one. Many of the fighters could be classified as boys. A number of the better-known warriors and leaders were in their late teens and early twenties. The fighting uniform was the clothing they had adopted from the miners and ranchers in the area. Despite some of the glorified descriptions and drawings of Modoc fighters, dungarees, boots, shirts, and bandanas were worn.

One extraordinary aspect of this war is often overlooked. Modoc women and children, numbering somewhere around 100, were with their men in the lava bed throughout the entire six-month war. When battles were fought, the women and children were there. There are records of women actually being armed and fighting.

Captain Jack's Stronghold was two miles long and 300 yards wide. Pit-like depressions and broken lava tubes forming caves served as dwellings for the Modoc warriors, women, and children. The Modocs had acquired a herd of 100 cattle. These animals were driven in and maintained as sustenance for the Modocs. The stronghold had deep chasms running through the fortress, allowing the Modocs to move easily from one end to the other. Jack's men dug additional trenches to strengthen their position. Where the natural terrain did not provide protection, they constructed artificial barriers of stone about four feet in height with loopholes to shoot through. Lookouts posted throughout the stronghold could easily see movement to the east and west.

The Modocs knew their own battlefield intimately. In preparing for battle, they had placed piles of rocks at strategic spots. These markers had no significance for the military, but had a deep importance to the Modocs as they slipped from one point of cover to another, using the rocks as guideposts. There were large mounds of rocks fortified and designed for a man or two to be stationed in each, giving the Modocs about a twenty-foot altitude advantage over the soldiers.

The stronghold was described by Lt. Thomas Wright, a U. S. soldier who fought and eventually died in the Modoc War, in this way: "The match for the Modoc Stronghold has not been built and never will be...It is the most impregnable fortress in the world."

The unique geology of the lava bed and the Modocs' understanding of how to survive in and use that terrain were the foremost reasons the Modocs were so successful. Bleak and forbidding, the jagged, sharp lava rocks became the allies of the Modocs, who used the land against their enemy in the truest sense of guerrilla warfare.

Curley Headed Doctor, spiritual leader and shaman to the Modocs, played a major role in the war, for it was his teachings that convinced the Modocs they were invincible. The shaman professed that no Modoc would fall in battle if they were to follow his beliefs.

Forward, March!

The battle to take the stronghold and force the surrender of the Modocs took place on January 17, 1873. It pitted approximately 300 regular U. S. military men, volunteers, and Indian scouts against the small band of fifty or so Modocs.

Lt. Col. Frank Wheaton was the commander of this battle. The military strategy for the upcoming confrontation was "gradual compression" or squeeze them out. Troops would move in and compress from both the east and west. To the north was Tule Lake and to the south was the inhospitable no man's land. The day before the battle, Wheaton wrote Gen. E. R. S. Canby, commander of the department of the Columbia, "I don't understand how the Modocs can think of attempting any serious resistance, though of course we are prepared for their fight or flight."

The day of the battle dawned cold, dismal, and foggy. Troops were readied, and the order was given to advance. Soldiers soon discovered that to obey this command was not the same task as it had been in other wars. Skirmish lines—a row of men marching forward in unison—were quickly found to be virtually impossible.

Not only were there rocks to be skirted, but also a seemingly level stretch of land would suddenly break into a yawning chasm. Fog had settled in and overhung the lava bed like a quiet sea. The soldiers found it difficult not only to know where the Modocs were, but also to determine the positions of their own units. In the confusion, the strategically placed Modocs were able to fire their rifles without revealing their positions. At one point Wheaton noted, "There was nothing to fire at but a puff of smoke issued from cracks in the rock."

One volunteer officer told of a very young soldier who had lost his way and ended up in the volunteer army ranks. The boy soldier was totally terrorized by the fighting. When the man next to him was shot and blood spurted out, the young man staggered back, retched violently, and then deliberately pointed his own carbine at his foot and pulled the trigger. He was through with soldiering for that day.

Howitzers, canons that fired projectiles in a curved trajectory, had been shipped to the lava bed specifically for this battle. They proved of no value when the enemy's position was hidden from view as it was in this battle. No one could tell where the rounds were landing. Afraid of hitting their own troops, leaders ordered the guns silenced. In Lt. William Boyle's words, soldiers were afraid they "would do more harm to our troops than to the enemy." It was back to rifles.

Maj. Green gave an insight into what the military faced:

It was impossible to make the proposed charge, the nature of the rocky ground preventing men moving faster than at the slowest pace, and sometimes having to crawl on their hands and feet. It is utterly impossible to give a description of the place occupied by the enemy as their stronghold.

At one point, Green became infuriated at his own men who when given the command to move forward, did nothing. In great frustration and disregarding the heavy fire, he leaped up in plain view of both soldiers and Indians and began a profane tirade on the character and ancestry of his men.

The Modoc were thrown off guard and absolutely astonished at this figure in blue jumping from rock to rock. Green snatched off his military glove and as he danced among the rocks, he pounded the glove into his other hand, punctuating his tongue-lashing with blows of his hand. For years to follow, the Modocs spoke of the magical properties of John Green's glove that protected him during the Modoc War.

After ten hours of battle, the U. S. Army returned to its base camp, bruised, completely demoralized, and having suffered twenty-five wounded and twelve killed. The soldiers' clothing was in shreds from crawling among the rocks, and their shoes were worn off their feet. Because of this defeat, Wheaton was relieved of his command, although many protested that move, and was replaced by Col. Alvan Gillem.

Before the battle had begun, Curley Headed Doctor had placed a tule rope dyed red around the perimeters of the Stronghold. He told the Modocs that not a soldier could cross that rope and not a Modoc would die.

He was right, and the Modocs were convinced they were invincible.

The Good Friday That Wasn't So Good

During the next three months, no major battle took place. The Modocs lived inside the stronghold with families living in lava caves and getting water from Tule Lake. A peace commission was officially established shortly after the battle for the stronghold. After the terrible defeat of the army, words now seemed to be a better route than weapons.

Good Friday, April 11, 1873, was the date set for the meeting of four U. S. peace commissioners and the Modocs. General Canby headed the commission. Canby was respected by Indian groups with whom he had worked, and he was willing to work with the Modocs to find a solution. He was entirely confident that the results of the peace conference would be positive and end animosity.

Alfred Meacham, the former Oregon superintendent of Indians affairs, had been with the commission since its organization and, like Canby, he had worked successfully with Indian groups. But unlike Canby, he had great foreboding about the conference. Toby Riddle, a Modoc woman, and her non-Indian husband Frank, were to serve as interpreters at the conference, and Toby had frantically warned Meacham that the Modocs were planning an attack at the conference. She and Meacham had become great friends when years before he had issued an edict that no white man could live with an Indian woman without marriage. As a result, Toby and Frank had married.

The night before the conference, the Modocs had met to discuss what was to be done. Modoc society operated on consensus. All decisions, both civil and war-related, were made by vote of the people. Captain Jack had stood in front of his cave with the Modocs gathered around him and made a plea for peace. But a Modoc jumped up beside him, placed a woman's basket hat on his head and a shawl around his shoulders. "You are a fish-hearted woman," the Modoc said.

When the final consensus was reached, the feeling was that by eliminating the leaders, the Modocs had a better chance for success. Any misgivings the Modocs had about killing the commissioners were swept away by memories of the Ben Wright massacre. The ghosts of Wright and his Modoc victims had found their way to the windswept, desolate site of the Good Friday peace conference.

The four commissioners—Canby; Meacham; Rev. Eleazar Thomas, a Methodist minister from Petaluma, California; and Indian Agent Leroy Dyar—came under fire at exactly noon. Captain Jack raised his gun from a distance of five feet, pointed it at Canby's head and fired. Reverend Thomas was shot in the chest by Boston Charley. "Don't shoot again, Boston. I shall die anyway," Thomas stammered as he rose to his feet. He, like Canby, was not to survive.

Both Meacham and Dyar had also come armed to the peace conference and Dyar made a quick retreat, threatening Modocs with a wave of his derringer. Meacham turned to run, tripped, and fell unconscious as a bullet creased his forehead. Boston Charley began to scalp him, a bit difficult, as Meacham was mostly bald. Toby Riddle, seeing her friend in deep trouble, yelled out, "The soldiers are coming," causing Boston Charley to dart away from Meacham. When soldiers arrived a half-hour later, they found Toby sitting beside the wounded Meacham and the naked bodies of Thomas and Canby where they had fallen.

Back to War

On April 14, the stronghold was once again attacked. But this time it was different. There were 650 men and they were primed for battle. Colonel Gillem was in command but was extremely unpopular with his men, even to the point of having his orders disobeyed at times. The three-day battle ended on January 17, and the soldiers entered the stronghold. Much to their amazement, only a few older, infirm Modocs were there. During the night, the Modocs had vacated the stronghold through a route running south through the lava beds. Scouts recalled how they had thought they had heard children crying during the night but had not investigated.

Where were the Modocs? That thought plagued Gillem, and on April 26 he sent out a patrol of approximately sixty-five military men. At around noon, the men took lunch, pulling off their shoes, and relaxing. They had no sooner put their shoes back on and started forward when the Modocs, under the command of Scarfaced Charley, attacked. It was short and it was brutal. Two-thirds of the patrol was wiped out, including the patrol commanders Capt. Evan Thomas and Lt. Thomas Wright.

Gillem delayed sending out a rescue patrol, and by the time he did, the weather had turned bitter with driving sleet and snow. "Never did men suffer as did the officers and soldiers on that night, hearing the wails of the dying and with the fearful spectacle of dead men packed on the backs of mules. The sufferings of that night's march made many a young man old," related Lieutenant Boyle. Many felt Gillem's actions were inept and following the Thomas-Wright Battle, Wheaton was reinstated.

Following the battle, dissention within the Modoc bands, accompanied by lack of water and food, signaled the beginning of the end for the Modocs. Over a thousand soldiers were now in pursuit. On May 22, 1873, the Hot Creeks surrendered, and on the first of June Captain Jack surrendered saying, "Jack's legs give out."

Thus came to an end one of the most grueling and expensive Indian wars ever fought. Even leaving out the huge expense of paying soldiers, estimates are that it cost $10,000 per Modoc—in 1873 money—to subdue these Indians in battle. If the cost were to be calculated in 2008 money, it would amount to $289,170 per Modoc.

Captain Jack, Boston Charley, Schonchin John, and Black Jim were put on trial for the peace commission murders and hung on October 3, 1873. They were buried at Ft. Klamath, although their heads were shipped to the U. S. Army Museum for study. Shortly thereafter, 150 Modoc men, women, and children were taken to Redding, California, and put on a train carrying them to Oklahoma Indian Territory.

Exhausted, hungry, and cold, on a bleak November day they arrived at their new home on the Quapaw Agency, near what today is Miami, Oklahoma. Having fought a battle that created international headlines in its time and that would spawn writings for over a century, history then turned its back on the Modocs. This tribe now started down an obscure road of little interest to the American press or anyone else.

They worked hard to adapt to their new life. As one Indian agent said, "The Modocs plow and sow and reap with the same resistant courage with which they fought." They were devastated by tuberculosis—almost wiped out by an enemy more lethal than guns. Poor government administration did not get medical supplies and services to them. For half a century they struggled to survive.

But survive they did. This was the tribe that wouldn't die, and today their descendants speak proudly of the tenacious staying power that carried Modocs through years of war, unrest, and disease. As long as the heart and soul of a people have tolerance, tenacity, and boldness, they will never die.

Editor's Note: the author is enrolled with the Modoc Tribe of Oklahoma and is the great-granddaughter of Modoc War warrior, Schkeitko, "Shacknasty Jim."

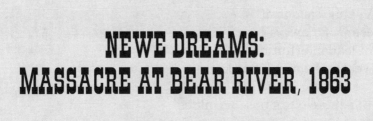

NEWE DREAMS: MASSACRE AT BEAR RIVER, 1863

By Rod Miller

I

Spinning in mist
thick with dim light
Tin Dup sees steel pony tracks
puncture the deep-blown snowfloor;
senses the shadowed
approach of distant blue tunics.

Beads of river splash
crackle and arc hard
back to black water.
He feels the throb of
hoofbeat drums, hears
the cadenced whine and cry
of frozen foot leather.

Snowfields roll 'round once more—
since painted with clay and ash,
stained with steaming scarlet
spatter and splash
of futures lost.

Anxious eyelids quiver:
Vexing visions of
crimson flowers blooming
in leaden eruptions on
weatherbeaten buckskin.

Bia-Wu-Utsee's nose wrinkles
at the stench of a yet imagined
reality intruding on her sleep:
the same reek riders make
marking mounts with fire.

But, in the phantasm at hand,
the stink comes as
her man's neck cracks
at the weight of a *toquash* boot
when a soldier bears down
on a carbine buttstock,
driving the fired iron taper of a bayonet
out the opposite ear sizzling
as mud fouls fresh flowers
fallen to mauled snow.

Tender red tendrils
drift downstream; icy wake for
baby floating cold...

FRONTIER WEST

Frontier West / Fiction

THE SPANIARD AND MERIWETHER LEWIS

By Rita Cleary

Don Carlos Dehault Delassus de Luzière, Spanish Lieutenant Governor of Upper Louisiana, slammed his silver-tipped cane across the mahogany desk. He was an aristocrat, son of an exiled count who had fled France in the Reign of Terror and he was angry. His family's lands, the Château de Luzière and all its dependencies, had been swept away by the peasant rabble in the French Revolution. Now, his new land, the vast Spanish province and former French colony of Louisiana, was about to fall to another rabble, the loose collection of former British colonies called the United States. Delassus himself had escaped from France to Spain, where he had enlisted in the Spanish Army and risen to the high position he held now. It was October of 1803, and if the dispatch he just received were true, he was about to lose Louisiana too.

He held the dispatch in his long fingers. He would have liked to burn it, but it held the seal of Colonel Juan Manuel de Salcedo, Governor General of Louisiana, his superior in New Orleans. His cold blue eyes moved from Salcedo's seal to the Delassus family crest that emblazoned the ring on his right index finger and his mouth curled in a cynical smile. He cursed the date, April 30, 1803 and exclaimed: "First San Ildefonso and now this." At San Ildefonso, Spain had ceded Louisiana back to France. Delassus swore: "Damn commoners and their legislatures, seekers of fortune, usurpers all. Damn Napoleon and his conquests! The

111

bloody Corsican thinks he's Charlemagne, sells Louisiana's riches so he can amass an empire. I will not be party to his conduct."

He tossed the dispatch onto his desk, swept the tails of his blue coat to the side and sank into his armchair. The tall, throne-like chair with lion heads carved into the angle of the arms gave him a sense of security and power. He cupped his hands around the carved beasts and rang for his manservant.

A short bespectacled man in black livery appeared with a bow. "You rang, Your Excellency."

"Yes, Manuel." Delassus tapped the dispatch nervously. Is the messenger who delivered this abomination still in the house?"

"He's in the kitchen, Your Excellency. Cook is feeding him."

"Summon him back. He must return to Salcedo with my reply."

Manuel shuffled out and Delassus waited. Brooding, he shoved the distasteful message to the edge of the desk, pinched his nostrils, fingered the silver medallion of his rank that hung on a link chain around his neck and snatched a blank page. Finally, he dipped a quill and began to write.

My dear Salcedo,

I have burned your dispatch of October 2nd. Its contents both dismayed and angered me. Like you, I will not recognize the purchase until I read the official document with my own eyes. And I will not implement its provisions without a direct order that I know is not forthcoming. Be assured that as of this moment, I have erased the dreadful news and its implications from my heart and mind. Please instruct the bearer of this message to do the same. As I have destroyed the hateful dispatch, I trust you will do the same with my reply. May the good God keep you many years and preserve our bounteous land,

He signed the letter with a flourish, folded it and sputtered: "I hope they paid in gold. I hope the Corsican demanded gold."

Louisiana had been French territory. Its population was French. Its inhabitants spoke French and kept their records in French, although Spanish had been the language of government for the last forty years. Spain's was a righteous rule, a good, kingly, Christian rule. The Corsican, Napoleon Bonaparte, was the product of an ungodly revolution, an aspiring *nouveau*, neither French nor Spanish. Delassus snickered to himself: "As if a title could buy him legitimacy." But now sale to the Americans, that dirty, untutored mob of woodsman, beggars and thieves, was a horror no proud son of the kingdom of France could countenance.

A soldier, a sergeant in a travel-worn uniform of the Army of Spain, appeared in the doorway and bowed obsequiously. Delassus raked over the man with cold blue eyes, applied a dollop of wax to his letter and stamped it with his seal. "Here is your reply, Sergeant. You are to deliver it directly into the hands of Salcedo himself, none other. If bandits, Indians, anyone threatens your safety, you will destroy it. Is that understood?"

"I go with armed escort, by keelboat, Your Excellency. There will be no threat."

"Good." Delassus snapped his thin lips shut. The soldier took the letter, turned on his heel and disappeared.

Pushing himself to his feet, Delassus retrieved his cane. He picked up the offensive dispatch, crumpled it with one hand and walked to the wide stone hearth. There was no fire because the day was warm and he passed a hand over his sweating brow. "So much for the Americans. May they come to a fast and inglorious end." He tossed the dispatch into the ashes, mumbling: "I must instruct Manuel to light the fire." Then he returned to the massive armchair and poured out a goblet of port from a silver decanter on the corner of his desk. He downed it, poured another, swallowed that, turned to the pages still left on his desk and began to read.

They detailed a plea, signed by more than forty commoners of St. Louis, requesting an end to the exclusive licensing of the lucrative Indian trade. Beaver was the commodity. Only men of influence and wealth could obtain the coveted licenses. He read the scribble of petitioners' signatures and paused at the name of Manuel Lisa – surely the organizer. But there were many more: Roubidoux, Vasquez, Sanguinet, the loudmouth Irishman, Reilly. Some were barely legible.

Delassus tossed the petition aside. Lisa should know better. The licenses to trade went only to highly-recommended, uprighteous men of impeccable repute – for a price. The system protected the coveted beaver from the likes of greedy entrepreneurs like Lisa. Licenses prevented every freebooting pirate from bribing the savages with whiskey, robbing them of their livelihood or inciting them to rob and pillage. The licenses produced significant revenue for his Catholic Majesty, the King of Spain. Commoners were not eligible. They were best settled on farms and dependencies, so that Spain could maintain her colony and prevent British and American incursions with a permanent population who inhabited and cultivated the land.

He downed his third glass of port and sighed. The sweet taste sharpened his thoughts. Spain had sent D'Eglise, Evans and Mackay north and they reported English activity on the Mississippi and Missouri Rivers. The British Hudson's Bay and North West men traded with Mandan, Arikara and Sioux. He dismissed any idea of threat and mumbled: "Surely they build only sparse trading posts, not settlements. The alternative is unthinkable. Open the beaver trade and our yeomen would abandon their families, leave their crops to rot in the field and run off in search of precious pelts. We would have unruly hordes swarming like so many ants on every river and creek. And Americans would come with their elections and meetings." Delassus was a lifelong royalist, had not forgotten the terror of mob rule or the crash of the guillotine and vowed: "I will keep Americans out. Beyond the Mississippi, they shall not pass."

Months passed and no further official reference was made to the sale of Louisiana to the fledgling United States. But like the mists that spread over the rich bottomlands, rumors expanded among the St. Louis merchants. Louisiana had been sold. Soon American settlers would arrive. Americans would descend on the fur trade as the fastest way to riches; they would not bow to government control; they would not cross the palms of grasping officials with gold. Free trade would benefit the merchants and traders of St. Louis. But to safeguard their profits, the merchants needed to secure their position now, quickly, before the acquisitive Americans arrived.

Lieutenant Governor Delassus ignored the rumors and paid no heed to the merchants' petition until a fateful day in early December when his manservant, Manuel, entered again. "Captains Amos Stoddard and Meriwether Lewis to see you, Your Excellency."

Delassus's head jerked back. "Stoddard, the American commander at Fort Massac?"

"The same, Your Excellency."

"And Lewis? Tell me where I've heard the name. Did they say why they come?"

"For a passport, Your Excellency. This Lewis requests permission to enter Louisiana. He needs supplies preparatory to an expedition he is launching to the Upper Missouri River. Word has it that he is seeking passage northwest at the behest of Mr. Jefferson. Stoddard accompanies him only for the purpose of introduction. Lewis carries letters of credit, Your Excellency, and begs your help."

"My help, when he is invading my province?" Delassus snorted, leaned back, arched his proud neck and resumed: "We will grant them an audience, Manuel, but not yet. First, I must calm myself. They will wait until I am ready. Come again in one-half hour."

Manuel did not question. Delassus picked up a quill and began to pen a billet to a young *señorita* he had met one week before at a ball in his honor. He had an eye, roving but discreet, for the ladies. He completed the letter, blotted it, sat back and contemplated how he would respond to Stoddard and Lewis.

Punctually, in one-half hour, Manuel ushered Captains Amos Stoddard and Meriwether Lewis into the room. Delassus remained seated in his armchair behind his massive desk like a king enthroned. Uncertain how to begin, Lewis and Stoddard bowed and stood. Delassus waited and stroked the silver medallion of his rank. He had often used delay to deflate an adversary. Finally, he nodded. "Gentlemen, I am not informed why you've come."

Meriwether Lewis stepped forward. "Your Excellency, I present to you a letter of credit signed by President Thomas Jefferson of the United States. It will explain our presence here." He handed it to Delassus who perused it cursorily and laid it on his desk.

Stoddard interjected: "I believe you have been informed, sir, that the United States has assumed the possession of Louisiana, by purchase in April of this year."

Delassus quipped: "I have received no such information, gentlemen."

Lewis gawked at Stoddard who stammered: "Seven months, time enough for the news to travel. Don Juan Manuel de Salcedo, your governor at New Orleans, was surely informed and would have sent word."

"Then perhaps his messenger has been delayed. The river is beset by shoals and eddies, harassed by pirates and thieves. But do tell me your purpose, gentlemen." Delassus smiled cynically. He would assure that whatever these two bunglers intended would favor His Catholic Majesty.

Lewis assumed an oily tone. "I am outfitting boats to ascend the Missouri, sir, to discover the extent of our purchase, the peoples, the flora and the fauna who inhabit her. Ours is a peaceful mission of exploration and discovery." He did not mention that he meant to assess the territory's economic potential as well and added: "In no way will we challenge your authority or incite the natives against Spain and her dependencies. We await only the formal transfer of Louisiana before we depart and seek permission to encamp on your shores and trade in your city."

Delassus was frowning. "You are aware of Spanish attempts to explore these very same lands, of Messers. D'Eglise, Mackay and Evans who had at their disposal the ample resources of His Catholic Majesty, the King of Spain? You presume to succeed where these have failed?" He glared down his long nose at the two plainly uniformed soldiers. "The cost of such an expedition would be prodigious."

"The United States has supplied us with sturdy boats, knowledgeable rivermen, interpreters and letters of credit to hire more men and purchase trade goods and supplies from the good merchants of St. Louis. I have faith, Your Excellency, that we will succeed."

"I see." Delassus tapped the letter of credit with an index finger. "Your request is honorable, gentlemen, but I cannot grant it." He handed the letter back to Lewis. "To my knowledge this province is Spanish, acquired from France by treaty at Paris in 1863. Emperor Napoleon now rules Spain but he has never assumed formal possession of Louisiana. The administration of Louisiana remains Spanish and I remain the servant of the King of Spain. How then can I concede that your country has purchased the territory from France when France has not first pursued her sovereignty and Spain has not been consulted?" When there was no reply, he continued: "You understand my position, gentlemen. And it has been Spanish policy not to admit Americans into Louisiana for trade, exploration, whatever purpose unless they

116

intend to become subjects of his Catholic Majesty and abide by the laws of Spain."

Meriwether Lewis arched his neck and sucked back his lips. "Then sir, there is no further reason to pursue this interview."

Delassus spread his hands, palms up. "I'm sorry, Gentlemen. There is nothing I can do."

The two Americans did not bow, but turned on their heels and left. Manuel directed them through the hallway, across the courtyard to the iron-studded door to the street. In silence, they marched out.

"He lies." Stoddard was the first to speak.

Lewis barely whispered: "He will never help us. We must find other means."

"I can supply muskets, powder, lead from the arsenal at Fort Massac and young, healthy men, fine hunters and boatmen. But as soldiers, they lack discipline."

"Will Clark can drill the devil out of them. But we'll forfeit the beads and mirrors which delight the tribes that I ordered from merchant Duquette here in St. Louis months ago. If we cannot collect our goods, Duquette will sell them to the highest bidder."

"Pay him well and he'll smuggle your goods across the river. You have good water and shelter where you camp by Wood River. Or send another, one who can blend with the half-breed denizens of St. Louis, one you can trust, to collect your goods."

Lewis smiled. "I have just the man. You know him, Georges Drouillard, Shawnee mother, French father. He speaks good French. And I'll alert Jefferson to our difficulties. He must forward copies of the purchase with all due haste to the Spanish ambassador and to this intransigient Delassus."

"Delassus will not accept the word of an American President."

"He will accept the word of his own ambassador."

"Not if the man is Bonaparte's hack."

They arrived at the dock where Lewis's boat was waiting to ferry him back across the river. Lewis stared at the swift, mud-brown waters of the Mississippi and mused: "The way is never clear, muddied by politics, stirred by intrigue and deceit. As if natural obstacles were not enough, we must contend with a tyrant."

Stoddard sensed his anguish. "It's December. You have all winter. Use it to amass your supplies and test your men. If Duquette denies you, we'll raid a Spanish boat coming upriver from New Orleans and blame the pirates. I leave you now. I go downriver to Massac and my command." He held out his hand. Lewis shook it and stepped into the waiting keelboat.

Pierre Cruzatte, a grizzled, eye-patched skeleton of a man, was at the sweep. He wore no uniform and shouted: *"Prêt, capitaine? Allons-y."* His crew of dirty rivermen hauled in the lines and shoved off into the river. Shaking his head, Stoddard waved from the shore and mused: "To cross a continent with such as these who cannot even speak English."

But merchant Duquette cast his lot with the Americans because Delassus had refused him one of the coveted licenses to trade beaver with the tribes. When the fog was thick and darkness descended over the river, his boats cast off from the backwaters near St. Louis bound for the Wood River and the camp of Lewis and Clark. They delivered glass beads, mirrors, silken ribbons and cloth to tempt an Indian's fancy. And they brought whiskey for Lewis's recruits. Captain Stoddard forwarded black powder and lead, muskets and seventeen sparkling new Harper's rifles from the arsenal at Fort Massac. And he sent men, rough, self-reliant frontiersmen. Some were heavy drinkers, others womanizers, men he could spare, not the cream of his garrison. Lewis left the discipline and selection to William Clark who melded them into a tough if unorthodox unit. Christmas came and went. The New Year was cold and ice formed on the river. Floes washed down from upriver with the frigid waters as the deliveries of goods increased.

Delassus ignored the smuggling. Christmas in the province of Louisiana meant colorful religious ritual, panoply, feasting, dancing, gaming and song. He forgot about the American challenge and gave his attention to the distribution of alms to the needy citizens of St. Louis and to another pretty *mademoiselle* who had stirred his interest. On February 5th, he sat at his desk in the favored armchair and wrapped his fingers around the lion heads carved into the arms when another sealed letter arrived by express messenger from his Most Excellent Señor Don Pedro Cevallos, Commandant General of the Internal Provinces of Spain. Delassus stood, grabbed the letter, broke the seal and read:

118

My dear Delassus,

On January 16, 1804, the president of the United States received official notice of delivery of Louisiana to the American commissioners by Prefect Laussat of France. I have the honor of enclosing a copy for Your Excellency's perusal. This negotiation is complete and there remains only for us to limit future American expansion and secure the boundaries of Texas, Mexico and California to the greater advantage of Spain. If upon receipt of this missive, Your Excellency finds himself still in command of the Upper Province of Louisiana, if no representative of the United States has yet presented himself, you must not hinder the further entry of Captain Meriwether Lewis to Louisiana, the Missouri River and beyond. And you are to facilitate the transfer of the government with honor and dispatch.

May the good God keep Your Excellency for years to come,

Delassus dropped the letter, fell back into his chair and waved away the bearer. "Begone. To the kitchen. There is food and drink."

The soldier bowed and stammered: "Thank you, Your Excellency, but I come with an escort."

"Feed them too, but leave me be and say no more." He waited for the soldier to exit before cursing aloud. Finally, he muttered: "Prefect Laussat, another ignorant peasant revolutionary, no doubt. I wonder can he spell his own name." Resting his elbows on his desk, he covered his face with his hands.

The man Lewis made no further requests nor did another official of the United States present himself. Weeks passed and another missive arrived on Delassus desk, this one from El Marqués de Casa Yrujo, Spanish Ambassador to the United States in its new capital at Washington. It set a deadline of March 15th for delivery of the province of Louisiana to the United States. Today was February 25th.

A hot fire was blazing on the hearth behind his desk. Delassus threw the offensive notice into the flames. He watched the corners curl and blacken and did not blink when the whole

119

burst into bright orange and crumbled to ash. They would expect him to prepare a ceremony for the official transfer. The whole effort filled him with disgust. Let Manuel make a fair job of it. Finally, he considered where he would go and what he would do in the aftermath. Would there be another lucrative assignment for him, an outspoken royalist, from the new rulers of Spain, from Joseph Napoleon, brother of the infamous conqueror? Would they trust him? Could he trust them? He had loved this place, St. Louis, named for the saintly French King, Louis IX. It was still a distant vestige of old royalist France. But no longer. He must find a place for himself where good breeding and upbringing were honored and respected.

On March 9th, Meriwether Lewis inspected his corps before boarding the boats for St. Louis. The sun shone and a warm breeze blew in the first breath of spring. The Mississippi crossing was calm. The Corps of Discovery disembarked on the western shore and climbed to the old French fort. The troops of His Catholic Majesty, King of Spain, in spotless uniforms and polished boots had assembled in precise ranks on the central square in front of a high platform where the flag of royalist Spain flapped briskly.

Stoddard's scraggly contingent from Fort Massac, grimy and shuffling, formed up beside them. Their clothing was plain but their new rifles gleamed and their bullet pouches bulged. Finally, Lewis's corps marched up to join them. When they saw the Spaniards, they pulled back their shoulders, stretched taller and lined their ranks straighter. At the command to stand at attention, they complied as best they knew how.

Don Carlos Duhault Delassus de Luzière arrived at the foot of the platform in a coach and four. Stepping out, he saluted his men and mounted the steps of the platform. For the Americans, he had not even a glance. The French consul followed. Then Meriwether Lewis, William Clark and Amos Stoddard clambered up behind him and Delassus stepped forward to address the crowd. Carefully, he enumerated the many benefits so graciously bestowed upon the populace of Louisiana by the King of Spain. His voice rang with imperial sovereignty. With his right hand placed over his heart, he turned toward the flag of Spain and watched it slowly descend. Rigid and reverent, he stood like a column while the Spanish honor guard collected the voluminous banner, folded it carefully and presented it to him. He clasped it tightly to his breast in trembling hands for the breadth of a moment. Suddenly, arching his spine and thrusting out his chin, he turned to face the troops. Then grasping tightly at two corners, with a wide sweep of arm, he cast the banner forth. The wind seized it and he watched it wave smartly one last time. Delassus smiled, gathered it in and wrapped it like the toga of imperial Caesar, about his person. Defiantly, he marched from the platform, down the steps to the captain at the head of the Spanish troop. There, solemnly, he saluted again. The awestruck troop returned his salute as he turned and stalked away to a waiting boat. The entire Spanish column followed in lock step.

Stoddard whispered to Lewis: "He cannot wait even to see the French flag fly. It's the tricolor of Napoleon's republican France and replaces his beloved king's golden *fleur de lis*. He cannot bear the sight."

The French consul raised Napoleon's blue white and red flag of liberated France which flew for one day. The next day, March 10th, 1804, Captain Amos Stoddard hoisted the American flag over Louisiana and the Corps of Discovery hooted and cheered. There were eighteen stars for eighteen states. Meriwether Lewis mumbled to William Clark: "The stars will multiply, Will, when we will have completed our journey."

Finally, on May 8th, the Lewis and Clark Expedition shoved off with forty-two men, one keelboat, two pirogues and over forty tons of supplies and trade goods. They headed into the Mississippi and up the Missouri, for the continental divide in the Shining Mountains where Napoleon's Louisiana ended. They would not stop there but press on to the land's end at the Pacific Ocean. They would walk where no Frenchman, no Spaniard, no white man had walked before.

When they returned, thirty months later, they hardly recognized St. Louis. All trace of Spanish domination had vanished. American settlers and traders mingled thickly with the French and Indian residents of the city. Their boats lined the shore. Their trade goods crammed the docks and storehouses.

In late September 1806, Meriwether Lewis sat at a rough table in the central square of the city passing out warrants for land in the new United States Territory of Louisiana, payment for their service to the loyal men of his corps.

Grinning from ear to ear, Amos Stoddard came to congratulate him. He slapped Lewis hard on the back and blurted: "Delassus would not believe it. What an impossible man."

"Not impossible, the product of his birthright. He could not adapt so he resisted. But have you heard where he has gone?"

"Mexico, so they say, where the tentacles of Bonaparte have not yet reached, to await the restoration of the monarchy in his beloved France, so he can reclaim his lands and his title."

KENNETH MCKENZIE, KING OF THE UPPER MISSOURI

By Bill Markley

Well-dressed men sat according to their rank at a long table. The king sat at its head. Servants set before them a prodigious quantity of the finest wild game and other culinary delights. The jolly company proposed toasts as they raised glasses of iced wines and liqueurs.

Did this feast occur in a European kingdom? No—the formal dinner party was a regular occurrence at Fort Union, the farthest outpost on the American frontier in the 1830s, almost 1,800 river-miles from St. Louis. The king, Kenneth McKenzie, ruled an economic empire larger in area than most European countries. How did this Scot rise to such power and influence that his friends and enemies called him King of the Upper Missouri?

Kenneth McKenzie was born into the Clan Mackenzie on April 15, 1797 to a distinguished family at Bradluck in Rosshire, Inverness, Scotland. He received a good education, immigrated to Canada in 1816, and went to work as a clerk for the North West Company.

For years, the Nor' Westers had been the only competition to the powerful Hudson's Bay Company. Confrontations between the two companies escalated into open warfare resulting in injuries and death. In 1821, the two companies merged retaining the name Hudson's Bay Company. McKenzie and many other Nor' Westers lost their jobs.

McKenzie and two friends, William Laidlaw and Daniel Lamont, drifted south to the United States frontier where they established the Columbia Fur Company with the Americans, Joseph Renville, James Kipp, Robert Dickson, and others. The Columbia Fur Company based its operations at Lake Traverse, where the current borders of North Dakota, South Dakota, and Minnesota meet. Lake Traverse is at the continental divide, a favorable setting for trading furs.

By 1823, the Columbia Fur Company had expanded its operations from the Upper Mississippi River into the Upper Missouri River region, building eight trading posts. The largest post and hub of their operation was Fort Tecumseh, located on the west bank of the Missouri River in present-day Fort Pierre, South Dakota.

McKenzie became an American citizen in 1822 emerging as the chief partner of the Columbia Fur Company and using Fort Tecumseh as his headquarters from 1822 to 1829. He was a good leader and a shrewd, but honest businessman who knew how to turn a profit and provide good merchandise for return business. In addition to trading with the tribes for beaver pelts and other furs, McKenzie and the Columbia Fur Company realized there was a strong market for buffalo robes in the eastern United States so they began to concentrate on this sector of the fur and hide market. By 1826, the Columbia Fur Company was trading for furs and buffalo robes with the Lakota, Arikara, Hidatsa, Mandan, Yankton, Ponca, and Omaha tribes along the Missouri River in present-day Nebraska, South Dakota, and North Dakota. Many of these tribes were hostile to each other; but at the forts, they put aside their differences to trade with McKenzie and his men.

The Columbia Fur Company was very profitable due to its buffalo robe trade with the tribes. John Jacob Astor, principal partner of the American Fur Company, a strong competitor, wanted to buy the Columbia Fur Company; but McKenzie and the other partners resisted. Astor's strategy changed to driving them out by building his own forts near Columbia's forts, angering McKenzie who further refused Astor's continued proposals. This extreme competition did not help the profits of either company. Eventually after long and tedious negotiations, Astor bought the Columbia Fur Company in July 1827 with the stipulation that

William Laidlaw, Daniel Lamont, James Kipp, Robert Dickson, and McKenzie become partners in the American Fur Company. The Columbia Fur Company's Missouri River forts remained semiautonomous and were renamed the Upper Missouri Outfit. McKenzie became the outfit's chief agent.

The newly enlarged American Fur Company began expanding further up the Missouri River into territory under the influence of McKenzie's old rival, the Hudson's Bay Company. McKenzie realized that to capture the trade from the Hudson's Bay Company, a fort was needed near the juncture of the Yellowstone and the Missouri Rivers along the present-day North Dakota-Montana border. In October 1828, he sent workers to the confluence of the two rivers where they built a small cabin to trade with the Assiniboine Tribe.

That same year, McKenzie began to tap into another area of potential profit—the free trappers or mountain men. He sent a team of men under the command of Etienne Provost to the Rocky Mountains to trade with the free trappers. This put the American Fur Company in direct competition with General William H. Ashley's Rocky Mountain Fur Company that had had exclusive trade with the free trappers.

In the fall of 1829, McKenzie sent workers to build a fort at the site of their trading cabin near at the confluence of the Yellowstone and Missouri Rivers and named it Fort Union. Fort Union had a twenty-foot high palisade and two stone bastions that housed iron cannon and brass swivel guns. In 1830, McKenzie moved his headquarters to Fort Union. It was the largest fort on the Upper Missouri until The American Fur Company built Fort Pierre Choteau in 1832.

It was at Fort Union that people began calling Kenneth McKenzie, who was now wearing a military coat, King of the Upper Missouri. They also began calling the American Fur Company "the Company" and called any competition "the Opposition."

McKenzie believed steamboats could travel up the Missouri River as far as Fort Union. If so, it would be a vast improvement on the movement of trade goods, furs, and hides. In August 1830, McKenzie traveled to St Louis to convince the other partners to buy a steamboat and send it upriver with trade goods. At first, they baulked; but McKenzie convinced one of the partners, Pierre Chouteau Jr., and together they swayed the other partners. The

Company paid to have a steamboat built and named it *Yellow Stone*. It was able to travel as far as Fort Tecumseh in 1831, but due to low water levels, it could not proceed further up the Missouri. The next year, on June 17, 1832, the *Yellow Stone* arrived at Fort Union to the firing of the fort's cannon and shouts from the crowd of onlookers. On board were Pierre Chouteau Jr. and the artist, George Catlin, who was painting and writing about the tribes of the west. Steamboats soon increased the Upper Missouri Outfit's efficiency to move furs, hides, and trade goods faster and easier.

McKenzie had wanted to establish trade with the Blackfeet Tribe. His chance came in 1830. The Blackfeet traded exclusively with the Hudson's Bay Company and considered all Americans their enemies as far back as their run-in with Meriwether Lewis during the Corps of Discovery's return from the west coast. McKenzie sent one of his men, Jacob Berger, to the Blackfeet inviting them to Fort Union to discuss trade prospects. Jacob was an old Hudson's Bay trapper and friend of the Blackfeet. He made contact with tribal leaders and brought a Blackfeet delegation to Fort Union. After McKenzie provided presents and promised a good exchange for their furs, the Blackfeet agreed to trade with the Company. They would also allow the Company to build a trading post in their territory. McKenzie sent James Kipp up the Missouri into Blackfeet territory and by October 1831, he had built the first of several forts, Fort Piegan, eleven miles downstream of present-day Fort Benton, Montana. Trade was brisk and by the spring, he had traded all his goods for Blackfeet furs. On November 1831, McKenzie developed and concluded a treaty of peace and friendship between the Blackfeet and Assiniboine Tribes. This was good for trade.

In mid-1832, John Jacob Astor sold his share in the American Fur Company to Pierre Chouteau Jr. and other partners. That same year, McKenzie authorized the building of Fort Cass on the Yellowstone River at the mouth of the Big Horn River for the Crow Tribe. McKenzie and the Upper Missouri Outfit now had trading relations with all the major tribes in the Upper Missouri River basin.

McKenzie traveled to St. Louis and Washington D.C. on business and returned to Fort Union on June 23, 1833 aboard the steamboat *Assiniboine* accompanying the German Prince Maximilian of Wied and his personal artist Karl Bodmer. Prince

Maximilian had served in a regiment of the Royal Prussian Army during the Napoleonic Wars and had previously explored Brazil. He was now studying the native peoples and natural history of North America. Maximilian and McKenzie had similar interests and became good friends. McKenzie brought several new items to Fort Union including the first fireworks. On the night of July 5, McKenzie held a fireworks show for the fort's inhabitants and visiting tribes shooting rockets into the air and tossing firecrackers into the crowd to keep them on their toes.

McKenzie had a wide range of interests. He was a voracious reader ordering books for Fort Union's library including textbooks on medicine, chemistry, and "Natural Philosophy." He collected American Indian craftwork and natural curiosities. McKenzie brought the latest in home entertainment to Fort Union—a magic lantern, the forerunner of the slide projector, and an electric spark generator that must have livened up the party when he used it on unsuspecting guests. He sent to St. Louis for luxury items—brandy, gin, catsup, herrings, boxes of "Segars", and canisters of oysters. He even ordered from England a "good complete suit of armour (coat of mail, etc)." There is no record of his wearing the armor; but who would buy a suit of armor and not try it on at least once? McKenzie had peace medals struck with images of John Jacob Astor and later Pierre Chouteau Jr. The Company gave these highly prized medals to tribal leaders as tokens of friendship and good will.

When McKenzie arrived at Fort Union aboard the *Assiniboine* in 1833, he also brought a still to make whiskey. For years, trade with the tribes had involved alcohol. Lewis and Clark's Corps of Discovery had brought alcohol for themselves and for the tribes. Many tribes demanded whiskey and it had become part of the trading "ritual." Congress was concerned about selling alcohol to the tribes; and in July 1832, it passed a law forbidding the introduction of alcohol in Indian Country. McKenzie's old rival, the Hudson's Bay Company had no such restriction and continued to provide the tribes with alcohol as part of the trading process. McKenzie and other American fur traders believed as long as the tribes wanted whiskey they should provide it to them.

McKenzie had made a trip to Washington D.C. to try to change the law. Government officials told him there would be no change. On his return to Fort Union, McKenzie met with the Company's St. Louis lawyer who after reading the law concluded there was a loophole. The law stated alcohol could not be introduced into Indian Country, but said nothing about the manufacture of alcohol in Indian Country. McKenzie shipped a still to Fort Union, and hired a man to run it. McKenzie bought corn for the mash from the Mandans and had men raise a corn crop further down river.

The Sublette brothers and Robert Campbell began building Fort William three miles east of Fort Union to compete against the Company for the Assiniboine trade. At the same time, they were establishing posts near other Company posts. McKenzie was not going to stand for this, so during the fall of 1833 and winter of 1834 he paid exorbitant prices for hides and furs—higher than the Opposition could afford. He was on the verge of driving the Opposition out of business when they cut a deal with the Company's New York City representatives and sold out. McKenzie was irritated; he had wanted to wreck the Opposition after what they had done to him in 1833.

Back in the autumn of 1833, Robert Campbell, Milton Sublette, and Nathaniel Wyeth stopped at Fort Union heading downriver with their furs. Always the good host, even to the Opposition, McKenzie wined and dined them, and then showed them around the fort including the still. They wanted to buy liquor from McKenzie, but he refused thinking they would try to horn in on his business and sell it to Indians. They were angered at McKenzie's refusal and when they reached Fort Leavenworth, the furthest western US military post, one of them told the military officials about McKenzie's still. This brought about problems for the Company to the extent that it almost lost its government trading license with the tribes. The Company dismantled the still and shipped the pieces back down the river.

Prince Maximilian invited McKenzie to visit him in Europe and he took the prince's offer. McKenzie left Fort Union during 1834, and sailed to Europe on vacation to visit Prince Maximilian and probably to temporarily escape his whiskey still problems. In the fall of 1835, McKenzie returned to Fort Union and resumed his status as King of the Upper Missouri.

On June 28, 1836, a smoldering feud between some of McKenzie's men and the Deschamps family broke out into open warfare. The Deschamps were a mixed-blood Canadian family who had lived for years in the Fort Union area and had now moved into the abandoned Fort Williams buildings. They were a mean bunch—notorious for robbery, rape, and murder of both Indians and non-Indians.

Francois Deschamps, the family patriarch, had been an employee of the North West Company and was involved in a fight with the Hudson's Bay Company in 1816. The Nor' Westers won the fight. Afterwards, Francois walked over the field of battle killing every wounded Hudson's Bay man he found including their leader Governor Robert Semple.

In July 1835, Gardepied, a Fort Union employee, was out to kill Francois Deschamps who had roughly treated Gardepied's wife and had threatened to kill Gardepied. Catching Deschamps off guard in a room at Fort Union, Gardepied smashed in Deschamps' skull with a rifle barrel and beat Francois's son on the head. The son hid under a bed while Gardepied finished off the old man by disemboweling him. The men with Gardepied pleaded for the son's life who said he repented and Gardepied spared him.

Almost a year later, on June 28, 1836, with the arrival of the first steamboat of the season, the people of Fort Union and surrounding countryside celebrated with a drinking spree. Francois' widow, Mother Deschamps, spurred on her sons to murder Jack Kipling, a friend of Gardepied. Kipling's daughter ran to Fort Union and spread the news that the Deschamps murdered her father. When some of the Fort Union men went to see Kipling's body, the Deschamps shot at them. The men were enraged and had had enough. They went to McKenzie and asked for permission "to destroy them all." McKenzie remained silent. The men took his silence as permission to attack the Deschamps. McKenzie allowed them to arm themselves with Company weapons and take a Fort Union cannon.

Assiniboine women were living with the Deschamps. McKenzie did not want them harmed so the Company men called to the Deschamps to send the women out before they attacked. The Deschamps did not think they were serious; but after a few shots from the Company men, the Deschamps sent the Assiniboine women to safety. A furious battle ensued. Realizing the Company men had them outnumbered and trapped, Mother Deschamps tried for a ceasefire by walking out holding a peace pipe in front of her; but one of the Company men shot her through the chest. Her sons quickly shot and killed her killer. The attackers set the Fort Williams buildings on fire and shot the last of the Deschamps as they rushed from the burning buildings—so ended the Deschamps family.

McKenzie prized his well-trained horses called buffalo runners. His favorite sport was hunting buffalo by chasing after them on horseback and shooting them on the run. Buffalo hunting was dangerous, but essential to the existence of the fort. Buffalo meat was a major portion of the men's diet. A good buffalo runner was necessary to get close enough to a stampeding buffalo to kill it. The horse had to be quick and smart to dart away from an unpredictable buffalo that might try to veer and lunge at the horse with its horns. McKenzie acquired the best buffalo runners. He enjoyed nothing better than to gallop close to a fast moving buffalo and bring it down with a shot from his Northwest musket.

In the autumn of 1836, two Fort Union horse herders deserted, taking the fort's best buffalo runners including McKenzie's favorite horse. As the deserters tried to take a ferry across the river, the horses saw their opportunity to escape and galloped back to the fort. The two deserters soon surrendered. The Company men were angry with them, as their theft had left the men at the fort without the means to acquire buffalo meat. The Company men were all in agreement with McKenzie when he had the thieves shackled in irons, flogged them, and sent them down the river.

McKenzie had a son, Owen, by one of his three Assiniboine wives. McKenzie had Owen educated and later he followed in his father's footsteps entering the fur trade.

In November 1836, Augustin Bourbonnais, a free trapper, attempted to seduce one of McKenzie's wives. McKenzie caught the two together in his bedroom and beat Bourbonnais with a cudgel as he ran out of the fort. Bourbonnais' pride was hurt. For days, he stood outside the fort armed with musket, pistol, and knife boasting he would kill McKenzie. McKenzie met with the Company men and convened a court martial. It was unanimous—Bourbonnais must die. John Brazo, an expert shot, climbed up into a bastion, took aim, and shot Bourbonnais in the shoulder above the heart. McKenzie had Bourbonnais brought into the fort, nursed back to health, and sent down the river.

In the spring of 1837, McKenzie left Fort Union to work for the Company out of St. Louis. He returned to the Upper Missouri years later after the great smallpox epidemic of 1837 that killed thousands of American Indians. McKenzie's mission was to reestablished trade with the Blackfeet. In 1844, Francis Chardon and Alexander Harvey, Company employees, had killed a large number of Blackfeet, including women and children, with a cannon blast in revenge for the murder and scalping of Reese, a black servant. McKenzie reestablished a good working arrangement with the Blackfeet, burnt down the old fort where the offense had occurred, and had a new fort built for the Blackfeet trade.

McKenzie left the American Fur Company and started a wholesale liquor business. He married his fourth wife in St. Louis and had two daughters by this marriage. Business was good and McKenzie continued to provide lavish entertainment for his friends until his death in St Louis, on April 26, 1861.

McKenzie had many faults; but he was always willing to work with and trust people until they earned his mistrust. He dealt fairly with the tribes and worked to provide them the goods they desired. He strove to keep the Hudson's Bay Company out of American territory and hold it for the United States. The true measure of this man was that he forged a bond of trust and friendship with diverse Indian tribes, and kept that trust and friendship in a region and during a time when the United States government was nonexistent. Kenneth McKenzie truly was King of the Upper Missouri.

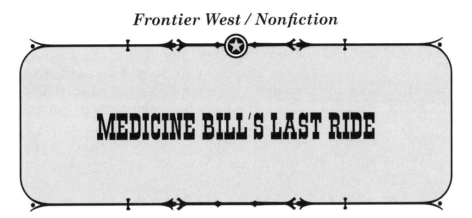

MEDICINE BILL'S LAST RIDE

By Susan K. Salzer

William Averill Comstock's star was on the rise in the summer of 1868. He was George Custer's favorite scout, Little Phil Sheridan requested his services, he owned a profitable ranch and he had just dodged a murder charge despite having killed a man in broad daylight before witnesses. Things were looking very good indeed for the handsome, 26-year-old plainsman when he was gunned down on the plains of western Kansas, his body left to rot in the hot August sun.

Even among a cast of characters shadowy as army scouts tended to be in those days, Comstock, a.k.a. "Medicine Bill," stands out. As Custer noted in his book, *My Life on the Plains*, a wise officer relied on his scout's skills but did not inquire too deeply into his personal life. "Who they are," he wrote, "whence they came or whither they go, their names even...are all questions which none but themselves can answer."

This was especially true of Comstock, Custer's guide during his early Indian-fighting days in Kansas. Everything about Comstock—his beginnings, the kind of person he was, the manner of his death and even where he is buried—is clouded in controversy and contradiction. Still today, 141 years after his death on that hot Sunday afternoon, it's impossible to know this elusive son of the West who made such a strong and lasting impression on all who met him.

One of the few things the record agrees on is Comstock's appearance. He was small in stature, wiry as whip leather and dark in coloring. People noticed his eyes. W. E. Webb, writing in the November 1875 issue of *Harper's New Monthly Magazine*, recalls the first time he saw the scout, standing in the doorway of a west Kansas stagecoach station. "He leveled those shining eyes at me with the precision a man would have used with field glasses...I felt that I had been photographed and could be hunted the world over by him did he ever have occasion."

The best surviving photograph, a carte-de-visite found among the papers of an army surgeon Comstock befriended at Fort Wallace, supports this observation; the eyes gazing back at you are arresting and challenging, the face oddly contemporary. Surgeon Theophilus H. Turner and Comstock roamed the prairies together hunting and finding dinosaur skeletons. Indeed, Turner—probably with Comstock's help—located a giant fossil in a ravine near an old Indian camp and alerted scientist friends in the East to his discovery. Eventually the bones, said to be those of an Elasmosaurus platyurus, were displayed in a Philadelphia museum and heralded as the longest of the sea saurians discovered up to that time.

Comstock wore his hair long under a wide-brimmed sombrero and dressed like an Indian in buckskins and moccasins. In fact, many of his friends, including Turner, thought he was half-Indian and Comstock did nothing to dispel the notion. He carried a sixteen-shot Henry rifle and was proficient in its use. Like Custer he seems to have had an affinity for dogs. Artist and *Harper's Weekly* correspondent Theodore Davis, who met and sketched Comstock in 1867, said the scout was accompanied by an "evil-looking" dog named Cuss.

He is most closely associated with Fort Wallace, Kansas, the westernmost and most Indian-troubled of the Smoky Hill Trail posts, where he served as chief of scouts from 1866 until his death. But he first appeared on the scene in 1860 when a census enumerator found the 18-year-old Comstock working as an Indian trader in the Nebraska Territory where he listed two employees and $500 in property. It was no doubt during this period Comstock began to accumulate the knowledge of the native inhabitants that later would serve him so well.

His first brush with celebrity occurred in May of 1865 near Fort Halleck, Wyoming, where Comstock worked as a hunter and army scout. On the 13th, a dark character and former Confederate soldier named Robert Jennings killed a well-liked innkeeper and threatened to do the same to anyone who came after him. According to historian John S. Gray, the local citizenry raised $1,000 and offered it to Comstock to bring Jennings in. After recruiting a posse of Arapaho braves, Comstock tracked his man down and delivered Jennings to Fort Halleck where he was hanged on May 20, a Sunday afternoon. Gray's description of the event is especially dramatic:

"The guard led the condemned man out to a long pivoted pole, or sweep, used to swing meat up and out of the way of bears and wolves. While they attached the noose to the long, slim end of the sweep, Jennings boasted that he would go to Hell a-roaring but as he was good at finding trails he would look for one to Heaven. At his final shout of 'Hurrah for Jeff Davis and the Southern Confederacy!' the indignant guards let go of the pole, which was so heavily counterbalanced that it sent the defiant outlaw flying twenty-five feet into the air, his neck already broken."

Later that year Comstock relocated to western Kansas and in the fall of 1865 settled on a piece of property that came to be known as Rose Creek Ranch. Its meadows produced fine hay—a valuable commodity in this arid, forage-bare country—which Comstock sold to the newly established Fort Wallace for $20 to $30 per ton. At 200 to 300 tons per year, the scout had a good thing going. Others took notice.

By August of 1866 Comstock was chief of scouts at Fort Wallace. That month he met W.J. Carney, an awestruck young Second Cavalry recruit.

"I had often heard of him," Carney wrote in a 1900 reminiscence published in *Collier's Weekly*, "his wonderful marksmanship and what a great Indian scout and fighter he was...so it was no wonder I was so anxious to see a real, live dyed-in-the-wool Indian scout like Billy Comstock." The impressionable young Carney bought Comstock's portrayal of himself as man born to the plains, a true son of the West.

"He was a person whose nationality would be hard to tell," Carney wrote. "He, himself, did not know whether he was a Mexican or not; or for that matter, where he sprang from, but he looked as if he might be half Spanish, or old Mexican and half Indian. He was simple as a child in regard to anything connected with civilization; never had been east of the Missouri River, had never seen a steamboat or a railroad—in fact, knew nothing about such things except to hear of them."

This was far from the truth, as we shall learn later.

It was at Fort Wallace that Comstock started making friends in high places. He chased horse-stealing Indians with Michael Sheridan, brother to Phil, struck up friendships with educated men such as Turner and Lieutenant George Armes, who later became Colonel Armes and wrote of their explorations together in his book, *Ups and Downs of an Army Officer.* "Comstock took me up on one of the branches (of the Republican River) where an old village of Indians used to be and where he lived with them some four or five years ago (1861 or 1862). He showed me the graves of a number of Indians he helped bury in the tops of trees."

Comstock also earned the admiration of Fort Wallace's new commander, Captain Myles Keogh of the recently formed Seventh Cavalry. When Keogh's boss, Lt. Col. George Armstrong Custer, needed a scout at Fort Riley he asked for Comstock and Keogh obliged, sending the scout east in January of 1867. In his letter of introduction Keogh described Comstock as "an eccentric genius and an ardent admirer of everything reckless and daring." In a postscript, Keogh added: "Comstock has never yet seen a R(ail) R(oad) train and his satisfaction I believe is improved by this accidental granting of his fondest wishes, viz: 'seeing Custer and the R.R.' "

Custer liked the scout Keogh sent him. "No Indian knew the country more thoroughly than did Comstock," Custer wrote. "He was perfectly familiar with every divide, water course and strip of timber for hundreds of miles in either direction. He knew the dress and peculiarities of every Indian tribe and the languages of many of them." He described Comstock as "perfect in horsemanship, fearless in manner, a splendid hunter and a gentleman by instinct, as modest and unassuming as he was brave."

It was during his time with Custer that Comstock met *Harper's* correspondent Davis, who drew a pencil sketch of him and three fellow scouts. Although Davis archly referred to frontier scouts as "Natty Bumppos," an allusion to the dated and quaint character from James Fenimore Cooper's Leatherstocking Tales, he was fulsome in his praise of Comstock:

"Will Comstock has lived in the far west for many years," Davis wrote. "His qualifications as an interpreter and scout are said by those best qualified to judge to be unsurpassed by any white man on the plains. He is moreover a man of tried bravery and a first-rate shot." Davis went on to say the scout was a "Kentuckian by birth" and "a reticent person."

Perhaps Comstock was too reticent to set Davis and his other admirers straight for he was not part-Indian, half-Spanish or Old-Mexican, he was not a Kentuckian and he had almost certainly seen the R.R. train. Contrary to the image he so carefully created, Comstock was in fact the son of a prosperous Michigan lawyer and state legislator who had built a fortune in the Chicago-Detroit Indian trade and military supply business. Not only that, but Comstock's great-uncle was none other than novelist Cooper, creator of the Natty Bumppo character to whom Davis alluded. There is no indication Comstock ever mentioned this kinship to anyone during his lifetime.

Why not? Family histories by his descendants and Gray's research reveal no embarrassing forebears—other than Cooper, whose portrayal of the noble red man was seen as ridiculous by the 1860s—nothing the scout might wish to conceal. Instead, his story, sadly, was not uncommon for the times. Comstock's mother died when he was four, his father suffered a reversal of fortune, and young Will was sent to live with relatives. His older sister, Sabina, eventually took him in perhaps even before her marriage to prominent lawyer Eleazer Wakeley in 1854. Three years later, when Will was fifteen, Wakeley was named district judge of the Nebraska Territory and the family moved to Omaha. By 1860, as noted above, Comstock was already an established Indian trader.

At some point along the way, probably during these trading days, Comstock picked up the moniker "Medicine Bill." Like so many things in his life, there are several versions of the story; Davis says Comstock got the name from the Arapahoes after he saved a tribesman's life by amputating his man's rattlesnake-bitten finger. Carney told it this way: "One day a young Sioux squaw, while trying to catch a rattlesnake, got bit on the finger. Bill, who was standing close by, without a moment's hesitation, grabbed the wounded finger and bit it off, slick and clean. From this time he was called Medicine Bill." Either way, the name stuck.

In the spring of 1867, Comstock accompanied Custer's Seventh Cavalry into the field with General Winfield Hancock's Indian Expedition, a harum-scarum campaign that did little to advance the reputations of Hancock or Custer. Comstock, however, distinguished himself, most notably in the episode involving Lieutenant Lyman Kidder and his ten men who disappeared while carrying orders to Custer in the field. Below, Custer quotes Comstock saying Kidder's party might be OK if he follows his Sioux guide's advice. Comstock must have been fairly well-schooled, coming from a privileged background and growing up in the home of a territorial judge, but he doesn't sound it if Custer's spellings and punctuation are accurate.

"Is this lootinent the kind of man who is willin' to take advice even ef it does cum from an Injun?" (Comstock asks.) "My experience with you army folks has allus bin that the youngsters among ye think they know the most and this is particularly true ef they hev jest cum from West P'int."

Informed that Kidder was not from West Point, but had just received his commission, Comstock said, "Ef that be the case it puts a mighty onsartain look on the whole thing..."

Eventually Comstock found the mutilated remains of Kidder and his party, victims of Cheyenne Dog Soldiers and Sioux. Later, Comstock may have guided Kidder's father, Judge Jefferson Kidder, to the site of the massacre so the old man could take his son's bones back to Minnesota for burial.

After the Hancock fizzle, Comstock returned to Fort Wallace. Perhaps it was during this period that he and Buffalo Bill Cody engaged in the famous buffalo-shooting contest Cody described his 1879 memoir, *The Life on Hon. William S. Cody*. As Cody tells it, the shoot-out occurred while Comstock was chief of scouts at Fort Wallace and Cody was hunting buffalos to feed the hungry men building the Kansas Pacific Railroad.

"Comstock...had a reputation of being a successful buffalo hunter and his friends at the fort—the officers in particular—were anxious to back him against me," Cody wrote. And so the game was on: the winner would be he who shot the most buffalos from horseback in eight hours. The wager was $500 but the stakes, especially for Cody, were much higher. As he noted, "My title of 'Buffalo Bill' was at stake."

Comstock's weapon of choice was his sixteen-shot Henry rifle while Cody was armed with the gun he called Lucretia Borgia – a .50-caliber breech-loading Springfield known on the frontier as a needlegun. "Comstock's Henry rifle, though it could fire more

138

rapidly than mine, did not, I felt certain, carry powder and lead enough to equal my weapon in execution," Cody wrote. And as it turned out, he was right. Buffalo Bill won the contest with sixty-nine kills while Comstock finished with only forty-six.

Other contemporary references to this event are nonexistent, although Cody said the railroad ran a special excursion train from St. Louis for more than 100 spectators, including Cody's wife and infant daughter, and champagne cocktails were enjoyed by contestants and onlookers alike. The *Kansas Historical Quarterly* in its summer 1957 issue placed the shoot-out in Logan County two and one-half miles west of Monument, Kansas, near the ruins of an old railroad station and recommended marking the site with a plaque. (Apparently, this was not done.)

In January 1868, Comstock became embroiled in a strange episode, one that contradicts his image as an amiable companion, hunting partner and, in the words of journalist Davis, one who overflowed with "kindly feelings for the human race." Comstock's kindly feelings, it seems, did not extend to wood contractor H.P. Wyatt, who cheated him on a business deal. Witness David Burton Long, then a hospital steward at Fort Wallace, recalled the incident in 1913:

"I was in the store (of post sutler Val Todd) at the time and heard loud talking, when Wyatt got up and was leaving the store; Comstock pulled out his six-shooter and shot Wyatt twice in the back. Wyatt ran out of the store and fell dead. During the trouble, as Comstock was shooting, I stepped up and tried to prevent Comstock from killing Wyatt, and he turned on me and said, 'You keep your hand off or I will kill you.' Wyatt was taken to the hospital dead room."

Wyatt may have needed killing; there is evidence he was the notorious Missouri bushwhacker Cave Wyatt who rode with William Quantrill at Lawrence and later with William "Bloody Bill" Anderson. Even so, Comstock was arrested and taken to Hays City for trial where it seems his friends came through for him. As Long recalled, the "rough element" of the community raised $500 for the scout's defense. Trial judge Marcellus E. Joyce, a justice of the peace from Leavenworth and a colorful character in his own right, appears to have been in Comstock's corner as well. Here, Long remembers Joyce's questioning of Sutler Todd, also a witness:

"'Did he (Comstock) do the shooting with felonious intent?'

'I do not know what his intentions were, but I did see Comstock shoot Wyatt and Wyatt ran out of the store and fell dead,' said Mr. Todd. Joyce said, 'If the shooting was not done with felonious intent and there is no proof that it was, the prisoner is discharged for want of said proof.'"

There is some indication the rough's $500 went not to Comstock's defense but directly into Joyce's pocket. Long believed this, saying the judge "was there to make more money..."

Lawton Nuss, a Kansas Supreme Court justice with an interest in frontier jurisprudence, is researching Medicine Bill's trial and its aftermath for an upcoming law journal article. He says Long may have been right about the good judge. Nuss unearthed an 1890 newspaper profile of Joyce which alleges a "cowboy" accused of murder managed, through a friend, "to quietly slip five hundred dollars into the hands of the judge." The so-called cowboy was acquitted of all charges.

"Certainly Joyce was not a law-trained jurist," Nuss says. "He may have been shady, or just a good man in over his head. Or he could have been a combination of things: untrained, opportunistic, greedy and a heavy drinker, as my research suggests."

However it came about, Joyce's decision seems not to have satisfied Wyatt's brother who placed an ad in a Denver newspaper offering a $500 reward for the "apprehension and delivery of William Comstock, late guide and interpreter, who on Jan. 14 shot and killed H.P. Wyatt at Fort Wallace."

Comstock beat a hasty retreat to his Rose Creek Ranch where he lay low, but not for long. The Indians started making trouble again and General Sheridan, who had replaced Hancock as commander of the Department of the Missouri, ordered Lieutenant Fred Beecher to assemble a crack team of scouts who could keep tabs on the hostiles and negotiate with them if necessary. (For the most part, Sheridan was inclined to agree with General William Sherman who dismissed peace talks with Indians as "senseless twaddle.") Beecher hired four men: Dick Parr, Frank Espey, Abner "Sharp" Grover and Comstock. Reportedly, Comstock only agreed to take the job after Sheridan personally assured him the Wyatt business was forgotten. At $125 a month, about ten times the wage of a private soldier, Comstock received the highest pay of the four.

Unfortunately, however, this assignment marks the beginning of the end for our hero. Beecher, whose own days were numbered, ordered Comstock and Grover to find the hostile village and persuade their chief to rein in the warriors wreaking havoc in the Saline Valley and along the Soloman and Republican rivers. By most accounts, Comstock and Grover entered the camp of Cheyenne chief Turkey Leg, whom both scouts knew personally, having lived with his people during their trading days, but it may have been that of Bull Bear, a leader of the Cheyenne Dog Soldier warrior society, as frontiersman George Bent later claimed. Bent, a mixed-blood who lived with a foot in both worlds, said Sheridan misidentified the village and unfairly castigated the Indians for what happened next.

"These scouts came into the camp as spies," Bent said in a letter to researcher George Hyde, "and the Indians would have been justified in shooting them as soon as they entered the village."

Either way, Comstock and Grover were counting on Cheyenne hospitality which held that a former friend would be safe in a man's lodge even if the relationship had soured. The two scouts went ahead with their mission even after learning Seventh Cavalry soldiers under Captain Fred Benteen had battled with Turkey Leg's warriors, killing four and wounding ten, just days before.

They found the village on Sunday, August 16. Accounts vary but Gray, whose research was thorough, placed it on the head of the Solomon River about twenty-five miles north and east of Monument Railroad Station. The scouts made it into the chief's lodge without mishap but midway through negotiations runners galloped into the village with news of the Benteen fight. Comstock and Grover left in a hurry.

What happened next will never be known for certain. The official report from Fort Wallace, written by commanding officer Capt. H.C. Bankhead and dated August 19, states: "The Indians then drove Comstock and Grover out of camp, and when about two miles away were overtaken by a party of seven, who at first appeared friendly, and after riding along with them, fired into their backs, killing William Comstock instantly. Grover remained hid (sic) in the grass during Monday—Monday night walked to the railroad, which he struck about seven miles east of Monument, and sent on to this post..."

In a letter to his father dated August 23, 1868, surgeon Turner mentions having Grover under his care in the hospital, shot through the lung but with a good prospect of recovery. Of

141

Comstock's death, Turner says, "I know of no one whose death would have produced so wide-felt an impression. He is certainly a great loss."

There were some who suspected Grover of doing his partner in to acquire his gold mine of a ranch. "Apparently, that was the opinion of several of the officers at Fort Wallace," John Adams Comstock notes in his *History and Genealogy of the Comstock Family in America,* privately printed in 1949. "There are some points in Grover's account that do not seem plausible."

For example, he finds it suspicious that Grover was sufficiently recovered from his wounds to lead Colonel George Forsyth's scouting expedition against the hostiles just a few weeks later. (That campaign ended in the now-famous Battle of the Arickaree in which Lieutenant Beecher was killed.) And he notes that Grover did indeed acquire the valuable Rose Creek Ranch after Comstock's death.

There are other tantalizing bits. In 1922, Frank Yellow Bull told an interviewer his father had been in the Cheyenne camp the night Comstock and Grover arrived. The two white men argued after leaving, Yellow Bull said, suggesting "maybe white man shoot white man..."

Still, it's difficult to believe Grover would shoot himself through the lung to escape suspicion. Forsyth did not think him guilty. In later writings, Forsyth said rumors of Grover's involvement in Comstock's death were spread by men who were "not to be depended upon." And Grover did not take immediate ownership of the valuable ranch but succeeded Comstock's employee Frank Dixon after Dixon, too, met a violent end.

At any rate, Grover's tenure at Rose Creek was brief. He was killed in a drunken saloon brawl in 1869. His assailant was not charged, alleging he acted in self-defense.

And there is one final question: what became of Comstock's body? Early on it was said the army recovered the corpse and reburied it in the post cemetery. Certainly the family believed this. Wrote John Adams Comstock: "General (sic) Bankhead sent out a detachment to bring the body of Comstock into the Post and he was buried there. The grave was in the third one south of the northeast corner of the post cemetery."

Except that it isn't. Even if one could make sense of the confusing coordinates, Jayne Humphrey Pearce, president of the Fort Wallace Memorial Association, says there is no record of Comstock ever having been buried in the Old Fort Wallace Cemetery.

Pearce, who lives in Wallace, has an archive of letters and manuscripts written by residents and Kansas historians who have sought Comstock's final resting place. The documents are difficult for a reader not intimately familiar with the terrain, they are in some cases incomplete and composed by men who have since joined the scout in the world beyond, but they tell an interesting tale. In one undated piece, longtime area resident Frank Madigan describes a conversation with Charles Cormack, a former Fort Wallace ambulance driver, in which Cormack says he buried Comstock's body on the north bank of the Smoky Hill River about 300 yards north of Hell Creek. Cormack died in 1944 at the age of 97, before he could take Madigan to the spot, but Madigan noted there are several graves in the area, "one in particular that has been covered with rocks as was described to me by Carmack (sic)."

This may have been the grave Leslie Linville of Colby, Kansas, found in 1941. At the time he thought it was that of an Indian but later, he came to believe it was Comstock's. "He was buried very respectfully in a very shallow grave perhaps 12 inches deep facing the Rising Sun," Linville wrote in 1970. "This was a must with the old Frontier Men." Others agreed, including Gray who mentioned the grave discovery in a footnote to his comprehensive 1970 article on Comstock's life published in *Montana, the Magazine of Western History*.

But in the end one is left to wonder about this, like so many things in Comstock's life. Given what is known about this elusive man, that's probably just the way he would have wanted it.

PRIEST'S LODGE

By Vernon Schmid

Where the Republican and Smoky Hill rivers
Come together, one spring morning
Each year the sun lights an altar,
Its equinox beam splitting the doorway,
Traveling to the far wall held in place
By the world's four corners, while nearby,
Blue jay, eagle, woodpecker, and owl
Listen for messages to carry to heaven.
Entering the sacred space, we are trapped
By a spirit resolute in its presence,
Refusing to abandoned that which knows
The direction of salvation, a promise of living
Stone and sand, tall grass hiding a tongue of flint.

WILD WEST

THE GHOST OF BILLY THE KID

By Matt Braun

Garrett awoke. His eyes opened, but he lay absolutely still. It took a moment for him to remember he was in a hotel room, rather than at his ranch. Yet there was no doubt in his mind that someone was in the room with him.

All in a motion, he levered himself erect. His gun belt hung on the bedstead and he jerked the old Colt from the holster, thumbing the hammer. The metallic whirr of the hammer was like a freight train in the stillness of the room.

"What the hell, Pat, you gonna kill me again?"

"Who is it?"

"You'll recollect I asked you *¿Quien es?* that night. And damned if you didn't shoot me anyway, Big Casino."

Once, decades ago, when they were friends, they were known as Big Casino and Little Casino. Garrett was six feet four and Billy was five feet seven, and whenever they entered a saloon, there was an amused murmur about their difference in size. Yet the nicknames had nothing to do with Garrett being broader and taller, or for that matter, tougher. Everyone knew the Kid was the killer.

Garrett didn't understand what was happening here tonight. But quickly enough, he understood that it was not of this world. He tossed aside the covers, rolled to a sitting position, feet planted on the floor. Fully awake now, he eyes widened in disbelief as he peered across the room. He knew he would never kill his visitor again, and he slowly lowered the hammer on the Colt.

Moonlight streamed through the window. A buttery patch illuminated one side of the room, dimly lighting a small stove and a straight-back chair. Billy the Kid, otherwise known as William Bonney, was seated in the chair. He was grinning.

"Took you long enough to recognize me, Pat."

"Goddamnit, you're dead!"

"You oughta know. You put me in a box and buried me."

Garrett and Billy had never worked together, even when they were both cowhands. Instead, they were sporting pals, rounders out to see the elephant when either of them was flush. They frequented the saloons and cantinas, vigorously chased señoritas and played poker, and drank copious amounts of tequila. Then Garrett got married and that all but ended the friendship. A wedding ring, or perhaps his wife, turned him into an ambitious man.

John Chisum, the cattle baron of New Mexico Territory, backed him in the political arena. Garrett was elected sheriff of Lincoln County, and he was ordered to bring in Billy the Kid, dead or alive. On a sultry summer night in 1881, in Pete Maxwell's bedroom at Fort Sumner, Billy barged through the door, spotted a shadowy figure seated next to Maxwell's bed, and asked, "*¿Quien es?*"

Without hesitation or reply, Garrett fired twice, killing him instantly. That was twenty-seven years ago, and now, on a crisp winter night in 1908, time seemed to have slipped its moorings. Billy the Kid sat grinning at him in a splash of moonlight.

Garrett frowned. "You're really dead?"

"I'm as big a ghost as you'll ever see."

"Where'd you come from?"

"Well, it shore wasn't the Pearly Gates. Reckon I killed too many men to make it past Saint Pete. These days, I live in hell."

"Got what you deserved."

"Yep," Billy said with a chuckle. "Me and the Devil are real good pards."

"Figures." Garrett paused, his expression suddenly curious. "Hot down there, is it?"

"Not what the Holy Joes make it out. They're just tryin' to scare folks with their fire and brimstone."

"How'd you get out?"

"*El Diablo* gave me a pass for the night. Tickled his funny bone, what I got in mind."

"What's that?"

150

Billy grunted a laugh. "Why, I've come to put you on notice, Pat. They're fixin' to kill you tomorrow."

"Who's gonna kill me?" Garrett demanded. "And for that matter, why would you give me a warning?"

"Guess you got a point there. You never gave me no warnin', did you? Just shot me down in the dark."

"When you asked me 'who is it,' what if I'd told you it was me? What would you have done?"

"Why hell's bells, Pat, I would've shot you. You'd already tried to kill me lots of times."

"So why would I answer back? Knowin' you'd kill me the minute I opened my mouth."

"We was once friends," Billy said crossly. "Wasn't no call to shoot me down like some blind dog. Specially when I didn't even know it was you."

Garrett thought otherwise. In 1878, he went from punching cows to operating a café, and he and Billy remained the best of friends. At the time, Billy was working as a cowhand for John Tunstall, an Englishman turned rancher and transplanted to New Mexico Territory. Tunstall was aligned with John Chisum in a bitter struggle with L. G. Murphy for political control of Lincoln County. Billy, who had never known his real father, became something of a son to Tunstall.

In early 1878, Tunstall was brutally murdered by the Murphy faction. A single incident, all in a moment, ignited what became known as the Lincoln County War. Enraged by his patron's death, Billy and a band of Tunstall supporters rode forth on a bloody vendetta. Over the next year, they killed several of L. G. Murphy's cohorts, as well as the sheriff of Lincoln County. Garrett, who had become friends with John Chisum, kept his distance from the killings. Neither of them supported the young outlaw, who was now known as Billy the Kid.

A truce was called in early 1879 by Lew Wallace, governor of New Mexico Territory. Wallace offered Billy a full pardon in exchange for testimony against the Murphy faction, and for a time, the violence subsided. But political considerations stalled the pardon, and Billy, disillusioned by failed promise, returned to the outlaw life. He formed a gang of gunmen and misfits, and began rustling cattle throughout the territory. Embittered by John Chisum's attitude during the Lincoln County War, he raided

Chisum's Jinglebob Ranch at every opportunity. The cattle baron quickly became his avowed enemy.

Chisum knew an ambitious man when he saw one. In 1880, he called in all his political chits to have Garrett elected sheriff of Lincoln County. Garrett, in return, agreed to bring his former friend to justice. Within a short time, Garrett and his posse fought three gunfights with the Kid and his gang, finally capturing him on December 23. Billy was tried and convicted for the murder of Sheriff William Brady in 1878, and he was placed in the Lincoln jail to await hanging. Four months later, the spring of 1881, while Garrett was out of town, Billy killed the two deputies guarding him and escaped. Garrett privately swore to Chisum that, next time, the Kid would be brought in dead.

On the night of July 14, 1881, Garrett kept his word. Billy was visiting his sweetheart, Celsa Gutierrez, at Fort Sumner. Late that evening, after an amorous interlude with Celsa, he felt like eating a steak and went to Pete Maxwell's bedroom to fetch the key to the meat house. Garrett was there, seated in the dark, questioning Maxwell on Billy's whereabouts, and instantly fired two shots. A coffin was hammered together that night, and the next morning the burial took place in the old military cemetery. Billy the Kid was just twenty-one the day they lowered him into his grave.

Garrett regretted nothing about the shooting. The incident made him famous, and with the help of a collaborator, he wrote a book entitled *The Authentic Life of Billy the Kid.* Yet tonight, seated across the room from Billy, he wondered if he'd taken leave of his senses. Here he was, arguing with a dead man, and he didn't even believe in ghosts. Still, the figure sitting cross-legged in the straight-back chair was definitely Billy Bonney. Ugly as ever, the same smart-alecky voice, and short as a stump.

Billy rose from the chair and walked to the window. As he crossed in front of the stove, Garrett suddenly realized he couldn't see through the figure. He'd always heard that ghosts were phantoms or spectral, or some damn two-dollar word that meant transparent. Then, as he looked closer, he saw that the moonlight spilling through the window cast no shadow of the Kid. Albeit reluctantly, he concluded he actually was talking with a ghost.

"Yessir, you're a real turd," Billy said, staring out the window. "Sold your soul to ol' man Chisum and killed me just to make your name. I won't never forgive you, Pat."

"Nobody asked you," Garrett retorted. "Hell turn you into a whiner, did it?"

"Oh, don't you worry yourself none about me. Told you why I was here."

"And you expect me to believe you?"

"I never lied to you before—not once,"

Garrett couldn't argue the point. Billy was many things, but never a liar. "Alright, let's have it," he said. "Who's gonna kill me?"

"Wayne Brazel."

"That's the biggest load of crap I ever heard. Brazel doesn't have the balls to kill anybody."

"Yeah, you're right." Billy turned from the window with a lantern-jawed grin. "He's hired Deacon Jim Miller to stop your ticker."

The name alone got Garrett's attention. He knew Jim Miller to be a hired gun, the most feared assassin in the southwest. Nicknamed "Deacon Jim" because he regularly attended church, he neither drank nor smoked, but he routinely performed murder when the money was right. Anyone with a grudge and a thousand dollars could hire his services, and he had reportedly killed fifteen men in Texas, New Mexico, and Arizona. His reputation was not one to be ignored.

Garrett stood, dropping his pistol on the bed, and crossed to the window. He stared hard at the Kid. "Where'd you get your information?"

"Down in hell," Billy said lightly. "Dirty tricks are the Devil's stock-in-trade. Not much goes on up here that we don't hear about—beforehand."

"Why would Brazel want to kill me?"

"'Cause you broke your word. Way it looks, that's reason enough for him."

"I never did any such thing."

"Sure you did, Pat. You got liar written all over your face."

Garrett winced at the cheery insult. Since killing Billy, he'd been a widely respected lawman and an utter failure as a businessman. In 1882, with the reward money for bringing down the Kid, he started a cattle ranch and slowly went broke. Then, in 1884, he captained a company of Texas Rangers organized to rout gangs of rustlers operating along the Texas-New Mexico border.

After that, he again went broke with an ill-conceived irrigation scheme in the Pecos Valley.

The years passed with various failed business ventures. Finally, turning once more to law enforcement in 1897, he was elected sheriff of Dona Ana County, New Mexico, and served two terms with considerable distinction. Afterward, Theodore Roosevelt appointed him customs collector at El Paso and he held the post until 1905, when he returned to New Mexico. There, back in Dona Ana County, he bought a horse ranch with grazeland bordering the Red River. He gradually lost all the money he'd saved while in Texas.

By early 1908, Garrett was in desperate financial straits. On the verge of losing his ranch, he sold the horses and made a handshake deal to lease the land to a neighboring rancher, Wayne Brazel. A month later he accepted a better offer from a man named Carl Adamson, and now, on the night of February 28, he was quartered in a hotel in Chamberino. Tomorrow, he and Adamson would travel to Las Cruces, the county seat, to sign a lease prepared by Adamson's lawyer. Until a moment ago, he hadn't given a thought to the handshake deal with Wayne Brazel.

"Doesn't make sense," he said. "I told Brazel the deal was off when he started grazin' goats on my land. Damn goats snip the grass clean down to the roots."

Billy shrugged. "Guess he figures it's a matter of principle. A man's word is his bond, and you done broke yours."

"Well, Jesus Christ, that's no call to have me killed!"

"We've both seen men killed for lots less."

"You're sure he's hired Miller?"

"Yeah, and Deacon Jim does good work." Billy flashed a peg-toothed grin. "'Course, no way he'll live long enough to beat my record. Way I hear it he's only killed fifteen or so."

"C'mon," Garrett scoffed. "You're not still claimin' you killed twenty-one men?"

"Damn tootin' I am! The Devil himself told me I pegged it right. Ol' Lucifer keeps a square tally."

"Way you murdered Jim Bell and Bob Olinger probably sealed your ticket to hell."

"Sticks in your craw after all them years, don't it? Me bustin' out of your jail, pretty as you please."

"Billy, there wasn't nothing pretty about it."

On April 28, 1881, Garrett had returned to Lincoln only to find both his deputies dead. At suppertime, while Bob Olinger was across the street at a café, the Kid pleaded a case of the trots and got Jim Bell to take him to the outhouse behind the jail. There, he retrieved a pistol hidden in the two-holer, thought to have been secreted by one of his ladyloves. Once back inside the jail, he killed Bell.

Bob Olinger heard the shot and came running from the café. As he rushed across the street, the Kid appeared at an open window and blasted him with both barrels of a double-barrel shotgun. The buckshot struck him in the head and neck, and he dropped dead in the street. The Kid then claimed Bell's gun belt and took a Winchester from the rifle rack in the office. On the street, he stole a horse and rode off, waving cheerfully to the townspeople. No one tried to stop him.

"Never meant to hurt Bell," Billy said now. "Figured to lock him in a cell after I showed him the gun, but he took off runnin'. Just didn't leave me no choice."

"You had a choice with Olinger," Garrett said. "Folks told me you called out his name, and when he stopped, you let him have both barrels. Damn near took his head off."

"Bob Olinger was a low-down sonovabitch. Wish't I'd killed him twice."

"Found your home in hell, didn't you?"

"Pat, I reckon I'm plumb blessed. Turns out death's a real hoot."

"How you figure that?"

"'Cause tomorrow, you're gonna join me in Hades. Be just like old times."

"Don't bet on it," Garrett said. "I'll deal with Jim Miller when he makes his play."

"Not the way it works," Billy told him. "The Devil explained it to me real clear after I'd been down there awhile. We're all slated to go out a certain way, at a certain time. Try your damnedest, you can't ride around it."

"Still don't understand why you'd warn me."

"You'll recollect you always said I was a jokester. I've just come back to put the joke over on you."

"Some joke."

"You get what you deserve, Big Casino."

"Says you."

A strange expression came over Billy's face. He stared out the moonlit window a moment, then turned back to Garrett. "I gotta go, Pat."

"You're leaving?"

"Yeah, my pass ends at midnight. From the looks of the moon, I'd judge I'm on my way."

"Hold on!" Garrett insisted. "You haven't told me the thing that counts most. What time will Miller take a try at me?"

"Ol' Lucifer's good, but he ain't that good. All he said was it'd be sometime tomorrow."

"Tomorrow covers a lot of ground. Dawn to dusk and everything in between."

"Don't worry on it so. I done told you tomorrow's your last day. Just take it like it comes."

"No damn way," Garrett huffed. "I'll beat it yet."

"You're a dead man, Pat, and I gotta go. I'll see you in hell."

"Wait!"

Billy seemed to vaporize in the moonlight. His form turned from corporal to shimmering mist, and then he was gone. The last thing Garrett saw was his crooked, jack-o'-lantern grin. The room was suddenly empty, and still.

Garrett shook his head in silent refusal. Billy the Kid, whether ghost or man, wasn't going to tell him how it would end. He was damned if he'd let himself be killed. There was always a way out.

A wild idea popped into his mind. He thought he might write another book and tell the world about his midnight visit from the ghost of Billy the Kid. His first book, written after he'd killed Billy, had been a national sensation.

But then, on second thought, a book about tonight's encounter seemed somewhat improbable. No one would believe it.

In fact, there was an even larger question: Why should he believe Billy? Wouldn't the ghost of the Kid want to haunt him, scare him so badly he'd never sleep again in his life? Perhaps, as Billy had said just moments ago, it was the joke of an inveterate jokester. Frighten him out of his wits and then laugh all the way back to hell. Perhaps the warning about Wayne Brazel's plan to kill him was stuff and nonsense. Nothing more than the work of a rascally jester.

Then again, perhaps not.

* * *

Chamberino was some fifteen miles south of Las Cruces. Garrett and Carl Adamson left the hotel early that morning, traveling by horse and buggy. The skies were clear, but the weather was chilly, and both men wore overcoats. The wagon road out of town bordered the Rio Grande.

By midday they were within five miles of Las Cruces. Their appointment with Adamson's lawyer, where they would sign the lease, was scheduled for two o'clock. Off to their right, east of the river, were the Organ Mountains, and to the west were the saw-toothed peaks of the Potrillo Range. The terrain west of the road was broken by arroyos and rugged hills strewn with boulders.

To Garrett's amazement, Wayne Brazel appeared ahead of them on horseback, riding from the direction of Las Cruces. Brazel was mounted on a sorrel gelding, his hat pulled low against the noonday sun, and the expression on his face was stern. Garrett was instantly on guard, searching for a second horseman, Deacon Jim Miller. He exchanged a glance with Adamson as he halted the buggy at the side of the road.

"What the hell's this?" he muttered. "Where'd Brazel come from?"

"You got me," Adamson said. "Watch yourself, Pat."

"I generally do."

Brazel reined his horse to a halt beside the buggy. "Garrett, we've got some unfinished business," he said in a hectoring voice. "You're not gonna lease that land out from under me."

"How'd you know I'd be on this road?"

"Don't matter one way or another. We shook hands on a deal and you're gonna keep it."

Garrett looked past him, scanning the broken hills west of the road. He heard Billy's warning from last night, and he was wary that Brazel might have stopped him at this spot in the road for a purpose. His eyes darted among the boulders lining the hills, but he saw nothing of another man. His gaze swung back to Brazel.

"You broke the deal," he said. "You and your goddamn goats. That's an end to it."

"No, by Christ, it's not," Brazel snapped. "Only the sorriest son-of-a-bitch goes back on his word. Don't try to welch on me."

"Or what?"

Garrett pushed his overcoat aside. He placed his hand on the holstered Colt and tapped the hammer with his thumb. Brazel stared at the pistol for a long moment, sitting perfectly still in the saddle, his hands clasped across the saddlehorn. He finally looked up at Garrett.

"You got no call to threaten me with a gun."

"Not a threat," Garrett said. "I won't tolerate rough talk from any man. Never have, never will."

Brazel scowled, wagging his head. "I'm just makin' my case for what's right. No harm in that."

"I drunk enough coffee at breakfast to float a cow. You go right ahead and make your case. I gotta take a piss."

"You know how to insult a man, don't you?"

"Why hell, you're lucky I don't piss all over you. Keep your hands where I can see 'em."

Garrett stepped down from the buggy. He unbuttoned his pants and pulled out his pud, splashing a hot stream in the dirt at the hooves of Brazel's horse. The sorrel snorted, dancing away from the sharp odor, and Brazel took a firm grip on the reins. Garrett watched him, eyes bright with contempt as he emptied his bladder. He finished, shook himself off, and looked at Brazel with an ugly smile.

"You and your horse ought not be so skittish at a little piss."

A rifle shot cracked from the hills to the west. The slug struck Garrett in the temple, and the other side of his head exploded in a spray of blood and brains. His knees buckled, and as he fell, another slug ripped through his chest. He dropped face down in the road, pants still unbuttoned.

Brazel swung off his horse. He walked forward as Adamson clambered out of the buggy and joined him in the road. They stood watching as blood puddled in the dirt around Garrett's head. After a time, Brazel woofed a sour chuckle.

"Dumb bastard never knew what hit him."

"No, he didn't," Adamson agreed. "Just like a duck in a shooting gallery."

"We got Deacon to thank for that."

"Yes, no question about it, he's a true-blue professional."

Deacon Jim Miller appeared from behind a boulder on a hillside and walked down to the road. He was carrying a Winchester carbine and the look on his face was one of a stoic craftsman satisfied with his work. He stopped beside the other men, glancing at Garrett with only casual interest. His job was done.

"Nifty shot, Deacon," Brazel said. "You blew his brains halfway to kingdom come."

Miller grunted. "Most generally, I hit what I shoot at."

Brazel pulled a wad of bills from his pocket. He'd already paid half the gunman's fee and now he handed over another five hundred dollars. Miller stuffed the bills in his mackinaw pocket, clearly unconcerned that the count was right. Nobody tried to stiff an assassin.

"Guess you'd best take off," Brazel said. "I'll be in touch if I need you again."

"Whenever you got work, I'll be around."

Miller trudged back up the hill and disappeared behind a boulder. A few moments later, they heard the sound of hoofbeats, fading slowly into the distance. Adamson, silent until now, let out a gusty breath.

"Coldest man I ever saw," he said. "No way I'd want to get on his bad side."

Brazel nodded. "You stay here while I ride into town and get the sheriff. Just make damn sure you stick to our story."

"Don't worry, you bought yourself a witness. Besides, I wouldn't go back on you anyway. You might sic Deacon Jim on me."

"Carl, I like the way you think."

Brazel mounted his horse and rode north toward Las Cruces. Adamson watched after him a moment, then turned and stared down at the body. He thought it was a poor end for the man who had killed Billy the Kid.

Fame, like the philosophers said, was fleeting.

* * *

Garrett and Billy were reunited in hell shortly after twelve noon on February 29, 1908. Billy, ever the jester, needled Garrett about their moonlit conversation last night. He thought it hilarious that Garrett believed he could forestall fate and dodge his date with death. Every man crossed over whenever God—or the Devil—snuffed the candle.

Garrett, surprisingly, took it all in stride. Dead was dead, and if he'd let himself be ambushed so easily, then the fault was his alone. He even displayed a certain equanimity about being consigned to hell, for he was more sinner than saint, and as Billy had told him, all that fire and brimstone stuff was mostly hokum. He largely ignored the Kid's ribbing, and their old friendship blossomed in no time at all. Big Casino and Little Casino once again.

A year later Wayne Brazel was brought to trial for murder. The county prosecutor openly scorned his contention that he'd killed Pat Garrett in self-defense. After the shooting, at the arraignment hearing, Carl Adamson had testified on his behalf, asserting Brazel had fired only after Garrett had drawn a gun. The sheriff's investigation indicated otherwise, and a grand jury promptly returned an indictment of premeditated homicide. The district court judge, rumored to be in Brazel's pocket, allowed him to post bond.

All the screws came loose when the case went to trial. Carl Adamson, the key defense witness, was by then incarcerated in a California prison. A few months earlier he'd been convicted for smuggling Chinese slave girls into San Francisco, and California authorities denied a subpoena for him to attend the trail. There were no other witnesses to the killing, and though the prosecutor trumpeted cold-blooded murder, Brazel's assertion of self-defense went unchallenged. The jury, lacking reasonable proof of guilt, brought in a verdict of not guilty. He breezed out of court a free man.

Ironically, almost exquisitely so, the day Brazel was acquitted in New Mexico, Deacon Jim Miller was hanged in Ada, Oklahoma. Hired to kill a troublesome lawman by local bootleggers, he ambushed the marshal on a country road with a shotgun. But he was tracked down by a band of vigilantes, and along with the three bootleggers, dragged into a livery stable and lynched from a rafter. The vigilantes, proud of their handiwork, took a photograph that appeared in newspapers across Oklahoma.

Garrett and the Kid had a good laugh about it in hell. Billy joked that Deacon Jim Miller, the notorious assassin, had been strung up like a common cow thief. As for Wayne Brazel, the Devil told them the rancher would be thrown from a horse and stomped to death exactly four months and three days after his acquittal for murder. Carl Adamson, the conspirator who had duped Garrett the most, was serving his time as the pass-around girlfriend for a bunch of lustful cons in a California prison. All in all, for Garrett and Billy, it was a good day in hell.

That evening, Satan summoned them to take seats by his throne. They were always impressed that he possessed none of the bestial qualities attributed to him by preachers and priests. No horns, no cloven hooves, no spiked tail, and yet somehow fiendish, affably diabolic. His gaze fell on Garrett.

"Are you pleased with the day's results?"

"Yes, Master." Garrett had by now learned his place in Lucifer's realm. "Telling me of Brazel's fate was kind of you. Miller gettin' hanged was icing on the cake."

"You are a vengeful man, much like your friend here."

Billy all but squirmed with glee. "Well, sir," he said, "some men just needed killin' and I obliged 'em. That's all."

"Vengeance is mine sayeth the Lord," Satan quoted with a roguish smile. "Of course, as you may imagine, I dispute the claim."

Garrett looked interested. "You know God, do you? Personally, I mean."

"Only too well," Satan replied. "Although we haven't spoken face-to-face in many thousands of years. He comes to me in my dreams."

"Your dreams," Garrett said, intrigued. "You don't mind my asking, what does he say?"

"Nothing memorable," Satan said. "We are the rulers of our own kingdoms, and I alone govern evil. I am, after all, the Prince of Darkness."

Billy beamed. "You're sure enough my Dark Angel. Treated me square ever since I got here."

"Goes for me, too," Garrett said. "Hell's made to order for the likes of Billy and me."

Satan nodded. "You both show unusual promise. I may yet install you as my disciples."

"Hear that, Pat!" Billy whooped. "We're gonna be the Devil's disciples!"

"Careful, young Billy," their host said indulgently. "I prefer my proper name, Satan."

"How about Beelzebub?" Garrett asked. "Preachers back on earth sometimes call you that."

"A pejorative term," Satan said. "But then, I treasure their scorn in the way priests cherish holy water."

Billy grinned. "By golly, ain't hell the life! Learn somethin' new every day."

Satan, always partial to killers, lectured them as he would acolytes. They listened attentively as he remarked on the vagaries so often imposed on mortals. He explained that life was never all you wanted, and seldom turned out just the way you expected. The trade-off, if you were lucky and appreciated the finer points of irony, was that you got to be happy most of the time. The rest of the time, he told them with a wry smile, life was like ten piglets and a mama sow with only nine teats. Someone always went hungry.

Later, off by themselves, Garrett commented on the wisdom of what they'd heard. The Devil, he noted, dealt in parables, and taught those in hell that their new lives were no better nor no worse than their lives on earth. Hell, he told the Kid, was just a longer journey. A slow trek through eternity.

"Yessir," Billy joked with a nutcracker grin. "And the fun don't never end down here."

"What the deuce are you talkin' about now?"

"Why, looky there, Pat. Here comes Deacon Jim!"

Deacon Jim Miller marched through the gates of Hell. His neck was crooked over from the hanging, but otherwise he looked much the same. Stoic, if a little pissed off.

"I'll be damned," Garrett said. "I killed you and he killed me, and we're back where we started. How's that for irony?"

Billy laughed. "Told you it'd be just like old times."

And it was.

THE LAST NIGHTMARE OF COMMODORE PERRY OWENS

By Tom Carpenter

The old sheriff had come to expect the ghost. It didn't matter whether he slept in bed or fell asleep from too much whiskey in the chair by the fireplace, every night for the past week, the ghost would lean into his dreams as if to leave a house through an open window. The old sheriff knew the ghost. It was Andy Cooper, gut-shot, with blood running through his fingers clutching his spilling bowels. Andy's mouth was closed, but Commodore Perry Owens could hear a banshee wailing from somewhere behind him.

The apparition had haunted his sleep through the years, but never two nights in a row. Was this the sixth or seventh night? Commodore wondered. It wasn't the apparition that frightened him as much as the frequency of these visits. He could understand the ghost. After all, he had killed the man a long time ago, but these repeat visits were wearing on him and he wondered what they meant. Whatever they meant, Commodore Perry Owens knew it couldn't be good.

His wife found him in the kitchen before sunrise. "You slept in your chair again last night."

"I did."

"I thought you were coming to bed 'shortly'."

"So did I."

She took her favorite cup, the one he'd given her when they married, from its hook beneath the kitchen cabinet. She yawned as she dropped two sugar cubes into the cup and filled it with coffee.

163

She looked into his tired brown eyes and touched his bristled cheek. "You can't keep this up, C. P."

C. P. looked at the floor to allow her hand to linger. "How'd you sleep, Elizabeth?"

"Not so good," Elizabeth said. She took her seat at the table by the window that overlooked her garden plot. The purple hills to the west and north were taking shape, and the long shadow of the house began to separate itself from the fading darkness. "It got cold last night. I missed my heater."

"It was colder than a ding-dang." He stooped and grabbed a chunk of cedar from the wood box and shoved it in the stove. He peeked in the oven, and then took his customary seat across from his wife. "Should warm some. Sky's clear." He took a sip and placed the thick mug softly on the table.

Elizabeth sniffed. "Biscuits?"

C. P. grinned. "Just about."

When the biscuits were ready, they moved easily and without speaking between the cabinets and the drawers getting plates and tableware and marmalade.

C. P. finished his last biscuit. "Elizabeth," he said. "Do you believe in ghosts?"

She looked into her empty coffee cup. "I suppose that depends on what you mean by ghost, C. P. If you mean a spirit that sort of occupies space with you, like my dead Momma watching over me, then yes, I suppose I do."

"Nope," C. P. said. "I'm talking about an apparition. A real honest-to-goodness ghost, a specter, a visitation by some dead soul."

Elizabeth looked out the window for a moment. C. P. watched her thinking. She picked up her dishes and his. "Well then, I guess I don't believe in ghosts. Do you?"

"I'm beginning to."

Elizabeth poured hot water from the big kettle on the stove into the sink and began cleaning their dishes. C. P. went into the bedroom and finished dressing. He stomped his feet into his old boots and returned to the kitchen while buttoning his denim shirt.

He grabbed a canvas coat from a peg by the back door. He took his time buttoning it. He watched the weather vane waggle atop the big shed. "Guess it won't be as warm as I'd hoped."

Elizabeth turned. "I know you don't want to do this."

"Not particularly. No." There was nothing in his tone to betray anger or a change of heart. "I said I'd do it."

"I know," Elizabeth said. "You can't go on like this. Not sleeping. It's going to kill you."

He sagged a little. "I'm fifty-six years old, darlin'. Something's bound to get me sooner or later."

"Well, I'm thirty-one and I'm not looking forward to spending the rest of my days a widow." The edge in her voice turned his head.

He started to smile and speak.

"Don't say it, C. P.," she said. "Don't make light of this. I love you and I don't want to lose you."

He frowned. "Don't get your hackles up. I said I'd go and I'm going." He picked up the Winchester .44 propped by the door. "Seemed like a good idea at the time, marrying a nurse."

"You know damned well it is, you old fool." The edge in her voice was still sharp. "Where are you going with that?"

He didn't answer. Sometimes he took the rifle with him on his morning walk. Sometimes he didn't. The wind caught the door as he stepped outside. It closed harder than he would have liked, but he didn't open it again to apologize. Instead he walked across the yard, through a barbed-wire gate and kept walking for half a mile without looking back.

A train whistle filled the valley air. C. P. stopped and turned to look back toward the town. He could see the train drooping like a slack rope from the ridge to the west, headed east and moving fast toward the cluster of buildings and shade trees that lay along the north side of the tracks.

It was a long one with three engines pulling at least a hundred cars, C. P. estimated. When the caboose disappeared around the bend in the track east of town, C. P. turned and resumed his walk.

He saw a herd of antelope grazing on a distant knoll. He raised the Winchester to his shoulder and took aim. His hands were steady and his eyesight clear and sharp. He sighted in on the chest of the buck that stood atop the knoll alert and watching him.

C. P. lowered his rifle. "Three hundred yards," he said to the antelope. "That would be a helluva shot." He watched the antelope turn and trot out of sight behind the hill. The rest of the herd followed.

A gust of wind chilled his face and hands. He tucked the rifle into the crook of his arm and jammed his hands into his coat pockets. His stiff fingers felt gravel and cold bullets in each. He kept walking. His legs were sore behind the knees from sleeping with his feet propped on a stool. His neck hurt, too.

"What day is it?" he asked the hawk circling overhead. "Tuesday? Wednesday? Tuesday? Must be Tuesday because Tuesday is the day I promised Elizabeth I'd go with her to see ol' Philbert Havatone up at Pine Springs."

A prairie dog barked from atop his hole. The soft soil muffled C. P.'s steps and with the wind in his face he had reached the edge of a vast prairie dog colony without his scent raising their alarm.

"Goddamn prairie dogs," C. P. said. He raised his rifle and shot the barker. The critter exploded with the impact of the .44-caliber cartridge.

C. P.'s ears rang and the valley air vibrated with the echo of the rifle's report. He swung his rifle and took aim at another dog frozen with fear atop the mound surrounding the entrance to his burrow. The swift sure movement, swinging the barrel to the next target, the quick aim, like snapping a chalk line between the muzzle and the heart of the target, the automatic release of tension in his shoulders and arms as his breathing paused, all of those old mechanical habits that made him a dead shot with a rifle flowed through him like water.

The air wavered and blurred and C. P. lowered his rifle. The landscape before him changed as though a playing card had been turned over. The high desert landscape he had lived in for the last twenty years just up and disappeared.

In its place was a dusty street in Holbrook and he was standing in front of the Blevins's house. It was September 4, 1887, about 4:00 p.m. on a Sunday. Somebody was frying chicken. He was thirty-five years old again. His long hair obscured the Apache County Sheriff's badge pinned to his shirt. He wore a heavy pistol in a holster on his hip and he carried the Winchester .44 in the crook of his left arm.

He glanced over at the railroad depot down the street and saw some men smoking and watching him. He didn't nod and neither did they.

The house was a small, wood frame with four rooms. An unsaddled horse stood tied to a cottonwood tree in the yard.

C. P. approached the house. He noticed a woman at the window, silhouetted by the thin drapes. He stepped onto the porch and knocked on the door.

Andy Cooper opened the door enough to speak, but not enough to reveal whether he was armed. "Well, if it isn't Sheriff Commodore Perry Owens," he said with his familiar smirk.

C. P. said, "Yup. How you been, Andy?"

"I been good, C. P. How 'bout you."

"I've been better," C. P. said.

"How so?" Andy closed the door a smidge and shifted his weight.

C. P. looked him in the eye. "I have a warrant for you and I want you to come along with me."

Andy didn't move a muscle. "What warrant is it, Owens?"

"The warrant for stealing horses."

Andy kept his gaze steady for a moment, and then glanced over C. P.'s shoulder at the horse.

C. P. said, "Are you ready?"

Andy Cooper said, "In a few minutes," and started to close the door.

C. P. moved his left foot and blocked the door before Andy could shut it.

Andy Cooper shouted, "No, I won't go," and raised a pistol he'd been hiding behind his back. Without shifting his Winchester, C. P. turned and fired it from the crook of his arm and shot Andy Cooper in the stomach. The bullet went through Andy and shattered a bowl on a table behind him.

C. P. stepped back on the porch and levered another round into the chamber. A woman inside the house started wailing. A second door on the porch opened slightly, and John Blevins fired his pistol at C. P. He missed from a distance of four feet, but struck the horse, which reared and broke free of the tree and galloped down the street. Blevins slammed the door shut. C. P. fired his rifle through the door and hit Blevins in the shoulder and knocked him down.

C. P. heard a window open on the east side of the house. He ran into the street. He saw Andy Cooper on his knees pointing his pistol out the open window. C. P. fired another shot through the wall of the house and hit Cooper in the right hip. Cooper dropped out of sight.

Gun smoke hung like a curtain in the still air. C. P. felt his heart beating slow, but forcefully, like a pump being worked deliberately by a tired man who needed water.

From inside the house he heard a boy's voice shouting, "Where's the son of a bitch? I'll get him."

The door flung open and the boy, Sam Houston Blevins, fifteen, pulled free of his mother's arms and charged onto the porch with a blood-covered pistol in his hand.

C. P. raised his rifle and shot the boy in the chest. The impact hurled young Blevins backwards, and he fell dying at his mother's feet. C. P. stepped back into the middle of the street, keeping an eye on the woman in case she decided to pick up the gun. He heard a commotion on the east side of the house and sidestepped in that direction. Another man, Mose Roberts, had barely cleared the window when C. P. stepped into view. Roberts raised his pistol, and C. P. shot him in the chest.

C. P. stood for a minute or so looking at the house. Through the open door, he watched two other women join Mrs. Blevins kneeling beside her dead son. All were covered with blood and wailing in terror and sorrow. No one else moved in the house, although he could hear groaning from the men he'd shot.

He turned and walked away through the pall of gun smoke hanging in the street. His friends from the railroad platform approached him. They met him beside the dead horse in the street.

"Did you finish the job?" one asked.

"I think I have," C. P. said.

Did you finish the job? Did you finish the job? Did you finish...

The hawk overhead swooped out of the sky and snatched a prairie dog. C. P. shook his head and began to recognize the landscape again. He turned to see if his house was still there. It was. He could see Elizabeth hanging wash on the line.

C. P. walked slowly back home. Elizabeth stood in her fallow garden plot.

She smiled as he approached. "Was that you shooting?"

C. P. nodded. "Prairie dog."

"That's a lot of firepower for a little ol' prairie dog," she said. "I don't think the last frost is behind us yet."

C. P. nodded. "I don't think so."

"I'll wait another week to plant."

C. P. nodded and went inside. He tossed a log in the fireplace, took a seat in his easy chair, and began to clean his rifle.

Elizabeth entered the room. "How long will it take to get to Pine Springs?"

"By wagon? About three hours."

"We should be going soon."

"Yes," C. P. said. "I'll just be a few minutes, then I'll hitch the team."

The wagon road to Pine Springs followed the contours of the valley, snaking along the edges of grassy knolls that looked subtle from town, but out in the midst of them, they were a chore to negotiate. C. P. kept the mule team pulling slow and steady.

Elizabeth sat beside him. At their feet sat a basket with food and water for the trip and an apple pie for the man they were going to visit. In the back, she had placed a bundle of clothes for the trip. The wind hadn't picked up as it usually did. The sky had a few clouds, but none that looked like rain.

"My sister wrote to me," Elizabeth said. "I got the letter yesterday." She pulled it out of her coat pocket and opened it.

C. P. grunted. "And how is Mrs. Abigail Fleet and her extraordinary children?"

"I was going to read the letter to you," Elizabeth said. "But now I'm not."

C. P. gave the mules a little tap with the reins to get them interested in making it up the next rise. "Fine with me. I am not particularly fond of your sister, nor her children."

"Abigail can be a little bossy," Elizabeth said.

"A little bossy? She makes Teddy Roosevelt look downright timid. And those children of hers..."

"Lyle and Emily Anne can act a little spoiled."

"Like sour milk."

"You've never forgiven those children."

"Nobody puts a live lizard in the boot of Commodore Perry Owens and lives to tell about it."

"They're just children, C. P.," she said.

"It makes damned little difference. Besides, I hate the way she always talks about her kids. It's like she's making a point about us not having any."

"She's not doing that," Elizabeth said.

169

"The hell she ain't."

She watched his face darken beneath a frown. "Yes, dear." She put the letter away and patted his arm gently.

Philbert Havatone was chopping wood in front of his brush hut when the wagon rolled around the last bend. There were half a dozen other huts much like his, all rough, brush-domed wikiups with low corrals nearby and dogs everywhere running loose and barking. A mongrel ran up to the wagon and snarled at the mules, making them shake their harnesses. Philbert tossed a rock at the mutt and hit it in the side. The dog yelped and ran off.

Philbert approached the wagon with a smile. "Mrs. Owens. I wondered if you would come." He turned and yelled toward one of the wikiups. A thick short woman in a shapeless shift stooped below the opening and stood outside at the doorway.

"Juanita," he said. "This is the woman."

Juanita didn't move or change her blank expression.

Philbert turned back to Elizabeth. "She doesn't trust white people. Even if they treat an infection that saves her child's life." That last he spoke loudly, turning his head toward Juanita.

The boy who'd had the fever poked his head out of the wikiup. Juanita swatted his forehead and followed the boy back inside.

"It's a long ride," Philbert said. "Come on down from there and let's get out of the sun."

Philbert grinned at the apple pie Elizabeth gave him and took it into the wikiup. He led C. P. and Elizabeth to the shady side of the house where they sat on logs and drank water poured into tin cups from a canvas water bag. The sun was still high in the sky, so the shade felt good to C. P. and Elizabeth. C. P. took off his hat and wiped his brow with a bandanna.

Philbert said, "My oldest boy, Squibby, told me what you want, Mrs. Owens. I said to him, 'Are you sure that's what she asked?' because Squibby is a boy who dreams too much and I wanted to be sure he wasn't dreaming this."

Elizabeth said, "My husband is plagued by nightmares."

"They're not nightmares," C. P. said. He scratched an X in the dirt with a stick.

Philbert said, "If they're not nightmares, what are they?"

C. P. scratched another X in the dirt.

Elizabeth waited for C. P. to speak. When he didn't she said, "A ghost. C. P. has been seeing a ghost."

170

Philbert looked at C. P. until C. P. looked at him. "This ghost is someone you know?" Philbert asked.

C. P. nodded. "Andy Cooper. I killed him some years ago."

"You have come to me with a serious matter," Philbert said. He picked up a stick and scratched his own X in the dirt at his feet. He turned to Elizabeth. "I thought my boy Wendell had the influenza when I brought him to the doctor in town. The doctor was gone and you were the only one who could help. My boy is better. I was afraid then. I am afraid now. This is a different fear."

C. P. tossed his stick aside. "Fear's got nothing to do with it. The son of a bitch woulda killed me, but I got him first. Simple as that. I can live with his ghost."

Elizabeth said, "Maybe you can, but I can't. I see what it's doing to you. You're aging—"

"I turned fifty-six last week, Elizabeth. I ain't no spring chicken."

"It's more than that, C. P. It's draining you. Every morning you look a little thinner, more tired. Like you're fading."

"I ain't fading," C. P. snapped. "I did what I had to do in Holbrook. People talking, saying I was soft on Cooper and his thieving family. Hell no, I didn't want to kill him. I knew Andy. But goddamn it, he forced my hand. They all did." He jammed his hat back on his head. "Philbert. I thank you, but we should be going. Elizabeth, dear, let's get back home. We've taken enough of the man's time."

"No," Elizabeth said. "You gave me your word, Commodore Perry Owens, and I mean to hold you to it." They stood glaring at each other in their stubbornness. C. P. made a move to the wagon, but Elizabeth didn't budge.

Philbert spoke quietly from where he had remained seated. "I saw my first ghost dance at Grass Springs." He traced circles in the dust with his stick. "I was a young man then, almost twenty, and I still remember feeling the power of that magic running through me like a flash flood. Of course, it was all a lie. The promise of raising our ancestral dead back to life and all the vanished game, too, all of it was a lie."

C. P. and Elizabeth returned to their seats.

"You can't understand," Philbert said. "No white man understands what was at stake for my people. The ghost dance was supposed to restore our lands to us. Our ancestors were to join us and drive the whites away forever. When the chief's uncle died, the shaman convinced us that our power was such that we could bring him back to life. We rested his body sitting against a pole and for three days we danced without stopping, until the stench of his decomposing body drove the truth through our hearts. We had no power. We could not change anything. We were doomed. We chased the shaman from our camp as a liar and charlatan. He never returned."

"If you have no power," C. P. said, "then what are we doing here?"

"C. P.!" Elizabeth barked.

Philbert said, "No, it's true. The ghost dance didn't give me or anyone else the power to bring the dead back to life." He snapped the stick in his hands. "But it did give me something it gave no one else. I see ghosts."

C. P. snorted. "Hell, I see ghosts."

"So you say," Philbert said. "But can you see my ghosts? Or her ghosts? Or can you only see your ghosts?"

"She doesn't have any ghosts," C. P. said.

Elizabeth said nothing.

"We all have ghosts," Philbert said. "I didn't tell anyone at the time, because I was afraid. I had nowhere to go if I was banished from my band. Besides, I was so young, I thought I was hallucinating, so I kept the secret."

C. P. kept looking at Elizabeth and at the wagon.

Philbert said, "You gave your word to your wife and I have given mine. I'll keep my word. Will you keep yours?" He turned to Elizabeth. "Did you bring the clothing I asked of you."

Elizabeth nodded. "In the wagon."

"You can change in the shed over there. When you're ready, come back here and we'll take a walk."

Elizabeth rose to her feet and C. P. followed.

"This is the damned fool-est thing I've ever done," he hissed at Elizabeth.

She didn't say anything. She retrieved the clothing from the wagon, marched to the shed, and stepped inside the shadows. "It's too small for both of us, so you can just wait your turn."

C. P. looked back toward the wikiup, but he couldn't see Philbert. "This is crazy, Elizabeth. Crazy."

He heard fabric rustling in the darkness. C. P. scanned the landscape. Juniper trees covered the hills. Their scent felt light in his nostrils. There were no clouds overhead, and the sun looked small in the cool blue air.

Elizabeth stepped out of the shed dressed in a clean, white shift. The cloth was thick enough to be opaque, but C. P. could still see the contours of her body that kept his loins responsive.

"This isn't the time and the place, you old lech," she said, smiling. "Your clothes are inside. Now get changed."

C. P. grunted and grabbed a handful of her ass.

"C. P.," she protested, but she didn't swat his hand or pull away.

In the shed C. P. took off his clothes and donned a pair of white pants and a white shirt.

"These'll be brown with dust in about a minute," he said as he stepped into the sunlight with the bundle of their regular clothes under his arm.

"Put those in the wagon," Elizabeth said. "And let's find Philbert."

They saw Philbert on a trail leading away from the wikiups. He wore only a breechcloth and moccasins, and he had covered his entire body with white chalk.

Philbert turned as they approached and led the way without speaking. He stopped at a level place on the far side of the hill. A charred cedar stump occupied a dusty circle. Faint footprints cluttered the ground.

He turned to C. P. and Elizabeth. "This thing we are about to do, I don't know how or why I am able to do it, but I can. Come and join hands with me. We will form a circle around this stump. It was a pole for the ghost dance I witnessed as a young man. Others burned it when they realized the dance could not raise the dead. I have come to it many times since because it is where this strange power of mine resides."

C. P. said, "Just what is this power?"

"I can travel to the land of the dead," Philbert said. "Actually, what I can do is travel to the world ghosts occupy and move among them. Not only that, I can take anyone with me I choose."

C. P. looked at Elizabeth.

Elizabeth said to Philbert, "Your son told me you were able to stop ghosts from haunting."

Philbert frowned. "Not exactly. I can travel to the place and time where a ghost was created, the moment of death, and

173

sometimes I can help the ghost finish whatever it is that keeps it from making the full journey to the other side. If the ghost can make the full journey, then the haunting ends."

"So, you're going to convince ol' Andy Cooper to let me sleep at night?"

"I don't know. Here, take my hands."

Elizabeth and Philbert and C. P. joined hands around the stump.

"Think about him," Philbert said. The hand holding C. P.'s started to tremble. C. P. started to release him, but Philbert held tighter.

Philbert said, "You must fight the fight again."

"What?" C. P. said. "How do I do that?"

"Remember it. Every detail. That will enable us to travel together."

"We travel?" C. P. asked. "Now wait a minute. Why does Elizabeth have to do this?"

"She doesn't."

"I'm coming," Elizabeth said. "And that's that."

C. P. looked at Philbert. "I guess she's coming. So, what's next?"

"You must fight the fight again," Philbert said. "You must kill again the man you killed before."

"How?"

Philbert said, "You'll know when we get there."

"What about you, and Elizabeth? Where will you be?" C.P. looked at Elizabeth and tried to hide the alarm in his eyes. She squeezed his hand and gave a wan smile.

Philbert squeezed C. P.'s hand. C. P. turned to him. Philbert said, "I don't know where I'll be and I don't know where your wife will be, but we will be there."

"What if I miss, what if Andy or one of the others gets me first?"

Philbert shook his head. "That must not happen."

"But," C. P. shook his head vehemently in response. "It was danged close the first time. They killed a horse that was tied up right behind me—I can still feel the breeze from the bullet on my cheek. What if it does happen? What if I get killed this time?"

"Then you will become a ghost and Elizabeth and I will have no way back."

C. P. shook his head slowly. "A good night's sleep seems hardly worth all this trouble. I've been getting used to ol' Andy's visits."

"It's killing you, C. P.," Elizabeth said. "I see it."

He looked at Philbert. "See what happens when you marry a much younger woman?"

"I wouldn't know," Philbert said. "I married an older one myself."

"Gentlemen," Elizabeth said. "Are you finished?"

"This won't take long, C. P.," Philbert said. "Just start thinking about that day. What happened?"

"Well, I'd been up on the Puerco River north of Holbrook making my way south to town. I'd been following the trail of a string of stolen Navajo horses, and a couple of Hashknife cowboys out that way said they'd seen Andy Cooper pass through with horses just the day before. I remember standing in the stable up the street from the Blevins House talking with a fellow named Brown, the livery man, and thinking I needed to clean my pistol before I went down and served the warrant. It was warm and the stable smelled pretty ripe..."

C. P. glanced over at the railroad depot down the street and saw some friends smoking and watching him. He didn't nod and neither did they. There was Philbert standing at the edge of the loading platform all covered with white chalk and looking pretty darned foolish next to the other men.

The unsaddled horse stood tied to the cottonwood tree in the yard outside the Blevins' house. As C. P. approached the house, he noticed a woman at the window, wearing a white dress, silhouetted by thin drapes and shadows.

"Elizabeth?"

He stepped onto the porch and stopped. Elizabeth was in the house! He turned and stepped back off the porch. His hands trembled, and the weight of the rifle in his arm seemed too much to bear. He looked down the street. Philbert and the other men stood motionless on the platform. He looked in the window again. Elizabeth parted the curtain ever so slightly and smiled. C. P. inhaled deeply and closed his eyes for a moment. Then he stepped onto the porch and knocked on the door.

Andy Cooper opened the door enough to speak, but not enough to reveal whether he was armed. "Well, if it isn't Sheriff Commodore Perry Owens," he said with that old smirk.

C. P. said, "Yup. How you been Andy?"

"I been good, C. P. How 'bout you."

"I've been better," C. P. said.

"How so?" Andy moved the door a smidge and shifted his weight a little to the left.

C. P. looked him in the eye. "I have a warrant for you and I want you to come along with me."

Andy didn't move a muscle. "What warrant is it, Owens?"

"The warrant for stealing horses."

Andy kept his gaze steady for a moment, and then glanced over C. P.'s shoulder at the horse.

C. P. said, "Are you ready?"

Andy Cooper said, "In a few minutes," and started to close the door.

C. P. moved his left foot and blocked the door before Andy could shut it.

Andy Cooper shouted, "No, I won't go," and aimed a pistol he'd been hiding behind his back. Without raising his Winchester, C. P. turned and fired it from the crook of his arm and shot Andy Cooper in the stomach. The bullet went through him and shattered a blue bowl on a table behind him.

C. P. stepped back on the porch and levered another round into the chamber. A woman inside the house started wailing.

Was it Elizabeth?

A second door on the porch opened slightly and John Blevins fired his pistol at C. P. He missed from a distance of four feet, but struck the horse, which reared and broke free of the tree and galloped down the street. Blevins slammed the door shut. C. P. fired his rifle through the door and hit Blevins in the shoulder and knocked him down.

C. P. heard a window being opened on the east side of the house and ran into the street. He saw Andy Cooper on his knees pointing his pistol out the open window. C. P. fired another shot through the wall of the house and hit Cooper in the right hip. Cooper dropped out of sight.

Gun smoke hung like a curtain in the still air. C. P. felt his heart beating slow, but forcefully, like a pump being worked deliberately by a tired man who needed water.

From inside the house he heard a boy's voice shouting, "Where's the son of a bitch? I'll get him."

The door flung open and the boy, Sam Houston Blevins, fifteen, pulled free of his mother's arms and charged onto the porch with a blood-covered pistol in his hand.

C. P. raised his rifle and shot the boy in the chest. The impact hurled young Blevins backwards, and he fell dying at his mother's feet. C. P. stepped back into the middle of the street, keeping an eye on the woman in case she decided to pick up the gun. He heard a commotion on the east side of the house and sidestepped in that direction. Another man, Mose Roberts, had barely cleared the window when C. P. stepped into view. Roberts raised his pistol, and C. P. shot him in the chest.

C. P. stood for a minute or so looking at the house. Through the open door, he watched two other women join Mrs. Blevins kneeling beside her dead son. All were covered with blood and wailing with sorrow. Elizabeth tried to stop the bleeding, but the boy's blood spilled over her dress and covered her hands. She looked up at C. P., her eyes wide and with tears streaming down her cheeks as if the boy she held was her own.

No one else moved in the house, although he could hear groaning from the men he'd shot.

He peered through the window into the room where Andy Cooper lay writhing in pain from the wounds to his stomach and his hip.

"The boy's dead now," C. P. said. "You'll be dead by midnight and Mose'll be dead in two days."

Andy said, "I wasn't going to shoot."

"The hell you weren't, you lying son of a bitch," C. P. said. He raised the Winchester and took aim. "I ought to just end it now."

"Do it then, you sorry bastard," Andy Cooper said. "But tell me this. What the hell are you doing, all dressed in white?"

C. P. pulled back the hammer. He said to Andy Cooper, "You hear them women wailing? They'll be wailing for you soon enough."

Elizabeth touched her husband's arm. "C. P.?"

C. P. aimed for the center of Andy Cooper's forehead.

"C. P.! Don't. You've done what needed to be done. Don't do more."

C. P. shook off her blood-stained hand and renewed his aim. He held the bead, and held it, aiming for a speck of dirt stuck to the middle of Andy Cooper's forehead.

"C. P.? Please don't shoot again."

C. P. lowered the rifle. He looked at Andy Cooper on the floor; the blood puddle beneath him had reached the edge of the rug. "Stop haunting me, you understand! Stop haunting me!"

Andy Cooper lay back in pain and bewilderment, staring at the ceiling.

C. P. and Elizabeth walked away. They met Philbert and the other men beside the dead horse.

"Did you finish the job?" one asked.

"I think I have," C. P. said.

Philbert joined hands with C. P. and Elizabeth. They closed their eyes. All C. P. could think about was the scent of juniper and the warmth of the sun.

He opened his eyes to see the charred stump. His hands were sweating in the hands of Philbert and Elizabeth. His clothes clung to him like a wet sheet.

"Did we do it?" C. P. asked Philbert.

Philbert said, "You'll find out tonight."

C. P. and Elizabeth changed back into their regular clothes. They gave the white garments to Philbert who said he would burn them. "No sense dragging anything back from where we've been," he said.

The wagon ride home took longer after dark. C. P. and Elizabeth didn't speak. When they got home, they hauled and heated water so they both could have a bath. It was midnight by the time they got to bed without having spoken a word.

C. P. fell to sleep immediately. Elizabeth listened to his snoring and in it recognized his restful repose. Smiling, she caressed his warm feet with her cold ones and closed her eyes.

Later, when she opened her eyes in the dark room, the bleeding Blevins boy lay in her arms. His dying eyes begged her to save him.

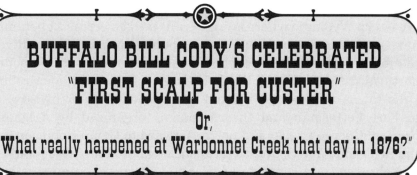

BUFFALO BILL CODY'S CELEBRATED "FIRST SCALP FOR CUSTER"
Or,
"What really happened at Warbonnet Creek that day in 1876?"

By Paul L. Hedren

Cody, Carr, Collins, and Townsend could hardly restrain themselves as their exuberance and stories poured out. On a hot afternoon at Fort Laramie, Buffalo Bill was his customary ebullient self, straight and slender and resplendent this day in a dashing showman's outfit as he promenaded in the shadow of John Collins's post traders store. Backslapping Fifth Cavalry Lieutenant Colonel Eugene Carr was at his side, as was Fort Laramie's ordinarily serene commander, Major Edwin Townsend of the Ninth Infantry. All were old friends who had not been in each other's company for a long while. Cody, now a successful touring performer, had appeared on an Eastern stage as recently as two weeks before. But it was mid-June 1876 in isolated Wyoming, in the midst of an Indian war, and these veterans were together again.

In the baking sun and with Cody the center of attention, the throng of friends kept the conversation lively. Others peered on and shouted their hellos. First Lieutenant Charles King of the Fifth Cavalry, like Carr, another Cody pal from earlier days in Nebraska and Kansas, chimed in and recalled with the celebrated scout other Indian campaigns on the plains. Among all, confidence ran unchecked. Recollected one veteran Fifth Cavalryman: "All the old boys in the regiment upon seeing General Carr and Cody together, exchanged confidences...that with such a leader and scout they could get away with all the Sitting Bulls and Crazy Horses in the Sioux tribe."

This was not the only day of commotion at Fort Laramie in this pulsating Centennial year of the nation. Positioned on the prairie of eastern Wyoming where myriad trails necked across a glistening new iron bridge spanning the turbulent North Platte River, the fort's denizens had watched steady streams of traffic bound northward to the luring Black Hills gold fields and such robust Hills towns as Custer City and Deadwood; and northwestward to Fort Fetterman and the campaigns organized by Brigadier General George Crook; and northeastward to Camp Robinson and the Red Cloud and Spotted Tail agencies in the Pine Ridge country of Nebraska; and south to Cheyenne and the glistening rails of the Union Pacific. Since 1849, in fact, Fort Laramie had protected such trail traffic, but now the pace was all the more intense, the gleam of gold in prospector's eyes more immediate, and the fear of Indian trouble, especially along the Black Hills road straight north, disquieting, and on too many occasions alarmingly real.

Fort Laramie's summer garrison was pitifully small, with but single cavalry and infantry companies tending the post's internal business and the ceaseless demands for emigrant protection on the trails and such wearying duty as telegraph line maintenance. The fort's other horse and foot companies were long absent, having joined Crook's Big Horn and Yellowstone Expedition in northern Wyoming. At last report, the general's column was preparing for a movement into Montana, but that was old news.

Especially stirring to Fort Laramie's inhabitants this June was the streaming arrival of these Fifth Cavalry companies. Fresh from service at forts Hayes and Leavenworth in Kansas, and before that engaged in prolonged and bloody warfare with Apache Indians in Arizona, the Fifth was among many new cavalry and infantry outfits directed by Lieutenant General Philip Sheridan to this all-out war with the Sioux.

Soon eight companies of the Fifth were outfitting at a cavalry camp located mid-way between the fort and the North Platte bridge, and with horses to shoe, leather gear to repair, missing equipment to replace, and munitions and rations to be fully issued and packed, the troopers were plenty busy. When opportunity allowed, the men also stole away to Collins's well-stocked traders store, where tastier foodstuffs, candies, alternative kerchiefs and hats, and all-important chewing and smoking tobaccos lured those with loose change in their pockets.

At Sheridan's direction, the Fifth was bound for duty on the Black Hills Road north of Fort Laramie, where, until directed again, they would safeguard this heavily used prospector's and freighter's road, especially where it crossed the infamous Powder River Trail. That latter avenue was the principal pathway west for thousands of Sioux and Northern Cheyenne Indians who resided, at least seasonally, at the Nebraska agencies. This year, the lures were both the vast buffalo herds in northern Wyoming and eastern Montana, and also Crazy Horse's and Sitting Bull's warrior camps.

With Carr in the lead and Baptiste "Little Bat" Garnier scouting the front (Cody momentarily side tripping to Camp Robinson with General Sheridan), some three hundred and fifty officers and men of the Fifth Cavalry departed Fort Laramie on June 22, bearing northward toward the Black Hills. Sergeant John Powers of Company A remembered, "The boys are all in good spirits and eager to be in active service." The trooper's glee at having joined this great Indian war was shaken just the next day, however, when news came via Fort Laramie that Crook had engaged the Sioux on Rosebud Creek, Montana, on June 17, but instead of pressing any advantage was retiring to a base camp in northern Wyoming. Retiring from the scene of combat was not a good sign.

The Fifth's spirits were shaken all the more on July 6, when Buffalo Bill led a Fort Laramie courier straight to field headquarters to deliver devastating news that Custer and nearly half of his Seventh Cavalry had been annihilated on Montana's Little Big Horn River on June 25. The pall was heavy. "Few words were spoken," remembered Lieutenant King, "the camp… stilled in soldierly mourning." Quietly the officers speculated that surely now they would be ordered north to Crook. Thus far, their meanderings on the Black Hills Road were fruitless, with rarely an Indian seen. The Indian's Powder River Trail was unusually quiet.

On July 12, the Fifth received orders to return to Fort Laramie, hurriedly resupply there, and embark for Crook's camp on Goose Creek in the foothills of the Big Horn Mountains. Crook was concentrating additional troops before renewing his campaign on the northern front. Colonel Wesley Merritt now commanded the regiment, having arrived in the Fifth's Cheyenne River camp on July 1. A Sheridan protégé and Custer peer, Merritt hurried his regiment southward toward Fort Laramie anxious to refurbish and depart for more active campaign country.

Within an easy day's ride of the fort, however, on July 13 Merritt learned from Townsend at Fort Laramie that hundreds of Cheyenne Indians were reportedly bolting Red Cloud Agency and were bound, so it was said, for Crazy Horse's camp in Montana. In the wake of the army's Powder River, Rosebud Creek, and Little Big Horn disasters, this was disquieting news in military circles. Merritt promptly dispatched Major Thaddeus Stanton, one of Crook's emissaries, and Captain Emil Adam's Company C directly to Camp Robinson to investigate the story.

In a breakneck ride to Camp Robinson and back, Stanton confirmed the news that, indeed, as many as eight hundred Northern Cheyennes and some Sioux had departed the agency to join Crazy Horse, and were traveling westward on the Powder River Trail. Trusting that Sheridan and Crook would prefer that he intercept and turn back these potentially hostile Indians rather than continue the trail to Fort Laramie, Merritt promptly countermarched north to the small infantry camp on Sage Creek in the Hat Creek Breaks, and then turned east into northwestern Nebraska to an intersection of the Powder River Trail at its Warbonnet Creek crossing. Ever after, the officers and men of the Fifth Cavalry reveled in this heroic ride, traversing some eighty-five miles in a thirty-one-hour forced march to place themselves immediately in front of unsuspecting Cheyennes.

Only as the sun rose on July 17 did Merritt and his men fully comprehend their surroundings. They had come to this Warbonnet Creek camp well after dark, but now they could see the creek's high cut banks immediately east in front of them. That cover was perfect—it could hide a regiment. Protruding from the broad, elevated flats beyond the cut banks were two conical hills, each affording perfect views of the Powder River Trail running onto them, as well as miles of rolling prairie stretching all around, and the Pine Ridge to the south, and Black Hills to the north, the latter barely twenty miles away. Merritt immediately ordered observers to the hilltops. Cody's pal and ever after the fight's ablest chronicler, First Lieutenant King, occupied the southern hill, while trooper Christian Madsen, who later became a famous Oklahoma lawman, was posted on the northern one.

Buffalo Bill, meanwhile, seized an opportunity in the breaking light to ride a wide route eastward in search of the Indians, doubtless not far away. Back at the creek, at about 4:15 p.m. King and an enlisted man from his company were the first to spot Indians, a small band of riders who had come over a ridge a mile or so away. These warriors, including Beaver Heart, Buffalo Road, and Yellow Hair, were members of Morning Star's band of Northern Cheyennes. These wolves or scouts had been sent ahead to look for soldiers. The main Indian camp was but a few miles behind.

Quickly the Cheyennes saw troopers, not the secreted Fifth Cavalry companies well concealed beneath Warbonnet's tall banks, but instead two couriers advancing ahead of Merritt's distant and plainly visible supply train ambling forward on the soldier trail. Believing that they were the hunters and not the prey, the warriors furtively pressed westward down a broad dry swale leading straight to Warbonnet Creek, and seven companies of well-hidden Fifth Cavalry.

As the drama unfolded, Merritt, Carr, and Cody, the latter having just returned from his daybreak scout, joined King on the southern hillock and assessed the lively scene. Behind and below them they saw the regiment, the men having closed tight on the creek's high banks where they waited, dismounted and fidgeting with their weapons and mounts. Ahead they saw the Cheyenne warriors cautiously advancing westward to cut off the unsuspecting couriers. And in the distant rear, Cody and the officers saw two equally unsuspecting troopers riding pell-mell toward their comrades, whom they could not see but whose trail was plain and barely hours old.

Buffalo Bill was the first to recognize the unique opportunity unfolding before him. By now always the showman, Cody was appropriately dressed this morning in a colorful Mexican vaquero outfit straight from the stage and featuring a triple-wide leather belt and large silver-washed buckle, crimson silk shirt, flared pants of black velvet and ornamented with silver braid and buttons, and a broad-brimmed beaver felt hat. Colorful, even gaudy in the extreme, this was the outfit Cody wore in his current play, *Scouts of the Plains*, and here was his chance to validate it as the genuine attire of a plainsman. But appropriate dress was but half of the prospect. Cody saw where he and a handful of followers could easily whip those Indians coming toward them while the rest of the regiment corralled the distant camp. Merritt concurred, telling everyone to get in place and ordering King to give the word at the appropriate moment. Cody, his close pal Jonathan "Buffalo Chips" White, and several men from King's Company K scampered to the mouth of the long coulee that the Indians were now descending, while Merritt and Carr positioned themselves at the base of the hillock below King to lead the cavalry companies when they ascended from the creek bottom.

A few minutes passed. Adrenaline pulsed. King cautiously peered at the Indians through his field glasses, his hatless brow barely rising above the crest of the hill. Southwest several hundred yards away King could see Cody and his small clutch of followers. Behind and below, King could see his superiors, and behind them against the creek walls were the near three hundred men of the Fifth Cavalry, and all were poised to surprise these unsuspecting Cheyennes.

The warriors closed to within ninety yards of Warbonnet Creek when King jumped up and shouted down to Cody, "NOW, lads, in with you!"

Instantly, Cody and his followers spurred their horses out of the creek bottom, confronted the utterly surprised warriors fanned in the near distance, and loosed a volley from their Springfields. King fired too. The startled Cheyennes returned fire toward both Cody and King. After the initial exchange, those supporting Cody sought cover in the meanders of the ravine, and so did those riding with Yellow Hair. Alone, both Cody and Yellow Hair fired rounds directly at each other, Cody's shot hitting Yellow Hair's horse and causing it to tumble. Cody's horse stumbled too, perhaps in the soft earth of an animal burrow. Cody quickly fired again, this time killing the young warrior.

In the ensuing years, this deliberate and careful exchange of carbine fire between two skilled marksmen would be described and embellished as a highly dramatic hand-to-hand duel, and with Yellow Hair often described as a sub-chief or chief instead of a plain-fact capable warrior. These fabrications certainly made great fodder for show business publicity and a colorful action scene on the stage. And Cody shamelessly exploited the embellishments, often to the chagrin of other Fifth Cavalry veterans present during the skirmish who winced at the superfluities. In fact, however, the

Cody-Yellow Hair "fight" did amount to mortal combat, with each warrior facing the other's bullets and only one surviving.

Cody rode over to the fallen warrior as several Fifth Cavalry companies passed by. Sergeant John Hamilton of Company D offers the best survey of the scene, having ridden within yards of the dismounted Buffalo Bill. Yellow Hair was laying face down, Hamilton recalled, with his arms folded under his head. He wore a paint bag, a scalp of yellow hair from some young white woman (thus his name, Yellow Hair), tin bracelets on his arms, war feathers, a neck charm, beaded belt, and a cotton American flag for a breechcloth.

As soldiers came on, Cody pealed off Yellow Hair's top knot, a circle of scalp about two inches in diameter with flowing black hair about fifteen inches long. He waved it aloft and amid a raucous cheer bellowed out:

"The first scalp for Custer!"

Buffalo Bill collected Yellow Hair's feather bonnet, shield, bridle, quirt, firearms, and scalp, which he later boxed and mailed to a friend in Rochester, New York. The regiment, meanwhile, scampered after the scattering Cheyennes. In their hurried flight back to Red Cloud Agency, the tribesmen littered the prairie with blankets, foodstuffs, and other weighty items. The regiment incurred no casualties in the fight and chase, aside from one private hurt when his horse toppled down an embankment. Yellow Hair was the lone Indian casualty. Remarkably, after the Fifth Cavalry gained the Red Cloud Agency near the close of the day, many of the Cheyennes came to the soldiers' bivouac to talk the episode over with them. At the agencies, enemies in the morning could be friends at night.

At first blush, and compared with other battles and skirmishes of the bloody and uniquely protracted Great Sioux War of 1876–1877, the affair at Warbonnet Creek, Nebraska, on July 17, 1876, seems hardly worth a mention. Only one casualty was recorded, not hundreds like at the Little Big Horn or dozens so common at places like Rosebud, Slim Buttes, Red Fork of the Powder River, Tongue River, and Muddy Creek.

But for the first time in the dreadful initial months of the war, Sheridan's army could boast of a successful encounter with the northern Indians, who until then had held such powerful sway over the frontier regulars. Warbonnet Creek did offer a celebrated "first scalp for Custer," itself an act of atonement for the horrors of the Little Big Horn. And many of the Cheyennes never made it to Crazy Horse's or Sitting Bull's camps, through certainly some did later.

Warbonnet's lasting importance emerged some time after the war. The "first scalp" episode became a highly memorialized public drama repeated for decades in Buffalo Bill's stage and Wild West shows and on the silver screen in a number of Cody movies, including his own celebrated 1913 film, *Buffalo Bill's Indian Wars*. Warbonnet, too, has been featured on an inordinate number of well-developed canvases by some of America's foremost artists and illustrators, including Charles Russell, Irving Bacon, and Robert Lindneux, rivaling Little Big Horn in the pantheon of American Indian wars battle art. Today, Warbonnet Creek is venerated in two on-site cobblestone monuments at a site that is still virtually lost in distant northwestern Nebraska. But perhaps most importantly, Warbonnet Creek is indelibly burned into the psyche of those who, to this day, are captivated by the events, large and small, of the Great Sioux War, America's greatest Indian war, and characters so compelling and true as William F. "Buffalo Bill" Cody.

FOR FURTHER READING: Paul Hedren unblushingly recommends two of his own works, *First Scalp for Custer, The Skirmish at Warbonnet Creek, Nebraska, July 17, 1876* (Lincoln: Nebraska State Historical Society, 1980; rev. 2005); and "The Contradictory Legacies of Buffalo Bill Cody's 'First Scalp for Custer,'" *Montana The Magazine of Western History* 55 (Spring 2005), 16-35.

SUN CITY, KANSAS (1903)

By Red Shuttleworth

Sightless, leg stumps
From the buffalo hunting trail,
Wesley Carter roosts
At the Baptist church,
A boar skull on his lap.
Some days he is naked,
Lesions here and there.
At Easter the children
Bring muffins and lilies.
Carter lifts the skull,
A greenish-yellow cracked thing,
Above his grizzled head,
This is our hero, General Custer.
There's a cruelty to surprise the cruel.

CONTEMPORARY WEST

DEATH COMES TO DEACONVILLE

By Johnny D. Boggs

Deacon Dutchover never had any luck. I mean, this town's named after him, yet you won't find his photograph in the historical display at the Visitors' Center. We used to have a little Historical Society Museum, but that's gone, and hardly anyone goes to the Visitors' Center now, except to park illegally and walk over to Wild Bill's Slots and Video Poker. Most visitors never make it that far into town anyway, hijacked into casinos on the outskirts of what once was Deaconville proper, or winding up the road to this highfalutin' Silver Lode Resort, Spa and Casino on the mountainside overlooking our historic town.

But I was talking about Deacon Dutchover. He wasn't a deacon, and the surname he was born with wasn't Dutchover. We know he was German. My grandmother told me that much, just as she told that interviewer with the Federal Writers Project in 1934. When the founder of this town enlisted in the 5th U.S. Cavalry, the soldier filling out the enlistment papers—Deacon Dutchover couldn't read or write English, but none of you would know that, would you?—was having a hard time of it, so the officer in charge said, "Hell, that man's Dutch all over." Thus, he became Dutchover. Deacon, we think, was a nickname given to him by the troopers of the 5th. He was a pious man.

He knew something about mining, though. Where he learned it has been lost to history, but Deaconville wouldn't exist if he hadn't been chasing Indians sometime in 1879 and

191

found promising-looking ore. He and a handful of buddies made a note of it, and when their enlistments ended the following year, they returned to prospect. They found paydirt, filed their claims. Placer mining then; the hard-rock mines, stamp mills and smelters wouldn't come about till long after Deacon Dutchover was dead.

Which didn't take long, because, like I said, Deacon Dutchover never had much luck. He had struck it rich when he was jumped by Indians and killed. His buddies found his body, and when log cabins, false-front buildings and adobe shacks started to replace the tents and lean-tos, his partners honored his passing by naming the growing boomtown after him. Deaconville or Dutchover City was put to a vote. Deaconville won. Personally, I always thought Dutchover City sounded better.

The gold rush didn't last long, because the first streams played out, and the parasites who came to towns like these in the 1880s couldn't hack a winter in the Rockies. Back then, at least. Winter hasn't stopped parasites recently, has it? Anyway, Indians were also raiding, and a correspondent for the *Denver Republican* noted that in the summer of 1881 alone, seventeen prospectors had been murdered by Indians around Deaconville's claims. The next summer, most people lit out for Bromide Gulch forty-one miles up what's now the Silver And Gold Expressway when gold was discovered there, and our town's log cabins, false-front buildings and adobe shacks were pretty much vacant by 1882. Deaconville died...but not really.

One man stayed put, you see, and, if you ever stepped outside of this fine establishment, you'd find his photograph, grainy as all get-out, at the Visitors' Center on Front Street. His name was Philip Pye, and he had seen maybe the same thing Deacon Dutchover saw in those rocks and streambeds. He knew that surface veins never lasted long, that you had to dig deeper to find the really rich ore. He was a hard-rock miner, and when he opened Pye Number 1, the second rush to Deaconville was born. Pye Number 1. That reminds me that you used to be able to get Pye Number 1 at Diana's Place, usually apple, sometimes strawberry-rhubarb, even huckleberry when Diana was of a mind. But the diner's long gone. Anyway, Philip Pye tried to persuade the newcomers to change the name of the town to Pyeville. He was vain, I mean to tell you. Glance at that picture of him at the historical display in the Visitors' Center.

He looks like one stuck-up SOB. Luckily, his proposal was laughed down, and that was a good thing, I guess. Who'd want to visit a town called Pyeville?

Bromide Gulch had stamp mills already, but the good men of Deaconville did not want to send their ore over the mountain to their nemesis city. Instead, they used a bunch of old peasant women, all of them Mexicans, to crush the ore using *arastras*. That's no way to run a gold mine, if you ask me. Think about it: Using *arastras* is not much different than using stones to grind grain. Eventually, though, the old Mexican women and their *arastras* went away as the stamp mills came to Deaconville, freighted all the way from Kansas City.

Other mines discovered richer veins, but not gold. When Sergeant Levi McClure filed on the Zelma Mine, only a mile from where Deacon Dutchover was killed—you used to be able to take tours into the Zelma from Memorial Day through mid-October—silver began to replace gold as this town's bread and butter. The *Santa Fe Daily New Mexican* called Deaconville "the richest, highest and most gorgeous town in the Rockies." That's why, today, you see all the signs on the state highways that proclaim: Rich—High—Gorgeous.

Bromide Gulch's newspaper took exception to this, noting in the *Weekly Telegram's* June 12, 1883 edition that in the past year Deaconville had been "the site of 412 fights with fists, 39 fights with pistols, 58 fights with dirks or Bowies, 147 fights with spurred cocks and 15 fights among hydrophobic dogs."

But overall, back then, life was good in Deaconville. Indian troubles would permanently end within a few years. Quickly, we had some one hundred buildings and as many as 2,000 residents. In 1884, according to the sole surviving copy of the *Deaconville Independent Examiner*, there were two butchers shops, a confectionary, apothecary's shop, Chinese laundry, two hotels, the largest one now being the Lucky Lady Hotel & Casino (although it's the second, no third, incarnation of the hotel), two boarding houses, fifteen saloons and a dressmaker's shop.

The dressmaker's shop was owned and operated by Virginia Bitterman. She was the first "respectable" lady to arrive in Deaconville. The men of Deaconville decided they needed good women if their town was to survive, so they offered free lots to the first ten unmarried ladies who agreed to move to Deaconville.

193

Apparently, the founding fathers of Deaconville didn't consider the Mexican peasant ladies, old and hard as they were, respectable. Maybe they were already married.

So, Virginia Bitterman was the first "respectable" single woman to arrive in Deaconville. They built her a house on the corner of Allen and Carmichael streets—we've never been able to figure out how Allen and Carmichael got their names—and she opened her dressmaker's shop on Second Street. Soon there were other "respectable" ladies in Deaconville, and Alex MacKin earned a position on the town council when it was announced that he was the father of the first child born in Deaconville. It did not matter that the mother of his daughter was not "respectable."

Shortly after that, civic leaders proposed that a church be built because having no place of worship in a town called Deaconville seemed repugnant. On September 3, 1885, the nondenominational Deaconville Meeting House opened to two baptisms and a funeral.

The funeral was for Marshal Jim Lane—no relation to the Jim Lane of the Kansas-Missouri border wars infamy—and his funeral used to be reenacted every Labor Day weekend from 1930 to 1963. It was a big to-do in Deaconville, with women dressed in period attire sobbing oh-so-beautifully, and pallbearers wearing six-shooters and passing a whiskey bottle as they carried the coffin to Boot Hill, which was never called Boot Hill, by the way.

What people forgot was the rest of the story. Jim Lane was killed by George Anderson, who was promptly shot down by Marshal Lane's posse, then unceremoniously dumped into his prospector's hole. During our Labor Day festivities, George Anderson was always portrayed as a mean *hombre* dressed all in black and smoking a foul cigar, straight out of an old-fashion melodrama. The truth is that George Anderson was a black man, a former slave, who had been run off his claims twice but kept coming back. Blacks couldn't legally file on a claim back then, but it didn't stop George. So the town leaders talked Jim Lane into arresting George, maybe stretching his neck, but George put up a fight no one expected. He killed the town marshal, and the town killed him.

The NAACP began protesting our Labor Day celebration, and in 1963, Deaconville was back in the headlines. We even got written up in *Time* magazine, although it wasn't a long article. The Jim Lane festivities ceased, and Deaconville started to die again.

Just like it almost died in 1885. Three months after Jim Lane's funeral, the first fire swept through town.

It started at Forrester's Saloon, when Old Man Forrester went into the back room, and, apparently, forgot he was smoking a cigar when he stuck his head into a whiskey barrel to check on how much forty-rod was left. Or, it started in one of the cribs behind Forrester's Saloon, when a prostitute, high on opium, accidentally knocked over a lantern. We don't really know for sure, as neither Old Man Forrester nor the prostitute survived the conflagration. The crib and saloon burned to the ground, as did practically all of Front and Second streets. It could have been much worse, but our valiant bucket brigade managed to stop the fire, saving Virginia Bitterman's dressmaker's shop and the rest of town.

Winter came early, and a number of people left, leaving charred ruins and ashes, and others decided to abandon town for Bromide Gulch, lured by Bromide's promises (lies) printed in the *Gold Leader*, saying that Deaconville was dead, and that the future resided in Bromide Gulch, "home of two newspapers, three churches, the Terra Gold Stamp Mill, and gold, gold, GOLD!" Yet, come spring, reports began circulating as far away as Topeka that the Denver & Rio Grande was going to run a spur line to Deaconville. Those proved not just rumors, and before the first rails started to be laid, Bromide Gulch had turned into practically a ghost town, and the Terra Gold Stamp Mill was freighted over the mountain to Deaconville.

A new Deaconville went up, more wooden facades, more picket and log houses. A stage line was put in, and a telegraph line established. Bromide Gulch lost its status as county seat to Deaconville in 1886, and Railroad Day became an annual celebration after the first locomotive pulled into Deaconville on July 27, 1887.

The truth is the railroad would never have reached Deaconville if it hadn't been for those Chinese workers, who soon established a virtual Chinatown on the town's east side. On Christmas Eve, 1887, another mob added another blight to Deaconville's history, deciding to rid our town of the Chinese. They came through that night with torches, Winchesters, and clubs, sweeping through Chinatown like the plague.

Any idea who came out Christmas morning to help those poor people? It was the prostitutes. They walked through wreckage and ruin, the dead and the maimed. They turned into nurses, and, in some cases, undertakers. Now, I'm not saying those soiled doves all had hearts of gold, but that's a story not many people remember about Deaconville. You won't find it in the historical display at the Visitors' Center, and Virginia Bitterman certainly never mentioned it in her diary, first published in 1932, which we used to sell at the Historical Society Museum before it went belly-up.

More people remember the second fire, the one that changed the face of Deaconville forever. That happened the following spring. It was April 3 or 4, 1888, when The Big Fire swept through town, wiping out six blocks. It began in what was left of Chinatown. Some believed that a tramp started a fire to keep warm, and the fire spread through the ruins that nobody had thought to clean up. A few blamed a spark from a Denver & Rio Grande locomotive. Others suggested that it was a lightning strike sent by a vengeful God. Unlike the previous inferno, this one claimed no lives, but once again Bromide Gulch, hanging on like grim death, started preaching again, or praying once more, that Deaconville was dead.

Once again, Deaconville wasn't about to be buried. Not with all that silver to be mined, not with a town so rich, so high, so gorgeous. It became even more gorgeous after The Big Fire. When Deaconville was rebuilt, gone were the buildings with the false fronts. Up went red granite, transported from Jensen's Quarry, and brick, transported by the railroad. When you step into the Lucky Lady, you'll notice the floors as well as the red granite walls. Those floors are the original imported Philippine mahogany, put in because Hans Dieter, who owned the hotel then, wanted to show everyone how rich he was, and Philippine mahogany cost one dollar a board foot. Last time I checked, Philippine mahogany still cost about a dollar a board foot.

A good portion of the town's population started staying in Deaconville permanent, even during the winter.

I'm not sure if Deaconville would have really turned into what it has become today if not for those opulent buildings. Look at the Grand Mountain Opera House, or I should say the Grand Mountain Casino. When the great singer Obdulia Renault and her thespian husband, Harold J. Monroe III, arrived for a one-week engagement, back when the Grand Mountain really was an opera house, our town leaders laid out a walkway of thirty-two ingots of solid silver so the great entertainers wouldn't have to touch our dirty streets. That's why you'll find thirty-two bricks painted silver on the doorsteps there.

But don't think that Deaconville was Utopia, a paradise in one of the West's richest mining districts. Not then, and certainly not now. We had our smelters, our railroad by then. Imagine the constant noise of cam-driven hammers at the mines and the locomotives of the Denver & Rio Grande. I can taste mercury amalgam, and smell the sulfur. I can feel heat from the smelters. The water was horrible, undrinkable in some places, and it's a miracle the big cholera outbreak of 1889 killed only fifteen. Forests were torn apart. Practically overnight, they vanished. Killing trees for the sake of progress isn't something developers started in the 20th Century. Our forefathers did it, too.

Yet, all that didn't stop Deaconville's glory, like when *The New York Times*—that's *The New York Times*!—reported, "In the monotonous, dreary regions of the inhospitable Southwest mountains, Deaconville shines as an oasis. If silver is king, then Deaconville is the queen city of the territories."

She was queen, too, until 1893. Then, she died again, and this time it looked as if Lazarus, the Phoenix, whatever you want to call her, would rise no more.

I shouldn't have to give you a history lesson about the Panic of '93. You could read about it in our historical display at the Visitors' Center. The bank failures. The railroad failures. The collapse of the silver market. Mines shut down. Even the Zelma, which was our biggest employer then, ceased production for a while. It wasn't just Deaconville, of course. About an hour north up the road, if you look carefully, you'll find an historical marker the state put up in 1957. That's all that's left of Bromide Gulch, where the mines had started to play out long before the 1890s national financial collapse.

People started leaving Deaconville. "Only the most hardy remain," the *Denver Republican* reported. Or the foolish, the reporter should have written. The last train pulled out of Deaconville in 1897, a year after we lost the county seat. According to the census of 1900, the population of Deaconville was 172.

Deaconville became an empty shell of brick and granite, but she just wouldn't, couldn't, give up the ghost. There would be

197

rebirths here and there. Coal was in demand during World War I, and the Denver & Rio Grande ran again along those narrow gauge rails for a couple of years, then stopped, forever. Deaconville's days had to be numbered.

Only now came the dredge boats. The first one tore up the river in 1920. All those stones you see along the highway? Those are the product of dredge-boat mining. By the 1930s, there were mountains of tailings left by those god-awful boats. Piles and piles of gravel, dirt, sand, rocks, dug up by dredges searching for one last bit of paying ore. The water became even more polluted, but the dredges meant work, so Deaconville held on.

She boomed a bit in the 1930s, when gold rose to $35 an ounce. Will Rogers stopped by once to give a speech at the Grand Mountain Opera House, and Tom Mix stayed two weeks to film one of his last Western movies. It was about then that Deaconville discovered there was gold to be found in tourists dollars, so, in addition to Railroad Day, we started putting on Old Deaconville Days, complete with Jim Lane's funeral and George Anderson's death. There was even talk about bringing back the railroad, but the Great Depression ended those rumors, and Deaconville fell relatively silent until Pearl Harbor.

If you ask me, the best thing to come out of World War II was Order L-203, which the War Production Board passed on the fifteenth of October in 1942. That stopped all dredge-boat mining. Stopped mining for precious ore, really. Of course, there was also a demand for steel, and that's why the railroad tracks were dismantled in '43. No, there'd never be another train to Deaconville. No point in celebrating Railroad Day when there was no train, not even rails, so we quit observing that holiday.

After WWII came some attempts at placer mining, by greenhorns mostly, and a few people tried to make the hard-rock mines profitable, but mining has always been ticklish. You're foolproof one day and plain fool the next. Zinc was in demand for a spell, and coal turned a bit of a profit until the trains, and practically everything else, no longer needed coal.

Deaconville's population dropped to just under a hundred, except during Old Deaconville Days, when we saw that grow to upwards of eight-fifty, and even more than that in 1963 when all the newspapers and television reporters came to town along with the marchers of the NAACP. I don't blame them at all, either, and

I think it was a good thing to end that George Anderson spectacle. One of those protesters, turns out, was a man from Hollywood. He'd been blacklisted in the 1950s, so he was a big supporter of Civil Rights in the 1960s. He came with the NAACP, but he also secretly took a liking to Deaconville, and in 1968, George B. Schwartz bought the Grand Mountain Opera House and the Lucky Lady Hotel.

Likely, you've never heard of George B. Schwartz, but if you watch old movies on TV, you've seen some of the Westerns he produced for Paramount in the 1960s. They aren't very good, B-flicks with bad actors who had grown long in tooth but still needed money for Lucky Strikes and Jack Daniel's. I never met him, but I'd see him in town, driving a Cadillac Coupe DeVille down Front Street like he was Ben-Hur. They tell me George B. Schwartz was a big gambler, and loved to play all-night poker, so he'd invite his friends from California to come to Deaconville. Unlike Tom Mix, George B. Schwartz never made any movies here, and after Paramount fired him in 1971, he sold the hotel and opera house, and retired to Palm Springs, where he died of lung cancer in 1977.

Yet George B. Schwartz knew a lot of players in Hollywood, and one of those was P.J. Knox, a second-unit director whose son, you know, is Adam Knox. That's Adam Knox, who produced, starred in and directed *Death Comes to Deaconville*. That's the movie, they say, which started the rebirth of the Hollywood Western in 1989, winning its four Academy Awards, two Golden Globes, a Spur and a Wrangler. They filmed it on location, restoring the ruins of Deaconville into a lively city. I thought it was funny how they turned the Woolworth's into a whorehouse, but there was no truth to anything in Adam Knox's script. He never once visited the Historical Society Museum, yet ninety percent of the tourists who come to Deaconville—those who get past the casinos—believe everything they've seen in that movie. Don't get me wrong. When that movie opened, I drove the sixty-one miles roundtrip to the county seat to see it, and I kept on seeing it. I must have watched that movie on the big screen six or seven times. I'd hoped they might film more movies in Deaconville, but Hollywood's Western revival didn't last long. Within a year or two, everyone was complaining how they don't make Westerns anymore.

Still, Adam Knox took a fancy to Deaconville. He liked the area. He liked the solitude, loved the view—hell, everyone raves about our views—and he became fascinated by the fact that one year after *Death Comes to Deaconville* won all those awards, the civic leaders of Deaconville campaigned for the return of legalized gambling. In 1990, a measure was put on the state ballot, and when it passed, limited stakes gambling was allowed in our commercial district, all profits earmarked for education and historic preservation. Yeah, right. That's where all that money went.

The governor herself came down on the following Labor Day to stick a coin in the slot machine at the Lucky Lady and pull that first lever amid the flashbulbs of cameras and the cheers of Deaconville's citizenry.

I clapped, too. I didn't know better.

Nobody knew what gambling would do to Deaconville. Likewise, folks thought it was a great idea when Adam Knox returned with plans to build a $13 million resort on the mountainside overlooking town. People started driving from three or four states just to visit Deaconville. I mean, we'd get tourists before gambling was legalized, but mostly history buffs, campers, hikers and dropouts from society. Or folks who were really, really lost. Now, like the advertising campaign said, it was "Destination: Deaconville." At first, they only came on the weekends, but soon this town was full seven days a week, sometimes even in the dead of winter. In the 1880s, most miners had the good sense to flee the Rockies before the first snowfall. Funny how people change in a short century or so.

We just didn't know.

Yes, I like history, and I love my town. I was born here. My grandfather worked in Deaconville's mines, my father worked in Deaconville's mines, even when hardly anybody worked in Deaconville's mines, and I worked in Deaconville's mines, mostly as a tour guide, but I worked. Now I found myself watching Deaconville morph into something... I don't know what the right word is, but it wasn't right.

I bought comic books at the Woolworth's. My father would stop there for a tin of aspirin and a Coca-Cola on his way home. There were memories in that old building, but it was the first to go. In 1992, it became Triple 7 Slots.

Wild Bill's Slots and Video Poker—Wild Bill Hickok, by the way, never came within 100 miles of Deaconville—is where I used to spend many an hour at the Historical Society Museum, and what galls me is the fact that the carpenters hired to remodel that place had as little respect for history as did the new owners. I didn't even know the museum had closed down, and when I came through town one day, my head splitting from the *ching-ching-ching-ching* of a thousand slot machines up and down Front Street, I saw the carpenters tossing all those historical artifacts into a trash dumpster. I yelled at them, but they ignored me, and a couple of them laughed when I climbed into that dumpster to salvage what I could.

Oh, not all of it was thrown away. Some of it was stolen. I have no idea whatever happened to Jim Lane's .44-40 Colt, although I found his badge on eBay eighteen years later, and tried to get it, but it sold for a whole lot more money than I could afford. Most of the stuff you see at our historical display in the Visitors' Center is what I saved from the dumpster, including the lock of Virginia Bitterman's hair. That photograph of the *Molly J.*, Deaconville's first dredge boat, wasn't always ripped. You can blame that on the carpenters, or the consortium that owns Wild Bill's Slots and Video Poker.

The closest gas station is fifty miles away on the Silver And Gold Expressway. You spotted all those billboards on your way up, and if your customers didn't gas up on the way here, they'd fill their tanks on the way home. *If they have any money left.* Well, we used to have a gas station in town. That's right. Here in Deaconville. Billy Floyd would pump your gas and clean your windshield long before those concepts went out of fashion, but Billy sold out, and I can't blame him, and moved to Destin, Florida. Where his gas station once stood is now covered with asphalt at Gold City.

I'm not a prude. I gamble. I've lost as much money betting on the Broncos as anyone around here. Men have been gambling in Deaconville since the days of Deacon Dutchover and Phil Pye. It's documented that even Virginia Bitterman favored the horse races they used to run west of town. I voted to pass that law that changed Deaconville forever.

It was a mistake.

No one realized what Adam Knox and gambling would do to this town. When this resort was being built up here, we locals called it "The Eye In The Sky." Thought it was funny. But it hasn't been funny for a long, long time.

Not with taxes on our property soaring, the prices driven up by all these newcomers from Hollywood, Atlantic City, Vegas, Houston. More and more developers arrived in town, to build upscale homes, condos, luxury hotels, and stupid, fifty-acre ranchettes. To ruin our views, like this place spoils this mountainside. To destroy our town. You can't find a decent meal in town. Diana's Place is now a cigarette and six-pack shop.

People even started losing their homes. They couldn't afford to live in Deaconville anymore. Adam Knox finally got sick of the whole thing, the crowds, the noise, the headaches, and sold his interest in his resort and went back to California, although I read on the Internet that he recently bought a new ranch outside of Livingston, Montana.

And what did you new investors of this grand Silver Lode Resort, Spa and Casino decide to do? You decided you needed more land. Wanted to expand. Had to, you said, to compete with those big-name places that built up Deaconville, saying to hell with our preservation building code. Demanded to add a golf course!

You decided that you needed to buy the land that was the Zelma Mine. You bet I protested that one. I wrote letters to the governor, Congress, the newspapers, Adam Knox's production company and the estate of George B. Schwartz. I pleaded to historical preservation societies that I was fighting for Deaconville. I found a hotshot lawyer to fight for my rights, to fight to save Deaconville. He wrote a bunch of letters till he spent all of my retainer. Then he wouldn't take my phone calls. Maybe y'all bought him off.

You said I was a crazy old man. A recluse. A hermit living alone in a dark mine, frightening children, pretending to give tours 1,237 feet into Grand Mountain at the Zelma. You said the place should be condemned, that it was nothing short of a miracle that no child had been hurt, even killed, in that damp, dark place. You pointed out that the place wasn't handicap accessible. You pointed out that I had been dishonorably discharged from the United States Army. That I had threatened you peace-loving owners of the Silver Lode Resort, Spa and Casino with bodily harm. You said that the Zelma had to be sealed up forever.

The Zelma. You've never set foot in that mine. You know as little about it, and Deaconville, as you do about me. My grandfather died in that mine, killed with twenty-two others in The Palm Sunday Tragedy of 1918, and it was that mine that claimed my father, breathing all that bad air, hammering away through granite with a Widowmaker drill, although my father took fifteen years to cough himself into a coffin. We Dutchovers have no luck, do we?

That's right. I'm a descendant of Deacon Dutchover himself. Well, sort of. He married. Did you know that? Of course, you didn't. You don't have a clue. Married her shortly after he joined the 5th Cavalry. He sent Zelma to her sister's in Indiana when he quit the army to find his fortune, and when she came to Deaconville after his death, the Widow Dutchover fell in love, and married Sergeant Levi McClure. The children's reading room in the Carnegie Library is named after her, but who goes to a library in Deaconville these days?

No, my name isn't Dutchover, and maybe old Deacon's blood doesn't run through my veins, but I'm bonded to his memory nonetheless. That's why I never sold out. That's why I've given my heart and soul to this town. My father, his father, my grandmother, my great-grandparents. They're all buried in the cemetery here, and somewhere near the Zelma rests Deacon Dutchover.

You won, of course. People like you always win. Got me discredited as an old fool. Got the Zelma condemned. Condemned for the good of society. Or something like that.

Well, there you have it. You wanted to know, and I've told you. That's what brings a sixty-two-year-old retired miner, a former demolition's man in the army, a Baby Boomer and Vietnam veteran, a historian and native, born and raised, Deaconville's most patriotic son. That's what brings me into your damned casino with twenty-six sticks of dynamite in my daddy's old suitcase, and a detonator in my right hand. The way I figure it, I can blow up your casino and bring down half of this mountain. Bury Deaconville, and keep the highway department busy for eighteen months trying to dig out the Silver And Gold Expressway.

Now, it's your turn. You give me one good reason why I shouldn't press this button and do what the Indians couldn't do. Do what Bromide Gulch's best citizens couldn't do. Do what the racists who killed George Anderson, who ran out the Chinese, couldn't do. What cholera, fires, and cave-ins couldn't do. What smelters and dredge boats couldn't do. What the Panic of '93 and the Great Depression couldn't do. And what the precarious commerce of mining couldn't do over the past 125-plus years.

You tell me why I shouldn't kill Deaconville.

Finally, and forever.

JOHN STONE'S TOMB

By Wayne Davis

John Stonecipher knew he was dying. It was about time, he reckoned. *But not like this.* His last breath should be of fresh Chihuahua desert or Guadalupe mountain air, carried away on the wind instead of lost in the stale atmosphere of a sickroom in a nursing home. If only he could rise and somehow make it to the little place he and Grace still owned on the edge of town and get a saddle on one of his horses, at least he could ride out into the sand hills east of Carlsbad to breathe his last. Even a cloud of gunsmoke or face down with caliche dust in his nostrils would be better than this. But where he really wanted to be was high up on that mountain amidst the smell of pinyon, jumper, pine, and cedar. That's where he wanted to breathe his last and that's where he wanted to be.

His large nose crinkled as he squinted his faded blue eyes in search of the writing materials among the various articles on the bedside table. There might be a way. There was someone who would see to it, if he possibly could.

It had been a long time, but John knew where he was. No one else knew he was still alive. But John knew. And he would come, too.

Fingers that had once been strong and nimble fumbled to get paper and pen into position. The nurse would mail the letter for him.

* * *

The brush-scarred green pickup with welded side racks was similar to others that could be seen on the streets of Carlsbad on any given day, except for the Arizona plates. A fellow rancher would only wonder casually at a work truck so far from the home range, and the average citizen wouldn't even notice. So it was of no concern to Wallace Bledsoe as he steered his vehicle through the gathering twilight in search of the Riverside Nursing Home.

Grace saw him in the lobby of the nursing home. But he turned away before she recognized him, if indeed she could after all these years. After she passed through and on out the door, he hurried down the hallway to John's room. Wally's grip was swift and firm, and John silently marveled at the difference in degree of preservation between two men of the same generation. The black eyes, still efficient without glasses, flashed the old mischievous fire as they laid their plans.

Wally hid in the closet when the nurse came for the evening bed check and dispensation of medication. Then he helped John get dressed, and assumed his vigil against the wall by the slightly opened door, watching patiently for an opportune time to slip past the office and out the main door.

Wally had to half-carry John outside. They exited the parking lot with John mumbling directions.

Wally cut the lights and killed the engine and coasted the truck to a stop on the side of the road a hundred yards short of the corral.

John described the two mounts he judged the best trail horses, and remained in the truck as Wally made his way through the moonlight to the barn. The line-back dun and the blue roan were not difficult to catch and he soon had them bridled and saddled and out to the truck and loaded. Then the overloaded pickup with two old men and two young horses eased through the blinking traffic lights of the sleeping town and headed south as a rosy fringe of dawn seeped into the blackness on the eastern horizon.

Nervously Wally watched the asphalt ribbon on the El Paso highway fall away behind him in the rearview mirrors on the doors of the battered Dodge pickup. Ahead and off to the southwest the distant ridges of the Guadalupes rose up on the horizon. Anticipation stirred John's vitals. He straightened up against the back of the seat, rolled the window down a bit, and lifted his head to fill his lungs. It felt as if the crisp desert air inflated his heart as well; the oxygen seemed to pervade his disease-ravaged body and a feeling of revitalization gradually spread to his extremities.

Wally slowed the pickup almost to a stop as they approached the turnoff. The "rip...rip" of the tires crossing the pipes of the cattle guard marked the transition from paved highway to the gravelly surface of the Bureau of Land Management road that zigzagged a southwesterly course toward the distant peaks.

John gazed intently through the top part of his lenses at the sprawl of country sloping off toward the Black River bottoms. Through the windshield he could perceive a light haze of dust rising above a group of cattle pens that had been set up just off the road. He squinted at the late-model pickup and homemade stock trailer parked near the pens to see if he could recognize them.

"Wallace, if you'll take a gander over yonder at the squeeze chute, you'll see a feller who's got some of the same blood as you in his veins. That's your brother Ben's grandson, his daughter's boy, Winston Brittain. His father was killed in World War II and he grew up on the ranch."

Wally almost lost control of the steering wheel for gawking at the man as they rumbled past the corrals.

* * *

Winston Brittain was hazing an open heifer into the proper holding pen when the overloaded pickup lumbered past. But his red-headed hired hand, O.C. Kirkes, was perched upon a top rail awaiting Winston's return to the headgate before he should booger another Bar BX heifer into the squeeze chute.

"You see that?" O.C. screeched, staring after the departing dust cloud.

"No, what about it?"

"That old pickup damn near turned a wheelie. They got two ol' ponies in the bed and they was swerving and a-swaying and churning up the road like a coyote dodging bullets. I thought they was gonna lose 'er for sure."

O.C. worked through the remainder of the morning speculating on who the men in the swerving truck might be and what they were up to.

207

"One of them ponies was a blue roan. You don't see very many of them around these parts."

When Winston announced they would take a lunch break soon as he inoculated the next cow, O.C. lifted the Styrofoam cooler out of the bed of the pickup and set it on the ground on the leeside by the rear wheel out of the wind. "What kind of sandwich did the li'l woman fix for us today?" he wondered aloud as he pulled the lid and claimed two of the wax paper bundles. He opened a door and slid onto the seat, pulling a wrapper away with his teeth as he clicked the key into the power position and turned on the radio. Within a half a minute he was mumbling angrily to himself.

Winston took a seat on the running board between the door and the fender after digging out a sandwich for himself.

"Something wrong with your sandwich?" Winston asked.

"Naw. It's just this damn radio! All you can get at noon is the news and that damn crazy music. Can't pick up no Western music nowhere. That damned rock 'n' roll stuff has done took over! I'd sooner listen to the news than that stuff," he said resignedly, and left the dial on a local "news at noon" program.

"You hear that?" he asked, poking his head out of the cab.

"Old John Stonecipher's done disappeared. Just plumb vanished out of that nursing home where they had 'im. When they went in to check on him this morning he wasn't there no more. Neither was his clothes."

"Probably became disoriented from some of the medication and wandered off in the night," O.C. said.

"That's what they figger, but not a soul has seen hide or hair of him. They gave a description of what he's wearing and asked for anybody who thinks they might've seen him to call the police or the sheriff.

"Sheriff might be callin' you in on this'n, Win, seein's how you been knowing old John for so long," O.C. said.

"Oh, I doubt it," disagreed Winston. He'd been appointed as a special deputy for the isolated southern end of the county. It was a part-time, on-call position that usually required very little of his time. The meager salary for his services was nonetheless a welcome addition to the family budget, as was his wife Barbara's salary as a junior high school history teacher.

208

* * *

The blue roan stood with head down and sides heaving when Wally reined in for a rest stop and dismounted. He noted the paleness of John's face and moved quickly to assist him as he laboriously hauled his right leg across the cantle to effect a painful dismount. His steadying grip on John's arm was all that prevented him from staggering to a rocky spill on the narrow trail. When John was securely seated on a flat-topped boulder with canteen at hand, Wally turned to loosen the cinches.

"Better give these ol' ponies a chance to blow before we go on up to the ridge." He pulled the black Stetson from his silver crown and tilted his head to survey the heights that towered over their position on the side of the mountain. "The last couple of hundred yards was always the worst," he recalled.

"Steep, and lotsa slick rock," John agreed. "We'd best lead the horses the rest of the way."

Wally gave him a suspicious eye. "You up to climbing, pard?"

John scrutinized the steep tangle of rocks and scrubby brush that obscured the dim switchback trail to the rim. "We got plenty of daylight, so we can just take it a little bit at a time... We'll be campin' on Lonesome Ridge tonight!" he said with a grin.

* * *

True to O.C.'s prediction, the sheriff called after they got home from the cattle pens and asked Win to visit Mrs. Stonecipher. Barb volunteered to go with him, thinking the old lady might open up more readily to another woman, and especially since Barb already had a certain rapport with her.

In order to make the subject of history more meaningful for her students, Barbara developed a class project wherein taped interviews were conducted with old timers in the area. Grace had reluctantly agreed to some interviews. Because of her extreme age and the delicate situation Barb always accompanied the two students who interviewed her. She actually seemed to enjoy the attention once she got used to the idea.

Winston and Barb had decided to travel together, leaving early enough to see Mrs. Stonecipher before school started. Barb would take the school bus home if Winston was not there to pick her up.

"I sure hope she'll open up to you," said Winston when they were underway.

"Oh, I think she will. She even told me some rather confidential things when we interviewed her for class. Off the record, of course."

"Confidential eh? She must've really took a liking to you."

"Do you know what she told me one day after the kids had left?" asked Barbara indignantly. "People used to call her Racy Gracie."

"I always heard she had a certain reputation," Winston admitted.

"Well, I think that's just awful! She's been faithful to her husband for what...close to seventy years? Just because she had an immature fling with some ne'er-do-well before she got married, she's had to carry the stigma all her life."

"She told you about *that*! There's hardly anyone left who knows about it!"

"You know about it, I gather," she said with an expectant look.

"Obviously, one thing Mrs. Stonecipher *didn't* tell you is who the desperado was!"

"She mentioned some Indian name he was called. Choctaw, I think it was." Barb looked expectantly at Winston.

Winston cut his eyes at her in order to see her mouth fall open when he said it. "The Choctaw Kid...also known as Wallace Bledsoe!"

"Bledsoe! You mean...?"

"My great-grandfather was Anson Bledsoe, who founded the Bar BX in the 1880s. His older sons were my grandpa Ben and his brother Charlie. After their mother died, Anson married a half Choctaw woman."

"Wallace Bledsoe's mother."

"Right."

"And the older boys resented him."

"That's putting it mildly. They never accepted him as part of the family—just referred to him as 'the Choctaw's kid.' Folks picked up on it and from that they commenced calling him the Choctaw Kid."

"Mrs. Stonecipher said he was accused of killing one of his own brothers. I guess that would be your grandfather's full brother, Charlie Bledsoe."

"Evidently when old Anson died in 1894 the older boys kicked Wallace off the ranch. He rode off on a Bar BX horse he considered his personal mount. Charlie tracked him down and tried to repossess the horse and got shot for his trouble. Charlie lived for several weeks after he was shot. He claimed Wallace pulled a 'hideout' pistol and shot him without any warning. He described the weapon as a silver-plated, long-barreled Colt's Peacemaker."

"How observant of him."

"A weapon has a way of getting special attention when it's aiming at you, I reckon."

"Where did Wallace get the gun?"

"I doubt there's anyone left amongst the living who can answer that question, except Grace. Like she told you, she ran away from home to be with Wallace. And John Stone—he would know for sure."

"You mean John Stonecipher."

"He was also known as John Stone in the old days. He was Wallace Bledsoe's closest friend. They were 'pardners.' But John always denied taking an active part in the rustling."

"Rustling?"

"Yeah, at first it was confined to driving off a few head of Bar BX stock now and then—like Wallace was collecting on his 'inheritance' the only way he could. But after Charlie died, Ben put a price on Wally's head and soon Wallace joined up with some other cow thieves running a full-fledged rustling operation out of a remote camp in the Guadalupes. Finally the ranchers had their fill of losing stock and a large posse was organized to find the hideout and clean the rustlers out of the country. Yet all of the gang slipped away but one, and he was dead when they found him."

"I'm guessing they found Wallace Bledsoe."

"They found Wallace's horse at the bottom of the Lonesome Ridge cliff. And a body battered beyond recognition wearing a fancy Peacemaker. Not long after that, John Stonecipher showed up at the home ranch with a new bride."

* * *

Grace Stonecipher sat with her spine as rigid as her old ladder-back chair, her hands folded on top of the cane across her lap. She didn't get up to open the door—just hollered for them to come on in.

Winston stopped in the middle of the room and removed his hat.

"Miz Stonecipher—" Barb stepped around the coffee table and sat down on the end of the divan near Grace and gently clasped a pale, blue-veined hand between her own—"is there anything that needs doing around the place that Winston can take care of for you?"

Grace started to shake her head no, then stopped. "Come to think of it, I didn't feed Johnny's pet ponies yesterday. There was such a hubbub around here and all, you know," she said in a voice made throaty by the years. "There's plenty of alfalfa. Just go ahead and fill the hayrack. And scatter about five scoops of Omolene in the trough—one for each head."

Winston re-entered the house sooner than Barb expected and she could tell from his expression that something was amiss. "What's the matter?"

"Miz Stonecipher, didn't you say there were *five* horses out there? Well, there's only three in the horse trap now—an appaloosa, a bay, and a bald-faced sorrel."

"They all came up for feed day before yesterday," Mrs Stonecipher said with a frown.

"Can you describe the two missing horses, ma'am?"

"Of course. Johnny also had a line-back dun and a blue roan."

A blue roan?

Could the blue roan O.C. saw the previous day be the missing blue horse? And if it was, did the theft of the horse have anything to do with the old man's disappearance?

Winston decided to go get O.C., and try to locate the overloaded pickup he'd seen.

* * *

Winston stood on the cab of the abandoned pickup truck and searched the countryside with his field glasses. They'd found the pickup with a flat tire, plunged into a patch of creosote bush alongside a remote and scarcely maintained BLM road.

Winston peered through the glasses at the rugged Chihuahua desert environment sloping up to the base of the Guadalupe escarpment. The riders could be anywhere among the myriad washes, knolls, rincons, and patches of tangled brush within the range of his binoculars and never be seen. He and O.C. had no choice but to trail them on horseback if they were to discover what the mysterious horse thieves were up to.

O.C.'s grunt of surprise brought Winston's attention back to the immediate surroundings. "Well, I'll be switched," O.C. exclaimed, "this here's a Arizony tag!"

O.C. took a moment to ponder the western horizon. "Shoot, they could've taken the old Indian trail to Lonesome Ridge and be plumb on top of the mountain by now."

"O.C., I think you're on the right track. Having come this far, where else is there to go? Well, it's too late to follow them up yonder today, even if we'd brought horses with us.

"I've got an idea how we might do a little catching up. There's a solitary trail on the ridge—only one way they can go until they get off the ridge and into the trees on the main part of the mountain. We'll load up and leave before daylight and take the Dark Canyon road up into the Guadalupes as far as the road is passable for our pickup and stock trailer. Then we'll ride horseback on across to the Lonesome Ridge trail and see if we can cut their sign."

* * *

John awakened with the first light of a new day—perhaps it would be his last. He threw back the flap of the sleeping bag Wally had supplied and sat up. Wally heard him stir and arose from his squatting position on the rim overlooking the precarious switchback trail they'd climbed the previous afternoon and walked back to their makeshift camp among the rocks and thorny brush. He knelt down to pour John a tin cup of coffee from the pot that was warming over a small campfire.

"You hungry?" said Wally. "I opened a can of vy-eena sausages."

"No thanks—haven't had much of an appetite lately. Let's just saddle up and get on up the trail."

"Shore looks different," was Wally's dry comment when they broke through the pinyon and juniper screening the grassy cove beneath the bluff.

"A place changes a lot in seventy years, Wallace, especially compared to the way a feller has it built up in his mem'ry," John said. "Still looks good to me."

A shadow flashed across the rocks. "Buzzard!" John said disgustedly. "Well, ol' son, just let me get back up yonder on my perch one more time and you're welcome to this here old carcass."

Wally's eyes followed the direction of John's gaze and he joined in watching the lazy circlings of the vulture for a few moments. "So the ledge is what you've got in mind, eh? Kinda like the old Plains Indian way."

213

* * *

For the second time in as many days the Bar BX pickup roared down the El Paso highway in the early morning darkness toward Carlsbad. The late model Chevy towed a homemade stock trailer loaded with two fresh horses and it was O.C. Kirkes who shared the cab with Winston.

No sooner had Winston and O.C. rolled up to the corrals the previous evening when Barb had come out from the house to tell Winston that Sheriff Hawkins was on the phone. He said that Mrs. Stonecipher had called the sheriff's office and insisted she didn't want the case of the missing horses pursued. When he tried to pin her down as to why she'd made such a demand she'd hung up on him. The sheriff wanted Winston to talk to Mrs. Stonecipher again. So Winston was not on horseback in the Guadalupes at daybreak as he'd planned, but in town knocking on Grace Stonecipher's door.

"Wal, wha'd she say?" O.C. straightened up in the seat and turned the radio down when Winston opened the truck door upon his return from the Stonecipher house.

Winston slid under the wheel, slammed the door, and turned the ignition.

"Getting information out of that old dame is like trying to punch a gopher out of the ground with a piece of baling wire."

"Didn't find out nothin', didja?"

"All I know is there's something she's not telling us."

"I'll bet she knows where John's at. And she don't want him found."

"It's got something to do with those missing horses." Winston was silent as he negotiated the truck and trailer through town and on out to the secondary road to Dark Canyon. Just when O.C. was about to turn the radio up, he spoke. "When Barb talked to Miz Stonecipher yesterday she mentioned as how John had been protesting the fact of spending his final days cooped up in a nursing home."

"He busted out, didn't he?"

"Maybe. But how could a weak, sick, stove-up old man...?"

"Two horses—that old buzzard's gone and got hisself somebody to help him, ain't he? Somebody from Arizony."

"But how. And *who*?"

* * *

"I do believe I've done found what we've been lookin' for," O.C. called out to Winston.

They'd hauled the horses to the end of the graded mountain road and proceeded to the Lonesome Ridge trail on horseback, searching for sign of the elusive riders' passing.

Winston nudged his horse alongside O.C.'s. "Yep, somebody rode across this stretch of softer ground not too long ago." O.C. glanced at the sun. It was well past its highest point. "What do you think our chances are of catching up to 'em before sundown?"

Winston peeked at his watch. "Slim to none. We'd best get back to the truck before it gets too dark." Winston reined his horse around. "We'll come back here and start looking for more sign tomorrow at daylight."

* * *

John propped himself up on an elbow and cocked an eye at the bluff that would be his tombstone. The sun had long since cleared the summit and was already settling into the tops of the trees on the west side of the clearing. It was too late to do any rock climbing today.

He'd gone back to sleep soon after they arrived at the old hideout. He guessed he needed the rest after the long climb up the mountain. Maybe he'd feel like trying the cliff tomorrow.

* * *

At the same time Winston Brittain and O.C. Kirkes regained the place where they'd seen the hoof prints the day before, John Stonecipher was making another tardy exit from his sleeping bag a few miles away. He was thankful for one more day. That's all he needed to do what he'd set out to do.

"Ready for coffee, pard?" Wally said.

"Don't mind if I do," said John, fumbling in his shirt pocket for his eyeglasses. When he got them on he took a deep breath and gazed all about, taking in all the smells and colors of the mountain hideaway.

Wally lifted the fire-blackened coffee pot off the flames, watching John from the corner of his eye. "Hard to leave it all behind, ain't it?"

"At least I got a last look at it, thanks to you." John's gaze came to rest on the ledge. "Now if I can just get up yonder without falling and breaking my neck..."

"I won't let you fall, pard. No more'n you let me fall, seventy-some years ago."

Wally was silent for a moment, thinking back on that fateful day.

"So they thought that dead owl hoot you dumped over the rim was me. I never thought me and ol' Rafer favored that much."

"But you did, basically. And he was beat beyond recognition before he took the dive. And it was your horse, and your pistol."

"I hated to lose that fancy Peacemaker. Wonder what become of it."

"I expect your brother Ben toted it off with your saddle and anything else he could scavenge."

"Reckon he sold it?"

"I doubt it. It's the gun that killed Charlie and a symbol of his revenge. It's prob'ly stashed away somewhere down yonder at the Bar BX."

"That Winston feller, he ain't like his grandpa, I hope."

"No, he's *bien gente*. The whole family's good, upstanding, church-goin' folks."

Wally pondered a moment. "This is Sunday, right?"

About the same time O.C. Kirkes told Winston Brittain he thought he'd caught a faint whiff of wood smoke on the air, Wallace Bledsoe kicked out the remnants of his campfire and went to get the ropes from the saddles.

John Stonecipher drank the last of his coffee, holding the cup in both hands lest he spill it. From the way he felt, Wally wouldn't have to wait around very long to be sure the mission had reached its ultimate climax. He just hoped he could hold out long enough to get to his chosen resting place.

John reached his hand for Wally to help him to his feet. "No sense waitin' any longer. Nothing to it but to do it!"

* * *

When Winston and O.C. heard the horse whinny it was the only clue they'd had as to the whereabouts of the mysterious riders since O.C.'s whiff of wood smoke.

The dun lifted his head to sound another greeting to the horses he'd heard and smelled a few moments earlier. Now they were in sight of the edge of the clearing.

"One dun horse, no blue roan," said Winston.

"Which means one of 'em's done lit a shuck and the other'n's still here. I bet they's a neat little grave around here somewhere."

Winston heaved a sigh. "We'd best check it out. You go around the clearing that way and I'll ride around this direction. Holler if you find anything." He nudged the buckskin into motion.

O.C. held his mount. "Why don't we just let him rest in peace, Win?"

Winston pulled his horse around. "O.C., I can surely understand why old John would want to be laid to rest up here and I wouldn't like it if our investigation should result in the relocation of his body. But I've got my duty to perform."

O.C. continued to hold his mount and scowl at Winston.

"Look, O.C., I don't like it any better than you do." He turned the buckskin. "Come on! *I'll* look for the grave."

Winston and O.C. were about to collect the dun horse and ride out of the clearing when the piercing scream of a red-tailed hawk drew their attention to the bluff.

Winston watched the hawk circle once and drift out of sight beyond the summit. When he refocused his attention on his companion, O.C. was still staring at the bluff.

Winston's eyes followed the direction of O.C.'s gaze. "What are you looking at, O.C.?"

O.C. snapped to attention. "Nothing! Let's get outa here!" he urged the bay into motion.

Winston continued to scrutinize the bluff. "Hold up a minute! There's something up yonder on that ledge, isn't there?"

O.C. drew rein and gave Winston a hard look. "*I* don't see nothing up yonder, Winston."

Winston returned O.C.'s glare for a moment. "Then I don't see anything either, O.C. Dab a rope on Miz Stonecipher's pony and we'll be on our way."

O.C. exposed his tobacco-stained teeth and winked a pale blue eye. "Yes *sir!*"

It was well past noon by the time the Bar BX pickup pulled the homemade stock trailer loaded with three horses up to the corrals on the home ranch. When Winston and O.C. turned the horses into the horse trap they were surprised to see the Circle S blue roan there with the Bar BX remuda.

"I'll bet that old pickup's halfway back to Arizona by now," said Winston. "He'll probably trust his spare to get him to El Paso before he stops to get the flat fixed."

"When he leaves El Paso he'll still have a lot of New Mexico to cross before he gets home. You could put out a A.P.B. on 'im."

"What for? What's he done that's illegal?"

"Nothin', I reckon. I'd just like to know who he is."

"Come on, O.C., let's go get something to eat."

Winston put his hand on the hood of Barb's station wagon as he walked past, ascertaining from the heat that the rest of the family had arrived from church just ahead of them. They entered the kitchen by way of the back door.

"What's wrong?" said Winston, taking in the morose expression on the women's faces.

"Someone broke into the house while we were gone," explained Barbara.

"I guess they found what they were looking for when they got to the storage closet," said his mother. "They ransacked that box of old relics I was planning to donate to the municipal museum in Carlsbad."

"They stole some antiques?"

"Just one. That old pistol your grandfather said he found at the bottom of Lonesome Ridge back in 1894."

O.C. looked at Winston, "Wal, it 'pears the owl-hoot's committed a felony! Are you goin' after him now, Win?"

Winston pushed his hat back and a knowing smile relaxed his features.

"Why should I? It's his gun!"

ASHES

By Arthur Winfield Knight

1

A week after his wife had died, Sam asked a friend, "What do I do now?" Each morning he awakened, expecting to find Sara in the kitchen making coffee, or on the deck smoking a cigarette, looking out across the Pacific. She'd only made it to thirty. Her dying first had never been a possibility. He was fifty, and had lived hard.

The third day Sara was gone he'd taken her clothes to a hospice on the Coast Highway. He'd piled her shoes, her dresses, everything, into a huge cardboard box he'd placed on the counter at the hospice, leaving before the gray-haired Mexican lady behind the counter could thank him, because he was confounded by conversation. Sara's ashes were the only thing he had left.

Sam's friend watched the light bleed out of the sky. There was just the glow of his cigarette, the glint of the Coors can he drank from, and the vanishing horizon. Finally, Karl said, "Now you find someone else and go on with your life."

Sam wasn't sure he wanted to find someone else, wasn't even sure it was possible, but he didn't want to die, either. He wasn't ready for that yet. He remembered an assistant director he'd worked with. Gene was in his thirties when his wife died. She'd had a history of heart disease, but no one imagined she'd be dead in her early thirties. It was never easy to imagine death.

219

Gene had been a nominal Catholic, but, once Helen was gone, he'd attended church each morning, kneeling before a statue of the Virgin Mary. It was easier to think about someone being gone, rather than dead. Gone was nicer, but it didn't help when you lay in bed alone at night. Sam realized that now, realized how much pain Gene must have felt, but Sam still didn't want to be like him.

Gene had kept Helen's name on his checks years after she'd died, and Helen's clothes were still hanging in his closet when his house burned a decade later.

Sam finally stopped asking Gene how he was doing, because Gene always said, "I'm doing as well as the Lord allows," but everyone at the studio stopped asking.

He left Malibu at dawn, heading north again, but he was alone this time. Months ago, Sara had been beside him. Now, her ashes were in an urn on the seat next to him. He felt numb, but hopeful, his hands resting on the steering wheel of the old Cadillac.

He'd let the road take him wherever it wanted, although he'd never been much of a mystic. He was impatient with Tarot cards and Ouija Boards and the people who believed in them, although Sara had seen omens everywhere. Nobody said you had to be consistent. Sam wanted to believe he'd find the perfect place— somewhere—to scatter Sara's ashes, to let go, to live again.

2

Sam parked the Cadillac at the foot of Partington Ridge in Big Sur, because he'd photographed Sara there. She was wearing white shorts, sitting on the front fender. You could see the ocean behind her. The seaweed turned the waves pale green; the sky was immense.

Henry Miller had lived at the top of the ridge. Sam had met him in the mid-50s, when Henry's books, *Tropic of Cancer* and *Tropic of Capricorn*, were still banned. Henry was bald, in his sixties, but he had more vitality than most of the people Sam knew in Hollywood.

Henry was curious about everything: flying saucers, lost continents, why kangaroos have two penises. His third or fourth wife must have been twenty years younger than Henry, but Eve had died prematurely, too.

Sam remembered driving up the winding, gravel road to Henry's house. It was so poorly constructed that Sam imagined a BB could penetrate the walls, but Henry didn't seem to need material things. When the weather was warm, he'd walk to the mailbox wearing a jock strap and a fireman's hat, pulling a red wagon. He claimed he was the happiest man alive. Sam believed him.

They were eating salami and Swiss cheese sandwiches made with French bread when a rat ran across the weathered wooden floor, hiding beneath a cabinet that was in worse condition than the house. Henry did a kind of Charlie Chaplin dance, waving his walking stick, then he sicked the dog on the rat, but the dog just sniffed at the cabinet.

Henry said, "Such a good dog, such a good dog," then the rat ran outside again. Small bits of colored glass and shattered pieces of pottery that were laid into the cement patio glittered in the striated sunlight. Henry stood there, laughing, while "good dog" wagged its tail and the seagulls swooped and soared over the vast ocean.

Hucksters stood in front of the restaurants along the wharf in Monterey. Some of them wore topcoats and top hats. They could have been extras in *My Fair Lady*. They were giving away samples of clam chowder and seafood stew, and you could tell they were desperate for business. Not many people were on the boardwalk. Immediate seating was available everywhere, but it didn't matter to Sam. He didn't have anyplace to go.

Sam got a window table at a restaurant near the end of the wharf. He ordered sand dabs, rock shrimp and a bottle of Chardonnay. He was still used to ordering for two. Being alone took getting used to.

Sam sat there watching some small children and dogs run along the beach, sat there watching the sky fall. It turned a robin's egg blue just before the coming of complete night. The waves were iridescent in the moonlight.

Sam walked along the pier, slowly, after dinner. A young woman sat on a bench in front of a geegaw shop, crying. She was wearing a silver fox fur coat. Her creamy skin was dotted with freckles, and she had red hair. Sam knew someone who believed redheads were descended from a lost continent. Mu or Atlantis. Sam couldn't remember which, and didn't care. A lot of people told him a lot of things.

A blond guy whose crew cut made him look bald put his arm around the redhead. The moon was a stone. He said, "Blood coming out of your ear is not good. It is definitely not good. You have to go to the emergency ward," but the redhead only cried harder.

3

The pears were gone from the trees along Delta Highway 160 as Sam headed north toward Cortland. A huge mowing machine threshed the dried cornstalks in a field to the east, and the dust hung in the air until the land looked like a yellowing antique photograph in the amber light of noon. The sky was like molten white glass, even though summer had ended.

Sam pulled into the parking lot next to The Rhyde Hotel, because he and Sara had spent a night there. It was built in 1928, during the Prohibition Era, and it had been owned by Lon Chaney's family at one time. Al Jolson and Dashiell Hammett stayed there, along with other movie stars and mobsters, and Herbert Hoover announced his presidential candidacy from The Rhyde.

People came to The Rhyde from all over California, many of them arriving on steam wheel paddleboats, and its downstairs casino and speakeasy were famous. The speakeasy's original door was still in place with its peephole, and there was a fainting couch in the ladies' room. Sara told him women commonly fainted in those days because most of them wore corsets that were too tight. Sara had never worn a corset, but she'd fainted earlier that summer, days before Dr. Music told her she had leukemia.

Sam remembered going to Locke with Sara. It had been built by and for the Chinese in 1915. It was still frequented by the Chinese, although it had a world famous bar and restaurant named Al the Wop's and several antique shops. Sara had bought a ceramic coffee mug with high-key black and white photos of Jean Harlow and Clara Bow on opposite sides, but Sam had given it to the hospice, along with everything else. This time, he sped past Locke.

The sunlight looked like gold foil as it filtered through the pear orchards outside Cortland. Sam stopped at the only restaurant there. He sat at the bar and ordered two tacos and a glass of water from the Mexican bartender, who doubled as the cook and bottle washer. He was young and overweight and wore a dirty white shirt he didn't tuck into his pants. He kept biting his lower lip. Sam was sure no one ever tipped him.

Someone sitting three stools away from Sam wore army fatigues. His left hand and leg shook continually, although he'd told the bartender he made guitars for a living. Sam imagined him running through the jungle in Vietnam, his lungs scarred from Agent Orange, his mind gone. He nursed an eight-ounce beer, holding the glass with both hands, his elbows resting on the bar. He looked at Sam and said, "Do you know what fish do in water?" It was a joke attributed to W.C. Fields.

"I don't want to think about it," Sam said.

4

Sam had spent a month, living alone, at a cabin on Tomales Bay when Karen left him. It was his second failed marriage, but he'd spent a lifetime failing at everything, except filmmaking, until he'd met Sara.

Sometimes seals came up below the deck. They were so close he could have hit them with a head of lettuce, but he'd just stand there, awed, watching their bodies slide through the water. Sometimes deer came into the yard facing Highway 1. They were beautiful creatures, but some of the aging hippies on the bay disliked them because they ate the marijuana plants.

Egrets nested in the trees at night. The sky turned a smoky purple and red, as if someone had fired a forge on the far side of heaven. Sam barbecued steaks and corn wrapped in foil because there wasn't much water and the well was broken. It almost never rained, but when it did the rain blew off the water, like spun glass across the sun. Sam drank martinis, turning the steaks, while he watched the light change. It was different everyday.

Some people claimed you could see the blue beginnings of eternity if you looked across the bay long enough, but they were more mystical than Sam. His neighbor collected old cars and had a long, gray beard and eyes that burned like a mad prophet's. Sam didn't know what he saw. He reeked of machine oil and marijuana, but a lot of people on the bay grew it. Someone Sam met cut out red cardboard circles the size of tomatoes, hanging them on the plants, to fool helicopter pilots looking for dope as they hovered over the bay, but it didn't work. The plants were confiscated.

Poppies were in bloom everywhere when Sam drove to the Marshall Post Office to pick up his mail each morning. Someone had posted the message JUST ANOTHER DAY IN PARADISE on a bulletin board, and it was easy to believe most days, even if you were getting a divorce.

Sometimes Sam would go to Nick's Cove for shrimp cocktails in the evening, or he'd drive to Point Reyes Station and play liar's dice with the bartender at The Western. On his way home, the bay was as yellow as paint in the moonlight. It would be a beautiful place to scatter someone's ashes, but it had never been home to Sara.

5

Sam drove through the redwood forests along the Russian River. The trees looked as if they were draped with mercury in the late afternoon light, the branches glistening. He ordered a hamburger at a place called Pat's on the main street of Guerneville, then it was evening. Stars fell as softly as pearls through the dark water, and the sky was so clear it was as if clouds hadn't been invented yet. There was a gibbous moon.

He and Sara had spent several days exploring the river country. They ate salami and French bread and huge bowls of minestrone soup at the Union Hotel in Occidental, and they discovered a small restaurant in Jenner just after it had rained one day. The sun's rays pierced the fog, and the waves were ethereal. Artificial flowers bloomed in a beer bottle on the table, and the air was so damp you could almost squeeze it. Frank Sinatra was singing a song about love on the radio.

There were vineyards along both sides of the highway. The sun was finger-painted against the sky, fluorescent, and wild mustard had turned the hills a translucent yellow after the rain. Sam had to stop so a flock of sheep could cross the road in front of them. He had no idea where they were, but they could see the ocean in the distance.

Sara liberated some daisies and daffodils from another restaurant in Duncans Mills, where Black Bart had robbed his first stage. Sara's blonde hair glistened in the brilliant sunlight, and her blue eyes shone like morning glories.

Aging hippies sold flowers from the backs of their station wagons and VW buses, and young women with flowing black hair sold tie-dyed clothing from roadside stands. Sam remembered someone saying, "Old hippies never die, they just move north," and it seemed to be true. They were everywhere.

Sam walked out onto the beach when he came to Gualala, because he and Sara had camped there one night. They'd listened to the wild boars running through the woods while they drank sauvignon blanc from a dented tin cup they'd shared.

He held the urn, as if it were a divining rod, before him. A strange light hovered over the waves, and there was a shining cloud above a ruined red barn in the distance. This was the perfect place to scatter Sara's ashes, but he wasn't ready to let go.

6

The young man at Tony's Place was drunk, but so was the bartender. Sam had been told Tony served the best steaks in Sonoma County. It was the only thing he served, besides fried chicken, but that was all right with Sam. He ordered a steak and a dry martini, then watched Tony go back to the far end of the bar. He and the kid were playing cribbage.

Tony had one winning hand after another, but he hardly looked at his cards. It was as if he were psychic, but he was just drunk. He told the kid, "My life makes Studs Lonigan's look like nothin'. You should write a book about me." Sam wondered why anyone would want to be a writer these days, but why did anyone do anything? You had to be nuts to make movies.

Tony said, "I was a bush pilot in Alaska, but I got tired of flying around above all that nothin'. I come back to Petaluma so I could help my family run the bar there, but they didn't want me around so they bought me this place." It was a historic roadhouse, five or six miles out of town, and President Grant had spent a night there when it was a stage stop. Black Bart was supposed to have been there, too. The guy got around.

Tony had a ruddy, pockmarked complexion, and the sleeves of his shirt were rolled up. He had huge biceps, but he was putting on weight around the middle. Tony said, "They claim I insulted all the customers. I didn't do nothin', except shoot one guy by accident. I was showin' him my fast draw when the pistol went off. The son of a bitch practically flew off the barstool. It was like a scene from a Sam Bonner movie." Sam wondered which of his films Tony was referring to, but he didn't ask. He liked being anonymous. "I took the guy a box of chocolates later, when he was in the hospital, but he told me to shove them. Some guys don't appreciate nothin'.

"I think the whole thing would have blown over, but the pistol belonged to a deputy sheriff who'd left it in the bar when he was drunk, so the shooting became a big deal in the papers."

A blowsy cook named Rose brought Sam his steak. She was in her mid-forties, and her hair smelled like cigarettes. Sam was aware of it, because he'd been off them for a month. Quitting was the second hardest thing he'd ever done.

A guy who looked like his feet hurt came into the bar. He was wearing a wrinkled corduroy jacket, and his tie was unknotted. He was a traveling salesman or a college professor who'd had a bad day. When he ordered a Budweiser, Tony yelled, "What do you think this is, a beer joint? Get the hell out of here."

The guy asked, "What's wrong with you?" then left hurriedly. Tony didn't notice. He and the kid were playing cribbage again.

7

Sam took the Petrified Forest Road to Calistoga. He passed a faded red barn with the words *Chew Mailpouch* painted on its side. He'd photographed Sara there. She was wearing Levi's with the two top buttons undone, and she was nude from the waist up. The framed 8 x 10 black and white photograph was one of the few tangible things he'd kept after she'd died, but he had all the memories. They were enough.

Tourists came to Calistoga for the mud baths or to bathe in the mineral springs. Probably no one believed the baths had any therapeutic effect, but the town had become fashionable, a spa taken over by the rich. Sam liked it better in the 50s, before the over-priced restaurants and hotels had come. Ordinary people could still afford to go there. You could see old people sitting in wicker chairs in the pale sunlight or wandering the streets as if they were dukes of despair, counting away the hours, the minutes. The hills faded away like ruined silk.

He'd visited a monastic-looking winery built out of stone one afternoon when he'd come to the valley with Edie, his first wife, and her younger sister. It was early spring, and the shadows from the new leaves were as faint as the shadows of an eclipse.

Elizabeth had turned twenty-one that day, so she was able to drink, legally, for the first time. A fervent young waiter kept bringing her new wines to try, eyeing her hopefully, until the manager asked to see her I.D. He was polite without being obsequious. You could have cast him as the maître d' in a Cary Grant film.

Elizabeth had forgotten her driver's license, but Sam assured the manager she was twenty-one. She was wearing a sundress, and you could see the tops of her freckled breasts. She was certain she was never going to be old.

Sam said, "I'll sign a paper, swearing to her age." The whitewashed walls were the color of salt in the brilliant afternoon light that refracted through their wineglasses. Everything seemed oblique. "You can put me in jail if I'm lying."

The manager said, "That won't be necessary, sir." He might have come from England. Or Hoboken.

Sam thought the guy had a lot of class, but he must have been relieved when they left.

8

Nearing Sonoma, Sam remembered: he and Sara had visited the Buena Vista Winery with a gay poet she'd known in San Francisco. It had been more than a hundred degrees that afternoon, so Paul had taken them to the limestone caves where the wine was stored in thirteen hundred-gallon casks made of oak. It was a way to get out of the heat.

The winery had been founded by Hungarian Count Agoston Haraszthy in 1857, and it was the oldest in California. Paul told them Haraszthy had disappeared in a Nicaraguan swamp, reputedly eaten by alligators. It could have happened, Sam thought, but it sounded like something a good press agent would dream up.

Wooden plaques describing the winery's history lined the walls, but Sam was particularly interested in one that read, "These tunnels were carved by Chinese XXXXXX labor." The word coolie had been scraped away by some well-meaning citizen who wanted to protect people, to preserve what he or she imagined to be good taste.

Sam hated it when someone tried to rewrite history. He'd always tried to tell the truth in his films, which is probably why so many of them had failed at the box office. A lot of people couldn't face up to the past.

Sonoma had the largest square in California, covering eight acres. It was originally laid out in 1835 by General Mariano Vallejo for troop maneuvers, and it was where the Bear Flag Revolt took place in 1846. Now you could see the square in television commercials.

The mission across from the square was the last to be built by the Franciscan monks, and it was the farthest north in the state. Miwok and Pomo Indians had been buried beside the mission, but the cemetery had been paved over a century ago, and tourists now stepped on their graves. Even the dead had to make way for what people called progress.

9

Burma Shave signs used to line the highway to Sacramento, but they'd vanished, along with a lot of other things. They had black letters on an orange background, and they were fastened to fence posts; there was still a lot of open country in the 40s and 50s. Each sign had a phrase on it, like a line from a bad poem. Sam remembered one. "He rounded the curve/ as a fast train neared./ Death didn't draft him./ He volunteered." Sometimes the poems dealt with large, dreadful questions, but maybe Sam imagined that. Maybe he'd fixated on death since Sara had died. Maybe that was what this trip to scatter her ashes was all about: coming to terms with life. Moving on.

10

The walls in the Georgetown Saloon were covered with stuffed birds and animals: deer heads, badgers, wolverines and hawks. The barmaid said, "When I tell kids I shot all those animals, it really freaks them out," and she laughed, her breasts shaking. She was a hundred pounds overweight. The hotel was built in 1856, shortly after the gold rush, but it burned down and was rebuilt forty years later.

There was a painting of some cowboys playing cards and another of some dance hall girls hanging above the Wurlitzer. Sam expected to hear Gene Autry singing "Tumblin' Tumbleweeds," but someone whose voice he couldn't place had a broken heart.

The walls were also decorated with American flags and framed slogans. One proclaimed, *Saloon closed for hangings.* "It's no joke," a cowboy said. He was wearing a straw Stetson, pushed back on his forehead, so you could see his blond hair. "We had us a hanging about ten years ago." He seemed cheerful about it. "The person was gay and wanted to open a business here, but he wasn't welcome. This is a small town, and the people can be pretty prejudiced. They didn't kill the guy, but they let him dance on the end of a rope a few times." The cowboy shrugged, sipping his beer. "No one ever saw him again."

"I wonder why," Sam said.

11

The lady behind the bar told Sam they had a coyote howling contest every May. Why not? he thought. There were eighty-two people in Coulterville, and they had to have some fun. You could probably hear the jack rabbits jumping through the brush at night. Sam ordered Coors in a bottle, rather than a draft beer, because the glasses behind the bar looked greasy. Someone must have stolen the towel the barmaid used from a service station, but a coot who came in tugging at his yellow suspenders ordered Budweiser on tap. The boards creaked beneath his feet. Coulterville was one of those places you sped by unless you needed a drink or gas or had lost your way. With a little luck,

229

you might be able to get a hamburger that wasn't rancid. The bar was probably more than a hundred years old, although someone had named it Yosemite Sam's and there was a painting of Sam brandishing his pistols on a sign hanging out front. The coyote howling contest interested Sam the most. It was something you could put in a film. The barmaid said, "There's a five-hundred-dollar first prize," as if that amount were unimaginable. She had a voice like Gravel Gertie's, and she probably had holes in her underwear. "I'll have to practice my howling so I can come back next May," Sam said. He remembered the night he'd howled when Sara was dying. It was something he didn't want to think about.

12

Only a few homes even made the pretense of having lawns in Tonopah—the name meant Little Wood, Little Water in Shoshone—and a lot of houses were abandoned. The windows were broken or boarded up, and the doors hung lopsidedly from their hinges. Several of the houses had graffiti painted on their sides. One said, JESUS WEPT, which was easy to believe in Tonopah.

There were some sparse Joshua and tamarisk trees, but not much else was living, except for a few lizards. When Sam was shooting a film in the area, he'd met someone who sat on his back porch, waiting for the lizards to run across the yard. Ed would shoot them with a .22 pistol. He said it gave him something to do besides drink.

Sam passed several churches that looked like small recreation halls that needed paint; the sun had withered the boards and barren crosses. Even the whorehouses seemed forlorn. Tonopah was a piss stop, midway between Reno and Vegas. Highway 95 ran through the center of town, but most of the streets were unpaved.

Sam passed a collapsed windmill and some miners' shacks with rusted roofs made out of kerosene cans. The scorched hills were covered with chewed-up rocks and rusting pieces of mine machinery. Sam expected to see wild dogs running and yapping past the slag heaps, but he didn't. Maybe the heat was too intense.

Tonopah looked like an over-exposed photograph in the blistering sunlight. Sam had forgotten how desolate it was.

A rancher and prospector named Jim Butler discovered silver here when his mule wandered off in a windstorm and Butler threw a rock at it. Later, he realized there was silver in the rock, and a boomtown was born, briefly. Jack Dempsey and Wyatt Earp had come here during the 1920s, but Tonopah's heyday had already ended. Neither man stayed long, but it was difficult to imagine anyone staying.

Sam went into the bar at the Mizpah Hotel. It was decorated with red, white, and blue crepe paper left over from the Bicentennial. An old guy who needed a shave was telling the barmaid, "I named my mine The Wild Goose, and it was the most aptly named place in the history of Nevada. I never found nothin'," but the barmaid seemed bored.

She had sagging breasts, and she wore a red, white, and blue Uncle Sam hat made out of cardboard. She told Sam, "I could hardly wait to leave when I was growing up here. I got a job tending bar in Elko when I was nineteen, too early to drink legally, but no one cared. The sheep herders were all cross-eyed from staring at my boobs." She bent over when she served Sam a lukewarm martini with too much vermouth. "I don't know why I came back. I must have been crazy."

"Me too," Sam said.

They'd brought in some whores from Tonopah when Sam was on location in the Valley of Fire. One or more of them had been infected, because almost everyone in the cast got the clap. It was years before Sara had come into his life.

Sam had slept with a whore named Honey. She had long black hair, and was naked except for a garter belt and some mesh stockings.

Sam thought about looking her up, since he was in Tonopah, but he didn't have the heart for whorehouses any more.

When Sam was a child, someone told him the Big Dipper was a milkman's wagon pouring out its milk into the foamy stars as it made its way across the sky. It had almost seemed possible when he stayed at his grandfather's ranch near Bass Lake. In Tonopah, it seemed absurd.

13

Sam held the urn before him, carefully. A bird painted like a shadow against the sky hovered above him, then disappeared in a burst of light. He'd parked the Cadillac at the end of Whitney Portal Road, more than eight thousand feet above sea level. He'd planned to walk the final eleven miles to the top of Mt. Whitney, because Sara had wanted him to bring her to the high country at the end. He'd probably gone two or three miles when he gave out. It was as if he walked under invisible weights. The air was crisp as cellophane, and there was no lower edge to the sky; it kept rising forever. The summit was over fourteen thousand feet.

Sam's hands shook as he took the lid from the urn, then tilted it into the burning ends of the wind. He could feel Sara disappearing into the aqueous air, feel her merging with the sky, penetrating the quilted light. Somewhere a bird sang in the high trees.

PADDLE YOUR OWN CANOE

By John D. Nesbitt

I met this guy named Arlie Buford in the prune orchard. We were working behind the machine, picking into small boxes, so it was something a guy could do by himself. Buford had the row next to mine on the right, and he kept about the same pace as I did. The row on my left had a man and his kid, about sixteen, working together. The two of them got out ahead of us the first morning, so I didn't see much of them. But I saw Buford off and on all day. He didn't have a water jug, but the boss left off a ten-gallon can, the galvanized kind with two handles, and in the afternoon I helped Buford go back and carry it up to where we were working. Then we took a break at the same time.

He drank from a tin can that hung from the handle on a wire hook. I drank from my one-gallon Clorox jug that I filled and put in the freezer compartment every night. I knew what it was like to drink warm water out of a hot can when the temperature was over a hundred, so I offered him a drink out of my jug. He said, no, he was fine. Then he shook out an L&M and lit it. He had his hair combed back on top and on the sides, and he didn't wear a cap or hat. From the looks of him I thought he'd be just as natural working in a tire shop or pool hall as in a prune orchard.

"This isn't too bad," I said. "But nobody's gonna get rich at it."

He flicked his ashes, and his blue eyes had a faraway shine as he said, "Not you or me, anyway."

I didn't know how to take that, so I said, "Did the boss give you any idea about how long this'll last?"

"Oh, I'd say about two weeks."

He stared off at his row of trees, and I got another look at him. He had light skin that blushed more than it tanned, and his hair was somewhere between blond and light brown. I figured him for a good five years older than I was, which doesn't seem like much, but when you're just nineteen, someone twenty-four or twenty-five might have been around and seen a lot more.

Still, I felt I had more experience in this area than he did. For one thing, I knew to wear a hat. Mine was a regular straw hat, which was fine for working on the ground. If I'd been working on a ladder I'd have worn a cap. This guy didn't wear either one, or even bring his own water, and he didn't seem to know that prune season lasted at least a month. But I figured there were plenty of things he knew that I didn't, so we were probably pretty even where we were.

As we got to talking, I found out this was the first time he had done any kind of orchard work. That didn't matter much, though, because a fella could learn just about any of these jobs in a few minutes, or at least learn what he was supposed to do. After that, it was a matter of getting the hang of it.

Take this work we were doing. The machines went through first—a shaker and a set of catch-frames that got eighty to ninety percent of the fruit. Some years the fruit shook better than others, and a year like this one, guys like us had to strip the trees with long poles. There were a few tricks to that. Then when the tree was stripped, a guy picked up all the scatters—some of them he knocked down himself, and others had fallen past the reach of the catch-frames. After that he picked up the strip of fruit that fell from the gap between the two frames, and the little heap around the trunk, and then there was usually a handful of prunes in the fork of the tree.

All the fruit went into lug boxes, stacked so there was room for the wagon to come through with the swampers. On this job they gave us a piece of chalk to write our number on the end of every box. My number was forty-nine, and I had blue chalk. Buford had yellow-orange chalk, and his number was thirty-seven. At twenty-five cents a box, we were both making about a dollar and a half an hour, which was two bits more than if we were getting paid by the hour.

It didn't take much brains, just the desire to stick with it and try to make a living. None of it ever lasted very long, so a guy made as much as he could. After all, if he was going to get up at five in the morning and put up with the heat and the mosquitoes all day, he might as well make the most of it.

Buford finished his second cigarette, and we both went back to work. We didn't stop or talk for the next couple of hours. When we knocked off at five, he asked me if he could get a ride into town. I said sure. I wondered how he'd gotten out to the orchard that morning, but I didn't ask. As a general rule, I don't ask a lot of questions. I don't want to seem like I'm prying, and most of the time I figure I'll never see this person again anyway, so whatever he tells me on his own is good enough. Then I can decide how much of it to believe.

My old Oldsmobile was hot as an oven inside, so we rolled down the windows and I stepped on the gas. He told me he was staying at the Star Hotel, which was an old hotel off Main Street, the kind that charged two or three dollars a night for a small room with the bathroom down the hall. I asked him if he had a way to get to work the next morning, and he said no. I offered to pick him up.

"That'd be damn good," he said. "If you want to get some gas now, I'll chip in."

He gave me a dollar, and I put up two more. Gas was twenty-nine cents a gallon, so my gas gauge was looking better when I pulled out of the station. I left Buford off in front of his hotel, and I drove to my cabin court.

First thing I did was fill my plastic jug and put it in the freezer compartment. Then I opened a can of macaroni and put it on to heat while I fried two slices of Spam. The cabin was hot and stuffy, and it took the squirrel-cage swamp cooler a good ten minutes to put out cool air.

It was all right, though. The place was costing me forty a month for a little kitchen and a main room. I could have had it for fifteen a week, but I went ahead and paid for a month, figuring I'd save money one way or the other. It had an iron-rail bed with bare springs and a mattress, plus a dresser and a narrow couch. The showers and toilets were all together in the middle of the court. It was a place for working men. I never saw anyone who looked like a bum, and I never saw a woman go in or out of any of the rooms.

After I cleaned the dishes I went and took a shower. When I came back, Slim was sitting in front of his cabin. He was an older man about forty-five or fifty, not as tall as most guys who went by Slim, and not all that skinny, just slender. I figured he got the name when he was young, and it stuck. He was an old-time Cat skinner with a weathered face and squinty eyes. He wore khaki shirts and smoked Pall Malls.

"Hello, Tom," he said. "Do any good today?"

"Regular, I guess."

"As much as you can expect. Hotter'n a son of a bitch, ain't it?"

"Sure is." I glanced at the water jug sitting next to his chair with water seeping onto the cement. It was a one-gallon wine jug with a burlap sack sewed tight around. I could see he had filled it and wet down the burlap, and I imagined he would wet it down again before he left in the morning. I knew that kind of jug, how to keep from chipping the mouth of it on a faucet when you filled it, but I knew what it was like when the jug broke, too. Then it was a bundle of crunching glass. Time to get another burlap bag and bum a jug from the sheepherders. Slim was a neat, careful guy, but everyone with a jug like that would break one sooner or later. Drop it on the pavement, crack it on the track of the Caterpillar.

"I'm gonna go in and watch TV in a little while," he said. "Come by if you want."

"Thanks, Slim. I don't know if I will tonight."

"Some other time."

"Sure." I went into my cabin and hung my towel to dry. I was wearing a clean shirt and pants, so I got my wallet from my work pants and stepped out into the evening.

Two blocks from the cabin court was a Frostie stand. The girl who worked there didn't look down her nose at me, so I'd gone there a few times. She was by herself again this evening, so I smiled as I stepped up to the window.

"Chocolate?"

"Yep."

I watched her as she swirled the soft ice cream onto the cone. She was just a normal-looking girl in her white uniform, with her blond hair tied back and her face not all done up with make-up. Her blue eyes didn't skate away as she handed me the cone and took the quarter I set on the ledge.

"Here you go."

"Thanks, Patty."

"Thank you. We'll see you later."

She slid the window shut, and I walked back to the cabin court as I ate the ice cream and cone. No hurry, I thought, and even if I did get the nerve to ask her out, there was always the chance she would turn me down.

* * *

I heard Slim moving around in the next room before my alarm went off, and I heard him pull out in his old Plymouth while I was making my sandwiches. He was off to a day of sun and dust, diesel fumes, and the ear-splitting crack of a D7 or D8. I had done some of that, and whenever I thought of it I could still hear the noise of the engine, along with the creak and clack of the tracklayer. Slim said none of it bothered him, he just stuffed his ears with cotton and lined up the radiator cap with a mountain peak on the other side of the valley, and pulled the throttle.

Knocking prunes was peaceful work by comparison, with the sound of the machinery at the other end of the orchard like the gunfire in a war movie. It was still lousy work, though. You never knew when you were going to stick your fingers in a prune that had fallen a week earlier. You went right into the mush, and then you were sticky with prune juice, but time was money so you didn't try to keep your hands clean. Even if you did, there would be another rotten prune beneath the ripe ones in the crotch of the tree. So your hands were sticky one way or the other, even when your palms rubbed clean with the knocking pole and the lug boxes, and when you picked the fruit off the ground, the dirt crusted on the sides and backs of your fingers. Then you slapped a mosquito and got a smudge on your face, and so on. It was no place to stay clean or look good. But it didn't matter.

I pulled out of the cabin court at five-thirty. The town was quiet and still like small towns are before sunup. Buford was waiting on the sidewalk with a little bundle of lunch wrapped up in a paper bag. When I stopped, he took a last drag on his cigarette and flipped it away, sending a few sparks along. He got into the passenger's side, and we rolled out of town. Lights had come on in a few houses, but no one was out and about. It gave a fellow a superior feeling, for what little it was worth, to be going to work before most of the rest of the world even got up. Clean, decent people—the kind that noticed if you came in from the fields with a dirty face and crusted fingers.

Buford and I ate lunch together that day, and he told a little about himself. He said he had been in the army, had worked around the oil rigs. That was good money, not like this, but his car blew up on him and he had to get back on his feet. He drove a truck in the oil fields, but he knew how to do all the roustabout jobs as well.

"You could learn it, too," he said. "Make three times as much as you can make at this."

"How do you get on at a job like that?"

"Aw, hell, you just go up and tell 'em you want to go to work."

"You need to know somethin' about it, don't you?"

He was eating a bologna sandwich, and he brushed away the crumbs from his mouth. "Not much to know. You can learn it as you go along. I could get you on, as far as that goes."

I always wondered why people who could make good money doing something else were working in the fruit fields, but I just said, "Somethin' to think about."

We worked on in the prune orchard for a couple more days, both of us getting sweaty and dirty and making about fifteen dollars a day. Buford rode back and forth with me, and on the fourth day we worked together he gave me another dollar for gasoline.

Then he said, "What would you think if I bought some porkchops, and we cooked 'em up at your place? I can't cook in my room, and I'm kinda tired of eatin' cold food out of a can."

I had already told him what kind of a place I was staying in, and his idea sounded reasonable enough, so I said okay. We went to a grocery store, where he picked out four porkchops, two cans of fruit cocktail, and a loaf of bread. Then at the cash stand he asked for two packs of L&Ms. He paid with a five-dollar bill and got two dollars and some change. He asked me if I needed anything else, and I said no.

Back at my place I fried the porkchops, and we ate them along with half a loaf of bread. Then we each had a can of fruit cocktail. It was a simple meal, but it was pretty satisfying, and the swamp cooler had made the place comfortable. Buford pushed back from the little table where we had eaten, lit a cigarette, and dropped the match in an empty fruit can.

238

"This place isn't too bad," he said. "Do you think it's big enough for two people?"

I shrugged. "I don't know. There's a couple of cabins where two guys stay, but I think they're a little bigger."

"I'll tell ya, I'm only lookin' to stay here for a couple of weeks, and I could sleep on that little couch easy enough. I could give you, say, a dollar a day. That way we'd both come out ahead. Then when I get ready to take off, if you want to go work in the oil fields, I can help you get on. If not, then I'm out of your hair."

"I don't know," I said, looking around.

"Naw, hell," he said. "That's okay. I don't want to crowd you. It's just that I'd rather be givin' money to you than to the folks at the hotel."

I gave it some thought. I could see where he might like to have me go with him to the oil fields, so he could have transportation, at least to get there. And the idea of making more money was a good one to me. On the other hand, if I was going to get tired of this fella, I ought to know it in a week or so, and I could get rid of him just by telling him I didn't feel like moving on.

Meanwhile, a dollar a day was nothing to sneeze at. Everything was on a two-bit scale, it seemed to me. A quart of milk and a loaf of bread both cost two bits. So did a pack of cigarettes. I didn't smoke, but I knew that much. Gas was two bits a gallon or a little more, depending on where you found it. The hourly wage was a dollar and a quarter, and I was averaging a dollar and a half at two bits a box. A dollar a day to have some guy sleeping on my couch for a week or two didn't seem all that bad, and sharing a room was still better than sleeping in my car, which I had done before and might be doing again before long.

"Yeah, why not," I said. "If it doesn't seem like a good idea after a few days, we can go back to doing things like before."

"Oh, hell, yeah," he said as he flicked his ashes in the fruit can. "Last thing I want to do is make a pest of myself. But if it's a go, I can let 'em know at the hotel, and I can take my stuff with me in the mornin'. I'm already paid up for tonight, of course."

"Sure."

"Well, that sounds good, Tom. And I'll tell you, I appreciate it. It's harder'n hell to just get by, and when someone helps you, you remember it."

"It's all right," I said, and I felt pretty good about being able to help out another guy.

* * *

He was waiting on the sidewalk the next morning, with a striped pasteboard suitcase next to him and a little traveling bag in his hand. I pulled over to the curb, and he opened the back door and put his belongings inside. Then he got in on the passenger's side of the front seat, and we were off for another day of work.

The early-morning farm program was on the radio, and Webb Pierce was singing "Wonderin'." Buford sang along as he rolled down the window and lit a cigarette. When the song ended he said, "There's somethin' I've been wonderin' about, too." He pronounced it "wanderin'" like the singer did.

"What's that?"

"Why in the hell do they call 'em prunes? I thought prunes was when they were dried, and plums was when they were fresh."

"That's somethin' everyone finds out before long. You've got fresh plums, and you've got fresh prunes. Then when they're dried, they're dried prunes."

"The hell."

"Oh, yeah. These guys that grow 'em, they're particular about it. And you go to work at a dryin' yard, you might find where they've got dried peaches, dried apricots, dried cherries, dried plums, and dried prunes. All of 'em. Whatever you call 'em fresh, that's what you call 'em when they're dried, and vice-versa."

"Well, by God, I never knew any of that."

"I didn't either, at one time."

He smoked his cigarette down and flicked the butt out the window. As I saw the sparks in the rear-view mirror, I wondered if he was just trying to make me feel smart.

* * *

We worked through that day without much to mention. It was a Friday, and the boss came around in the middle of the afternoon and paid me for everything through noon that day. Then he went to talk to Buford. He seemed to be making the rounds, and he didn't stop to talk very long with either of us.

240

We cashed our checks at the store where we bought our groceries. I cashed mine first and paid for all the groceries, which the kid in the green apron put in a cardboard box for me. I carried it out to the car and waited as Buford cashed his check and bought a carton of cigarettes. As a general rule I don't look at other people's wallets or money, so I had no interest in knowing how much he had gotten paid. When he came out of the store and climbed into the car, he gave me eight dollars for his half of the groceries.

That evening while he was taking a shower, I put away sixty dollars of my money. In the bottom of my traveling bag, beneath a couple of pairs of folded pants, I had a copy of an old book called *Topper*. The title of the book and the author's name, which I remember was Thorne Smith, were in staggered letters across a dull brown cover. I never read the book, but I remembered seeing parts of the television program, which was a slow-moving comedy about a ghost and odd things that floated on the air. Anyway, I ended up with the book, so I used it as a place to stash money whenever I got a little ahead. Then I dipped into it when I ran low between jobs. I always knew exactly how much I had, so I didn't have to count it, though I did from time to time. The amount I just put in made two hundred and forty.

When Buford was done with his shower, he pulled a chair outside and sat near Slim. He had made friends with the old Cat skinner, and the two of them would sit in the shade and talk as they smoked their cigarettes.

I took a shower and put on my clean clothes, and then as I often did, I went out for an ice cream. Patty was working by herself, as usual. She smiled as she handed me the cone.

The sense of having money stashed away made me feel good about myself, like I wasn't some run-of-the-mill fruit tramp. Still, I didn't think I'd known her long enough to talk about going out, so I just paid her and said, "See you later."

Back at the court, the door was unlocked and the room was empty. I could hear the television going next door, so I figured Buford was watching TV with Slim. I checked in my traveling bag, and there was the same old *Topper* with the two hundred and forty dollars safe and sound. I told myself that I was making myself worry, that putting in the sixty dollars hadn't made any big change except to remind me that I had the money hidden there.

241

* * *

We worked Saturday and Sunday just like any other day. When fruit was in season, it was nothing to work thirty days straight, and we were just getting started on this job. Buford plugged right along, working at the same rate as I did. For as much as anyone could have his heart in work like this, he didn't seem to have any feeling for it. He wasn't like the people who hated field work, but as soon as he was out of the orchard he acted as if he had never seen a picking bucket. By the time he had been staying with me for a week, I found myself wishing he would move on. There wasn't anything specific that I disliked—just that he and I weren't on the same wavelength. And he hadn't said much more about Bakersfield and the oil rigs.

One thing did get on my nerves a little, and that was his singing. Once he had gotten familiar with me, he took to singing out loud. I could see that he thought quite a bit of himself in that way. One day he came right out and said it. We had finished eating lunch and were sitting in the shade, and he had just lit a cigarette.

"If I could get the right break," he said, "I could be a singer. A lot of these guys have never had music lessons, much less voice lessons, and look at them. What have they got that I haven't? They got a break somewhere along the way, and now instead of workin' in a truck stop they've got someone drivin' their bus."

I nodded. "Who are you the most like? I mean, if you got to be a big singer, who would you be like?"

His answer came quick. "Webb Pierce."

"Really?"

"People tell me I sound just like him. When I want to. But I can do George Jones, Ray Price—you name it."

"Buck Owens?"

"Sure."

I could tell he was serious, and I didn't know enough about any of it to say otherwise. So I asked, "How about 'King of the Road'? Can you do that?"

"You damn right I can." He sat up, stubbed out his cigarette in the dirt clods, and sang that song as if he was Roger Miller himself, dropped down in a prune orchard.

"That was pretty good," I said.

"I just like to sing. If I get the right break some day, maybe you'll hear me on the radio."

* * *

On Friday, the boss came around again and paid through noon of that day. With the deductions, my check came out at a hundred and one dollars and some change. When we cashed our checks, Buford gave me eight dollars for room rent and five for gas, so I put an even hundred in with the rest of my hoard. Buford was in the shower, so I took the time to count the bills. It was all there.

After we ate, he went over to Slim's to watch TV, and I got cleaned up and went to the Frostie stand. I'd been there only once during the week, and I hoped the girl was glad to see me. She seemed like maybe she was. She smiled as she took my order and then handed me the cone.

As I paid her I asked, "Do you ever get tired of workin' all the time?"

"Sometimes, but there's not much else to do."

"Do you ever go out?"

"Once in a while."

My heartbeat picked up, and I was afraid of saying the wrong thing, so I just asked, "Where do you go?"

"Depends."

"Depends on..."

"Depends on who it is and what they want to do, and whether I can do it."

"Like whether it's bowling or the drive-in?"

"I can't go to the drive-in because it's out of town."

"Oh." I noticed the ice cream was starting to slip, and I didn't want to lick it right in front of her. "Well," I said, "there's no law against me askin' you next week, is there?"

"No, but I don't work Monday, you know."

"I remember that. So what if I come by on Tuesday?"

"No law against that."

Back at the room, Buford was still watching TV next door, and all my money was just as I left it. I sat around and killed time, thinking about how I was going to ask the girl to go out with me.

Buford came back at about nine. "Might as well turn in," he said. "Day starts early tomorrow."

We went through the same routine as every night except that now, just before I pulled the string on the overhead light, I noticed something for the first time. He had a tattoo on his right ankle. It looked like a row of numbers, nothing fancy, not like a girl's name that some guys had on their arm or shoulder. I thought he caught me looking at it, but then I shut out the light and neither of us said anything.

* * *

We went to work the next day, and everything seemed like normal. At a little before noon, Buford was gone for a while, like he'd been to the outhouse at the end of the orchard, and he came back.

"Say," he called as I was setting a lug box on the stack. "This old boy and his kid are goin' into town for a few minutes and then comin' back. They said I could go along. I need to wire some money to my brother, and the Western Union might be closed later on."

"Your brother?" This was the first time he had ever talked about any family.

"Yeah. My twin brother. I don't think I'll be gone more'n an hour."

I shrugged. As long as he didn't ask me to take him in, I wasn't going to lose any time. "Go ahead," I said. "I'll help you get caught up on your row when you get back." That was no skin off my ass either, because everything I picked would go into my box and get marked with a forty-nine in blue chalk. I looked at his stack, with the numbers all written in yellow orange, and I thought, I really couldn't worry about how much he made.

I worked on through the afternoon, and he didn't show up. I thought I heard that other car come back, and doors slamming at the edge of the orchard, so when I found a good stopping place I walked over a couple of rows and down toward the end where I could hear the man and his kid whacking branches and plunking fruit in a bucket.

The old man didn't have much to tell me. He said Buford offered him five dollars to take him to town, and when they got there, Buford asked him to leave him off at the cabin court. And that was it. I didn't know what to make of that, so I went back to my row. I picked a couple of more boxes, and then it got to eatin' on me, so I went to find the boss.

He was just turning into the orchard, driving a tractor and pulling an empty trailer with two swampers sitting on it, smoking cigarettes. He stepped on the clutch, cut the throttle, and tossed his head in a question.

"I was wondering if you knew what was up with this other guy, Buford," I said.

He shook his head. "I don't know. Why?"

"He went into town, and I thought he was coming back."

"I don't know. I thought he rode with you."

"He did. But he caught a ride with this guy and his kid."

"That's more than I know. I hope he doesn't go on a drunk."

"Well," I said, "I think I'm done for the day anyway. I guess I'll find out when I get back to town."

* * *

When I went into the room, I knew right away. Nothing was out of place, but all of his stuff was gone, and the key I had gotten for him was sitting on the dresser. I felt a sinking in my gut as I reached down by the far side of the bed and hauled up my traveling bag. I reached under the folded pants and brought out the old brown copy of *Topper*. I turned to the back cover, where I had always tucked the bills, and it was as bare as the front.

A hopeless, empty feeling set in as I held the book in my hand. This was what a person got, I thought. Try to go straight, help someone else, and they play you for a chump.

I didn't feel like eating or taking a shower or doing a damn thing, but I made myself eat a can of sardines and a couple of slices of bread. Then I went outside to tell my story to Slim.

He didn't seem surprised. "You can bet one thing," he said. "That bird's long gone. You just don't know which way."

He was right. The busses ran north and south through this town, a couple of times a day each way. I shook my head. "What a son of a bitch. Said he had to send money to his twin brother. And then he does this." I was having a hard time with the whole idea, like I was falling and hadn't stopped yet.

"It's just the kind of guy he is. He'll probably piss it away, then go on to the next place."

"I'd like to know where that was."

Slim made a little spitting sound. "That's another thing you can bet. You'll never see him again."

"I imagine." But I knew I'd be on the lookout for him everywhere I went. "There's one thing I was wonderin' about," I said.

"What's that?"

"Do they put a tattoo on your ankle when you're in the army?"

"Not that I know of. Why?"

"This guy had one there."

"Ohhhh..." said Slim. "They do that in the joint. And unless he was in the army first, that would have kept him out."

"So that was probably just another lie. All I was was a patsy for him."

"Well, I'm sorry for you, kid. But things like this are supposed to teach somethin'. Help you learn to paddle your own canoe. Make you tough, help you get back on top. "

Get back on top. It was like a capsized canoe and my hands kept slipping. "It doesn't feel that way."

"Not yet."

I shook my head again and tried to pull in a deep breath. I knew that as much as anything, it was the idea that the guy had gone into my room, reached into my bag, and opened that book—probably not the first time, either. And I had trusted him.

"It's like I've been walked all over," I said.

"Look, kid, I know this is easy for me to say, but you need to get the best of this. Look at it this way. You've still got a job and a way to get there. As for this other money, it's shot in the ass. You're never goin' to see it again, or that cheap bastard either. Just start over."

I knew he was right, but I also knew I couldn't make myself feel a certain way. I was just going to have to get through it. There was one thing I could do, one thing I knew how to do. I could go back to work alone and look out for myself. No one else was going to do it for me.

THE BELLS OF GOLD

By Miles Swarthout

Corporal Taylor had gotten hold of a bottle. The unshaven veteran was well into it, gulping the golden cactus juice away from the campfire's light, so he didn't have to share any with his tent mates in Troop G, 11th Cavalry, command of Second Lieutenant Harding Polk. Alcohol had been banned from General Pershing's Expedition into Mexico to chase Pancho Villa and his bandit gangs around to punish them for attacking and killing unsuspecting civilians and soldiers in a surprise raid across the border into Columbus, New Mexico, the violent night of March 9, 1916.

Now it was a chilly night in May at 5,200 feet on a wide plateau not that far from the rocky ridges of the fabled *Sierra Madres*. But if you were cagey and had the money and connections to obtain Mexican liquor, getting drunk off-duty was passably tolerated as long as you didn't make a spectacle of yourself. This *was* the United States Army.

Sergeant Sturges stirred the embers with a stick, sipped his coffee. His green recruit, Private O'Daniels, hunched next to the non-com, tight as a flea near a dog's anus, others had commented.

"Don't we have leave comin', Sarge? Two months ridin' hell and gone all over Mexico, seems to me we're owed some."

The lifer scratched under his wool collar with a dirty nail, seeking an elusive flea moving far from his ass. "We are, kid.

Prob'ly a week to hitch a ride on one of the empty supply trucks back to Columbus. Gives you a couple days up there to drink and debauch in the coochie houses across the border."

"Least they're American girls. I can't seem to work up an interest in these brown-skinned gals."

Their drunken tent mate chortled from the shadows. "They're all the same color in the dark, kid!"

Sergeant Sturges smiled at the time-worn riposte. "I was talkin' to this Mex yesterday, guy who sells us our vegetables. He mentioned this lost town up in the *Madres*. There's supposed to be bells left behind in its church's belfry. *Solid* gold."

Their newest recruit was skeptical. "Who in the world would abandon gold bells? Not Mexicans."

"Sounded phony to me, too, but this Mex, Roberto, swore it was true."

The gangly young man was all ears, and big ones, too. "Then let's go get 'em. Think the Lieutenant would let us look?"

Sergeant Sturges shrugged. "We can ask. Polk owes me a favor, after I shot that *Villista* at *Ojos Azules* who had a bead on him from the roof of that big *hacienda* when we rode in through its front gate."

"You speak enough Spanish?"

"Savvy more than I speak, but I talk with tradesmen every chance I get. You hear more from the locals than you ever will from our officers." He spoke over his shoulder. "You wanna go hunt gold with us, Taylor?"

"Maybe. Cheaper booze down here. But we'll probably find Pancho Villa quicker than any damned gold."

Sergeant Sturges squinted into the fire and nodded. He projected a hard brow and a hard jaw when he was thinking. A *taut* man, everybody agreed.

And then Corporal Taylor made a spectacle of himself, noisily sucking the green worm from the bottom of his clear bottle. The alcoholic crunched the caterpillar larva between prominent yellow front teeth, like a snapping turtle. His tent mates watched him swallow his fiery snack down his gullet and smiled at each other.

Surprisingly, Lieutenant Polk was amenable to his Sergeant's request for leave, even to somewhere besides Columbus. Something about paying a bet to another Lieutenant manning a scout detail presently at *Corrales*, a little town southwest in the mountains, the same direction they wished to go.

"You deliver a note and a bottle of whiskey from me to Lieutenant Charles Eby. And both better reach *Corrales* unopened or I'll take a stripe, Sergeant. Requisition food from the mess and I'll write you a seven-day pass. Two days ride each way and another three to—what was it you men wanted to do?"

"Search for treasure."

Lieutenant Polk stared for a moment, then shook his head. "Not likely. I owe you a favor, Sturges, which I'm repaying with your little jaunt. You're more likely to run into *Villistas* then dig up treasure. Three men, you wouldn't stand a Chinaman's chance against Pancho's boys. Then I'd have to mount the whole troop to fetch your carcasses back for burial, if enough of you was left. And I'd catch hell from Major Howze for allowing this foolishness... You *understand* me?"

"Yes, sir." Before turning on his heel, Sergeant Sturges even remembered to salute.

The soldiers rode out the next morning right after daybreak to get a good jump on their trek. Sergeant Sturges had spoken to the vegetable man again, but history remained vague. A forgotten village up in the *Madres*, somewhere beyond *Corrales*, bells of gold, solid, *buena suerte*, Señor. Sturges figured he'd have a better chance of shooting and cooking a wild goose on this particular chase.

They trotted their cavalry mounts away from the tent camp, which General Pershing was already turning into his main supply depot for all the troops of cavalry and infantry he had out scouring 94,000 square miles of Chihuahua for Pancho Villa and his bloody pals. Day and night, ton-and-a-half Jeffrey Quad truck trains chugged at fourteen miles an hour back and forth a hundred miles north to the American base in Columbus, which connected by rail to permanent Ft. Bliss in El Paso. The Expedition had been roaming around northern Mexico since January, and their engineers had managed to turn a long trail to the border into something resembling a road. Still rutted dirt, but navigable.

The three riders passed along the stream running through *Colonia Dublán* four miles below their camp. *Dublán* was one of

249

nine large colonies established in Mexico by Mormons at the turn of the twentieth century after conflict with the U.S. authorities over America's new polygamy laws. Two-story brick houses, wide dirt streets, fruit trees, and once-green lawns now unseeded made *Colonia Dublán* look like a prosperous Midwestern community reassembled in Old Mexico. But they were now empty except for caretakers left behind to make sure their homes weren't looted and to tend their cultivated fields. A few of them hired out as bilingual guides for the army, but most of these Mormons and their many wives had high-tailed it back up to the States. Too dangerous for whites during a revolution in Mexico. *Buenas tardes, gringos!*

The well-worn trail to *Corrales* was easy to follow as it led up into the foothills of the *Sierra Madres*. Their horses were fresh and good climbers, even under full loads of armed men and stuffed saddlebags behind their McClellan saddles, plus rain slickers and blankets strapped on, too.

They camped the first night in a rocky defile between the first ancillary peaks over six thousand feet, closer to seven. Adjusting to this thinner air, they didn't talk much, letting Taylor subdue his hangover in peace as he built a cook fire. Their horses needed to be fed while it was still light. All Sturges had been able to get for this unimportant trip were sacks of native corn, rather than the expensive oats usual on military patrols. So Sergeant Sturges and Private O'Daniels had to first spread out a sackful of dried corn kernels across a woolen blanket and pick out by hand the small pebbles among the feed. They needed to locate all the tiny rocks, for once a horse bit a stone it stopped eating from that nosebag, regardless of its hunger.

Corporal Taylor stopped tending the fire to pull out the "makins," loose tobacco from a sack and a paper to roll himself a smoke.

"I can't believe Mexicans would leave gold bells behind, hanging out in the open. They dig gold from these mountains all the time and love it to death, just like we do."

"My vegetable man said it was because of evil spirits, *espíritus malos*, and jaguars around this lost place, so no one would go there."

"*Jaguars!*" O'Daniels snorted. "Those spotted cats aren't big enough to prey on folks, are they?"

"Not like the bigger mountain lions down here," agreed Sturges. "You ever hear one of those cougars scream in the dark, you'll believe in evil spirits. Immediately!"

They laughed. "Mexicans are mostly Catholics. Spiritual folk. These peasants are very taken with old myths and superstitions," added their scholarly Sergeant.

"Well, if they did leave any gold bells behind, they're gone by now," groused the Corporal, rubbing his aching forehead. "Not everyone's that stupid, or superstitious."

After supper they tucked in, pondering jaguars and noises in the night. Sturges and his protégé huddled together in single wool blankets for warmth. Across the fire, Taylor sawed wood noisily, sweating *mezcal* from his system.

They arose early again, unlimbering stiff joints in the cold spring air as they warmed up currying and feeding their horses. A hasty breakfast of hardtack and coffee got them on their way again to a hoped-for hot meal at the cavalry outpost that night.

There wasn't much of *Corrales* to see that late afternoon. It lay between two mountain ranges—a spatter of adobe hovels, a stable, a blacksmith, and a cantina with a small store attached. As they trotted in they saw vegetable gardens and patches of corn planted behind some dwellings. Chickens and pigs rooted between the hovels, and shy niños peeked at the cavalrymen from around corners. Mongrel dogs wandered out to bark greetings.

First Lieutenant Eby and his squad were bivouacked in a dilapidated adobe. The cavalrymen's eight horses were tied to a lariat line strung between the stick-built outhouse and a short tree out back, which his companions used while Sturges reported.

Lieutenant Eby rested in a hammock inside the adobe, hung from *viga* timbers in the dwelling's low ceiling. Several of his men were playing cards on the dirt floor. The officer smiled when Sergeant Sturges handed him the unopened bottle of Kentucky whiskey.

"Compliments of Lieutenant Polk, sir."

Charles Eby stroked his sandy mustache as he read the brief note from his buddy.

"You rode two days to deliver this?"

"I like Lieutenant Polk, so we did him a favor. We're jus' takin' a few days' leave, lookin' around... You ever hear of a lost village, in the *Madres* around here, sir?"

"Hell, they're *all* lost up here. We're only bivouacked here temporarily, thank God. Indian camps, mining claims, tiny towns, this huge mountain range is mostly unmapped, Sergeant. *You'll* get lost in the *Madres*, just trying to *find* some goddamned forgotten place."

The non-com nodded. Lieutenant Eby untangled himself from his sisal-woven hammock, sat up and stretched. "Talk to Estrella next door. Her husband, Esteban, runs the *cantina* and she works their little store. This fine hovel she's renting us. Estrella knows everybody and everything going on in *Corrales*. Even speaks a little English."

"Knows where Pancho Villa is?" O'Daniels had followed Sturges inside.

Lieutenant Eby grinned. "Maybe even that. Go get a hot meal and a bath, boys, on your lovely vacation."

They didn't need a bath yet; it was only a couple days since their last one at the main base. But the three men from Troop G did enjoy hot plates of tamales and pinto beans in Esteban's cantina that evening. Besides some peasants drinking at the wooden bar, at another table in back Lieutenant Eby was treating his seven cavalrymen to shots of his prize whiskey amidst high spirits for all.

When the woman serving passed by their table, Sergeant Sturges indicated more rounds of *tequila, por favor*. When she returned with a bottle to pour more shots, Sturges queried her.

"*Señora Estrella?*"

"*Si.*"

"*¿Dónde están las campanas de oro?*" ("Where are the bells of gold?")

The well-built woman smiled, but kept pouring. "You hear thees story?"

"*Si.*"

She had the soldiers' attention. "Somewheres in thees *Sierra Madres*, thees lost village, thees golden bells, they hide. Don' know where? Or I rich, no?"

"Protected by Pancho Villa?" asked O'Daniels, obsessed by the bandit chief.

The proprietress laughed heartily and slapped a solid thigh. "Pancho keep thees bells, si."

"Would anyone around here know? In *Corrales?*" asked Sturges.

Estrella shrugged. "Natividad, may-be. Ol' Indian, up thees mountain, keep goats. You pay, may-be he show you?" The restaurant owner pulled a shot glass from her worn apron and poured herself a shot of tequila. Raising it in toast, she added, "*Por las campanas de oro! Mucha suerte, Señores!*" (Good luck, Sirs!)

All four drank 'em down. Estrella cupped a hand to her ear. "I hear them ringing now!"

They chuckled.

"Estrella! *Comida!*" At a shout from the kitchen, their hostess vamoosed.

There were no more hovels to rent, so the three soldiers picketed their mounts with the other patrol's horses, grabbed some weedy ground for their blankets out back and went to sleep without a campfire that starry night.

"How do these peons even make a living way up here, middle of nowhere?" O'Daniels wondered.

"We saw half-wild cattle in the brush riding in here," answered Sturges. "Vegetable patches and crop fields in the flatter places, maybe a little smuggling, too. Tenant farming at best."

"So signing up with Pancho Villa when he rides through, looks exciting to these young bloods," decided O'Daniels. "Guess I can't blame 'em."

Taylor was already snoring in his blanket.

"Good night, Sarge. *Gracias* for the *tequila.*" O'Daniels wiggled his stockinged toes, his big one poking through a hole. "Don't let those jaguars bite."

After a breakfast of eggs and beans and tortillas in Esteban's cantina, they were on their way, just as the cavalrymen in the adobe next door were rising. Sturges didn't welcome any more sarcasm from the First Lieutenant about what they were doing. They had only two days left of their leave to find anything and three days after that to return to the army's base at *Colonia Dublán*, so they had to move it.

The soldiers found the goatherder's place up the mountain trail an hour beyond *Corrales*. There was nothing else besides his lean-to shack of boards and dried ocotillo spines up there. Old

Natividad was outside milking a she-goat into a rusty iron bucket. The army men could see other goats across the mountainside munching sparse browse. The three dismounted for a breather, taking pulls from their canteens.

"*Natividad?*" Sturges asked.

Darker-skinned than most of the Mexicans he'd seen, the wizened old man probably had some Indian blood in him, Sturges thought. A tribe called *Tarahumaras*, fabled long-distance runners, inhabited these *Madres* mountains, and God knew who else.

The old man stroked a dusting of snowy beard and nodded.

"*Estrella en Corrales nos mandó. ¿Dónde están las campanas de oro?*" (Estrella in Corrales sent us. Where are the gold bells?)

Natividad looked them over, then smiled. He said something in Spanish, but he was missing a few teeth and he mumbled, so Sergeant Sturges couldn't understand him. He repeated the question.

The old Mexican smiled and pointed up the mountain, then his gnarled finger arced off into the distance.

"*¿Las campanas de oro?*" (The golden bells?)

"*Sí.*"

"*Llevanos, por favor. ¿O enseñenos donde queda?*" (Take us, please. Or show us where they are?)

"*No gracias.*" (No thanks.)

Sergeant Sturges pulled three silver dollars from the pocket of his pegged breeches and displayed them in his open palm.

Natividad wiggled his index finger negatively, then reached and tapped the sky several times in the direction he'd indicated before.

Sturges became more forceful, moving toward the oldster squatting.

"*Señor, por favor!*"

It had become a disagreement. The old Mexican pointed to the goat in front of him, then to his other goats scattered about the mountainside, indicating he couldn't leave his herd.

Sergeant Sturges bent and took the old man by his skinny bicep, lifted him to his feet. "Taylor, your Springfield."

The big Corporal knew what his non-com wanted. Yanking his .30-06 from his saddle scabbard, the overbearing man strode over to the two men and suddenly swung the wooden butt of his

254

rifle into the old man's stomach, knocking the wind out of him with a *"woof!"* Natividad went down on his tailbone among the rocks. Taylor raised his Springfield again, preparing to smash the toes protruding from his ancient leather sandals next, but Sturges stopped him.

"Not his feet or arms. He's gotta guide us, remember." Sturges yanked the old man back up, where he was met by an uppercut from the Corporal. Taylor was off-balance, holding his nine-pound rifle in one hand, so the sucker punch didn't do much damage, draw any blood. But Natividad had gotten the harsh message as Sturges pulled him once again to his feet. Holding his bony hands up to stop the punishment, the old man gave in.

"Si, si, vamos." (Yes, yes, let's go.)

Within a half-hour they were back on the trail heading up this higher ridge. Sturges took the point now, with Taylor second in line, pulling Natividad behind him on his burro by a rope halter. The Mexican's bare ankles beneath his white muslin pants banged against his burro's sides, but he was used to riding with no saddle from when he rode down to the village to trade a goat for supplies. As they crossed the ridge, looking back from his position in the rear, O'Daniels could see smoke rising from peasants' homes in the distance, back in *Corrales*.

Their day's journey was uneventful, up, then down into a dry watercourse, then back up an even higher ridge as they rode slowly, deeper into the *Sierra Madres*. Natividad was quiet. That night they camped in an elevated arroyo leading up between two higher peaks. No flat land to sleep on, even their campfire was built on a slant. Sturges was concerned about water. Hopefully this lost village they would soon reach would have some water source nearby. He shook a half-empty canteen at the old man, who was rubbing his sore jaw as he tied his burro to the horses' picket line.

"¿Hay agua cerca?" (Is there water nearby?)

Natividad grumpily shook his head. No water nearby.

They made do with a nearly dry camp that night. Corn for the horses and ripening bacon from the skillet and hardtack from their saddlebags. This was a feast for the old man and his burro. Sergeant Sturges drank his "cowboy coffee." It was a dark, bitter brew made by boiling water and coffee and allowing the grounds to settle in the bottom of the pot. He poured another tin cupful.

He had to keep this old boy functioning to guide them to the gold and then back out of this wilderness again. Natividad accepted his charity drink in silence.

O'Daniels was attempting to sew up one of his holey cotton socks.

"I heard Pancho Villa executed his prisoners, even the wounded. A guy in the 7th Cavalry told me Pancho would line up prisoners three or four deep and dispatch them all with one heavy bullet through the first one's head. To save ammunition."

"The *tiro de gracia*, mercy shot," commented Sturges.

"So you think that's possible?" wondered O'Daniels.

"Horseshit," said Taylor, picking his teeth after dinner with a dirk. "Mexicans are notoriously bad shots. They don't know how to use the front sights of the guns they steal from us or smuggle down here. Maybe it happened once, but they ain't makin' trick shots like that often."

"Heard Villa was fond of sweets and women. Won't touch alcohol, though," offered Sturges.

"Unusual for a bandit," Taylor concluded. "Don't trust a man who don't drink."

This was a colder night in the mountains, a sharp contrast to warmer days down on flatter lands. Sturges and O'Daniels raked away coals from their campfire with green brush, spread a tarp over the heated firebed, and then lay down fully clothed beside each other, pulling blankets and saddles on top of themselves. Taylor threw his blanket over his shoulders and took the first two-hour watch over their captive, who rolled up in his thin blanket and *zarape* next to his resting burro and went to sleep, well used to the altitude and the cold.

They made it through a restless night, what with all three soldiers having to sit guard without nodding off too long. Consequently theirs was a mostly silent breakfast, so they didn't fall into argument. As they hit the saddle, young O'Daniels blew his nose loudly, having developed a nosebleed from the higher elevation. The Americans were all partially hypoxic, having trouble breathing. Sturges did allow that this had to be their last day of searching, for even by pushing harder back to camp, three days would barely be enough time left on their week's pass.

They rode up into the ramparts of the *Sierra Madres* and the trees reflected this higher elevation—pines, cedars, and low junipers all around. The narrow trail was almost overgrown in places and didn't reveal any animal tracks, not shod ones anyway. After a couple hours, they rode slowly down into what looked like a box canyon. The burro had no problem, but the larger horses had to pick their ways carefully over the loose shale. The air became warmer again and the cavalrymen's drab green woolen shirts soaked up sweat and began to itch. To pass boring time, Taylor broke into song, which echoed off the surrounding cliffs.

"Oh I'd rather be handsome than homely,
I'd rather be youthful than old,
If I can't have a bushel of silver,
I'll make do with a barrel of gold..."

"Give it a rest, Taylor. Warn everybody for miles around we're comin'," cautioned Sturges.

"Who's *every*body? I ain't seen *any*body."

Natividad pulled his burro's guide rope, signaling the Sergeant to halt. The old man gestured to his right and the others peered along an offshoot slot canyon they hadn't seen from a distance. The Mexican pointed several times they were to take it. "*Rápidamente!*"

Spurring their mounts to a slow trot, they rode into this slot canyon for nearly an hour, through a gully between cliffs tight enough in places for only four horses to pass side-by-side, or one wagon. This must be the lost passage to paradise, Sturges figured.

The narrow canyon gradually rose upward again, until they came to a place where a dry arroyo bent sharply right. They followed this path at a walk, letting the horses blow, for their only option was to turn back the same way they had come into these narrow canyons. Finally, by early afternoon, they broke out of the slot canyons into another canyon, which was ringed on three sides in front of them by taller cliffs.

Sergeant Sturges pulled his Arabian stallion's bit to halt. Reaching behind, he drew his Bausch and Lomb binoculars from his saddlebag. The other riders bumped up behind him.

Below them, the ground gradually lowered and flattened into a canyon through which ran a stream, rushing from the spring rains. Sturges scanned the distance through the dual lenses a supply Sergeant had loaned him.

"Anything worth all this trouble?" demanded Corporal Taylor.

"Well...I see...what looks like a little village, ruined adobes, a couple better dwellings, too. Can those be brick? Oh, there's a bigger building, taller, could be a church, but it ain't whitewashed. Some kind of open structure on top. Fruit trees down there, no people. Not a soul, looks abandoned."

Their leader pulled the binoculars from his eyes and handed them to Taylor, who grabbed. Sturges sloshed the last water from a canteen down his parched throat. "Regardless, we've gotta get to that stream or our horses will founder."

"Me, too," muttered Taylor, still scanning the distant canyon bottom. "Don't see nothin' in that church tower, if that's what it is."

Private O'Daniels pointed excitedly into the distance, quizzing their guide. "*¿Las campanas de oro?*"

The old man nodded gravely. "*Sí.*"

They had to stop at the stream first. Their horses smelled water and took off in that direction. Upstream from the splashing animals the soldiers stuck their heads into the rushing waters filled from spring rains. They splashed their sweaty chests, wrung their wet hair dry. Sergeant Sturges dried off with a spare shirt before putting his brown peaked campaign hat back on. He scanned the village again through his binoculars.

"Couple houses look like they're built of brick. They aren't crumblin' like the adobes. How could anyone have gotten bricks in here? By muleback? Reminds me of those brick houses in *Colonia Dublán* the Mormons built."

"If Mormons were in here, Sarge, why did they leave? You could farm this canyon bottom land, run cattle and sheep in here," mused O'Daniels.

"Well, this place is isolated, far from any railroad, any bigger towns to sell your crops in. Looks like it's been abandoned for a good while. Five years ago they had Red Flaggers, the *Colorados*, storming across Chihuahua. The Major told me about 'em, bandit gangs who pillaged and killed and held for ransom anybody with money, especially *gringos*. That was, I guess, the second part of this Mexican revolution. Now we're in their third act. Villa and his armed gangs have scared most of the Mormons out of their colony at *Dublán* and elsewhere all over again."

"What about the spirits and jaguars?" said Taylor, grinning.

"Well, maybe those scared 'em out of here, too."

Young O'Daniels was excited. "Mormons *love* gold! I had a friend in Illinois, Mormon kid always trying to convert me. He told me about these golden plates inscribed with their sacred Mormon text, protected by an angel named Moroni. Mormons love gold. It's part of their holy scripture. Why not golden bells, too?"

Corporal Taylor was becoming impatient. "Who *doesn't* love gold? Let's go find some!" Taylor yanked his horse from the stream, tried to mount on the slippery grass.

"Fill your canteens *first!*" ordered Sturges.

They did so, reluctantly, but Sergeant Sturges couldn't hold his excited men back as they raced ahead on refreshed horses. Sturges and the Mexican trotted behind, Sturges pulling his rifle from its scabbard. They jumped off their horses. Taylor and O'Daniels were already running inside the bigger building, which did look like a crude church, with one larger wooden front door hanging from a hinge. Sturges took his careful time, pulling a 1911 Colt .45, the Army's newest semi-automatic weapon, from his holster. He pulled the slide and bolt on top back and let it snap forward, then thumbed up the safety before entering one of the sturdier brick and frame houses by pushing its wooden door open with the barrel of his Springfield.

The house was empty, its walls barren except of cobwebs. Pieces of wooden furniture were all he found in the three small rooms. The little home had been looted, cleaned out of anything of value. Sturges stepped back out into the daylight, blinking. Behind the brick home, what might have been an outhouse lay rotting in wood scraps.

A hundred yards away near the canyon's other wall he saw O'Daniels appear in the walled upper opening of the biggest structure. The twenty-year-old rousted several large birds, crows, from what might have once been a belfry with his yelling.

"No bells up here, Sarge! Gold or otherwise!"

Downstairs, Sturges could hear the Corporal banging around, busting up stuff in his fury. The Sergeant was perplexed, so he walked to another dwelling, one of the adobe and log hovels crumbling from hard weather and poked around inside it. The fireplace was blackened from use, but except for broken pottery and a tin bucket with a hole in its bottom, this home was also empty.

Outside again, Sergeant Sturges saw their horses idly munching new grass. Natividad squatted on his haunches beside three run-down citrus trees which needed pruning, near the brick house. The old Mexican got up to walk over to an *acequia*, which ran to these trees from the stream. He bent and pulled up a stone wedge at stream's edge so that water ran down this ditch that appeared to be mostly clean of weeds and grass. *Someone* had been irrigating these fruit trees regularly!

O'Daniels ran up to report. "Nothin' inside that old church, Sarge! If that's what it was?"

Taylor stalked up, fuming. "*Nothin'* here! Any bells would be very heavy, solid gold. If they weren't stolen, maybe they buried them. To come back later."

"Well, *fine*! We don't have time to go diggin' all around here, even if we knew where in hell to look." Sergeant Sturges walked his frustration around in a circle, like an angry rooster. He halted and threw his arms wide toward the elderly goatherd. "*¿Dónde están las campanas de oro?*" (Where are the golden bells?)

The old man looked from one of these tired, anxious, damp men to the next. Natividad turned to open his arms to the citrus tree near him.

"*Pero Señores, aqui están!*" (But Sirs, here they are!)

The soldiers stared.

And there, from the branches of the three trees, swinging gently in the breeze, shining in the sun, hung golden oranges. Natividad rose, picked a big one, fully ripened now in early May, and began to peel rind off with his strong, gnarled fingers.

The cavalrymen stood stunned, not quite comprehending.

The Mexican raised an orange half, tilted his head back and squeezed juice into his mouth. Orange pulp dribbled down his stubbled chin as he smacked his cracked lips in delight.

"*Delicioso!*"

"Oranges!" shouted O'Daniels. "The spirits tricked us!"

The big Corporal just shook his head, pole-axed. Their Sergeant was more circumspect. Sturges stepped to the nearest citrus, ripped off several good-sized ones and tossed an orange to each of his companions. Pulling a Barlow knife from his pegged pants, he sliced an orange in half and imitated the old man, squeezing the tasty juice overhead into his mouth.

"Ahhhhggg! It's good!"

Borrowing his pocket knife, soon all four were doing it, slicing oranges and squeezing juice into their opened mouths like chickens in the rain, laughing and slobbering, dancing a little crazy, men possessed.

As a ripe, golden sun disappeared slowly below the west rim of this hidden canyon's little village, lost in the vast silence of the *Sierra Madres.*

THE GREAT FILIBUSTER OF 1975

By Richard S. Wheeler

Now, I know you're going to disapprove. You'll be shaking your head, frowning, and concluding that I am the ugly American; that I threatened the comity of nations, acted recklessly, was utterly insensitive to the world's poor, and am stupid besides. And that's just for starters.

Actually, I would agree with you. I was all of the above, and I am quite contrite. Or at least ninety percent of me is contrite. The other ten percent—well, you have to understand that I am an aging juvenile delinquent. I look back upon that awful deed not as a moment of shame or folly, but as my own glorious footnote to History. After all, do you know of anyone else—even one soul— who has added to the territory of the United States? Especially by stealing it from a neighbor? Ah, now I have your attention! I committed a *filibuster* against Mexico.

But I have gotten ahead of myself. In 1975 I was at loose ends, having been put out of work by the great oil crisis and recession. It was a bad time for the United States. The sheiks had turned off the spigot. There was the little matter of Watergate. A lot of us were out of work, including me, John Arnold, indirectly descended from Benedict Arnold, but the family doesn't make it known.

By trade I am a newspaper editor. But in 1975 I had no trade at all, having been released from the desperate grasp of a certain Midwestern metropolitan daily that I will not mention for fear of embarrassing its stockholders. I am also a veteran bachelor, having attended a wife briefly in my youth and finding the whole arrangement without merit. I prefer to spend my entire salary on myself. At least when I have a salary, which I didn't, in 1975. As long as I was at loose ends, and the chances of getting a job in a recession were nil, I thought I'd squander my savings on adventure. So, I traded my Midwestern Buick for a used pickup truck and headed west, intending to end up in whatever trouble I could get into, wherever the wind blew me. That proved to be the Rancho Oro Blanco, right smack on the Mexican border of Arizona, southwest of Tucson, a place just about as remote as one can get.

Oro Blanco was, in fact, a venerable guest ranch, but so hidden that only the most intrepid guests ever found it. It spread over the eastern edge of the Altar Valley, a vast mountain-girt desert plain that extended north and south, from deep in Sonora well into Arizona. To reach it, one drove to the weary little town of Arivaca, perched solemnly in an arid plain and existing only because its few inhabitants were too tired and broke to depart, and from there one traversed an endless dirt road that meandered south and west, through cholla-choked canyons, and ocotillo-crowned hills, until suddenly one burst out upon a watered delta dotted with cottonwoods and verdant grasses, all of it shocking green. Here a giant arroyo burst out of the hills and emptied into the valley. It was dry, of course, like everything else in the Sonora Desert, but not far under its rough, sandy bed lay a water table that was the foundation of the Rancho Oro Blanco, the White Gold Ranch.

During the winter months the ranch did a lively trade, offering a thin warmth and horseback riding and bird-watching to guests from all over the world. The Oro Blanco was a venerable place, over two hundred years old, and owed its existence to a Spanish land grant dating back to the 1750s. The ancient dried-mud buildings hadn't changed much. The adobe guest quarters had beehive fireplaces and ocotillo ramadas. The corrals had been built of mesquite and rawhide. The old rancho itself had terra cotta tile floors, vigas, thick adobe walls strong enough to fend off the Apaches, and an array of heavy Mexican colonial furniture.

I had arrived in May, when the temperatures were already topping a hundred each afternoon, and not a guest was in sight. A room might be had for a very little during the Sonoran summer, and the use of the big kitchen came with it. The rancho did not employ much help during those furnace months. There was only the manager and his wife, and one wrangler to look after the dude string, as the saddle horses were called. Assorted Mexicans drifted in and out, on mysterious errands, occasionally as day labor. Whether they were legally on the north side of the line I could not say.

I settled in. The place enchanted me. There I was, in the middle of nowhere, three hours from Tucson but it may as well have been three weeks. They let me fool with a gentle horse, and if I got up at six I could get in a good ride before it got hot. The place twittered with desert birds, of such plumage and color as I had never seen, as if I had entered a land of a thousand fluorescent parrots.

I didn't know what to do with myself, but what did it matter?

The border itself was nothing but an ordinary four-strand barbed wire fence stretching arrow straight in southeast-northwest direction there. The desert on the other side was more ravaged by grazing than land on the United States side, but just as unpopulated and mysterious. The fence, I learned, was private property; it belonged to the Rancho, not the government. And its upkeep was not shared by the Mexican ranchers on the other side, who were too poor to maintain it. The border was demarcated by small white obelisks at five-mile intervals. One stood on the rancho. Occasional wire ranch gates had been built into the border fence here and there, and I could only surmise what for. Sometimes I saw footprints in the sand at those gates. There was traffic I knew nothing about, that probably passed in the night.

During my forays into the kitchen I got to know my hosts, Cap and Marcy Granville, and the wrangler, a blond kid from Wyoming named Willie something or other. If the Granvilles had social graces they reserved them for the guests in season. During the hot, dry, summer days of doing almost nothing, they grumbled at each other, complained, and vanished into their rooms for endless siestas. Willie was more taciturn, and apart from working some greenbroke horses in the cool dawn, forking some alfalfa hay, checking the wells, and smoking some contraband under his ocotillo arbor at twilight, he mostly slept. He obviously intended to squander the fierce Sonoran summer letting his thin blond beard grow to perfect scruffiness while avoiding declarations longer than three words. That suited me fine. I was more interested in the lizards and Gila monsters and exotic pink desert rattlers than in the riffraff.

In spite of their best efforts not to be sociable, I got to know them well. The summer isolation does that. Just when you think you've left the whole world behind, you hanker for companionship. I was quite content to spend days and hours saying nothing, avoiding the others, and doing nothing. After twenty years of laboring in the vineyards, I wanted to do nothing at all. The exotic land, so harsh and handsome, was enough for my soul at that time.

But society intrudes, even in that silent, remote corner of the nation. And where else but the kitchen? They cooked their meals, just as I cooked mine, and soon enough we were eating together.

Captain (where the title came from I don't know; there was nothing military about him, thank God) Theophilius Granville, it turned out, was a burly carrot-haired natural boor as well as the world's greatest expert, but he had the saving grace of conceit. He thought little of the neighbors to the south, whom he called "our brown brothers." I thought at first he was a home-grown racist, but he wasn't, exactly. Chauvinist would be a better word. He was simply jaundiced and cynical.

If the brown brothers had let a diesel engine burn up for lack of crankcase oil, that was something to nod knowingly about. If the brown brothers drilled a well in the bottom of an arroyo that drew off village sewage and they all got sick, that was something for Cap to dwell upon with sheer joy. If the brown mothers spent all their loose pesos on expensive Pampers at the port of Sasabe instead of changing diapers, that was something delicious to rail about. Cap found evidence every day to fortify his views. I found his bilious observations infectious in spite of myself. They were an entertainment that continued nonstop to while away a hot empty summer. The more time he spent with me, the less guarded he became, and after a few weeks I came to know Cap Granville as a rural raptor whose own vulpine esteem fed on the carcasses of his neighbors across the line.

Mexico offended him enormously, hugely, like some giant trash heap in the middle of Newport Beach. And there it was, just beyond the four-strand barbed wire fence, this monster of Granville's indignation, this habitat of cretins who guzzled cerveza that tasted like varnish, slaved in an adobe brick factory for eight cents an hour, and knifed each other on weekends and holy days for sport.

Marcy was kinder. She was Earth Woman, embracing brown brothers and sisters to her generous bosom. But I preferred to listen to the refreshing and uncivilized bile issuing from the Captain, which was an improvement over the bland talk radio one could sometimes pick up. Cap was an original, and from his jaundiced soul I fashioned a good idea of life across the border, a life I never witnessed because across that mysterious fence was nothing but barren rock, ocotillo, cholla, and silence.

Neighboring the ranch to the west was the small, crowded yard of a refrigerator smuggler, who dwelled on a hectare or so carved out of the great hacienda some eons ago, some peon's reward for a life of servitude. His casa could be reached only by traversing a violent two-rut road that wound and teetered westward into the broad Altar Valley and eventually joined a larger ranch road, and finally the unpaved Arizona highway to Sasabe. The refrigerator smuggler, one ChiChi Juarez, made his living by running used appliances into Mexico in his battered 1950s-vintage gray Ford stock truck. His adobe house stood so close to the line that he could spit into Mexico from his window. But his weedy clay yard was a phenomenon. Everywhere I looked, I beheld cancerous Maytags and Frigidaires, rusty swamp coolers, venerable Whirlpools and Kenmores and Generalissimo Electrics, all of them the offscouring of prosperous Tucson. You would suppose he was running an outdoor Laundromat. No nearby wire gate in the border fence ever revealed tire tracks through it, but every few weeks this amazing collection of rusty white rectangles would vanish, and then ChiChi's clay yard would be the home only of niños and tarantulas and Gila monsters, along with old batteries, mufflers, washing machine innards, and carburetors.

The source of ChiChi's wealth was simple. Mexico imposed a stiff import duty on manufactured goods, a duty equal to the cost of the appliance, and the result was that Mexico's campesinos could not afford new or even used washers or refrigerators or stoves or dryers or air conditioners or coffeemakers or freezers. So, it became ChiChi's inspired vocation to relieve suffering south of the border, by purchasing these objects in Tucson and then periodically running down dusty Sonoran trails, far from the eyes of the Federales, or maybe right under their eyes if he filled their extended palms, and sold his rusty iron in Hermosillo.

I considered ChiChi a hero, making Arizona a cleaner state and relieving the poor of their suffering. He could barely speak English, so I had little commerce with him, but he smiled a great deal, displaying a fine gold incisor. And judging from the perpetual distended condition of his esposa, I knew that his greatest achievement on earth was manufacturing niños, which he produced as reliably as stoves and washing machines.

And so my Sonoran summer progressed. The heat deepened. As May cooked into June, the furnace heat stifled the impulse to do anything but lie abed and enjoy the dry breezes wafting through open windows. Even the exotic birds headed for cover mid-day. I had never experienced a heat so oppressive or pervasive or inescapable, for there was no air conditioning at Rancho Oro Blanco except for a swamp cooler in the Granvilles' adobe. But I rejoiced. For the first time in my forty-two years, I was doing absolutely nothing, and not all the promptings of conscience warning me against a squandered and ruined life, persuaded me to do anything other than wander about like some war-ruined veteran, which in a commercial way, I was. I was adrift among sun-blasted rock heaps, cactus, scaly creatures, scorpions, and gaudy birds.

The Granvilles warned me that the summer monsoon season would start late in June, around San Juan's Feast Day. These would be sharp showers and would be over fast, and sometimes the rain would not even reach the superheated desert floor.

The day began just the same as any other, burning bright with a brassy sky and a ferocious sun. But then, to my surprise, clouds built over the mountains, and formed into towers of cumulus, sometimes tens of thousands of feet high, so one peered upward into a world of white walls. It did not rain that day, but plainly something had changed. The air was somehow different, softer, gentler, like baby's flesh. The following day the towers of cloud increased, and some of them formed black bottoms and I saw slanting streaks of gray rain falling from them. Lightning flickered in the heart of these white soldiers of the sky, and sometimes I heard the distant rumble of thunder. I had not yet witnessed more than a dozen drops of rain falling on the parched Sonoran desert, and I suspected the whole show might be smoke and mirrors. But I did enjoy the sudden freshets, the cold downdrafts, the whirlwinds of damp air that eddied across the rancho. And down in Mexico it was plainly raining, great gray sheets obscuring the horizon.

The third day of the monsoon season began sullenly, with angry clouds obscuring the heavens. These had flat purple bottoms, and rose so high I could scarcely spot the bold blue of the sky. Midmorning the wind kicked up, whirling dust, rattling desert sand against dusty windows, chattering doors, bending the palo verde and willow trees, and shooting icy tendrils into my room. I stared anxiously upon a grim heaven, bruised purple and black, that had driven Arizona's blue sky out of sight.

The rain arrived like cannon shot, rattling off the tile and tin roofs, banging the earth, raising puffs of dust, thumping against window glass, leaving muddy streaks as it coursed downward. A hum built slowly, an eerie whispering rumble unlike anything I had ever heard, and then sheets of rain swept in, opaque curtains of rain blasting everything in their path, instantly turning the barren yellow clay into brown gumbo. I felt the whole earth vibrate with the deluge; the rain gusted under the broad eaves intended to protect the adobe from water; it sluiced over the ground, instantly flooding every hollow, cutting channels before my eyes. And in the midst of this roar of water came lightning so constant it resembled the flickering of an arc light, and drumrolls of thunder that shot atmospheric bullets that I feared would collapse the building or rip away its sheet metal roof.

This Sonoran storm did not abate in minutes. Noon passed without change, and the afternoon turned black. Through the watery windows I beheld a lake; there seemed to be no dry ground anywhere. Instant rivers formed, scouring the corrals of the horse muck in them, knocking plants flat, pushing in around my front door and onto my tile floor, pooling at the base of my beehive fireplace. The electricity quit, and I could do naught but gaze upon a fearsome gray world in which visibility ceased scarcely ten paces distant. Rarely could I see the other guest quarters, or the main buildings of the rancho.

What pierced my consciousness then was a new sort of roar, the sound of rolling water tumbling ever downslope. I knew the great arroyo was running. It was called El Coronel, the Colonel, the wash that collected all the waters from the naked mountains to the east and north, and flumed them into Mexico. It was El Coronel that gave the rancho its wells; which supplied its water table, which nurtured the cottonwoods and willows and palo verdes and a hundred other desert shrubs and trees, which made the rancho an island of bright green even in the season of sunbaked drought.

El Coronel was roaring, and I ached to know whether it would wash away my building, or other ranch buildings. By two the storm had abated, and occasional shafts of sun poked through the gray cloudbanks. But El Coronel still roared, carrying hundreds of millions of gallons of water with it, straight through the rancho and across the border, where the arroyo flattened and widened into a great playa visible from the border fence.

That's when I heard Cap shouting.

"Hey, Arnold, we need you!"

I could not imagine why, but I hesitantly stepped outside into the mild drizzle, which wetted my jeans and tee shirt. The light rain was not unpleasant.

I found Cap, Marcy, and Willie all awaiting my presence, water dripping off them.

"Border fence is down," Cap explained. "Washout. This was a fifty-year storm, and El Coronel took two, three hundred yards of fence with it."

We slogged over surprisingly firm clay to the border, a quarter mile south, and beheld the devastation. The tan water still churned through the broad arroyo. The fence was nowhere in sight. I could not even see where the break started and ended.

"Jaysas," said Willie. That was about as exclamatory as he ever got.

Cap squinted at me. "We gotta rebuild fast. Keep the horses in. If they get into Mexico, we'll never see 'em again."

"I thought you told me the Mex ranchers always returned stock."

"Well, yeah, but these are good horses, and if the brown brothers find them, we ain't gonna see them again."

"Well, couldn't Willie get them into the pens?"

"Scattered to hell and gone now. Could be miles from here, up on higher ground." He fixed me with his pale gaze. "We gonna build fence. Fast. No one eats around here until we get that fence up."

I had never built a barbed wire fence in my life.

"Yeah, I'll help," I said, "But don't count on me knowing what I'm doing."

"Willie and me, we'll show you. Everyone here works, including Marcy."

I eyed that brown river dubiously. "How deep is that?"

"We'll find out."

Over the next hour we collected spools of barbed wire, staples, clips, a wire-stretcher, which worked in some manner beyond my fathoming, sledge hammers, a dozen metal posts, a few twisted mesquite posts, spades, hammers, and other mysterious gear, and loaded it into the battered ranch pickup, all the while keeping a wary eye on the border for renegade horses or Mexican bandidos creeping up to snatch the entire herd belonging to the hated gringos.

We piled into the ancient International Harvester and Cap steered it toward the arroyo, spraying muddy water over the windshield. By the time we returned to the border, El Coronel had reduced itself to a braided trickle. The unfenced border yawned at us. The last of the storm clouds vanished, and the late afternoon sun shot golden light over the drenched Sonoran desert. The quiet was eerie. The cool air was intoxicating. On the Mexican side, a vast silvery lake, a playa, shimmered where only tawny clay had stretched before. We began looking for the border fence, which was no where in sight.

I walked into Mexico, oddly enjoying the undocumented visit. Not a soul observed our progress. We found the west wires first, twisted and tangled on the ground, the metal posts lying flat but still connected to the barbed wire. We followed that for some distance until we came to undamaged fence.

"At least it's mostly still here," Cap said. "But we're going to have to free every post from the wire and start over."

The downed wire at the eastern end was shorter because the ground rose above the arroyo.

"All right, Willie and Marcy, you work at this end, free up those posts, and Arnold and I will work the west end," Cap said. "We gotta hurry; get this done before dark, or at least a couple strands anyway. Wear gloves."

That was good advice. It wasn't long before my hands were bleeding, even with gloves on.

The wire was fastened to the steel posts with little clips that were the devil's own invention. But slowly we freed post after post and left them lying in the sodden ground, well inside Mexico. Off in

271

the distance, we could see Willie and Marcy slowly working toward us, and sometimes even hear the murmur of their conversation.

"Damned Messicans. Why don't they help us? They get the benefit of the fence without donating a dime," Cap grumbled, wiping a bloody hand on his jeans. "They just feast on us. You know that over in Sasabe, half the women live on Pima County welfare checks? They get a little domestic work up to Tucson, and next thing you know, they get unemployment comp and stuff like that, and that keeps 'em flush for a year and then they work a little on a green card and go back to sucking money out of the country," he muttered. "If they didn't have suckers like us paying their way, they'd earn fifty dollars a year in the adobe brick factory."

I could see the direction his thoughts were rolling and kept quiet. The work was exhausting, wet, and miserable. At least it wasn't cold. The temperature had cooled down into the eighties and the air was pleasant.

El Coronel had swept the ranch fence forty or fifty yards into Mexico. We worked steadily, freeing the posts and wires, until finally we reached the broken ends of our strands. Marcy and Willie had finished before us, and were hauling posts back toward the border.

"I don't know how we'll ever get the damned fence straight," Cap grumbled. "We don't have the equipment to lay it right along the line. We'd need a surveyor..."

We rested a while, sucked Coronas around the back end of the pickup. The air had cleared and now we could see up and down the international border. We could even see the white pylon far to the east, but not the one to the west. I can date the filibuster to that very moment.

"To hell with all that," Cap said. "We gotta keep the brown brothers from borrowing our horses."

"We could eyeball it," I said. "I'll go to the first upright post to the west, and Marcy can go to the first standing post to the east, and we can sight down a line and drive a few in as sort of guidelines. We'll yell the directions to you."

Cap snorted. "They're always getting welfare checks from us," he said, a remark I did not yet fathom.

Willie got the idea before I did, and grinned crookedly from pot-shot eyes.

"We're just gonna bend this here fence a little," Cap said.

I thought he was joking, but he dropped a steel fence post slightly inside Mexico, walked about a rod and set down another one a couple of feet farther south. "Pound these in," he said. Get that little flange part of the post well into the clay. It's soft."

He began laying out the posts in a great arc that bent gently southward. Willie began hammering the posts at the east end, and I pounded on the westerly ones, while Marcy sorted the tangled strands of wire as best she could. Some of it would have to be cut out and thrown away.

Cap returned to help me.

"We'll get into trouble," I said. "They'll just make us do it right."

"When were you gelded, Arnold?"

"I don't think this is a good idea."

"It's called getting even."

"For what?"

"What are you, some wimp?"

That hurt. Well, the hell with it. I figured I'd be leaving soon anyway. My money would run out. Maybe the recession would be over. I'd get away from that crazy place.

Hammering posts drained me of whatever strength I had left. The rain-softened clay accepted the steel readily enough, but there were a lot of steel posts to pound home, and a lot of rock in the way, and I knew I would never become a ranch hand if I could help it.

The air continued to clear and as the sun settled lower, it lit the land with a golden light that gilded the arrow-straight border fence. We were clearly building fence five or six yards into Mexico. I kept eyeing the mesquite trees south of the line, waiting for a squad of Federales to pounce, but we saw nothing, not even a stray cow.

I kept worrying and wimping. The rest built fence and laughed and celebrated the liberation of turf from the Republic of Mexico. I have to give them credit. Once they got into the mood of it, they were transformed into a gang of filibusters scything through prostrate Mexico like a small army.

We got the posts in around six, and took a break, but Cap wanted the wire up before dark, so we started in again. The wire stretcher proved to be useless. We needed to anchor it to a good wooden post in order to ratchet the wire taut, and there were no good wooden posts, nor was our new fence a straight line. So we tugged, bloodied our hands, wrapped pieces of barbed wire around the metal posts, and jerry-built a border fence. Now, with the sun low, we could clearly see the bulge. I guessed we were copping maybe an eighth of an acre, and being very bad neighbors, but I had shut up and was working silently. Willie and Cap were sucking beer now, tossing the empties into the truck bed, pissing on the posts, and making smart remarks about Mexican fence-builders.

Cap justified it all. "If it'd been them, instead of us, they'd have snatched twice as much ground," he said, and belched.

We got the top and bottom strands stretched, after a fashion. That would be enough to keep stray livestock in, and we were pretty beat.

Cap squinted at the dying sun. "That'll hold until tomorrow," he said. "But Willie, you go find them horses and run 'em into the pens if you can."

Willie nodded. We threw the loose gear into the old truck and rattled back to the Rancho, feeling we had done a lick of work. The ranch looked strange, scoured clean of every plant and stick and pebble. The lower three feet of the adobe buildings were stained brown in spite of the broad eaves intended to keep rain away from the mud walls.

"That 'dobe plaster, it's got some emulsion in it that resists water," Cap said. "They sell it up at Tucson. Got put to the test this time, but I don't see any crumbling mud heaps."

The Rancho Oro Blanco would be all right, but I wasn't sure the border would be. Some day, some federal official accompanied by some Mexican would come knocking.

I slept hard that night.

The next day, a breezy and balmy one, we finished the fence. We packed our tools and hiked to the east edge of the arroyo. From the rising slope there, one could peer across the bottoms of the Coronel, and discover that certain territory bordering Arizona, formerly in the possession of the Republic of Mexico, had been transferred to the Stars and Stripes.

"Ain't that purty?" Cap asked. "Serves them brown brothers right."

I just shook my head, wimpishly, but Cap was watching.

"We've made history. We should go down in the books," he said.

The rest of the Sonoran summer passed quietly, and eventually I left the desert and found a job in an Illinois town surrounded by endless cornfields. It was such a bucolic place that I began to regale the locals with yarns about my Sonoran adventures. Especially my filibuster. Like all good stories, this one grew with the telling. The good burghers for whom I produced a five-day-a-week paper listened to my border tales with secret envy and vast disapproval, and the more they disapproved, the grander my filibuster became. No longer did I assert that we had commandeered an eighth of an acre. The figure grew to half, then one, and finally "several." No longer was I, John Arnold, the wimp of the filibuster expedition, worried about unneighborly conduct and international incidents. Instead I became the swashbuckler, a filibuster armed to the teeth with howitzers at my hips, an inciter of uproars, and a famous liar.

I relished my notoriety. Who else, after all, had increased the territory of the United States? I don't know whether the fence ever got fixed or rebuilt along the line. My guess is that it still bulges south, and the local ranchers on either side still return the strays without telling the officials about it. That's the way life is in Sonora. I never saw Cap and Marcy and Willie again; they are merely phantasms now. But together, we were a conquering army.

TWO ROADS DIVERGED

By Susan Cummins Miller

Dodging raindrops and lightning bolts
I ducked into the split-log bar
in Montello. Bud Country, but Dave
rustled up a warm Guinness
from the back.

My brown hair was long then, twisted
up off my neck and secured
with a piece of leather
and a wooden pick, sharpened
at both ends.

Played pool with three geologists
and a cowboy—just a way to pass the time,
a way to drive the geologic puzzles
from my mind so I could sleep. Lost,
on both counts.

Walking back to the motel
in the sultry darkness, under restless stars,
the Leach Mountains at my back
the valley stretching east forever—
or to Utah,

whichever came first—I passed
that cowboy, smoking behind the store.
He tossed out a proposition
like a half-smoked Camel.
Unfiltered.

The wind riffled the cottonwood leaves.
Black shadows played tag. A killdeer piped
from the sage-covered slope.
A horned owl answered.
Awkwardly,

laughing, I turned on my heel,
grinding the metaphorical butt
into the muddy road. Yet,
thirty years later, I'm still
wondering.

NOVELLA

THE BIG GUNS:
Or,
Whose Little Lily Is She?

By Andrew J. Fenady

Long-legged, trim-waisted and high-pocketed, she was tired and dusty from the ride but still she was the prettiest thing ever to step off a stagecoach in Hot Rock.

And while they didn't know it, two men were there waiting for her—Big John Bender and Ready John Roades. They'd been partners until five years ago when they had that fight. Nobody ever found out how it started, but everybody knew how it ended—both men battered and bloody on their bellies sucking for wind.

They split everything down the middle. The horses, the cattle, the ranch right down to the last keg of nails—and each one still ended up with a bigger spread than anybody else in Arizona.

Big John and Ready John hadn't spoken a word to each other since. But here they were standing a few feet apart pretending they were looking in opposite directions while the passengers debarked from the Overland Stage.

Big John walked over toward the driver as the little man hopped off the coach.

"Shorty, you got something aboard for me?"

"Nope."

"Something for me?" Ready John came up and inquired.

"Nope."

Big John and Ready John glared at each other, then back at Shorty.

"Look here," Ready John frowned, "I got a telegraph saying there'd be something aboard this stage for me."

"So did I," Big John added.

"I ain't sayin' you didn't."

"Then go through that baggage and mail, you dumb bastard, and find out what it is."

"Big John, I know everybody and everything aboard my stage and I'm telling you there's nothin' for either of you."

"Oh, yes there is," the girl's voice interrupted.

The two big men turned and looked at her. Damn, she was pretty. And there was something familiar, more than something. Those dancing, blue eyes and generous mouth. Even the voice. Yeah, mighty familiar.

"I sent those telegraphs to both of you."

"Why?" Big John asked.

"Yeah, why?" Ready John added.

"For the same reason I came here."

"Why?" Ready John asked again.

"Yeah, why?" Big John added this time.

She looked at them a moment and smiled.

"To find out which of you two sons-of-bitches is my father."

The other passengers and some of the townsfolk heard what she said. She said it plainly enough for everybody to hear. The womenfolk were outraged and took a step back. The menfolk were interested and took a step forward. Big John cleared his throat.

"Are you Lorena's daughter?"

"I am."

"Let's go someplace more private," Ready John suggested.

"All right, Daddy."

"Don't call me Daddy."

"Well one of you sure as hell is."

"Not me."

"Me either."

"Let's go someplace more private," Ready John repeated.

The two men flanked the pretty girl and the three of them walked away amid the whispers and upraised eyebrows of the citizens of Hot Rock.

Deacon Adderly walked up to Sheriff Broke Baker.

"Sheriff, did you hear that?"

"I ain't deef."

"Well?"

"Well, what?"

"We can't have a situation like that in a decent community like this."

"You're forgettin' something, Deacon."

"What?"

"Who made this here community decent in the first place."

"Well?"

"Well, your ass. Hadn't been for Big John and Ready John and their guns, Hot Rock'ud still be an outlaw town and you and the other decent donkeys'ud still be hidin' your ears under your blankets."

"And you're forgettin' you're a public servant, Sheriff."

"Anytime you want this star you can take it and shove it..."

"Now, Sheriff, let's not either of us say something we'll regret."

"You say whatever you want, Deacon; me, I'm goin' to do a little drinkin'."

* * *

"To whose place are we going?" the pretty girl inquired as they walked down the main street of Hot Rock.

"Well, not to his," Big John responded.

"And not to his," Ready John confirmed while they walked on.

By now word of the unexpected arrival had ricocheted all over town. People were even leaning out of windows watching as the triumvirate entered the La Paloma Hotel.

"We want to rent a room," Ready John announced to the clerk.

"Who do...uh, who does?"

"We do," Big John said.

"You want to register...in three names?"

"No, you horse's ass." Ready John glared. "Register it in her name. We'll only be there a few minutes."

"I understand." The clerk smiled.

"No, you don't," Big John said as he lighted a stogie.

"Anything you say, Big John. And what is the....lady's name?"

Big John and Ready John both looked to the lady.

"Lily. Just...Lily."

283

"Very good, Miss...Lily. Room Six."

The two men and "just...Lily" started to walk away.

"Any luggage?" the clerk added.

"Send somebody down to the depot to pick it up," Ready John said without looking back. "And do not disturb."

Inside Room Six, Lily removed her hat and gloves and turned toward the two men.

"Well, here we are."

Big John took a deep puff from his stogie.

"Big John, you got another one of those ceegars?" Ready John asked.

Big John nodded and handed over a stogie.

"I'll take one, too," Lily said.

"To smoke?" Big John inquired.

"Light me," she answered.

Big John lit her. He started to light Ready John, but when he realized what he was doing he put out the match and let his erstwhile partner light his own.

"Let's get down to cases," Big John said.

"Let's," Lily agreed, blowing a perfect smoke ring.

The two men watched as the circular, blue haze floated across the room.

"Where's...your mother?" Ready John asked.

"Dead. Four years ago."

Neither reacted outwardly.

"She never married," Lily added. "If it's possible for a woman to have been in love with two men at the same time, then that's what happened. By the way, are you two married?"

Both men shook their heads.

"You mean you've both been 'true' to her?" Lily twitted.

"Well," Big John pointed out, "it *has* been over twenty years.... and...."

"What do we look like?" Ready John proffered. "A couple of monks?"

"But both of you were in love with her. I know that."

"How do you know?" Big John asked.

"She left me a letter to be opened on my twenty-first birthday. That was six months ago. She tried to explain what happened."

"What did the letter say?" Ready John asked.

"It said that during the war for the Confederacy, a young southern belle fell in love with two Yankee officers. They both promised to come back. But when they moved on she found out she was about to disgrace her family. So she ran away. She never told her family...or the two Yankees."

"Where did she, I mean..."

"Where were you born?" Big John finished.

"New York."

"No wonder we couldn't find her," Ready John said.

"Did you really try?"

"You're damn right we did, sister," Ready John blared.

"I'm not your sister. But I am glad to hear that."

"We're still not down to cases," Big John said. "What do you want from us?"

"I only want something from one of you. A name."

The two men looked at each other a moment, then Big John broke the silence.

"Excuse us for a minute, Miss."

"Does that mean you want me to leave the room?"

"No, we'll just walk off aways and whisper, if that's agreeable to you?"

"Agreeable."

Big John and Ready John eased over toward the window and spoke softly.

"First off," Big John said, "officially I'm still not talking to you. This is off the record."

"Same here."

"What do you think, Ready John?"

"I think she's out to hook one of us for all she can grab."

"Me, too."

"How do we play it?"

"Stall," Big John advised.

"Right."

The two men eased back toward the center of the room.

"Well," she said, "have you decided? Which one of you is my daddy?"

"We're trying to figure something out," Ready John said.

"What does that mean?"

"He means we're trying to figure *it* out. But it'll take some more figuring."

"What do you want to do, talk to your lawyers?"

"No!" Big John blared.

"Hell, you've waited twenty-one years. Can't you wait a little longer?" Ready John reasoned.

"Here's a hundred dollars for expenses in the meanwhile," Big John offered.

"I don't want your money."

"Not even if I'm your father?!"

"Are you?"

"I don't know…yet."

"Then I'll wait until you do know. And in the meanwhile, keep your damn money."

"We'll be talking to you," Big John said as he started toward the door.

"And vice versa," she smiled and blew another smoke ring.

"How long you been smoking ceegars?" Ready John inquired.

"About five minutes."

The two men paused outside in the hallway.

"We better sleep on this. I'll meet you someplace tomorrow," Big John said.

"Where?"

"Not in public."

"Suits me."

"Where the river narrows. Ten in the morning," Big John proposed.

"Suits me," Ready John repeated.

When they walked out of the La Paloma, Broke Baker was waiting.

"Sure is good to see you two fellas together again."

"We're not together," Big John said.

"Not now or ever," Ready John added.

The two men walked in diverse directions leaving Broke watching first one, then the other. He didn't see the two-up wagon coming along the street. It stopped directly in front of him.

Aboard the wagon was a good-looking fellow about thirty and next to him an older, thinner man wearing a tam-o'-shanter. The good-looking fellow spoke to Broke.

"You the Sheriff?"

Broke looked at the young man, then at the badge stuck on his chest, then back to the young man. That was his answer.

"My name's Courtland. Jess Courtland. This is Mr. MacIntosh, my assistant."

"Verry pleased to make your acquaintance, Sherrriff," Mr. MacIntosh said in a thick Scottish accent.

The Sheriff nodded.

"Mac and I are going to be in these parts for a time."

"You drummers?"

"No," Courtland smiled. "Surveyors. We're going to make a survey along the Hassayampa for the Territorial Governor."

"That's interestin'." Broke started to walk toward the Appaloosa Saloon.

"This the best place to bed in town?" Courtland inquired.

"Yep. 'Cept for Emma's hen house."

* * *

The next morning, just after sun up. Big John walked out the front door of his ranch house onto the porch. He was still strapping on the .44 as an arrow whizzed by and stuck into a post not more than the length of a lizard from his Stetson. The arrow impaled a black widow spider.

"Mornin', Reggie," Big John said.

"Right-o," the fellow with the bow rejoined, then commenced to walk toward his employer. Reggie was dressed in the wardrobe of his Comanche ancestors on his mother's side, but spoke when he did speak with the cockney twang of his Anglican ancestors on his father's side.

"Reggie, take a ride over to the south range and check out the herd."

"Right-o."

At about the same time, Ready John was departing from the outhouse at his ranch. His foreman, Maguey, approached the structure eating a chunk of stale bread spread with honey.

"Maguaey, better send somebody out to the south range, see if any of our beeves got stuck after the rain."

"Do it myself, Ready John, soon as I take a dump."

"Oh, is today Thursday?"

"Yep."

In town, Lily was breakfasting at the hotel restaurant. Broke Baker approached as Courtland and MacIntosh started toward the exit. Courtland never took his eyes off Lily and nearly walked into a wall.

"I'm Broke Baker, Sheriff of Hot Rock, ma'am. Could I sit down and talk to you for a short time?"

"Did I break any law?"

"No, ma'am. But you just might do some mendin'."

"I don't know what you're talking about, but sit down, Sheriff."

Broke sat down, produced a pint of whiskey from his pocket, and took a swig.

"You see, ma'am, I used to work for Big John and Ready John when they was partners. They come here years ago with the first herd outta Texas. But in them days, Hot Rock was loaded with desperados. Wartnose Bascomb and his bunch. A dozen of the meanest, dirtiest bastards ever breathed. And one day it come to a showdown. Bascomb and his bunch versus Big John and Ready John. Them two fellas rode into town just as cool as if they was goin' to a church social. Bascomb started blazin' away, but Big John and Ready John stood shoulder to shoulder and side by side, slingin' lead and grinnin' like good Indians. When the smoke cleared, Bascomb and six of his boys had got their halos gratis. The rest pulled for the border, including Bascomb's brother, Bentnose."

"Very picturesque," Lily said sipping her coffee.

"You damn betcha," Broke said swilling more whiskey. "Them two fellas prospered after that. Built up the biggest and best spread in the Territory and I was right along with 'em. Till five years ago when they had one hell of a remembered fight."

"About what?"

"They didn't say. It started in the saloon, proceeded into the street, went through the stable and ended up right where Bascomb fell...they was like two spent bulls and neither one with enough strength to roll over."

"Is that when you became Sheriff?"

"Well, I..."

"Couldn't choose between them. That it?"

Broke ignored the question.

"They ain't spoke a word to each other since—till yesterday when you come to town."

"They weren't exactly overjoyed to see me."

"Maybe not, but at least you got 'em talkin' to each other. And that might just be the beginnin'."

"Beginning of what?"

"Bringin' 'em together."

* * *

"You back-doorin' sonovabitch!" Big John was hollering at just that moment.

"Me! Why you sneaky, egg-sucker! Lorena was my girl!"

The two men stood across from one another at the narrow part of the Hassayampa that divided their ranches.

"*Your* girl?!" Big John growled. "I saw her first!"

"You might'a saw her first, but I was the first to..."

"To what!? Say it! And I'll tear the lying tongue right outta your jawbone."

"Come ahead, you big baboon and I'll finish what you started five years ago."

"I whupped you then and I'll do 'er again!" Big John grimaced.

"Why you're so out of shape you couldn't whup a sick schoolboy!"

"Hold on," Big John reflected. "This ain't getting us anywhere. Let's get down to cases. We can fight anytime."

"Well, then say what you came to say."

"Let's reason this thing out. Now, first off, I'm getting tired of hollering. Come on over here."

"You come over here."

"Meet you halfway."

"Suits me," Ready John allowed and started to walk toward the middle of the stream.

Big John did likewise.

They met halfway in the stream, stood cheek to jowl with water into their boots and up to their crotches. Neither spoke for a while until Ready John broke the silence.

"What you looking at me like that for?"

"I see it."

"See what?"

"The resemblance."

"What resemblance?"

"She's got your weak chin."

"Yeah, well take a look in the mirror if you ain't afraid of the sight and you'll see she's got your shifty eyes."

"Hold on, Ready John. We are going to call a truce."

"You started up again."

"Yeah, I did."

Another moment of silence. Big John lit a cigar, then offered one to Ready John, who accepted.

"Well, this powwow was your idea. You got any suggestions?"

"I say we both deny it."

"That's brilliant. *You* know it was one of us. *I* know it was one of us and *she* knows..."

"Hell, yes. But we deny it."

"What good'll that do?"

"That's just the beginning. We deny it, but we offer her money to go away."

"Think she'll do that?"

"Hell, yes," Big John said again. "That's what she's after. Money."

"She says she wants a name."

"She just says that till she gets some money. We'll split the bill."

"How much?"

Big John reflected for a few seconds as he puffed away.

"Five thousand."

"You're too damn anxious. I think it was you!"

"I should'a known better than to try to reason with some dumb hardhead."

"And I should'a known better than to trust a sneaking..." Ready John stopped short as he spotted the wagon approaching. "Did you tell anybody you were coming out here?"

"They're on *your* land."

The wagon with Courtland and MacIntosh pulled closer. The two men aboard were fascinated by the sight of Big John and Ready John standing in the middle of the stream with water up to their crotches.

"Hello," Courtland greeted them, tipping the beak of his cap. "You two fellows taking a bath?"

"If we were, it's in our tub," Big John replied.

"And who the hell are you, sonny boy?" Ready John added.

"I'm the sonny boy who's going to survey this Territory," Courtland answered cheerily.

Ready John waded toward the bank as Courtland got off the wagon.

"Look here, sonny boy, how'd you like your butt bounced over the rim of that hill?"

"I can think of more pleasant things."

"Then think of them on your way out."

Courtland took a folded piece of paper from his breast pocket.

"I have here authorization from the Territorial Governor to survey this river and the land on both sides."

Big John stopped smiling at the "both sides" part and waded over toward "sonny boy."

"It's already been surveyed."

"Yeah," Ready John said, "by us. About the time you were feeding off a nipple."

"And this river," Courtland proceeded, "feeds a large part of the Territory."

"So what?" Ready John said.

"So with a proper dam it could benefit a *larger* part of the Territory; and during a drought...."

"This river belongs to...us," Big John said.

"This river is a natural resource and *all* the people own a natural resource."

"Where'd you learn so much law?" Big John inquired.

"Harvard. And it was engineering, not law."

Courtland continued and waved the paper again. "But if either of you two water buffalos can read, you'll find that I'm well within the law."

Ready John snatched the paper from Courtland, tore it in two, and let it drop.

"Now, sonny boy, you're getting skin close to making me lose my temper."

"Let's leave," MacIntosh suggested.

"Just a minute, Mac," Courtland said. "If this rusty hinge wasn't so old and creaky I'd teach him some manners."

"Don't let that stop you, sonny boy," Ready John grinned.

Courtland extended both fists and circled Ready John.

"Marquis of Queensberry?"

"Any way you want to fry it, sonny boy."

But what followed was not what Ready John expected. Courtland danced and jabbed and danced away again, peppering

291

Ready John with smarting, punishing, short punches. Ready John's nose commenced to bleed and his brain swirled from the tattoo of knuckles.

Big John bellowed with laughter.

"Go get him, Ready John! He's just a schoolboy!"

"Stand still and fight, you frog-legged bastard!"

"Say when you've had enough, old fellow."

Well, Ready John had had enough all right. He kicked Courtland in the shank with the tip of his boot, proceeded to pull the beak of "sonny boy's" cap over his eyes and nose, then followed through with a kick in the rump that propelled young Harvard into the Hassayampa.

Ready John turned toward MacIntosh.

"The Marquis of Queensberry's a little damp behind the ears. You better give him a hand outta here."

"Yes, sirrr. Verrry good, sirrr," the little fellow purred.

MacIntosh proceeded to follow these simple directions as two riders approached in the distance, one on either side of the river.

Reggie and Maguey both riding like their britches were burning.

"What the hell's the matter with you two?" Ready John roared. "You want to ride them ponies to death?"

"Bascomb!" Maguey panted. "Rounded up everything on the south ranges! Pulling for the border!"

"Right-o," Reggie added.

"Bascomb!" Big John grunted. "He's been making a hell of a living off us all these years."

"He does have perseverance," Ready John responded.

"So do I." Big John went for his horse.

"Whose herd?" Ready John asked of Maguey. "Mine or his?"

"Both."

Ready John went for his horse.

Big John, Ready John, Maguey and Reggie topped out over the rim of Sentinel Hill and reined up. In the valley below, a dozen riders were urging a couple hundred head of stubborn beef southward. The brigands were led by Bentnose Bascomb and consisted of half-breeds, Mexicans and general hard asses.

Ready John looked at Big John.

"You got any particular play in mind?"

"This is no time for subtlety," Big John said as he pulled out his long gun. "You ready, John?"

"I'm ready, John."

They shot four rustlers in the back before the cattle thieves knew where the shooting was coming from. Two more bandits fell with arrows in their vitals. Bentnose and the rest didn't want anymore. They fired a few shots and went to their spurs.

* * *

Back along the Hassayampa, Courtland had laid his wet clothes over a branch of a live oak tree and stood naked rubbing his sore shank. At the sound of Lily's voice he grabbed his shirt off the tree and wrapped it around his middle.

"What is this?" the girl remarked. "A nudist colony?"

Broke Baker was on his horse beside Lily.

"There's a law in these parts against indecent exposure, boy."

"I was just…just drying off my clothes, Sheriff."

"How'd they get wet in the first place?"

"In the river."

"Uh-huh. Was you wearin' 'em at the time?"

"I was, " Courtland admitted with as much dignity as he could muster.

"You mean you *fell* in? A growed up surveyor like you fell in the river?"

"I was struck a foul blow," Courtland said, then turned his attention to Lily. "Miss, we haven't been properly introduced. I'm Jess Courtland."

"It's good to see you," she smiled.

Before Courtland could analyze the precise intent of her remark, Big John, Ready John and company appeared. Broke Baker beamed at the sight of the two men riding side by side.

"It sure is good to see you two fellas together again."

"We're not together," Ready John growled.

"And what the hell is going on here?" Big John added looking directly at Lily.

"I persuaded the good Sheriff to bring me out."

"What for?"

"Just to take a look at the ol' homestead."

Big John and Ready John took a look at each other. Their worst suspicions were confirmed. Ready John in his mounting frustration turned his attention to Courtland.

293

"And didn't I tell *you* to get your…hide off my land?"

"Sheriff," Courtland petitioned, "will you please tell these gentlemen that I have proper authorization," he took the bisected document from MacIntosh's pocket and held a piece in each hand, "to survey this area. The Territorial Governor…"

"The Territorial Governor is a pettifogging, peanut politician," Ready John said.

"Nevertheless," Courtland continued, "he's given me the authority…"

"And I'm giving you about ten seconds," Ready John concluded.

"Now just a minute fellas," Broke said. "Let's all cool off. I got to think on this. Meantime, young fella, you come back to Hot Rock—and you too, Miss Lily."

"All right," Lily agreed. "I have to look for a job anyhow."

"What kind of job could a girl like you find in Hot Rock?" Big John asked.

"Oh, I don't know," Lily replied. "What kind of job pays a girl like me the most money…in Hot Rock?"

* * *

Bentnose Bascomb and the remnants of his gang made it back across the border to their headquarters, the Toro Toro Cantina in Sedona. Halfway through his second bottle of whiskey, Bascomb was still cursing the two Johns.

"I'll get them two bushwackers one of these days," he grumbled. "I'll stake 'em over an anthill and pour honey into their eyeballs. They ain't heard the last of this."

And neither had Bascomb's gang. They'd been listening to his vows of vengeance for over a dozen years and knew Bentnose'd go right on filling the saloon with idle threats until he passed out drunk again tonight like he did every other night.

Back in Hot Rock the patrons of the Appaloosa Saloon were hearing sounds they'd never heard in those parts before. The source of these sounds was Lily. She wore a blouse that was definitely décolleté and a split skirt that allowed those long legs to show through when she glided around the place. Damn if she didn't have a pleasant voice to boot.

Broke was still trying to decide what to do about that surveyor fellow, but Harvard seemed in no particular hurry. Since Lily got the job he just sat at a good table and stared.

On the third night, things came to a head—sort of. Big John and Ready John approached the Appaloosa at exactly the same time—from different directions, of course. Officially they still weren't talking. But their coincidental convergence called for some sort of explanation.

"Thought I'd wet my windpipe," was the best Ready John could come up with.

"Me, too."

They stood at the batwings a minute while Lily sang inside. Appropriately she was singing "I'm Lily, Lily of the Valley." Both men winced a little as they listened.

"All I know," Big John said, "is that no daughter of mine would be working in a place like this."

"Mine either."

The two men went through the batwings. The Appaloosa was full. Standing room only. The two Johns stood.

A large percentage of the patrons was made up of the boys from "Bar-26." They'd come in especially to see "that there filly named Lily, who sang mighty pretty," as Snot Johnson, their poet laureate, put it. But the Bar-26 boys weren't all poets. They prided themselves in being tough as a two-bit steak and meaner than a tiger with a toothache.

The brouhaha began when the Bar-26 foreman, Gotch Higgins, grabbed a hold of Lily's décolleté. Courtland was up like a shot, but not for long. Gotch never heard of the Marquis of Queensberry. Somebody else went after Gotch and that blew the lid off.

Lily disappeared temporarily in a tangle of Stetsons and elbows while Big John and Ready John busted their way toward her general direction. Their fists ploughed a clean furrow of humanity until they got to her. Courtland was up by now and dismissed all thoughts of the Marquis of Queensberry. He was slugging from behind and utilizing his boots and whatever bottles he could find in the best barroom tradition.

Lily was no bystander either. She had somehow straddled the chest of the fallen Gotch Higgins, grabbed a hold of his hair with both hands, and was banging his head onto the sawdust. That's when the double-barreled shotgun went off. That quieted things down. Broke Baker walked off across the room with both barrels still smoking.

Neither Big John nor Ready John could conceal the look of pride as they lifted Lily from the limp, unconscious form of Gotch Higgins.

"It sure is good to see you two fellas together again," the Sheriff beamed.

"We're not together," Ready John growled. "I just came in to wet my windpipe."

"Me, too," Big John said.

The two Johns walked toward the door. They went through the batwings and paused out front.

"By God," Ready John smiled, "that girl's got gravel!"

"Yeah," Big John agreed.

Then they walked off in different directions.

The events of that evening held particular interest to a weasely fellow—Schemer Scroggins. The Schemer had been in the Appaloosa and witnessed the proceedings from under a table where he wisely ducked at the first ripple of unpleasantness.

After the fight, Scroggins wasted little time in stealing a horse—riding south to Sedona—explaining his scheme to a bleary-eyed Bascomb—and claiming ten percent of the profits for putting together the package.

The next couple of nights, Broke Baker and his shotgun walked Lily to the hotel after the Appaloosa closed up. That was just in case any of her new-found admirers got any amorous ideas.

But the third night instead of the Sheriff, Jess Courtland was waiting. He explained to Lily that Broke had to deliver a prisoner to Piedra and wouldn't be back until morning. Courtland also explained to Lily that he was in love with her. She took the news in her stride. This sort of put a crimp in Courtland's style. He took a more direct approach.

"Lily, I want to marry you."

"I can't marry anybody...yet."

"Why not?"

"I'm an old-fashioned girl," she smiled.

"What the hell's that got to with it? Old-fashioned girls've been getting married for years."

"That's not what I mean."

"What do you mean?"

"I mean I have to get daddy's permission."

"Then get it."

"First I've got to get a daddy."

Before Courtland had an opportunity to reply, he was hit on the head from behind with a barrel of a forty-four. Two men grabbed hold of Lily, gagged her, bound her hands and tossed her into a wagon that appeared out of the shadows. One of the men pinned a note on Courtland's coat, then jumped into the wagon as it rolled south toward Sedona.

So far the Schemer's plan was working 100 percent.

* * *

Big John, Ready John, Courtland and Broke were gathered in the Sheriff's office the next morning as Big John read the note aloud.

> "Dear Big John and Ready John—you bastards. Do not follo for 48 hours. Your dawter is being held prisoner at the Toro Toro in Sedona.
> Just the 2 of you come up with $20,000 in gold. Be here by Saterday mdnite if you want to see her alive.
> Bascomb
> *PS: I won't molest her till you get here.*"

"Well?!" Courtland said.

"Well, what?" Big John answered.

"What are you going to do about it?"

"Why the hell should I do anything. She's not my daughter."

"Mine either," Ready John added.

"Now, goddammit, she's got to be one of you fellows' daughter. Everybody in the Territory knows that."

"Maybe she is," Ready John admitted, "and maybe they do. But what the hell do you expect *us* to do?"

"I expect you to do what the letter says for you to do."

"These boys go down there," Broke mused, "they'll never come back. Bascomb's been waitin' for years to get even."

"You're the one that let 'em take her," Ready John said. "*You* go down."

"I haven't got twenty thousand—and even if I did," he added quickly, "Bascomb said for you to come."

"And get our asses blown off," Big John observed. "To hell with her. She was just out to grab what she could from us in the first place."

297

"Yeah," Ready John agreed. "To hell with her. We were trying to figure a way to get rid of her anyhow. Bascomb did us a favor—and so did you, you bonehead."

"I can't believe my ears. You two are the most unfeeling, uncivilized bastards I ever met."

"We'll excuse that remark, sonny." Big John squinted. "But don't repeat it."

"Well," Ready John said, "might as well mosey along. Lot of work to be done out at the ranch."

"Yeah, me too," Big John said.

"But they'll kill her!" Courtland cried. "Or worse!"

"Spose they will," Ready John nodded.

"She did have gravel," Big John admitted.

"You got to give her that," Ready John agreed. "Well, at least I hope they get it over with quick."

"Yeah," Big John concluded, "wouldn't want the poor little gal to suffer too much."

* * *

"You just wait until my daddies get here," Lily was saying.

"That's exactly what we *are* waiting for," the Schemer smiled.

"You sure they'll come?" Bascomb questioned the Schemer.

"Oh, they'll come all right," the Schemer smiled again. "I'm a rare judge of the human species and I tell you they're both nuts about this kid."

"You're damn right they'll come," Lily said. "Shoulder to shoulder and side by side with their big guns blazing away, blowing you and your whole gang to bits."

"Ha, ha, ha," Bascomb snorted.

This conversation was taking place in the back room of the Toro Toro with Lily tied to a chair. Bascomb walked over to the chair and started to loosen the rope.

"What are doing that for?" the Schemer questioned.

"She's been tied up like that for hours. Just thought I'd let her stretch her legs."

Lily still wore her saloon outfit and those legs were very much in evidence. The evidence hadn't gone unnoticed by Bentnose Bascomb.

"I still can't figure out how a girl can have two legs... I mean two daddies."

298

"What do you care, Bentnose," the Schemer said, "so long as you get those two Johns and twenty thousand gold…less ten percent."

"Yeah," Bascomb glowed, "plus a neat little bonus."

His long, hairy arms went around Lily and he pulled her close. At the same time she jerked her right knee hard into his crotch and Bascomb screamed. Yes, screamed.

A couple of Bascomb's boys came in from the saloon to see the fun. What they saw was Bascomb buckled over rubbing his groin.

"What's wrong, Boss?" one of the boys inquired.

"I think I'm having an appendicitis attack," Bascomb gulped. "Tie her up again."

"How come you untied her, Boss?" one of the boys queried.

"Do like I tell you," Bascomb groaned, "and mind your own goddamn business."

* * *

Three o'clock in the morning and everybody in Hot Rock slept except the four people conferring in the Sheriff's office and one other person. The conferees consisted of Big John, Ready John, Sheriff Baker and Reggie. The other person consisted of Jess Courtland. He'd seen the four of them skulk in there about fifteen minutes earlier. Courtland figured that by now they'd be deep in conversation and he could sneak up and listen.

"It's awful risky, boys," Baker was saying, "but maybe it'll work."

"It better work," Ready John whispered.

"Right-o," Reggie added.

"But I still think you need a fourth," Broke suggested.

"What for?"

"Well, Big John, somebody's got to go 'round back and get her while all that's goin' on. Yep, you need a fourth. So, I'll be goin'."

That's when the door flew open and Courtland proclaimed:

"Like, hell!!"

"Get in here and close the door, you damn fool," Ready John said, "before you wake up the whole town."

Courtland closed the door and repeated softly.

"Like, hell. If anybody else is going, it's me…I. And don't think you had me fooled with all that talk about leaving her down there. I knew you were going after her."

"Yeah," Ready John said, "but we don't want the whole town to know. Bascomb might have spies."

"Well, I'm going with you."

"Look here, Harvard," Big John said, "you don't know saddle from spur."

"Maybe, but I'm going."

"Why?" Big John asked.

"Because I love Lily and I intend to marry her."

"Right-o," Reggie said.

By Saturday afternoon the four of them had ridden across the border and were hiding out until dark. Courtland wore a sombrero, a serape and was made up to look Mexican.

"You sure you can talk enough Meskin to get by if anybody asks you some questions?" Ready John wondered.

Courtland let fly with a muzzle load of Spanish and might still be talking it if Big John hadn't stopped him.

"Okay," he said, "get on your mule and get going."

Courtland was on his way.

"Reggie," Big John said, "it's dark enough now. Circle to the south and come in that way. And here."

He handed Reggie a canvas bag.

"Right-o," Reggie nodded and was on his way.

After the Anglican-Indian left, Ready John commenced to re-inspect his artillery.

"Don't think this makes any difference."

"What the hell are you talking about?"

"I'm talking about us. I haven't forgot. When this is over you can go straight to hell."

Big John checked the chambers of his .44.

"And vice versa."

* * *

Eleven-thirty. Bascomb was getting drunker and madder by the minute. His gang was pretty drunk, too. Nobody paid any attention to the Mexican who came in a couple of hours ago and nursed a bottle of tequila at a corner table.

"Bring me another bottle!" Bascomb bellowed, then he turned his attention to Scroggins. "And Schemer, if they don't show up pretty soon I got a scheme for you."

"They'll be here." Schemer tried to convince himself as well as Bascomb.

300

"Because if they ain't," Bascomb went on, "I'm gonna cut out your tongue—so think on that. Meantime go back there and make sure that little bitch is still tied up."

The Schemer followed orders and Courtland's eyes followed the Schemer.

Eleven forty-eight. One of Bascomb's men ran into the cantina and said that Big John and Ready John were in town and riding toward the Toro Toro.

Bascomb went to the batwings and looked out at the two horsemen approaching slowly.

"Well, there they be, by God. Shoulder to shoulder and side by side." Then he commenced to laugh. "But I sure as hell don't see any big guns blazing. They look like a couple of whipped dogs from here."

As Bascomb took a step onto the boardwalk, he spoke to his gang still inside.

"Cover me, boys. Any sudden move—cut 'em down."

Big John and Ready John stopped just across from the cantina.

"We're holding up our end of the bargain, Bascomb," Ready John said.

"Hold it up so's I can see it," Bascomb replied. "All twenty thousand in gold. But hold it up slow and in your right hand."

Each of the two men held up a heavy satchel that was tied to his saddle horn.

"Ten thousand in each satchel," Big John said.

"Where's the girl?"

"She's in the back room, none the worse for the wear…yet," Bascomb said. Then he hollered to one of his sentinels at the end of the street.

"They bring any help?"

"No," the voice came out of the dark. "All alone."

Bascomb repeated the question to the sentinel on the opposite end of the street and got the same answer.

"Well, you two are dumber than I thought. Here's where the real fun starts. Now drop them satchels."

That was the signal.

Reggie from the rooftop across the Toro Toro already had his bow strung with the lit stick of dynamite tied to the arrow.

As the satchels dropped he let fly the arrow. Before Bascomb and his gang knew what happened the arrow stuck in the front of the Toro Toro and forthwith blew half the place to bits. Big John and Ready John were off their animals, standing shoulder to shoulder and side by side with their guns blazing.

Stumbling and coughing, Bascomb and what was left of his gang tried to shoot it out, but none of them, including Schemer, survived the barrage from Big John and Ready John's forty-fours. Bad men were dropping onto boardwalk and gutter.

During the fireworks, Courtland went in the back room, untied Liliy and got her out through the rear door. Just for good measure, Reggie let fly another arrow with dynamite attached and that about broke the Toro Toro to a finish.

As the smoke cleared, Lily came over to Big John and Ready John.

"It sure is good to see you two fellas together again," she said.

"We're not together," Ready John growled as he ejected the empty shells.

"You're damn right we're not," Big John said.

Lily smiled her knowingest female smile.

"You can fool the rest of the world, but you can't fool your own flesh and blood. Now what started this damn feud in the first place?"

"Well," Big John said, "he passed some remark about your mother..."

"Me! Damn it, Ready John, it was you! You're the one who bragged how you were first to..." Big John's voice trailed off when he saw the tears in Lily's eyes.

"I told you before," she said, "if it was possible for a woman to be in love with two men at the same time—then *that's* what happened."

"Awww come on, Lily," Big John drawled. "No daughter of mine's gonna bust down and cry."

"Mine either," Ready John added.

***

Well, Jess Courtland got a lot of surveying done along the Hassayampa that summer...and Lily got herself a name.

It was the damndest wedding Hot Rock ever saw.

Right up to the last minute there was one more argument to be settled between Big John and Ready John.

Who was going to give the bride away?

Everybody in Hot Rock, including the bride, was waiting to find out.

"Lily, excuse us for a minute," Big John said.

"Yeah," Ready John added. "We'll just walk off aways and whisper, if that's agreeable to you."

"Agreeable," she smiled.

Big John and Ready John eased away from the front of the church. After a moment of silence, Big John spoke.

"Ready John, you give little Lily away."

"Well, hell, Big John, that's damned decent of you. But why me? You've got just as much right...."

"No, I haven't. You've *got* to be her father."

"Why me?" Ready John repeated.

For the first time in his life Big John stammered more than just a little.

"Because Lorena and I didn't...that is, I didn't... Well, I just didn't!"

"You didn't?!"

Ready John went pale.

"I didn't either," he admitted.

Both men looked at the bride and whispered.

"Whose little Lily *is* she?"

"Well," Big John finally grinned, "what the hell's the difference? Are you ready, John?"

"I'm ready, John."

Like I said, it was the damndest wedding the West ever saw— or the world for that matter. Not just because of the eating and drinking and celebrating—that was part of it all right—but also, it was the first time ever recorded where two fathers gave away the bride.

AUTHOR BIOS

D.L. Birchfield

D.L. Birchfield's *Field of Honor* (OU Press, 2004) won the Spur Award for Best First Novel. He is a member of the Choctaw Nation of Oklahoma, a graduate of the University of Oklahoma College of Law, and is Professor of Native American Studies at the University of Lethbridge in Alberta.

Kent Blansett

Kent Blansett (Cherokee) is a PhD Candidate and Andrew W. Mellon Fellow in History at the University of New Mexico, Albuquerque. His dissertation is a biography on American Indian student leader and activist Richard Oakes (Mohawk) who led the takeover of Alcatraz Island in 1969.

Johnny D. Boggs

WWA President Johnny D. Boggs is a four-time Spur Award-winner and five-time finalist who has also won the Western Heritage Wrangler Award for his fiction. A frequent contributor to *True West*, *Wild West* and *American Cowboy* magazines, Boggs lives in Santa Fe, New Mexico, with his wife and son.

305

Matt Braun

Matt Braun was born in Oklahoma to a ranching family. A WWA Spur and Wister Award winner, Braun is the author of fifty-six books with over 40 million copies in print worldwide. Two of his novels, *Black Fox* and *One Last Town*, were adapted into television movies on CBS and TNT.

Tom Carpenter

Tom Carpenter is an award-winning newspaper columnist. His nonfiction has appeared in *Arizona Highways* and *True West* magazine. He is the Director of Graduate Admissions and Services at Northern Arizona University in Flagstaff. He has been a member of WWA since 1995. He lives in Flagstaff, Arizona.

Rita Cleary

Rita Cleary has written seven novels, various short stories and articles for *True West, We Proceeded On* of the Lewis and Clark Trail Heritage Foundation and various other historical and horse publications. She was President of WWA in 2004-2006. With her late husband, John, she spearheaded establishment of The Homestead Foundation that supports WWA's educational and award-granting missions. In 2006, she was recognized for her writing as a "New York Woman of Distinction."

C.K. Crigger

C. K. Crigger lives with her husband and three feisty little dogs in Spokane Valley, Washington, and crafts stories set in the Inland Northwest. She is a two-time Spur Award finalist, in 2007 for Short Fiction, and in 2009 for Audio. She reviews books and writes occasional articles for Roundup magazine.

Wayne Davis

Award-winning Western Novelist Wayne Davis grew up in Southeastern New Mexico where he owned Quarter Horses and hired out for day work on area farms and ranches. Wayne and Joan and their horses currently reside on eight acres overlooking the Rio Blanco in the Texas Hill Country.

John Duncklee

John Duncklee has been a cowboy, rancher, quarter horse breeder, university professor and award winning author of eighteen books and myriad articles, poetry and short stories. He is a Western Writers of America Spur award winner. He lives in Las Cruces, N.M. with his wife, Penny, an accomplished watercolorist.

Andrew J. Fenady

Andrew J. Fenady has been an actor, playwright, television writer and producer, songwriter, screenwriter, and novelist. He created and produced the TV series *The Rebel* (and wrote the hit theme song for Johnny Cash), produced the Western series *Branded* and *Hondo*, and wrote and produced the John Wayne film *Chisum* as well as several TV movies. In 2006 he received the WWA Wister Award for lifetime achievement.

Paul L. Hedren

Paul L. Hedren is an award-winning historian and retired National Park Service superintendent living in Omaha, Nebraska. His publications include more than 60 essays, and seven books, of which *First Scalp for Custer* (1980) was his first, and *Great Sioux War Orders of Battle* (in press, 2010) his latest.

Paul Andrew Hutton

Paul Andrew Hutton, editor of this collection, is Executive Director of the Western Writers of America and holds the rank of Distinguished Professor in the University of New Mexico. He is the author or editor of eight books and has published widely in both scholarly and popular journals. He is a frequent "talking head" on television, and has written a dozen documentaries. Among his many writing awards are four WWA Spurs, six Western Heritage Awards from the National Cowboy and Western Heritage Museum, and the Billington Prize from the Organization of American Historians. He was President of the WWA in 2002-2004.

Cheewa James

Born on the Klamath Reservation in Oregon and enrolled with the Modoc Tribe of Oklahoma, Cheewa James was raised in Taos, New Mexico. James is a professional keynote speaker, using Native American philosophy and stories for emphasis. She is an award-winning television producer and on-air talent. James has published in *Smithsonian, National Wildlife*, and U.S. newspapers. Her latest book is *MODOC: The Tribe That Wouldn't Die.*

Elmer Kelton

Elmer Kelton, author of more than forty novels in his half century writing career, is one of America's most popular and honored writers. The WWA has awarded him a record seven Spur Awards as well as its lifetime achievement award. He has won four Western Heritage Awards from the National Cowboy and Western Heritage Museum in Oklahoma City and in 1990 received the Western Literature Association Distinguished Achievement Award. The Texas state legislature proclaimed Elmer Kelton Day in April 1997. He was President of the WWA in 1962-1963. He died on August 22, 2009.

Arthur Winfield Knight

Arthur Winfield Knight has published more than 3,000 poems, short stories and film reviews, and he is the author of six novels, an imaginary autobiography (of James Dean) and a real autobiography. He is listed in Who's Who in America, Contemporary Authors and Contemporary Authors Autobiography Series (volume 27).

Bill Markley

Bill Markley has written *Dakota Epic, Experiences of a Reenactor During the Filming of Dances With Wolves* and *Up the Missouri River With Lewis and Clark* as well as many articles about the Old West. Bill and his wife, Liz, live in Pierre, South Dakota.

Rod Miller

Rod Miller is the author of a Western novel and two historical books, most recently *Massacre at Bear River: First, Worst, Forgotten*, from Caxton Press. He has also written a number of magazine articles, several anthologized short stories, and numerous poems about cowboys and the West.

Susan Cummins Miller

Tucson, Arizona writer/geologist Susan Cummins Miller, an affiliate of the UA's Southwest Institute for Research on Women, pens the award-winning Frankie MacFarlane, Geologist, mysteries (Texas Tech UP). She edited *A Sweet, Separate Intimacy: Women Writers of the American Frontier, 1800-1922*, and her poems have appeared in regional journals and anthologies.

John D. Nesbitt

John D. Nesbitt has written short stories, poetry, song lyrics, magazine articles, scholarly essays for literary journals, and both contemporary and traditional Western fiction. His novel *Trouble at the Redstone* won a 2009 Spur Award. He lives in Torrington, Wyoming, where he teaches at Eastern Wyoming College.

Dusty Richards

Dusty Richards has been a pro rodeo announcer, auctioneer TV anchor and rancher. He has written more than sixty books under his own name and pseudonyms and has twice won the WWA Spur Award. In 2004 he was inducted into the Arkansas Writers Hall of Fame. He and his wife, Pat, live on Beaver Lake in northwest Arkansas.

Susan K. Salzer

Susan K. Salzer is a graduate of the University of Missouri School of Journalism. Her short fiction has appeared in literary journals and anthologies. She has won awards for short fiction, most notably a 2009 Spur from WWA. Salzer's first novel, *Up From Thunder*, will be published in November 2009 by Cave Hollow Press.

Vernon Schmid

A Kansas native who has been a rough stock rodeo competitor, radio personality, wrangler and trail guide, horse trainer and journalist, Vernon Schmid is a prize winning poet whose work has been published internationally. A columnist for the National Foundation Quarter Horse Journal, he lives in Maryland, where he and his spouse, Susan, raise Quarter Horses.

Red Shuttleworth

Red Shuttleworth's *Western Settings* (University of Nevada Press) won WWA's first Spur Award for poetry. *True West* magazine, in 2007, named him "Best Living Western Poet." His poems appear in many journals. Red's plays on the West have been presented widely, including the Tony Award-winning Utah Shakespearean Festival.

Cotton Smith

Cotton Smith is past President of Western Writers of America and author of fifteen western novels, including *Death Mask*, *Spirit Rider* and *Stands a Ranger*. He was co-creator of the musical, *First Light*, produced for televising the world-famous Country Club Plaza Christmas Lighting Ceremony. Smith lives in Kansas City with his wife.

Miles Swarthout

Miles Swarthout wrote the screenplay for *The Shootist*, John Wayne's last film, as well as the Spur-Award winning novel *The Sergeant's Lady*. He has recently completed a sequel to his father Glendon's novel *The Shootist* entitled *The Last Shootist*.

Robert M. Utley

Robert M. Utley is a former chief historian of the National Park Service and the author of sixteen books on western American history. His most recent are a two-volume history of the Texas Rangers. He is now working on a biography of Geronimo. He lives in Scottsdale, Arizona, with his wife, historian Melody Webb.

Richard S. Wheeler

Richard S. Wheeler is a five-time winner of the WWA Spur Award and recipient of the Owen Wister Award for lifetime achievement. He has authored more than forty books. He lives in Livingston, Montana.

COVER ARTIST

Thom Ross

Thom Ross is a Seattle-based Western artist whose work appears in art galleries throughout the West as well as in the permanent collections of several museums including the Buffalo Bill Historical Center in Cody, Wyoming. He is well known for his evocative book illustrations and cover art that, although historical in inspiration, are contemporary in style and mythic in meaning. He is the author of *Gunfight at the O.K. Corral: In Words and Pictures*.

WESTERN WRITERS OF AMERICA, INC.
Qualifications for Membership

WESTERN WRITERS OF AMERICA welcomes all published writers who derive their livelihood, in whole or in part, from writing about the land and the peoples of the American West, past and present. Our membership includes novelists, historians, essayists, journalists, poets, screenwriters, publishers and others. Applications for membership are judged on an individual basis and the requirements for the different levels of membership are somewhat flexible.

BENEFITS:
- All members receive a $30 subscription to the *Roundup Magazine*
- Network with professional Western writers, editors, publishers and agents
- Annual national convention, awards and opportunities for leadership
- WWA regional, state and local seminars and signings
- Professional membership fee is tax deductible

MEMBERSHIP LEVELS AND REQUIREMENTS

ACTIVE: Active Membership in the Western Writers of America, Inc., may be granted to authors who derive their livelihood, in whole or in part, from the writing of books, stories, articles, screenplays, or teleplays pertaining to the traditions, legends, development, customs, manners, or history of the American West, or early frontier, if published or produced without financial assistance of the author. An applicant must have written at least three (3) published books or at least twenty (20) short stories, articles, or poems or three (3) screenplays or nine (9) teleplays. At least one-third of such published/produced work must pertain to the American West, or early frontier. Annual dues are $75.

(continued next page)

ASSOCIATE: Publication of one (1) book about the West or at least five (5) short stories, articles, or poems or one (1) screenplay or three (3) teleplays will qualify you for Associate membership. Such works may be produced with or without the financial assistance of the author. You may also be eligible for an Associate membership if you currently are participating in one of the following occupations, and if your work substantially concerns the West: publisher, editor, bookseller, literary agent, literary reviewer, librarian, film or television producer or director, artist or illustrator. Associate members have all the rights of Active members, save that only Actives can vote for WWA officers or on proposals to amend the constitution and bylaws. At least one-third of such published/produced work must pertain to the American West, or early frontier. Annual dues are $75.

SUSTAINING: Any Active or Associate member who wishes to contribute further support to the WWA may become a Sustaining member by paying annual dues of $150. Sustaining members retain all rights and privileges of their Active or Associate status.

PATRON: Companies, corporations, organizations and individuals with a vested interest in the literature and heritage of the American West may become Patron members by paying annual dues of $250. Eligible organizations include but are not limited to publishing houses, presses, libraries, museums, and wholesale and retail booksellers. Active and Associate members of the WWA who choose to become Patron members retain all rights and privileges associated with their professional membership status.

For more information, visit the WWA Web site at
www.westernwriters.org

Ordering Information

For information on how to purchase copies of *Roundup!,* or for our bulk-purchase discount schedule, call (307) 778-4752 or send an email to: company@lafronterapublishing.com

About La Frontera Publishing

La frontera is Spanish for "the frontier." Here at La Frontera Publishing, our mission is to be a frontier for new stories and new ideas about the American West.

La Frontera Publishing believes:
- There are more histories to discover
- There are more tales to tell
- There are more stories to write

Visit our Web site for news about upcoming historic fiction or nonfiction books about the American West. We hope you'll join us here — on *la frontera.*

La Frontera Publishing
Bringing You The West In Books ®
2710 Thomes Ave, Suite 181
Cheyenne, WY 82001
(307) 778-4752
www.lafronterapublishing.com

OldWestNewWest.Com
Travel & History Magazine

It's the monthly Internet magazine for people who want to explore the heritage of the Old West in today's New West.

With each issue, **OldWestNewWest.Com Travel & History Magazine** brings you new adventures and historical places:

- Western Festivals
- Rodeos
- American Indian Celebrations
- Western Museums
- National and State Parks
- Dude Ranches
- Cowboy Poetry Gatherings
- Western Personalities
- News and Updates About the West

Visit **OldWestNewWest.Com Travel & History Magazine** to find the fun places to go, and the Wild West things to see. Uncover the West that's waiting for you!

www.oldwestnewwest.com

La Frontera Publishing's eZine about
the Old West and the New West